The Christopher Landon Omnibus

The Christopher Landon Omnibus

Ravette London

This edition published by Ravette Ltd
© Ravette Ltd 1986

Typeset by Input Typesetting Ltd
Printed and bound in Great Britain for Ravette Ltd
3 Glenside Estate, Star Road, Partridge Green,
Horsham, Sussex RH13 8RA
by T. J. Press (Padstow) Ltd., Cornwall.

ISBN 0 948456 07 8

Contents

Ice Cold in Alex

Contents

CHAPTER 1

They served it ice-cold in Alex . . .

For the moment that he shut his eyes, he could see every detail of that little bar in the lane off Mahomet Ali Square; the high stools, the marble-topped counter, the Greek behind it. Then the sound of the place came back . . . the purr of the overhead fan, a fly, buzzing drowsily, the muffled noise of the traffic seeping in through the closed door.

'If I think of that long enough, there might be a chance of forgetting this bloody noise.' But it didn't help.

Then he thought about the beer itself, in tall thin glasses, so cold that there was a dew glistening on the outside of them, even before they were put down on the counter; the pale amber clearness of it; the taste, last of all.

It did not help much either. It did not shut out the sound of the endless shells that screamed over his head—only delayed the inevitable visit to the back of the truck for another whisky. Perhaps, more than anything, it made him realize that for the first time he was entirely afraid.

Jerry had got a ring of their 88-millimetres right up now and were banging the shells on to the edge of the escarpment. The ricochets—perhaps they were doing it for that effect—were screaming out over the harbour in flat trajectory like a curtain of wailing rain. It was doing no damage, except to minds. But that was far the worst.

There had always been noise in Tobruk; in the first siege, the regular, expected pattern of dive-bombing and shelling, to be sworn at and endured; then the lull of a year, with only daylight stuff coming over high from the west and their growing confidence in the numbers of Allied aircraft ready there to meet it. But now everything was back to where they came in—all the soft-skinned stuff coming back inside the perimeter, the noise of the guns getting closer and closer—and then this last thing, this steady stream of hail that wailed just over their heads.

He knew that the fear had come to stay now—not coming and then draining away, as it had for the last two days. His mind reached back to the first time, when it had come and flapped its dark wings in his face for those few seconds in the moonlight on the Gazala road. The night when those two ambulances had not come back and the CO had gone to look for them; when the CO had not come back either, and he had gone to look for them both. It had gone away afterwards—but now it was back, all the time, sitting on his shoulder like a vulture, waiting . . .

He had been scared before—but so had everyone. Perhaps, in a way, it had been a relief from the drab routine of the unending flog up and down the desert between Mersa Matruh and Benghazi. But it had gone on for so long—two years in the wearing-down process of so many days of heat and half-meals, so many nights of no sleep—or, worse, half-sleep, when every little noise is translated by the watching brain into the clatter of tank tracks—that it was not adventure any more. And when it stopped being adventure, he had started drinking.

He shifted his position in the shade of the truck and looked at the nearness of his slit-trench, wincing at a burst of the screaming overhead; that empty aching feeling was welling up from his stomach to the back of his throat now, it was a question of how long he could hang on before he made that move . . . think of something . . . anything . . .

Two years ago. His mind reached back wistfully to what it had been like then: the rising tide of preparation under clean desert skies before the dash forward to lock in battle with an equal enemy, a few days of excitement before the withdrawal from an honourable stalemate, the break of leave in Cairo or Alexandria before the cycle started all over again. It had gone—all that, and now he was so bloody tired the whole of the time. No one had noticed, no one had said a word; but he had started to drink all the time—just to keep going. He never got drunk; perhaps that was the worst part, that he could not get drunk.

It was snapping point now. He got out, almost levering himself upright against the weight of screaming horror overhead. He went round to the back and groped inside the hanging sheet. Just inside on the floor was an old ammunition box, padlocked, with his name and PRIVATE stencilled on it. Inside, piled on top of his personal stuff, were four bottles of Haig. He lifted one and held it up in the dim light so that he could see the level of the liquid—half full—against the label. Then he made a mark on it with his thumbnail, a quarter inch below.

'There—and no farther.' He tilted it back, feeling the raw spirit in his throat and the beginnings of its warmth reaching down to the pit of his stomach. He knew that it would not make the tiredness any better—only allow it to be borne. The cork went back into the neck with a soft sound; he stood for a moment, holding the bottle, thinking back to how it had all begun.

There had been no thought of a general retirement when the Germans started their attack on the Gazala line. Even when they got through in places, the scraps of information that got back to Tobruk were smoothed over with the comforting thought that their armour was now boxed on the wrong side of the line, cut off from their own supplies, with no hope of repair, a sitting duck for our tanks to come in and squash, the moment they chose. The withdrawal of the ambulances from a forward position had followed as a routine movement: a little farther back from the battle would make them easier to control. It had been so casual that he had not even bothered to radio the orders; he had taken them up himself in the car. It had been an excuse to escape from the monotony of Tobruk and he had found the shelling and bombing no worse than he had expected. But as he was on his way back, something started to happen . . . out here, to the south of him, as he motored back to the fortress . . . over the lip of the escarpment, in the flinty plain between Knightsbridge and Bir Hakeim . . .

He heard the distant thunder of the guns as he drove; heard, in the hours that followed the breath of rumour that swept through the fortress. That something had gone a bit adrift in the smashing up of those Jerry tanks . . . that 150 Brigade 'box' had gone in the middle of the line, and that the German transports were streaming through the breach to replenish their armour.

Like most of the rest that heard it, he didn't quite believe. And no one seemed to care very much.

The first real personal impact came later: when the last report of the new disposition of the ambulances came in, there were three blanks—three, that had been ordered to leave their old location far south on the line, had not arrived at the new. He spent an hour hanging round the wireless truck with the CO—dapper, friendly Major Brooker, the only doctor in that odd formation, a motor ambulance convoy. The operator had twiddled his dials, three times they got a firm, laconic 'No' from the new sites, but there was only silence and the crackle of static from where they had been.

At last, the major had straightened and smiled: then he said, 'I'm going to pull them in, George. Shan't be long—keep an eye on things.' He had got into his car and given that half-wave, half-salute of his, and driven off towards the eastern perimeter, into the darkness in a stream of dust. And never come back.

After four dragging hours, Anson knew he would have to do something.

It was one of those things that happened so often: someone like the CO—whom you had eaten with, argued with, slept beside, and seen frightened—would get into his truck and say, 'I'm going to swan over and see old Joe,' or, '—look at that well,' or '—get some beer from the NAAFI'. There would be a grin and a wave, the truck would be swallowed up in the night to the fading beat of the motor, or dwindle to a speck on the rim of the desert.

And that was that: they didn't come back.

Sometimes you found them afterwards. A riddled, burnt-out, twisted wreck, with an untidy bundle slumped in the seat or lying on the sand beside. And the face, always, caught in that last moment of all, was never the face of your friend. Something had gone from it.

But you did all you could: marked the position on your map and sent the identity disc back to the Graves people, there was the trench to be dug, as deep as the rock would let you go, with the stones piled on top to keep the dogs out. Perhaps later, months afterwards, in a moment of relaxation by the mess truck, someone would say suddenly, 'Do you remember Charles—the cunning old basket—the time he—?' But you didn't want to hear it—to remember anything. You shut your mind tight to it; wondered only if the sand was blowing the right way to cover it deeper, made the firm resolve to take a trip out there the next time it was in range and make sure. Then someone else would say, in a tight voice, 'For Christ's sake, shut up—and turn on the radio.' And the BBC crooner would always be in the middle of singing, 'Sand in my Shoes' in that don't-cry-in-my-gin voice. Which didn't help a lot.

Well, it had happened again. The CO this time. And Anson knew that he had to go and look for him, and those poor bastards in the missing cars. He was the senior officer now, the only captain in the unit. He had got up from his truck and gone over to where the duty officer was nodding in a chair beside the wireless truck.

'Paul,' he said, 'I'm going out to look for the old man.'

Paul Crosbie was the senior subaltern; he uncoiled his rugger-forward bulk from the chair and stood up towering over Anson.

'Corps HQ won't let you, George.'

'Corps won't know.'

Paul had shrugged. 'You're the boss. What shall I tell them if they come on the blower?'

He had hesitated for a moment. 'I don't want them told anything—I want you to wake Smith, to take over here—and I'd like you to come with me.'

It was quite dark now, with only the faintest glimmer of reflection from the stars, he could only see the faint shadow of Paul's face. He looked away, down to the ground, and added quickly, 'That's not an order, Paul. I'd—just like you to come—if you will.'

As if in answer, the edge of the moon began to creep up over the line of the escarpment. As the round of it grew, the red-orange flicker that painted the southern horizons like unending summer lightning began to pale; the gunfire—unending muffled roll of a deep drum—thinned and died to a pattern of separate sounds. He had looked over to it—the direction of the flinty plain of Knights-bridge where they would soon have to go—then down at the sand he was turning over with his desert boot. 'That driver of mine—he's beginning to get bomb-happy. And I don't want to go alone.'

'Of course I'll come.' The moonlight was bright enough then to show the glint of teeth as the craggy face broke into a grin; as the big man turned his head, Anson saw the eyes for the first time. And knew that Paul knew.

They had been on their way over to the Humber when he said, 'I had better take a map, I suppose.' He had come back with a map-board under one arm and a bottle of Haig in the other hand.

'Might get cold, Paul.'

'Yes.'

'Will you drive?—then I can stand up later—and get a better look-see.' He held out the bottle. 'One for the road?'

'Might as well.'

When he had taken the bottle back and had a swallow he remembered it was the ninth he had had since the CO had gone.

The Humber was an old, open four-seater: battered, sand-stained, but with an engine that had the heart of a lion. They had bumped out of the camp area and then moved quickly to the bridge that spanned the tank-trap on the western edge of the perimeter. There had not seemed to be much traffic moving on the roads inside the fortress that night—and when they had been checked and were through on the open road outside, none at all. None at all, moving their way. But Anson's heart had sunk lower and lower as he saw the endless line of vehicles, head to tail, sometimes two deep, facing towards them as they waited to get into Tobruk.

The gunfire over on the back of the escarpment had died to nothing, there was almost a complete silence. Only the hiss . . . hiss . . . hiss . . . of reflected sound as they passed each vehicle in the jumbled string of lorries, guns, even some tanks, that waited. Their side of the road was clear. They were the only thing that was moving west.

Hiss . . . hiss . . . hiss. Nothing but that and the occasional deeper snarl from their engine and the rushing sound of sand spewed from racing wheels as Paul had had to swing off the hard going to avoid the wider jams. Each vehicle rushed towards them and was then swept into the dust behind; each one, white and ghostly in the moonlight that was bright now; each one, silent and unmoving. It was like a horrid travesty of a bank holiday traffic jam.

There was no contact between them as they passed. Only for an instant had Anson seen the driver or passenger in the cab as they flashed by. They were still too, staring as if they did not really see the Humber, without interest. Things had gone wrong again.

Paul broke their silence. 'Another bloody balls-up—or should I go all official and say, strategic withdrawal?' He had sounded remarkably cheerful. 'Please God, Jerry doesn't come over and drop a load on this lot—it would be murder.' He spun the wheel with an expert flick and the engine roared and the tail bucked sideways' before they were round a tank and back on the road again. The solid line was thinning now to groups of two or three, moving slowly: there were long gaps between them. As with the long blocks, Anson had looked at each one in turn, searching for the smaller, square, biscuit-coloured shape of an ambulance car. But there was no sign.

Paul had braked suddenly, peering ahead, and said, 'Tanks.' A pause. 'All right—they're ours—Valentines.'

'Keep going,' said Anson. As they had passed the low, humped shapes strung out on each side of the road, their turrets pointing backwards, someone had shouted at them. Then there had been nothing but the empty road, a black ribbon stretching straight ahead on the whiteness of the desert in the moonlight.

They were doing a steady fifty then; Anson standing, gripping the top of the windscreen with both hands, the chinstrap of his cap cutting hard into his jaw, the wind of their passing roaring in his ears. The edge of the front seat pressed against the back of his legs and he pushed hard against it—to stop the shaking. It must be the cold . . . he bent for a moment below the shelter of the screen to wrap his white Syrian sheepskin coat closer round him. Something of the feel of it . . . the sight of Paul's big hands splayed out on the wheel, brought back a moment's vivid memory of those leaves in Beirut they had spent together, shared everything together. Until they had met her.

He sat down for a moment and reached for the whisky bottle from the dashboard compartment, pulled the cork and held it out, the other hand poised ready to take the wheel. 'I wonder what Ariadne's doing now,' he shouted.

If Paul heard, or saw the bottle, he did not react. The hands stayed steady on the wheel and it had seemed a long time before there was the faintest shake of the head as if to dismiss both offer and question. Then he said, 'I'd stand up, if I were you, old man. You might miss something.'

'Sorry.'

He had taken a quick hard swig at the bottle and then put it back. When he had hoisted himself to his feet, there was nothing ahead; nothing except the black strip that stretched on, unending, and the white plain on either side. It was then that he had started to search desperately, to find anything there, even the wrong kind of things; the shaking of his legs had nothing to do with cold then and the words that were torn from his lips, to be whirled away into the fog of dust behind, almost a prayer. 'They must open up—now. They can't let us go on getting farther and farther in—with nothing happening.' For the first time, he was horribly afraid. But they did not oblige.

Another mile and no relief—it would be relief—of those orange buds of tracer bursting into flower as they streaked towards them. Nothing; only the moonlight and the black and white. Then he made his last try.

'Paul—' he had bent, shouting down to the unmoving head, 'you know the old track we used to use up the escarpment—by that

black stone—about three kilometres on—? They might try and get
down there if they were in a jam. We'll try up that way.'

Paul had nodded—and another answer had come back to him
moments later. Far, far away to the south, beyond the escarpment,
three green star shells had climbed up into the sky; he knew that
one—the panzer signal for advance. He was just bending to pass
this on when he had seen something else: the black rock . . . nearer
than he had expected . . . farther from the road then he remembered
. . . much larger. Before he could speak they were on it and past it;
in the instant of passing there was no mistaking the tight-packed
night-laager of tanks . . . no doubt about the square, chopped-off
turrets of German Mark IV's. But they were by without the sound
or sign of a living soul.

That finished him. His legs were uncontrollable now and for the
next kilometre he managed to hold himself up by the strength of
his arms alone. Then he sat down suddenly. 'Stop her, Paul.'

Paul had thrown out the gear and cut the engine and let the
Humber coast to a halt. 'That track's about another kilometre,' he
said.

Anson tried so hard to gain control; he knew the moment he
spoke, that he had not succeeded. 'Did you—see that lot?'

Paul let his hands drop from the wheel. 'The squareheads? Yes.
Having a nice kip before the pounce.'

Anson had looked at his watch. 'It will be two hours—if we turn
back now. If they move—and straddle the road—we'll never get
back at all. We've done all—'

'Of course we have, George.' His voice had sounded a little too
casual. 'It's entirely up to you. If you say, "Go on"—we go; if you
say, "Go back," we do. It was your idea of a party. I'd rather be
in bed.'

Both had listened for a moment: except for the cracking from the
cooling engine, there was not a sound, only the soft moonlight
flowing over the black road and the white desert.

'We go back. And, for God's sake, get past that like a bat out of
hell.'

Paul had turned to stare at him. 'That's fine. What happens if
they have stretched a wire across the road. Would you like to drive?'

'No.'

'OK.' He had stabbed at the starter button and in two quick
reverse turns was facing back the other way. The moon was behind

them then, the way ahead clearer, empty, everything still. They could not see the thing that lay in front of them.

Paul had said, 'Well, here we go—first stop, Victoria,' and then the Humber had leapt forward in the full power of first gear.

He had crouched, watching the speedometer needle tremble and surge forward as the car accelerated up through the gears . . . sixty-five . . . seventy. Now the ribs on the sand-treads of the tyres were roaring so loud that he could not hear the noise of the engine. They must be very close now. He had looked up at Paul, straight and stiff behind that wheel . . . he could not duck. With all he had left, he heaved himself upright, gripping the top of the screen, and the wind struck him like a blow. The black mass—on their right—was rushing towards them . . . was it his watering eyes, or tortured imagination—but was that a gleam of something stretched across the road in front? HE MUST NOT DUCK. Fifty yards . . . he could see the damned wire now . . . he was certain . . . Then everything snapped, and with a scream of, 'Stop—stop!' he had collapsed back on the seat with his face buried on his knees. Paul had made a noise that was halfway between a grunt and a laugh and put his foot down to the floorboards. They were by—they must be by; but nothing had happened. He waited, hunched, for the roar of exploding mines or the tear of the wire that would overturn the car and decapitate Paul; but it had not come, not a shout, not a shot, nothing.

Slowly their speed had dropped, the tyres now giving a faint hum instead of that roar. Anson sat huddled in the passenger seat, stared down the empty black ribbon of road that unfolded in front of them, as he waited for Paul to speak.

He had waited, while the minutes dragged by in silence, staring into the moonlight as they closed nearer to Tobruk, thinking . . . Of all the fun they had had together, he and Paul, of all those leaves—the times in Alex and Cairo and Beirut.

Beirut most of all—because it connected them both in the web of Ariadne. Cretan Ariadne, with the slim grace and look of a deer; Ariadne they had met together, taken out together in perfect accord, the girl they had both loved in their different ways. Or were they different—? That was something he would never know now, that was why he was thinking of it all for the last time, for it would never be the same again. There would be no more leaves together. He had seen the look in Paul's eyes just before he had turned the car back down the road.

He had taken another pull at the bottle before Paul spoke.

'Don't you think you had better lay off that, Skipper?'

He threw the whisky back in the locker and they did not speak again until they had been challenged at the tank screen—so thin, so pitifully few. As they had walked back to the car after reporting their find to the squadron commander, Paul said suddenly, 'Has it struck you we could have stopped the car in front of them—got out and done a fan dance—sung the "Horst Wessel"—and there would not have been a cheep out of the lot?'

'Why, Paul?'

'They were just as scared as we were. It must have looked very like the setting of a trap.'

He had said, 'I'm sorry, Paul. I—'

'Forget it,' Paul's voice had been brusque but kind. But he knew that really it never would be forgotten.

The day had been almost normal.

There had been no word of the CO or the ambulances—and deep down inside him now he had known that there never would be. He had gone about his routine work in a dead, numb sort of way. He had not spoken to Paul.

The fear of the night had gone, but the hurt of it was still there: so was the whisky, and it did not remove anything of it. Only, it seemed to move the whole thing to one side, so that he could stand and watch it, disinterested.

All through that day the sound of gunfire had increased, had come closer, as the ring tightened. He hardly noticed it—or the raids: just went on with the job, hoping that no one would notice him. His brain had been quite clear; only there was a jerkiness in the way his legs moved as he walked and a numb tight feeling in the muscles of his face.

There had been a counter-attack at dawn and the ambulances were out again, feeling their way through the twisting paths in the minefields beyond the perimeter, running back with their load down the snaking road that led to the harbour and the cluster of tents and the one standing building that made up the General Hospital. It had taken all the morning to get them into the swing of their new routine, and it was not until after the midday meal that he had had the chance to go round the resting sections and talk to the men.

Stiffly, in that jerking stride, he had trudged round the camp, from vehicle to vehicle, squatting down at the bivouacs that were beside them, exchanging a few sentences with the occupants before moving on. Always with one eye cocked at the burnished bowl of the sky for the sign of a glitter of wings, one ear attuned to the mutter of gunfire.

The men . . . he knew them all. Most were hardened old sweats, stripped to the waist and capless in the high sun, burnt native brown, scarred on hands and knees with two years of desert sores. If they got their rations, their fags, and their beer—if they could be contemptuously affectionate to all in authority, that was enough. They had learned to accept the desert, to take the changing fortunes of its war with philosophy; after two years, England had almost vanished, Cairo and Alex were home. They ignored the nuisance of noise of any bombardment that was not personally dangerous to them: jumped unerringly for a slit-trench on the instant of anything that was. Through either, they would curse—foully, but again with a certain affection—at the giver.

They were just the same, as he had talked to them . . . almost. He did not get the change until he had been to three or four vehicles. It was something in their look, questioning, not quite holding his eyes, when they asked for news of what was doing. It gave him the first return of the feeling of the night before.

'When are we going in for another bash, sir?'

'Soon, I think. There was a counter-attack at first light and I hear it's going well.'

'Good, sir.'

But it wasn't good, because, for the first time, they were not believing him. They knew it was just words—that he hadn't got a clue.

The signal to report to the medical brigadier at Corps HQ came through at four. He changed into a clean bush shirt, had a quick pull at the bottle, and got into his car alone to drive down the hill. Everything was normal as he drove off the camp site and on to the road; the shelling had died in one of those uneasy lulls, and he was glad to see that the men had flattened a patch of desert and had unrolled their strip of coconut matting for a cricket match. He stopped to watch for a minute. Paul was there, bowling at that moment—crafty leg-breaks. He remembered that, apart from routine, they had not spoken since the night before. He let in the clutch and started down the road to headquarters.

The brigadier was a typical desert oddity. Medical officers, even on the staff, do not as a rule attract much attention, but 'Dangle-toes' was a name, apart from this reference to his stature. Always, as long as there were troops in the desert, he would be remembered for the fabulous tale of the day that his headquarters had been overrun at dawn by German tanks. He had got out of a delicate situation by the simple expedient of speaking a little German—and understanding Germans.

He had been asleep when the bother started, and before anyone had come to winkle him out of his dugout, had dressed quickly in his best tunic, with tabs, his best hat, with the maroon band. He had stalked out to storm at the bewildered commander of the panzer group, screaming, in his atrocious German, the facts of his own importance, insisting that they loaded his entire kit on his own truck and that he was driven by his own driver into captivity. They reacted, as he had hoped, to noise and brass: they did it. When he had moved off in state, and under escort, towards Tripoli, he had waited till dark and then slipped out sideways past the escort and regained Allied territory. He had arrived triumphant, but speechless with rage. Those—Jerries had forgotten, worse, deliberately omitted, to load his portable wash-stand!

He was small, very thin and, through some whim of hygiene, always kept his head shaved close to the scalp. He looked like a Hun—and was a bloody good bloke. At the moment Anson made entry to his dugout at Corps Headquarters, he had been sitting cross-legged in a tin bath, with nothing more on than a pair of rimless glasses. Anson had thought of Gandhi.

'Ah—Anson. 'Afternoon.' He reached forward, fishing for something in the three inches of grey scummy muck that was a week's water ration.

'Good afternoon, sir.'

'Well. Sit down. Let me finish this lot. How's everything?' He always spoke in jerks.

Anson sat on the one camp-chair and began the recital of the unit's state. As he listened, the brig still trawled the water in front of him with his hands: at last, with a grunt of satisfaction, he pounced to pull from the depths a fragment of what had once been a loofah. Without interruption, he began to scratch his back.

When Anson had finished he said, '—and there's no news about Major Brooker, or the ambulances?'

'None, sir. I don't think there is anywhere else to check. I've packed up all the kits—shall I—?'

Outside there was a crump—crump—crump, as a stick of bombs dropped quite close. The water in the bath had shivered in little circles and some sand fell with a soft noise from the sides of the dugout. The brig had not moved, except to lift one arm and explore the mysteries beneath it.

'Now—there's a thing,' he said. 'Never a moment's peace—for either side. Take a man going to the latrine. Why shouldn't he? Normal natural function. Then that happens. No wonder they get constipated.'

Anson's fingers had been slowly relaxing from the grip he had on the underside of the chair. The brig had shot a quick glance at him and gone on scratching.

'I think I'd like a drink, Anson—and I expect you could do with one, too. The Scotch is on the table. There's the water bottle. No, not that one—the next. That's real Charing Cross.' In the desert, the merit of various wells was judged as fine as a vintage.

When he had handed down a mug to the bath, his hand had stopped shaking. The brig went on talking as if there had been no interruption.

'Poor Brooker. I'm afraid he's had it. We shan't hear anything now. You are to be temporary OC by the way. I can't find a doctor that's suitable to take over—and your RASC don't object, so you can carry on.' He stood up in a rush of scum and reached for a towel. 'After all, there's no medical work in an MAC—just an ordinary Service Corps carrying job, even if it is a rather special load.'

'Very good, sir.'

The brig was finding his shirt and shorts. 'Now, immediate details. "A" and "C" sections to carry on just as they are—with the other two resting at an hour's readiness. Less six cars from "D"—that I have a special job for.'

'A special job—?'

The brig finished his drink. 'The nurses at the hospital,' he said, 'they're to go back to Alex—tonight.'

Anson had stared for a moment, trying to gauge what was going on behind the glint of those glasses. 'Is it—as bad as that, sir?'

The little man made an impatient movement. 'Good God, no, man. But it isn't very pleasant here—' He cocked his head and listened. The dull tattoo was beating up again from the south: now, close, something sighed overhead, to finish in a deep crunch, followed by a long rumble. 'Things like that,' said the brig.

He swung round. 'Anyway, I never wanted them here. It was Army that insisted, said it needed a woman's touch to make the poor bastards feel they were on the first stage of the road home. But that hospital isn't fit for that any more, Anson. It's too damned crowded. It isn't fair to the colonel—or the girls.'

He stopped suddenly to glare. 'And what the hell has it got to do with you?'

'Nothing, sir.' He changed the subject hastily. 'How many will there be going?'

'Thirty-two and the matron. No kit except essentials.'

'That will mean eight cars.'

'Eight—? Why eight? Why not send the whole damned unit if you're feeling so generous?'

'I was only thinking of the sleeping, sir. They are bound to be at least one night on the road. There are four bunks in each car—I thought eight cars would make it about right.'

'Five cars,' said the brig, gently, 'that's all they get, Anson. They'll have to double up—or sleep on the floor. They may be glad of one night's discomfort . . . soon.'

So it was like that—however much the brig tried to smooth it over. There was going to be another siege. Then the first thing was to think of his own men. He had weighed the situation for a moment and then said, 'Those caves, sir. The ones by the shore, east and below the hospital—you know them? There's no one there at the moment. We'd be nearer you—and the hospital, the troops would like the bathing too. Can we move in?'

The brig had smiled, not unkindly. It was the moment when both were certain of the other's knowledge. 'If there's room—and you're first, go to it.'

Anson had got up. 'Is there anything else, sir?'

'Not at the moment, Anson. Just five cars to be at the hospital for loading at seven. The drivers—I want nice types—' he looked down at his congealing bath for inspiration, '—married men.'

For the first time that day he had felt like laughing. It was typical brigadier. There was quite likely to be further embellishment. As he waited for the probable instructions on chastity belts he thought of the work entailed by this proviso in searching the company roll. But the brig did not seem to have anything to add; he realised in the same instant it was not a question of the nurses' virtue—it was only five, but the brig was getting five married men out of Tobruk as well as the girls.

'An officer to go with them, sir?'

'No. A good sergeant—to come under orders of the matron.'

Anson saluted. He was halfway up the dugout steps when the sharp voice called him back. 'Oh, Anson—in your movement order, give the sergeant explicit orders as to propriety.'

'Propriety, sir?'

The brig waved his hands. 'Dammit, man. They'll be two days on the road, and there's not a bush worth calling by the name between here and the delta. I imagine they'll want to powder their noses. Instruct the sergeant to take orders from matron; when she gives the word, to pull the cars off the road and form a hollow square—then leave them in peace.'

It was almost the last straw. 'And when they have delivered them, sir, where do they report back?'

'Here—or as near as they can get.'

Quite suddenly, he thought he had never seen the brigadier look so old.

Things had followed the expected pattern after that.

It was a vague unrelated pattern, for Anson was only a grain of the mass: he knew—but could not ask for confirmation, his only source to the higher, over-all picture, the brig, was closed to him now, because he knew that he knew. There would be no answer as to 'why'; only the rate of the 'how' of disintegration could reach down to his awareness in the narrow limits of his job.

It was after the ambulances had left for the hospital that the signal from the brig had arrived; it said, ALL CARS RETURNING EX PERIMETER TO REMAIN YOUR HQ AND NOT REPEAT NOT RETURN LOCATIONS. It didn't make sense and, as they were in the middle of the move to the new site at the caves, made extra work in directing the empty cars back. 'Hasn't Dangle-toes anything better to do—' Anson had snarled as he tried to sort the tangle out. It had taken him twenty minutes to find the five most married and moral for the hospital lift.

Then he had looked up to see Smith, the junior subaltern, poking his head into the back of the office truck. 'Well, what do you want?'

'Can you let me have some money from the Imprest, Captain Anson?'

'What do you mean—from the Imprest? It's the field cashier's job to deal with your advance-of-pay chits. The unit's not a bloody bank.'

Smith had looked uncomfortable. 'I know that. I'm sorry, but I can't find him.'

Anson stopped in his writing to stare. 'The field cashier? But he's just down the road man. Where he's been for months. I saw his tent this afternoon. He'll be back later—probably gone out to pay a unit.'

Smith stared at his feet. 'I've just been down there. The tent has gone.'

'Nonsense!' He had thrown down his pen. 'Get in the car and I'll take you down. I bet I find him.'

But Smith had been right. He wasn't there—or anywhere that they had the time to search. The place that they knew, where they had come to cash their cheques for months, was just a beaten square of sand with an untidy rim of sandbags pulled back from the edges where the tent had been struck. A few tattered shreds of paper were blowing across the open space. That was all.

Anson had lifted his eyes to the huddle of tents a little farther down the road ... the NAAFI. There was some transport there, and a lot of figures milling round it. He was all right now, he had had another drink and the whisky was singing high in his head. He knew what was going to happen. If the paymaster was gone, it was only a question of 'how long' before the NAAFI bonfire went up ... Then he had looked at Smith's face. There was just the same look there that the men had had that morning. And nothing he could say, nothing he could do about it. If the brig wouldn't tell him ... then he couldn't speak ...

'He's probably swanned off to find himself a cosy little cave—like we have. We'll find him later. Come back to the office now, and I'll cash that pay slip.'

On the way back in the car, he had pulled out his own wallet and counted. Three pounds and fifty-odd ackers ... but money wouldn't matter any more.

So to this wait by the truck—waiting, turning the whole thing over, wondering, afraid. Then this last bloody thing had started—that had just tipped the scales. And now he was going to drink when he knew he shouldn't ...

He was late for the rendezvous at the hospital; two sudden, vicious raids cost him half an hour crouched in the ditch by the side of his car. When at last he arrived, the broad turnround outside the main building was empty. The convoy must have gone. He had better go and find the CO to apologize for not having been there to see them off.

He ran up the steps into the main corridor. The whole place had a quiet, deserted feeling and he did not meet anyone. First turn to the left, then second door on the right, that was the colonel's office. He stood for a moment, looking at the plate with the CO's name on it before he knocked. There was no answer, so he pushed the door open and went in.

The colonel was not there, nor the carpet, nor the big desk, nor any of the things he remembered. The room was stripped of everything. Only bodies covered the floor now; wrapped in blankets, laid reverently side by side . . . but packed like sardines . . . about three deep.

The smell of wounds and guts and death beat about him with its horrible sweetness. He managed to pull the door fast and grope his way blindly towards the entrance. There, on the corner of the steps, all the defeat and bitterness and whisky of the last days won as he rocked to and fro, vomiting.

When it was over, the colonel's voice came to him suddenly. It seemed to be a long way off and when he turned his head to look he could not see for the tears that were blinding his eyes. The voice said, 'Drink this, George. And take the pills—you'll feel better.'

He groped for them, took them, and then bent forward, resting his head on his knees until the shaking had stopped. Then he turned to look at the man he had known and worked with for months. He was glad the voice had been the same, for otherwise he would not have recognized him.

There was a long white coat, buttoned to the throat, and it was stiff and stained the whole way down the front . . . all shades of red that merged to the edges in an older brown . . . like a butcher's smock that had been worn a long, long time. The face above it seemed so thin now, so sucked in at the cheeks, that it had taken the cast of a skull; the eyes had dropped back in the sockets and the little of them that showed had an opaque look.

'I'm sorry, Colonel. I went straight to your office—I didn't know—' He wiped his mouth on the back of his hand and looked away.

'It's I that should apologize, George. I should have put up a notice. The mortuary is full—there was nowhere else to put them.' There was a pause and then he had said, '—and we can't get any help in the burying . . .'

Anson said, 'But I'll send a squad down—'

'No, George. There's going to be plenty for your blokes to do without taking on outside jobs.'

For the second time he said, 'It's as bad as that, then?' and there was no attempt to brush the question aside as before.

The colonel said, 'Yes.'

The light had nearly gone then and, as often happened, there was a lull in the firing, a sort of respite before the night came up and the big bombers were over. They sat, in the peace, side by side, on the steps.

'Did they get away all right?'

'The nurses? Yes, just before that raid. It was good of you to be so prompt with the cars, George. It's a great weight off my mind.'

He said, 'They'll be OK. I got through to Eastern Control. There's an "all clear" report from there to the frontier. They should be in Egypt by dawn.'

'I know.' The colonel got stiffly to his feet. 'Stay a minute and I'll get you a drink. By the way—what's the time?'

'Twenty to eight.'

'About time I had a break. I've been operating since ten. I'll go and tell them.'

He sat quite still waiting for him to come back. The mutter of the guns started up again, the light flickering against the sky to the south. The evening breeze was coming in off the sea, making the few tattered palm fronds that were left whisper and rattle against the stems. Even the moving air felt heavy . . . like the moment before a thunderstorm.

The colonel came back carrying one glass and a small cedar box bound with a bright label. 'I won't have a drink, but I'll smoke a cigar. I've been thinking about that all day.' He looked affectionately at the box. 'My wife's last Christmas present—only it didn't arrive till February. I thought I'd save them for the next one. But—'

Anson took the drink. 'I shouldn't have this. I've been on it all day. I made a BF of myself last night.'

The colonel's thumb made a brittle sound as it broke the seal.

'It won't hurt you now—I've fixed your tummy. I knew there was something wrong. The brig told me.'

'But—'

'He just knew, George. But he thinks very highly of you. And, by God, he's going to need you.'

'Is it another siege, then?'

The colonel didn't answer for a moment. He pierced a cigar carefully, lit it, and then blew out a perfect smoke ring. He watched it for a moment before cutting it to fragments with a stroke of his hand.

'What has the brig told you?'

'Sweet Fanny Adams.'

'Then I can't tell you—can I—officially. But I think you will find out very soon—that we're for it. Beyond that—it's only guessing. Even *they* haven't got that far.' He stopped for a moment and stared out towards the pale flicker on the skyline. 'But I've made my plans,' he said.

'Plans—?'

'Yes, George. To go quietly into the bag with that lot.' He jerked his head at the bulk of the hospital behind him.

'But—you can't mean . . . ?'

The colonel just looked at him. 'I do. I think this place will fall like a pack of cards.' He looked out once more to the south. 'It's different this time—they are resolute, first-class troops, those Germans.'

'They couldn't take it before.'

'It was only the Ities then—and no treachery.'

'Treachery—?'

The colonel said, 'Perhaps that is the wrong word. You had better forget it. But I've heard some very funny talk.' He drew on a cigar for a moment. 'All I'm interested in is starting clear here when the balloon goes up. There's a hundred cases to get away. We've signalled for a hospital ship—but there's no answer yet.'

'Couldn't we lift them?'

'Far safer by sea—and they have always played fair with hospital ships. Over the desert—there might be accidents—even if you could get through—' He broke off abruptly and held out the box. 'Have one. And let's talk of something else.'

From time to time people came in and out of the entrance to the hospital, but none of them seemed to notice the colonel in his butcher's smock and the captain of the RASC sitting on the corner of the steps in the dark, smoking their cigars. They talked of many things as they sat there—the pubs of Nottingham; the best way to make steak and kidney pudding; rowing. Once an orderly came out and plucked at the colonel's sleeve, holding out a signal that he said was Most Secret and Immediate.

'Dear God,' the colonel said, 'they are all like that now,' and put it under the cigar box.

It was pleasant sitting there—and strangely peaceful. Anson began to forget everything. Then, from east and south, first in little wedges of sound that grew each moment in volume, the 88-millimetres started the second barrage that sent the hideous whine skating out over the circle of the harbour.

He remembered what the colonel had said. This was the first part of the softening-up process. And the fear of the night before came back to him, only this time it did not leave.

It was impossible to go on talking. The colonel bent close to his ear and shouted, 'I'll have to get back.' They both got up and walked over to the car, the colonel unfolding the signal he had retrieved from under the cigar box. 'It's too bloody dark,' he said.

'There's a masked light on the dash.'

The colonel climbed into the passenger seat and smoothed the paper out under the dim, shaded light. 'How nice of them. There's no hospital ship available—so they're sending a transport—with doctor—and eight nurses. Due in harbour at eleven. As there's no protection from the red cross, they must be away before moon-up—that's two. Only three hours.'

'How many cars will you want?'

'In the dark—better a few, and work fast. Five good ones.'

'All right. I'll lay them on to report to you at nine—to be on the safe side.'

'Thank you, George.' He got out of the car and then leaned back over the door. 'Here—take these.'

Anson's hand groped out to feel the bundle of cigars, wrapped in a slip of paper. 'I won't have time to smoke the lot,' the colonel said, 'and I thought you wouldn't mind doing something for me—I remembered earlier. My missis's address is on the paper. When you get out of this—please write to her. Say how you sat here with me—and that we smoked her cigars and enjoyed them. That I was well, but very tired. And we had done a good job.'

'You'll be able to do that before I can.'

'I don't think so. Good luck to you, old man.'

He turned away abruptly and soon the Humber was creeping back up the road to the centre of the perimeter. Then a sharp turn to the right and he was bucking back down the track towards the caves. As he walked towards the office truck after parking the Humber, he was not a bit surprised to see a thin streak of light

showing through the blackout, to find, having let himself through
the curtain, that the brig was sitting at his table, writing furiously.

'I'm sorry, sir. I'd no idea—'

'That's all right, Anson. Mr Crosbie told me you had gone to
the hospital. I've had a look round the new quarters. Very snug.'

He started stuffing the papers back in his briefcase and then his
glasses glinted in the light of the pressure lamp as he swung round
to stare.

'How are you feeling?'

'All right, sir.'

'Well, bring that map-board round here. I want to have a talk
to you.' He glanced at the orderly, sitting in the shadows by the
telephone—'Alone.'

'Go and get yourself a cup of tea, Corporal,' said Anson. 'I'll
answer that.'

When the corporal slipped out through the blackout curtain, the
brig pushed the map-board into the yellow circle of light, while
Anson leaned on the table beside him. From outside, over the quiet
hiss of the lamp, the sound of the bombardment was rising again;
but under the lee of the cliffs there was less menace to it . . . the
noise was more like that of distant surf. The brigadier started
talking in the quiet impersonal voice of a chairman addressing a
shareholder's meeting.

'There is a change in the whole tactical plan. We are going to
break off contact with the armour and go back to the "wire" '—his
finger traced the line that was the barbed-wire entanglement sepa-
rating Libya from Egypt—'re-form there, and then come in again.
It's got to the question of speed of recovery on both sides again.
But we command the air, so it should be easier.

'While this is happening, the plan is to hold as much of the coast
road as possible—but not as far as Tobruk.'

So the colonel had been right in fact—but how far would the
guessing prove to be . . . That fear surged up in him again, sick
and sour.

'And I suppose we stay inside again . . .' he said at last.

'Not all of you—and not for long. The estimate is that the garrison
will be contained for a maximum five weeks. And it will be
immensely strong this time. And lashings of everything they want
in the way of supplies already stocked.'

'But some of this unit will be with them,' Anson went on
doggedly.

'Yes. Twenty-five cars with one officer. To come under the CO of the hospital. They will provide all the medical transport for the garrison. How are you going to detail them?'

There was a long silence. He knew what had to be done; what he had to say.

'Unmarried men, sir—and myself.'

'The first excellent. The second—no.'

The relief made him feel ashamed, but he had to go on.

'I would like to stay, sir. I should stay. I wouldn't like those that have to—to think anything else. It won't be very funny for those in for the second time.'

The brig did not answer for a minute. He had pulled his pipe from his pocket and started filling it: as he bent forward in concentration, his shaven head shone like a billiard ball in the glow of the lamp.

'Look, Anson—though you may forget it, I happen to be a doctor as well as a brigadier on the staff. I suppose you would argue that I should stay inside with the hospital and set an example? Well, I'm not going to. For two reasons. The first is that my doctoring is so far behind that I wouldn't be any bloody good—I doubt if I could even give an enema properly. Second, and far more important, I'm too valuable to be frittered away in a gallant gesture. Corps HQ moves out of here at dawn tomorrow, and I'm going with them. The same thing applies to you. I want an OC back with me at the "wire", running the unit, not mucking about in here doing a subaltern's job.'

'I see—'

'Crosbie,' said the brig, 'he's the one for it. I don't imagine he suffers from nerves—'

'Nor does Smith, sir. Both are unmarried. And Crosbie did go through the last siege.'

'So much the better. He should feel quite at home. Crosbie it is, Anson.'

He said, slowly, 'Would you mind telling him—that—yourself, sir?'

The brig gave him a long searching glance. 'No. Get him here now.' He picked up his signal pad and started writing.

When Paul was found, they walked back together to the office truck in silence. The brig was still sitting at the table with two folded signal forms in front of him. He started without preamble.

'Crosbie, I've given Captain Anson certain orders with regard to the disposition of this unit. As a main part concerns you, I thought I would brief you personally.' He pushed one of the signal forms across the table. 'Here are your orders.'

Paul, so big, so broad, seemed to tower over the little man as he bent forward to read the message under the lamp. A long silence, with only the mutter of the guns coming through to them from outside, then the paper crackled as he folded it carefully and put it in his pocket.

'Quite clear?' said the brig.

'Perfectly, sir. I am to take over command of a section of this unit remaining on this site and coming under orders of CO hospital, Tobruk.' There was no expression in his voice.

'Any questions?'

'The rest of the unit—'

'That has nothing to do with your orders—but they are going back to Sollum.'

'I understand, sir. Will I have my own section?'

'No, Captain Anson will detail the other ranks staying. They will all be unmarried.'

'So—we're going to be boxed in again,' said Paul.

The brig hesitated for a moment. 'I think it is only fair to tell you, Crosbie, that Captain Anson volunteered for this job—but I refused him.'

Paul did not answer.

'Well,' said the brig, 'I'd best be getting back to Corps. We have all got a lot to do. Will you drive me, Anson?'

The three of them walked back to the Humber. When the brig was in the passenger seat, he turned to Crosbie, standing beside the door and leaned out to grip his arm.

'Well, so long, Crosbie—and good luck. I know I can rely on you. It won't be for long.' Five weeks at the most—and you'll be quite snug in these caves. I'll look forward to the time you and Anson dine with me in Alex—and we can have a good laugh about it all.'

'I can hardly wait for it, sir. Goodnight.'

Anson was just able to see the black shadow of him, outlined against the stars. He knew then that he would always remember that moment. He said, 'Will you check the nominal rolls while I'm gone, Paul? Put the names of all the single men in a hat. Then we'll draw sergeants, corporals and drivers as necessary, when I come back.'

'What about Mr Pugh?' Crosbie's voice came back to him out of the darkness.

'Who is Mr Pugh?' It was the brig.

Crosbie answered before Anson could speak. 'Mechanist sergeant-major, sir. He qualifies. A widower—since the blitz on Plymouth.' There was an edge in his voice.

'No,' said the brig. 'He goes with Captain Anson.'

The moved off, groping their way down the track and then on to the road; neither spoke until they were nearly back at Corps HQ. Then the brig said suddenly, 'I'm sorry about all that, Anson.' When he had got out of the car, he held out the other message form.

'These are your orders. The rest of the unit to move off at 02.00 hours. To reach the eastern checkpoint by 02.25. The senior subaltern to be in charge. They will go straight to the old location at Sollum. You will stay and tidy up detail with Crosbie. Then report to me at first light here. I'll come along with you.'

Anson thought for a minute. 'Can I keep Mr Pugh to come with us, sir? It will give him a little more time on the vehicles staying behind—and—'

'And what?' said the brig.

A raid had started. It was one of the usual high-level night pattern—so usual, that neither of them had taken much notice. To them, it was just a lot of extra noise. For a second both looked at the pale slanting fingers of the searchlights, the heavy flicker of the AA guns and the orange flare and crump of bombs.

'And what—?' asked the brigadier, again.

'Mr Pugh—he's sort of the keystone of the unit, sir. I think there may be a few rough edges over this business—and he'd be valuable in helping me sort them out.'

The brig had not answered for a moment. He was looking along the line of the harbour. A fire had started in one of the depots; little pinpoints of yellow and orange that licked and jumped out from the first explosion. Then, nearer, another patch of light appeared, starting this time without any explosion, without benefit of the burst of a bomb.

'Good of NAAFI,' said the brig, 'I thought they wouldn't miss the chance. Yes, keep your Mr Pugh, as long as he doesn't have too much kit. There is to be no question of him staying behind. Good night, Anson.' He got out of the car and scuttled off into the darkness that flickered in the lights of the fires.

All that followed after that was the vague, unpleasant, condensed pattern of a nightmare. The look of the men as they had waited for the names to be called out of the hat; the little sounds that gave expression of the relief of those not staying; the frozen silence of the others when they heard that they were. Paul standing beside him, calling out the chosen in a clear, expressionless voice, withdrawn, seeming already to have taken over control. There had been the rush—too eager, almost indecent—of those going down the road to prepare their vehicles and pack up. The deadly tiredness coming back to him, the furtive drinks. Last, and most clearly of all, his talk with MSM Pugh.

He had sent for him as soon as he had got back to camp. It was not the actual words that were said, but the way of saying them, that would always stay in his mind.

Mr Pugh had come in quietly through the blackout curtain at the back of the truck to stand silent, waiting. Tall and very thin, with a russet pippin of a face and the bluest of blue eyes. They had known each other for so long, and always the older man, the junior in rank, seemed to be cast in the role of parent.

'Hello, Mr Pugh.'

'Good evening, sir.'

Even after these years, their relations, in any circumstance, were always of the most formal.

Anson had leaned forward against the desk and knuckled his hands into his eyes, trying to think, trying to bring himself back from that dark sea of tiredness and despair. Then he pushed the bottle and a spare glass across the table. 'Sit down and have a drink,' he said.

'Thank you, sir.'

He had watched the sergeant-major tilt the bottle to pour a small tot, then swallow it neat. His eyes had taken in the dark stain of grease on the side of the jaw; the black worn nails of the hand that was holding the glass. Then the overalls, anonymous but for the gleam of the brass coat-of-arms on the sleeve. As always, Tom Pugh was on the job.

'You've heard?' he said.

'Yes, sir. I've started workshops on the division of spares. I wondered what—'

Anson held on to the edge of the table, fighting to say sparingly what had to be said.

'First—the cars that are staying. There'll be twenty-five. And

they're to be the best in the unit—regardless of who has them now.
You know which they are—so tell the platoon sergeants to get them
transferred at once.'

Tom Pugh wrote in his notebook: he looked up and said, 'The
present owners won't like that much sir.'

'I couldn't care less. And it will take that cocky look off their
faces when they start on that safe road east.'

'Very good, sir. And then—'

'Then—' He stopped to stare. Then—? He couldn't remember.
He looked all round the truck and then buried his head on his arms
. . . 'I'm sorry, Tom,' he whispered, 'I'm so bloody tired . . .'

It was the first time a Christian name had ever passed between
them, but the warrant officer took no more notice than to slip one
key in his form of address. 'You've had enough, Mr Anson,' he said
quietly.

Anson moved his head sideways, looking at the whisky bottle.
'You mean—of that?'

'No. Of everything.'

Four years of respect and understanding and something deeper
flowed between them in the narrow space while the pressure lamp
hissed and spluttered to break the silence. Then Tom Pugh got to
his feet. 'I'll look after it, sir. I know what you want. You get some
sleep.'

'Mr Crosbie—' said Anson, and stopped.

'I'll explain to Mr Crosbie. And I'll come back and see you before
you go.'

'But you're coming with me.'

The MSM stood quite still. In an instant he was the warrant
officer again. 'I'd rather stay, sir.'

'No. You can't be spared.'

'I'd rather, sir. I've nothing to go back for—'

There was another silence. Anson thought of that day in Matruh
when he had had to break the news of a house obliterated in far-
away Plymouth. 'Neither have I, but that's not the point. The
brigadier says we both are non-expendable—so we go. His direct
orders.'

'Very good, sir.' Tom Pugh looked down at the air-mattress that
was laid out under the table. 'You lie down—just for an hour. I'll
attend to everything. Call you, if necessary.' The soft Devon voice
sounded so very persuasive.

'Just an hour then—' He almost folded up as he levered himself out of the chair, rolled on to the mattress without even bothering to loosen his belt. 'Only an hour,' he said again.

'Yes, sir.'

There was the sound of the chair being moved and then the truck went dark as the lamp was turned down. He heard the scraping of boots and then two hands pulled up a blanket to his neck and tucked it in all round him. There was a patch of the night sky showing where the blackout was parted and the thump of someone jumping off the tailboard.

He stared for a moment at that chink of light, flickering, faintly tinged with orange, the reflection of countless fires. Then he went down into the sleep of exhaustion to the sound of the mutter of the guns . . . and something else . . . a new, different noise. Beyond the cliffs, on the road, the steady grind of an unending column of vehicles . . . creeping in low gear . . . without a light . . . winding out towards the east on the last night of Tobruk.

CHAPTER 2

Mr Pugh rolled over on his back and wiped the sweat out of his eyes. He said, 'I don't want no more of that kind of talk, Corporal Bellamy. Pass me a three-eighth-inch ring spanner.'

It was stifling in the narrow space under the engine of the lorry: the four blankets that were draped to the ground on all sides of the engine effectively prevented any air as well as light from escaping outside, while the four inspection lamps that blazed inside gave off the combined heat of an electric fire. As he turned on his back and adjusted the blanket to the contours of his body where it straddled outside, Tom Pugh winced at the sharp edge of a stone that was biting through the tarpaulin and into his left shoulder-blade. He marvelled again at the state of mind in base workshops and civilian garages that insisted on minimum facilities before they would attempt the renewal of big ends.

Above him, the bowels of the engine—gleaming crankshaft and loosened connecting rods, tied to the sides of the crank-case with wire—seemed to be grinning. It was a challenging grin—'what's wrong with me?' He stared back, up at the glint of metal, framed in the black space where the sump had been removed. 'It's easier for doctors,' he thought. 'Patients can talk. But machinery goes on uncomplaining, until it breaks.'

An arm holding a ring spanner came in through a crack in the blankets, groping its way towards him like a blind worm. Tom took the spanner. 'Thank you. When I've switched off the lights, you can come in and get cracking. Bring the split-pins and locking washers with you.'

He switched off the lights and then, with a grunting and a humping, Corporal Bellamy wriggled through the curtains to join him. Tom Pugh felt to see if the blankets were tight round both their legs and then switched on.

'Start on number four, Corporal. If you'd done that inspection properly, it wouldn't be necessary for a WO to have to get under here and show you your job.'

The corporal was a natural grumbler. 'If the mucking officers knew what they were mucking well doing—and what was mucking well happening—instead of boozing—none of us would be mucking about under this mucking son of a bitch in the middle of the mucking night—'

With immense skill, Tom Pugh flicked a gob of oil off the crank-shaft and into the corporal's left eye. 'Sorry, Corporal,' he said pleasantly, as the other rolled away, cursing and rubbing. 'When you're ready—hand me up some of those pins and tabs—and let's get on with it.'

As they worked on their backs, reaching up into the dark shadows of the crank-case, he went on with a monologue.

'You don't like being left here, do you, Corporal? Just nothing to do, except sit on the soft sand on your fat arse—and a nice little cave to run to when the bombs come down? You would rather be coming with the Captain and I—probably get shot up and chased all the way—just like it was at Sidi Rezegh, if you remember that?

'You wouldn't? Well, you will—if there's another word of that kind of talk—and under close arrest, on a charge of mutiny. That's a promise. And they aren't very kind to mutineers at these times, Corp, they find nice hard walls to stick them up against.'

There was a healthy silence.

'You heard what the captain said, didn't you?' Tom was tightening steadily.

'The captain—he didn't look too good,' said Corporal Bellamy reflectively.

'No. He's had too long wet-nursing clots like you.' Tom felt in the tin between them for a locking washer. 'But you heard him say—three or four weeks—no worse than last time. And I'll tell you something you don't know—and you can tell it to your precious friends—the captain volunteered to stay—'

'Go on, S'major.'

'Sir—to you,' Tom snapped, '—I happen to hold the King's Warrant. But tell your friends. I was there and I heard it.'

'Heard what, sir?'

'You know that little brigadier—the medic they call "Dangle-toes"? Well, when he was telling the captain what was going to happen, the captain said, "I must stay, sir," and when I heard that, I said, "I'd like to stay too." And the brig—he didn't half bawl us both out. Said "No" and that we'd bloody well got to obey orders.'

'That's different,' said Corporal Bellamy.

'Yes.' As he bent over the last split-pin and then ran his square fingers, lovingly, over the work done, he was thinking that it had been the only thing he could do to help—and at least some of it was true.

'This seems shipshape, Corporal. Get the sump on—fresh oil—and test the pressure. Don't let me ever hear again of you failing to report a low one on inspection—or you'll be on a charge.'

He switched out the lights and crawled out of the blanket tent.

Outside the flickering darkness and the noise that had been muffled by the blankets, almost unnoticed in his absorption over the repair, came back with a sense of surprise. He got to his feet and groped his way back to the running-board. Then he sat down and bowed his face on his hands. He was so very tired.

After a minute he stirred and looked at his watch. Better give the captain a little longer. What else was there to do? As duty, nothing, for all the vehicles were sorted out in the order of their going and the best shape he could have them in the limited time. From loyalty, so much—if he had been in a position to do it. He wondered where Mr Crosbie was, thought of him and Captain Anson and then wished he was not in uniform and could do what was necessary. Knock their two silly heads together . . .

An eruption of noise down by the harbour made him look up. The searchlights were circling in a cone and the orange reflections tinted the dark sea from the explosions on the point. A raid—and a bad one. 'Poor sods,' he said out loud. He was thinking of the drivers of the five ambulances, down there, so close to it while they cleared the hospital. Then his mind went back to the problem of his commanding officer.

It was a little thing that had started the essence of their relationship. On that overcrowded troopship, coming out. He, the just-promoted warrant officer, Mr Anson with one pip up. It had been the time when the first letters home had been due for censorship, and he had held his back for three days because he could not bear the thought that any other eyes should see the things he had written to Ann. Somehow, Mr Anson must have guessed, and sent for him, to that stuffy little cabin where he sat with piles of letters waiting to be read and stamped.

'Mr Pugh—I don't want to have to read your letters home. If you promise me that there will never be anything military in them that there shouldn't, seal them and give them to me personally, and I'll sign.'

In the moment of his promise, something had been born. And he had never forgotten it.

Nor the other time . . . In Matruh, when he had been told about Plymouth. Mr Anson had been so wise. There had been no fumbling, no awkward sympathy, no offer of leave that would have been an insult, just quiet orders for a reconnaissance of a well far to the south, and at the very last moment, before he set off, the news. Alone, except for the company of a moron driver, between clean sand and clear sky, he had had three days to get to grips with it. He had not forgotten that, either.

Down over the harbour the noise was dying. He could hear Corporal Bellamy swearing under the blankets. It brought him back to the present.

'Officers boozing' . . . He turned that remark over in his mind. If it had become so obvious, he supposed it was fair. He, watching the long slow change from a different angle, had not realized. And there had always been Mr Crosbie to help him shield it . . . until today. But something had happened—they were against each other now. It had been sudden, he could pinpoint it to last night . . . when they had gone out to look for the CO. It must have been something serious. They were avoiding each other; once, today, when he had seen them talking, he had not liked the look in Mr Crosbie's eyes.

Though he had meant what he had said in the first place, now he was glad he was going. He would pick the chance of seeing the final crack-up of the captain rather than have to spend the next month cooped up with Mr Crosbie in that mood. A month? . . . he wondered. It had all sounded very convincing, but he knew that the captain did not believe it . . . and he knew that the men did not believe the captain. That was the trouble of being a WO—you were too close to both sides . . . saw too much. He wondered if the brigadier believed it. No, it would be flannel from there too . . . flannel all the way down.

He looked at his watch. Time to wake the captain. Then he would stay close. Six hours before they left to pick up the brig, six hours in which he must keep those two apart or in the restraint of his presence. It must be done, now at the end. They had been such good friends.

He groped his way through the dark patches of the vehicle lines, past the shadowed quick movement of the men packing up, the purr of idling engines, subdued talk. The office truck was black and silent. He climbed up over the tailboard and when he had turned up the lamp, called, 'Captain Anson,' softly.

There was a sharp crack as the figure on the bed jerked up so suddenly that he hit his head on the underside of the table, then in one movement he had rolled sideways and was on his feet. Tom saw the eyes open, but not awake; the glisten of the tight skin on the cheekbones. This half-sleeping was the most dangerous thing of all.

'What's the time?' The voice jerked.

'A minute before 01.30, sir. I thought you would like half an hour before the convoy leaves.'

'Yes. Thank you, Mr Pugh—' The eyes had come back and were focused on the table. Then a hand strayed towards the bottle that was there. Tom said, 'Let me—' and grabbed the bottle quickly to pour out two small tots. ''Luck, sir.' He put the bottle down on the chair behind him.

Anson looked about him vaguely. 'You say they're nearly ready to go—is everything all right?'

'Yes, sir.'

'I suppose we'd better have a look round them.'

They went out into the darkness to the deeper shadows where the convoy was forming up. As they went from vehicle to vehicle down the line, Tom, from the feel of the ambulance or lorry, the faint glimpse of the driver's face, would give all details of load and fitness. The two subalterns who were going with them followed behind. Apart from Tom's quiet voice, there was hardly any sound: the men, standing by to finish the lashing down, were silent, with no spirit of the start of an adventure about them. Once in the darkness a voice passed them, calling, 'Timmy . . . Timmy . . .' and someone close said, 'Dodger's lost his mucking dog again.' Beyond, separated, watching, were the dim shapes of those that were staying behind.

Tom Pugh turned from the last truck. 'That's the lot, sir. They're the worst—as you said—but they shouldn't give any trouble.'

'Good.' Anson turned to the two lieutenants. 'We'll get in the rear ambulance—then I'll brief you. You had better come too, MSM.'

When the rear doors were closed and the ventilators stuffed with rag, they put on the inside light and sat in pairs opposite each other on the bunks. The interior of the car seemed very clean and white, smelling of new paint. Tom Pugh breathed a sigh of relief now that he could see the captain properly. That glassy look had gone from the eyes, the voice when he spoke was natural, firm.

'You, Smith, will command. Prosser take the rear and whip-in. Control are sending a motor-cyclist to guide you up to the eastern checkpost, but they're pretty vague about the state of the road beyond there—or the position on the flank. The best thing you can do is get cracking from there—non-stop—with at least a hundred yards between vehicles. Go to the old location at Sollum and put out a unit sign. Let the men have one bathe and then get them working.' While he had been talking he had scribbled on his message pad. 'There's the movement order.'

Smith said, 'Mr Pugh—does he come with us?'

'No. With me, later. I've got to report to the brig at first light. Unless he mucks about, we should catch you up fast enough to be at Sollum almost as soon as you are there. But I want Mr Pugh to do one or two things for Mr Crosbie before we go—'

He broke off suddenly. 'Has anyone seen Mr Crosbie lately?'

'He was in that far cave, fixing up his new cook-house, about half an hour ago,' said Smith.

'Good. I'll see him later.'

Tom was still watching. That muscle had stopped twitching at the side of the captain's face. Then he remembered something.

'Those five ambulances, sir. The ones that have gone to the hospital to clear it. What happens to them?'

'Hell, I'd forgotten them.'

'I fixed that direct with Crosbie, sir,' said Smith. 'He's sent five of his—so it doesn't matter.'

From outside, through the thin plywood and canvas walls, came the soft *chug...chug...chug* of a motor-cycle. 'There's your escort,' said Anson. He reached up to the light switch. 'See you for tea or supper, then, Prosser—I'll come up to the front with you, Smith, and see you off.'

They all went out into the dark that was not quite dark now as the tip of the moon was coming up over the escarpment. Tom walked up behind Anson and Smtih to the head of the column where the motor-cyclist, was waiting beside the lieutenant's truck. He heard the captain say, 'Look after them, Smithy.' Then the red-cap, who had been looking round, turned to kick his starter; like a soft wave passing down the column, the noise of the running engines was increased one by one. The vehicles started to move past them, lurching, gleaming ghostly in the beginnings of the moon. Dim faces looked out of the cabs, little puffs of sand spurted white from between the wheels, there was the soft snarl of power in low gear. Tom stood close behind the captain, counting, forty-six . . . forty-seven . . . forty-eight . . . then Mr Prosser's truck. That was the lot. The sounds faded into nothing.

The captain gave a deep sigh, but before either of them spoke, another voice came from behind.

'So I just missed the farewell party.' It was Crosbie.

Tom moved closer to Anson, instinctively. This was exactly what he had feared.

Anson said, 'Hello, Paul. How's it going?'

'All done—and ready for your inspection, sir.'

Tom moved a little closer, almost between them. He didn't like that tone. Anson did not answer for a minute, but just stared up into his friend's face. At last, he said quietly, 'If you read your chit from the brig, Paul, you would see that you came under orders from the hospital as from midnight. The colonel can inspect, if he wants to—I just wondered if I could help in any way.'

'You—' said Crosbie, and stopped, for Tom had cut in with a quick, 'Listen.' There was the noise of vehicles coming towards them and then four ambulances came round the edge of the hill, swaying ungainly as they bumped towards them down the track.

Anson looked at his watch. 'From the hospital—and about time too.'

Corsbie said, 'Only four—what the hell's happened to the other one?'

They pulled up abreast of them and a sergeant got out of the leading cab and came over. He saluted. 'It was pretty bad down there, sir. We got that raid right in the middle of loading. But we got them all on.'

'What's happened to the other car—hit?'

'No, sir. The colonel kept it. He gave me this note for you. Said you were to get it at once.' He held out a folded signal.

'Thank you, Sergeant.'

When the four cars had bumped off down the track to their lines, Anson unfolded the paper and held it up to the moonlight. All Tom could see was that it was very short.

'I thought you said that I was in command here now.' There was that edge in Crosbie's voice again.

Anson folded the note carefully. 'It happens to be addressed to me personally.' He looked at Tom. 'Are you very tired, MSM?'

'Not too bad, sir.' He had had no sleep and he was dropping on his feet, but he was wanted.

'Will you drive me to the hospital now? I must see the colonel.' Then he said, 'I'll see you when I come back, Paul.'

They were off the track and on the road leading down to the hospital when Tom said, 'What's the trouble, sir?'

'I don't know. The note just said, *Further complications, you must help me, George. Please come down at once.* Could be anything.'

Their arrival at the entrance to the hospital coincided with one of those complete lulls that made the silence more frightening than any form of activity. The moon was bright now and, in a way, that only seemed to make it worse. As they drove on to the wide gravel sweep in front of the main entrance, the ambulance, parked up against one wall, scarcely showed but for the darkness of its red cross. When they had stopped and got out, Tom was surprised to see an orderly standing near it. As they walked over he stiffened, gripping his pick-handle. But he did not challenge, for both of them were well-known.

'What's cooking, Corporal?' said Anson.

'Guarding the ladies, sir.'

'Ladies—?'

The corporal lowered his voice. 'There's two in the back. Nurses. They came up on that transport. Got left behind somehow. I'm here to see no one disturbs them.'

Anson said, 'Well, I don't know what the hell I'm supposed to do about it. Stay here, Mr Pugh. I'll go and find the colonel.' He ran up the steps into the entrance.

Tom moved off a few paces, away from the sentry and towards the back of the car. He pulled out a packet of cigarettes and lit one, carefully cupping his hands over the flame of the match. The moonlight was like soft silver water flowing over everything, smoothing out all the scars and wreckage that lay around. He drew deep on the fag, letting the coils of smoke float up like white snakes from his nostrils. He listened and there was nothing but the faint mutter of the guns starting up again far away, over the escarpment to the south. 'I don't like it,' he thought, 'these lulls—they're too frequent—too long. It's not like them to let up.' Then there was a different, closer sound. He turned quickly to see the back door of the ambulance opening.

At first there was only the widening band of black hat showed the darkened interior, then something slim and light slipped between, closed the door and came down the steps.

It was a girl—not a bit like a nurse, he thought—in those slacks and khaki shirt. As she walked over to him, he saw that she was slim and tall and, somehow, serene. The fair hair that was tied back tight behind her head glowed in the soft moonlight and the mouth, big and generous, was smiling. He could not see her eyes. She stopped in front of him and held out her hand.

'Good evening. You must be Captain Anson. I'm so sorry we're going to give you all this trouble.'

He saluted, but did not take the hand.

'Good evening, Miss. Captain Anson's gone to find the colonel. I'm his sergeant-major, MSM Pugh. We were sorry to hear you had been left behind—' he looked towards the ambulance—'but I thought the corporal there said, "Ladies"—or are you on your own?'

'No, there's another sister with me—but she's rather shocked and the colonel's put her to sleep for a bit. I had to come out of there. I was dying for some fresh air.'

He fumbled with his packet and offered her a cigarette and she lit it from the tip of his own. She blew out a cloud of smoke and turned to look around her while the moonlight pressed down on them gently. 'So this is Tobruk,' she said. 'How different from all that I had imagined.'

He said, 'It isn't always as peaceful as this.' Then, 'How did you manage to miss the boat?'

She laughed. 'Oh, it was all too silly. Sister Norton—that's the other one—should never have come on this trip. She's too highly strung—and very young. I don't suppose she has ever been in any real bombing before. While we were loading—she and I had come ashore to help—there was a raid. Things started coming down right on the harbour—'

'I saw it,' he said.

'Well, Sister Norton just panicked. She ran away. They could only spare two men to help me find her—and it was all so dark and strange. It took hours. She was right over on the other side of that lagoon thing, crouching by the water. Then she wouldn't come back—we had to carry her. And by that time the transport had gone—something to do with the moon. You can't blame them.'

She stopped as the sound of voices came from behind them. It was the colonel and Captain Anson coming down the steps.

The colonel smiled at Tom. 'Good evening, Mr Pugh.' Then he turned to the girl, 'How is she, Sister?'

'Still sleeping, sir.'

'Good. Sister Murdoch, this is Captain Anson.' As they shook hands, he added, 'Your trouble.' Tom had not taken his eyes from the colonel's face. They were old friends and now he was shocked to see how he looked. In this light he would hardly have recognized him, like a walking skeleton.

The colonel said, 'We seem to have made a mess of this all ways, Sister. Captain Anson's main convoy has gone—and he doesn't think much of the idea of trying to catch up with them.'

They were by the car now; Anson leant against the bonnet, rubbing his chin. 'It would mean special permission to go through the perimeter, sir. And that would take time. I don't mind taking one of Crosbie's vehicles—but he's got so few spare drivers—' He looked across at Tom. 'Of course, Mr Pugh could start on ahead with them—'

Tom said quickly, 'There's a couple of vehicles up there I should look at before we go.' It wasn't true—but neither did he want to go dodging about in the night with a couple of girls, nor leave Captain Anson to the mercy of whisky or Mr Crosbie.

Anson said, 'Well—if the sister doesn't mind—the best thing is to leave them here for the moment. It's only a few hours before we meet the brigadier, anyway. We'll come and collect you then, and go on my movement order. A sort of special convoy. And either I or the MSM will drive the ambulance.'

The girl said, 'That seems simple. We'll do whatever you wish, Captain Anson.'

The colonel looked from one to the other. 'And you'll deliver them, George?'

'I promise. Either I or the MSM will drive until there's—' he hesitated—'no risk. Then send them on with a sound man to Alex.'

'I'm profoundly grateful, George. I know they will be all right now. But I must get some sleep—so I'll say goodbye—and the best of luck—for the second time.' Then he turned to Tom and held out his hand again. 'And the best of luck to you, Mr Pugh.'

The three of them stood watching him; straight, tall, with the grey hair shining in the soft silver light as he turned and walked towards the entrance of the hospital.

Anson looked at the girl. He said, 'Get some sleep. In the morning we won't disturb you. One or other of us will get in the car and just drive it away. But I want you to keep in the back until I give the word.'

She smiled and said, 'We are under your orders, Captain Anson.' Then she turned and walked over to the ambulance. The big square door closed behind her.

The moon was going when they got back to the caves and the first breath of the dawn was coming off the sea; already there was that minute shading of colour in the sky between black and grey. They reached to the back of the car for blankets and sat with them huddled round their shoulders. The wind grew and it was colder.

'Time for an hour's kip, if you want it, Mr Pugh.'

'No, sir. I'm fine as I am.'

'Don't forget you may be driving those bloody women.'

Tom smiled. 'And don't forget you may be driving—the brigadier.'

There was silence while Tom pulled the blanket closer round him, taking off his cap and letting the wind ruffle his hair. He closed his eyes with no thought of sleep. He was too tired for that, he just wanted to think . . .

There was no problem forward—except the extent of the disaster into which they were plunging. That it was to be that, he was now quite certain. He did not have to wait to see the brigadier to be convinced—although he knew that would do the trick. The brig . . . that amusing, gutful, little flanneller . . . he was thinking of him, without disrespect, from the Olympian heights of a WO . . . in the morning he would get that stream of bouncing confidence, but he would be able to see the eyes behind those glasses while they told the tale. Which appeared to be more than his officers could . . .

He had seen all he wanted at the hospital, the colonel, a man he knew and trusted, resigned, calm, saying goodbye, and then going back to his job. And, from him, Tom knew.

He opened his eyes and looked towards the east, no sun yet. Perhaps it was good that a curtain lay between that and what would happen before it set again. There was no point in thinking forward then, only back . . . and there were so many things.

He thought of the garage. The little square whitewashed house with its two green pumps on the corner of the village crossroads by the post office. The village, deep in its hollow to the west of the Tamar, with the tall elms round the church, the thatch of the cottages and the smoke hanging straight on summer evenings. They had been so happy there—but now it was like a dream; as if it had never happened.

There was no link, no children—and thank God for that—nothing to draw him back . . . yet he couldn't stop remembering. How she had slaved at those cream teas in the summer, how they had scraped and gone without to put in the second pump, repair jobs, big and small, that had paved the way in the modernizing of the business that had been left him by his blacksmith father.

Then the war. The stirrings of conscience that he should do something. The arguments that he was too old, and then the tears that night he came home from Plymouth, sheepish, enlisted in the RASC. The kaleidoscope of north-country billets, postings and promotions. His meeting up with Mr Anson . . .

He turned to look at the hunched figure beside him, the head forward, nodding. The first fingers of real light were creeping into the east of the sky. He shook the shoulder gently. 'First light, sir.'

Anson stirred and stretched. 'I'd better find Mr Crosbie.'

'Shall I come?'

'No, stay and start her up. I'll bring him back with me.'

He watched the captain, stiff and awkward, get out of the car and walk away. A wave of feeling rose up inside him that almost stifled, it was the focus now—of everything, after a lost wife and the children that might have been. They had been together, up and down that desert, for so long, they had grown up, militarily, side by side—he to the highest rank that held any interest, Anson to captain. 'He should be a major soon,' he thought—then remembered the other things that had happened. His captain was not growing any more. He was withering, and that was, must be, Tom Pugh's only problem.

That day in Plymouth—the one he had heard of in Matruh—it did not hurt any more. Only, it was so terribly hard to understand. The chance that a one-day visit to her sister should coincide with the lone raider, the fighters on his tail, dropping his load on that distant suburb to get more speed for the desperate run home. There had been no hate in the mind that loosed those bombs, he knew, only fear. And in him, now, there was no hate either. It had happened. And there was nothing to go home to.

Voices behind him now, and the soft crunch of desert boots on the sand. He turned to see the captain and Mr Crosbie walking

side by side, yet apart. He got out of the car and stood waiting for
them.

'I came to say goodbye, Sergeant-major. I hear you have everything laid on for this trip—even female comfort.'

'We'll be seeing you very soon, sir.'

'I doubt it.' Crosbie was not looking at either of them, but far,
far beyond. The light was coming now. Grey.

Anson moved uneasily and said, 'Well, I'll say it. So long, Paul,
and good luck. We must get cracking—and I know you've a hell of
a lot to do.'

'I have.' He ignored the outstretched hand and threw up a stiff
mocking salute. 'Permission to fall out, sir?—and remember me to
Ariadne.'

'Paul—' the captain looked very old suddenly, standing there,
his hand groping.

'Permission to fall out?' As Crosbie repeated it, his voice went
brittle. Then he said, 'You ripe bastard,' very softly, and turned
away. Tom stared at the ground because he did not want to see
the captain's face. He heard the soft crunch of boots fading into the
distance.

When he thought it was safe, he said, 'We'd best be moving, sir,'
and Anson had answered, 'Yes,' in a flat voice, and they had got
into the car without looking at each other, and Tom had started
her up and driven down the track and on to the road without once
looking back. Dawn was with them now; it was easy to see the
details of the harbour, the black smudges of smoke still rising from
last night's fires, the dark line of the escarpment away to the south.
Still that heavy, uneasy silence clung to the whole place.

The ambulance stood like a square box against the run-in to the
hospital; there was nothing else there and no movement. He ran
the Humber alongside and then turned to look at the captain.

'Will you take the ambulance, sir?'

'No. You hop in and follow me down to Corps HQ. I'll get ahead
and meet the brigadier.' He was looking straight in front of him,
his voice still had that dead, flat tone.

When the Humber had moved off, Tom got into the cab of the
ambulance. It was a wide platform with no doors at the sides, the
bucket seats of driver and orderly separated by a gangway that led
to the door communicating with the back; the windscreen, top panel
hinged open, was smeared with oil and sand to stop the telltale
glint of sun that might be spotted by hostile aircraft. He sat relaxed

in the driver's seat for a moment and then turned round to look at the door beside him. There was no sound from the other side. After he had started the engine and adjusted the choke, he let her idle for a minute. He was leaning forward to put the gear lever into first when the door opened and the girl put her head out.

'Hello, Sergeant-major.' She smiled and he thought it was a very nice smile. He noticed all that he could see of her was as spick and span as he had thought it was last night in the moonlight.

'Are we off?' she said.

'Yes. To Corps Headquarters first. I think the captain has to get permission from the brigadier to move you.'

'And then—?'

He shrugged. 'Back to your hospital at Alex. Two days—if we are lucky.'

'Will it—?' she started, but he looked at his watch and then said, 'I'd best be moving—that brigadier gets very testy.'

She smiled again. 'All right. And we'll keep in the back, like Captain Anson said, until you give the word.' The door closed and he let in the clutch and went off up the hill after the Humber. He thought, 'I ought to have asked after the other girl—can't waste any more time now—must later.'

It was full light now and all the old scenes of the well-known road slid by one after the other as he turned and twisted up the loops climbing up from the harbour. Well-remembered, but now so different. He stared more and more intently as he swung from one lock to the other on the bends. He used this road so often . . . the last time only two days before . . . one was accustomed to a particular turn by the look of the camps that were close to it. Now it was all changed, for the camps were not there any more, only empty, untidy, turned-over squares of desert where the tents had been. A lot of people had gone in the night.

Farther on, up the higher slopes, there was a new pattern. The transport, pulled just off the road in long straggles. It was the tanks that made him stare hardest, for there were so many, far more than he had ever seen inside the perimeter before. Silent, canted sideways in the ditches, he could see their crews, wrapped in their ground-sheets, lying like grey slugs beside them. But they were not casualties, pulled in for repair . . . he saw no splattered holes drilled through turrets, no damaged tracks. He started to whistle.

In and out . . . in and out, as he pursed his lips. He tilted his cap on the back of his head and then the words came back to him

... 'Where do us be going ... and what be doing of there ... ?'
The old Devon song ... Tavistock Goosey Fair. It struck him that
he did not know where he was going any more than those poor
b—s by the side of the road did.

The song died suddenly as he stared down the straight stretch of
road ahead. If it had not been for the Humber drawn up on the
verge and the three figures standing beside it, he would not have
known he had reached Corps HQ. Like the other camps, it had
gone.

'God!' he said. 'They don't half get their finger out when they
do a swan.' He pulled up behind the Humber and got down.

The brigadier was standing talking to Anson, waving his arms,
and Tom could see that the captain was angry. Another
officer—remembered vaguely as a staff captain, medical—was busy
loading a pile of kit from the sand into the back of their car. He
saw the brig was wearing his best hat and tunic. A bad sign. He
went up to the correct distance and saluted.

The brig looked at him, gave a faint waggle with one hand, and
said, 'You're late.' Then turned back to Anson.

'I'm sorry. I sent my truck on with the Corps transport because
I thought your car would be quicker. Now I find you've involved
yourself with two sisters and an ambulance. Do you expect me to
trundle back to Egypt in convoy? No, I'll take the car—and Ponsonby
can drive it. *You can, can't you, Ponsonby?*' he roared at the staff
captain, who dropped the pack he was carrying and said, 'Oh, yes,
sir,' hurriedly.

'Do you want us to take our kit out?' It was Captain Anson and
there was a tremble in his voice. His face was very white.

The brig looked up from where he was leaning on the bonnet,
writing furiously in his message pad. 'No. Dammit, man—you'll
have the lot back this evening. We'll look after it.' Then his face
changed. 'Look—I'm ordering you, Anson. There isn't time for
argument.' He stabbed his pencil in the direction of the escarpment
to the south. 'They are making a strong thrust, east of here, towards
the road. Corps got out in the hell of a hurry, and I don't like being
too far behind the commander—it's uncomfortable. Here are your
orders—' he ripped a sheet from the pad—'in case we get separated.
These girls are your responsibility. To be delivered to Alexandria
by a reliable officer.'

Tom was thinking ... 'A thrust to the east of us ... on the road
... when and how did they manage to get that far ... ?'

The brig had jumped into the passenger seat. 'Come on, Ponsonby. Don't stand there. I'm in a hurry.' He turned to grin at the two of them. 'See you for supper,' he said. Then their cherished Humber bounded like a wounded animal as the staff captain let in the clutch with a bang and disappeared up the road in a cloud of dust.

They climbed into the ambulance in silence. Then Anson said in a tight voice, 'I'm going to catch that little bastard. How long would it take to lift the governor on this crate?'

'All of half an hour, sir. Not worth it—fifteen miles lost. And listen—'

During the argument, neither had realized how the sound of the guns had been growing, how the direction had changed so gradually from south to south-east. It had swung right round now over to the strip that held the coast road, the only access to the frontier of Egypt.

'Yes,' said Anson, 'perhaps, for once, Dangle-toes is right. Get cracking, then.'

Tom let in the clutch and soon the engine was snarling under its full thirty horses as they swayed round the last twist on the road before the long straight run to the eastern perimeter. They were high now, the escarpment clear to them, a long brown cliff that flanked the south about ten miles away. Ahead, the black ribbon of tarmac and the telegraph poles stretched out in perspective, empty but for a faint dot that might have been the Humber. Tom had his foot down on the floor now, tense over the wheel while the air roared in through the open screen. Once or twice he managed to flick his eyes over towards the escarpment. Was it imagination?—or was there a haze hanging over it?—vehicles moving? The second time, a little farther east, he saw something quite definite. A ripple of pale flashes that came from the crest. The noise of their passage was too great to hear anything—he did not see the bursts. He swung his eyes back on the road, keeping them there, not speaking. There was no point in telling the captain that they were outflanked already—and that Jerry was shelling the road.

Now the tank-trap on the perimeter and the huddle of tents near it were rushing towards them. He threw the gear into neutral and started coasting to a halt. There were only two vehicles there, a lorry and the Humber jammed up tight behind it. Remembering the advantages of dispersion, he pulled up a clear fifty yards behind.

There seemed to be some form of argument going on up there,

for the brigadier was standing up in the front seat of the car, waving
his arms as usual, clearly haranguing the MP who was standing in
the road. Anson said, 'I'll go and see what's happening,' jumped
down and started running up the road towards the checkpost. There
was still no sound from the back of the car. Tom unhooked the
captain's binoculars that were hanging from a peg behind the
driver's seat and then knocked softly on the communicating door.

'Yes—?' It had just opened a crack, only enough to see her face.

He said very softly, 'We're at the checkpost. There seems to be
a delay, and the captain's gone up to sort it out. How is she?'

'Awake—and terribly scared.'

He said, 'Look—Jerry's started shelling the road and it seems as
if we shall have to run the gauntlet. There isn't much protection in
these things—just wedge all the cushions and blankets beside you
to the right, and when we move off, lie on the floor. I'm afraid it
may be a bit bumpy.'

She took it quite calmly. 'I'll do that.'

'Are you sure—you can manage?'

'I'll have to.'

He said, 'I'm just going over to that mound there for a
moment—to see if I can see anything.'

'We'll stay put.' The door shut with a click.

He got down and went over to the little mound that was a few
yards off the road. He slung the glasses round his neck, then focused
them down towards the checkpost.

The lorry and the Humber looked misshapen and foreshortened.
The figure of Anson, covering the last few yards, moving in that
curious slow-motion gait of magnified distance. The brig had sat
down now and then he saw dust puff from under the wheels of the
lorry in front; a second later, the noise of the revving exhaust came
back. He swung his lenses out to the south, on the escarpment.

The sun was right up now, a blood-red disc that rested on the
edge of the desert, beyond the point where the straight line of road
and telegraph poles vanished to nothing. The colours to the side of
it had changed to a pattern of dun and grey and sage, it stretched
to the south as far as the ridge of the cliff. There, clear now, like
ants on an earth bank, was a host of transport. He thumbed the
fine adjustment to get them clearer . . . Yes, they were moving . . .
down the cliff towards them. There was no fear, only an aching
responsibility for their load.

He swung the glasses back on the way ahead. The lorry had

moved a distance now, across the tank-trap and on to the road. He could see every detail of the barbed wire and the minefield as it passed them, dwindling down the line of telegraph-poles. Suddenly, short and then in two groups over, slender columns like black and yellow poplar trees spouted from the desert to grow up in the sky. The 'crump' of them came afterwards, the lorry was invisible beyond in the cloud of dust. Perhaps it had got through, but Jerry had the range of the road.

The roar of an exhaust came back to him again, and he lowered the glasses quickly to the bridge of the tank-trap. It was the Humber being given the gun. He kept his eyes trained on it, hardly aware of the pound of Anson's boots coming back down the road, the shout of, 'Come on, Pugh, there's talk of closing the bridge.'

It was strange to see the foreshortened, open body of the car he had maintained and nursed so long dwindle like that down the black line of the road. The brig was standing up, arms waving, for a second the light caught the maroon band of his cap. Tom smiled, he thought of the stream of bad German that was being hurled at the enemy. He wondered if it would be effective at a range of four thousand yards.

He saw what happened—exactly, in slow motion—because he was looking straight at the car for that split-second of time. One moment it was there, the next, an orange flower seemed to burst into bloom on the right-hand side of the body; the long bonnet whipped round backwards as a running dog might turn to snap at a fly and then everything was lost in a blot of smoke and dust, with one dot that might have been a body turning slowly in an arc high in the air. When the dust cleared, there was just a spiral of black smoke climbing straight in the sky.

He lowered the glasses, feeling rather sick; the first thought was not for the men . . . or the car. His own tool-kit, the special set of ring spanners, that he loved and would not lend, they had been stowed in the back.

He looked down at Anson. 'They've had it . . . a direct hit.'

'Christ! Dangle-toes . . .' Anson was very white. Tom understood that thought so well. It was a blasphemy that a pillar of the desert could be obliterated for ever, just like that. Then the captain's hand was dragging at his sleeve, pulling him down the slope. 'Come on. Quick—while there's still time.'

As they ran back towards the car, Anson jerked, 'Are they—all right—inside?'

'Yes—I told them—what to do. The other—she's just come round.'

They scrambled in and started her up and Tom crashed into gear and accelerated towards the empty strip of concrete that was the bridge. But there were two figures running away from it now, down the road, in their direction. They were shouting—Tom could see the open mouths—waving their arms; no words came to them through the roar of aero engines that were coming in from the east.

'Get a move on, Tom.' Anson's voice rose and cracked through it. But the two figures had halted now, spread across the road, barring it, their tommy-guns at the ready. They were MPs.

When Tom had halted in front of them he leaned out of the cab and looked upwards, watching the glint of silver wings against the sun as the fighter-bombers circled in the dive of their attack towards the escarpment, then the shooting stars of tracer weaving their patterns to and fro, the fountains of sand spouting among the distant enemy transport. In seconds it was over and the planes were turning and climbing back to the height for their return to base. The noise of the engines died away. The voices of the MP—a captain—and Anson came clear to him from the other side of the cab.

'Sorry, old boy. I've got the orders. Close the road and blow the bridge. You'll have to turn back.'

Tom turned to see him standing with one foot on the step, the tommy-gun crooked under his arm. There was a sheen of sweat on his face.

Anson said, 'Don't be a bloody fool I've told you twice—I've got two nursing sisters in the back. And orders, direct from Corps, to get them back to the Delta. Look—' He fumbled for the brig's signal in his pocket.

The policeman stiffened. 'I don't care if you've got the Archangel Gabriel. That bridge is going up in a minute. So get back.'

'Drive-on, Sergeant-major.' Anson's voice was tight.

As Tom hesitated, the tommy-gun came up from under the arm until it pointed straight at Anson's stomach. He saw the finger curling round the trigger.

'I shouldn't, Sergeant-major. You'll have a dead duck beside you if you do.'

He put the gear lever into reverse. 'Best keep clear of any flying bits,' he said. Then he let in the clutch and the ambulance started backwards. The MP jumped on the step, holding the windscreen pillar with one hand, gun still pointing. Neither he nor Anson exchanged another word.

Straining round to look past the bulge of the spare wheel cover, he was surprised at the empty road behind them. Surely there should have been others, they could not be the last out. No, there was something else . . . a good way behind . . . heavy stuff, by the haze of dust it was making.

He heard the MP say, 'Thirty seconds . . . best turn sideways, or the blast may get your windscreen.' He locked the wheel hard down to back off sideways on the soft sand, then cut the engine. As he relaxed in the seat, Anson was knocking at the communicating door. He heard him say, 'Lie down, Sister—there's going to be a big bang—' over that, the voice of the MP chanting, 'Ten . . . seven . . . five . . . four . . .' He turned to look down the road to the bridge and then it heaved up slowly with bursts of orange and black between the cracks and the blast of it slapped him in the face. With the noise that followed, the whole thing dissolved into a cloud of dust and smoke; a block of concrete whistled through the air to bounce on the road in front of them, burst, and roll in smaller fragments to the side.

And that was that. They were inside. As Tom sat and watched the dust clear, he thought, without anger, without even bitterness, of the trail of incident that had led up to this moment; the different streams of thought that had caught him for a moment to pull this way and that; the brigadier, warm and comforting, the captain, fighting his own battle, patently not believing, but backing up manfully what he had been told to say; the chill of rumour, his own personal doubts. It was bloody hard for a WO—sitting in the middle.

Well, they had said Tobruk would be invested . . . but surely there could be no planned investment, if it happened at such a speed. He wondered how accurate they would be over the second part . . . its strength . . . the time before it was relieved.

The MP was talking to Anson. 'Sorry, old man. But I wouldn't have fancied your chances out there. Safer inside.'

Anson said, 'Sorry I created,' and they shook hands. The policeman slung the tommy-gun. 'Well, I'd better go back along the road and organize the stuff that's coming up.' For the first time, Tom noticed the clatter of tracked vehicles that was growing to a roar behind them.

They swung back on the road and started back towards Tobruk

and dropped the MP at the first screen of tanks that were coming up from behind. As they went on, the sight of the 25-pounders and the Bofors that crowded the road while they moved up in support gave Tom a little hope. They drove on, not speaking, without slowing, without a halt. As always, the red crosses of the ambulance gave them absolute right of way. Only when they had got to a road fork that branched right to the harbour had Anson said, 'Left, Sergeant-major,' and soon after that, as they ran along a higher ridge, parallel to the sea, were those earlier thoughts chilled.

There was a lot of transport there, a lot of troops in camps or resting at the side of the road. He saw some British armour and some of the Second South African Division. Trucks passed them or came in convoy from the opposite direction. It all looked very busy and impressive . . . until you looked very close.

Then the pattern of movement became aimless; the second's glance at the faces at the side of the road a little disquieting. There was a groping, bewildered look creeping over all.

Anson's voice cut across these thoughts. 'Did you check this crate for everything?'

'Only the petrol, sir. She's full—twenty-four gallons—but I couldn't very well get in the back to look at the water and rations. I know there are the usual small spares issued, and a front and rear spring.'

'Mechanically?'

'One of the best maintained in the company. Driver Grimes has always had her. He didn't half kick up when he had to leave her behind.'

Anson looked down to where a name was painted in white on the drab dashboard. 'Good old *Katy*,' he said absently, 'I suppose that's his wife?'

'I think so.'

There was a silence and then Anson said, 'Well, the first thing is to stop and check everything. I came this way to be nearer the supply depot. If the girls agree, I've got a kind of plan.'

He did not enlarge on it, but Tom guessed. He said, 'One thing—tools. We only have the issue kit. Not too good, sir. Mine is—was—in the back of the Humber.'

Only the snarl of the sand tyres on the tarmac came up to them as both thought of the blackened scrap-heap on the Bardia road, then Tom said, 'And we've only got one jack.'

There was a lull in the transport passing them now, a high bank on the left of the road that hid anything above; then round the next bend was a semi-circular indent cut into the side that looked like a road-mender's quarry.

'Pull in there,' said Anson. 'We'll talk to the girls—and work it out.'

When they had pulled off the road and cut the engine, the captain got up stiffly from the passenger seat and went to the door between them and knocked. 'Will you come out, Sister?'

In a moment her head appeared and she said, 'Where are we—? and what was all that noise—?'

Tom smiled at her. 'Still on the inside—looking out, I'm afraid.'

Anson said, 'Can you both come out here—we've got to have a talk.'

'I'll try and make her—but she's being awfully difficult.' The door was left ajar and while they lit up their cigarettes they heard her voice coming from the back, low and insistent, then the incoherent sobbing answer of her companion. The voice rose, there was the unmistakable sound of a slap. The two men's eyes met and held. Another complication. Then the fair girl came out into the cab, followed by her friend.

' . . . The wrath of God . . .' that was Tom's first reaction to her appearance, and he was not far wrong. He could see that at other times she would be beautiful; at the moment, the red, puffy eyes, the white, tear-stained face with the red mark of an open hand still showing on one cheek, were not appetizing. 'More trouble,' he thought.

She did not answer their quiet 'Good morning,' and slumped down in the gangway with her back against the door. Not quite crying, not quite silent, she looked like a crumpled khaki sack in those creased slacks and shirt.

Anson had got down to the road and was leaning on the windscreen pillar, facing back towards them; the fair girl had slipped into his seat. He said, 'I'm terribly sorry. We did our best—but we just didn't make it. They were shelling the coast road outside the perimeter when we got there. The brigadier had the first run—in my car. It got a direct hit. Then our people blew up the bridge over the tank-trap. That was the noise you heard. They wouldn't let us have a try at it—they turned us back at the point of a gun. Perhaps it was for the best. But I'm sorry.'

The fair girl said, very calmly, 'What happens now?'

'First the sergeant-major is going to check all the stuff we have

with us: petrol, water, food—everything like that. On that, if I
decide that it is possible, and—you agree, of course, there is one
other way to get you out.'

'And if you can't—?'

He smiled. 'Let's see if it's possible first—before we give in. Tom,
have a quick shufti, will you?' He was pulling out his cigarettes and
offering them round as Tom went round to the back of the car.

It did not take him long to check the cans and the sealed box
that held the emergency rations. He started whistling while he
worked; there was more than he had hoped of everything, and the
captain hadn't had a drink for hours . . . and didn't seem to want
one.

When he went back to the front, they were still in the same
positions. The dark sister—Norton, he thought her name was—was
sitting straighter now, looking better, though the hand that held
the cigarette still trembled.

He said, 'The vehicle rations are sealed, sir. That's seven days
for four people. Beside the tanks, there's five jerricans of petrol—say,
twenty gallons. Sixteen gallons of water in tins, and some, I can't
say how much, in the inside patients' water tank.'

Anson said, 'We could do it—'

The fair girl said, 'What—?'

'Break out—go south and turn up back to the road.'

'And the alternative—?'

'To take you back to the hospital—to wait for a ship—if there
are going to be any—'

'I think I would prefer—'

They had all been so intent on their problem that the build-up
of noise above them had passed unnoticed. The drone of engines,
the crackle of machine-gun fire had come gradually; the *bump-bump-
bump-bump-bump* of Bofors fire brought them back to reality and
then the scream of dive-bombers rammed it home.

It came down suddenly on them, rising in pitch and volume so
fast that in seconds it was almost more than ears could stand. Anson
was leaning back, staring upwards, shading his eyes. Then his voice
came, sharp, 'On top of us—quick—scatter.'

As Tom turned to pull the dark girl from the floor beside him,
he saw Anson dragging the other one down in the ditch on the far
side. As he touched her, she came towards him at first unresisting,
then reacted with terrifying suddenness. She jumped across him,
straight out into the road, head down, running with arms flailing.

He cursed and dived after her, making a flying tackle that sent them both sprawling into the far ditch. The noise above them had changed to the thinner whine of bombs. He was lying on top of her then, just before the ground seemed to come up and hit them, hard and quick, six times. It was all noise and debris then, with the warm dry dust filling his eyes and choking; the soft body beneath him had stopped shaking. He rolled over and peered through the fog for the others. They were both there, crawling back along the far ditch to the ambulance. He picked up the limp body and carried it back.

Apart from scratches, they were none of them touched and they decided that the dark girl, Norton, had fainted, pure and simple, from fright. They put her in the back and covered her with a blanket, then beat the dust from their clothes and wiped their faces, the yellow grit coming away in patches to leave the travesty of a stage makeup.

The fair girl scrubbed with the back of her hand. 'So this is what it will be like—until it's relieved.' There was the faintest tremor in her voice. 'I wish I could have a wash.'

Tom pulled out a large handkerchief. 'It comes off better dry. Take that.' She smiled as she reached over for it and then, for the first time, he touched her; something strange and from the past stirred inside him.

Anson said, 'I don't want to frighten you—but I shouldn't count on this place being relieved too quickly—if ever.'

She stared at him. 'What do you mean?'

'That Jerry will be in here before we know where we are. That he's only so slow about it because he can't believe it.'

'We'll go with you—your way,' she said.

'What about—her?'

'Norton? She's in no state to decide anything. But she won't be any trouble. I'll see to that.'

'All right. But I want you to know what we're in for. It will be difficult—perhaps dangerous.' He turned to look at Tom. 'Do you remember that track—the one to the south-west through the minefield—towards Knightsbridge? That one we used in the last siege?'

'I only went over it once, sir. It twists like anything and I bet the marking tapes will have gone by now. Probably been re-mined too.'

'I knew it well,' said Anson. 'I did it in the dark once. They

won't have re-mined it. No point up to a few days ago—and then
no time. It's worth a chance.'

'—That's the chance, is it?' said the girl. 'Being blown up if
you're wrong?'

'Yes. But I'll back my hunch. The next bit will be the tough
spot, getting through the ring outside if the place is contained. The
only chance is if they haven't enough troops to cover the whole
perimeter—that there are gaps. The minefield is wide and looks
strong where that track is, so they might leave it alone.'

'And if they don't—'

'And we run slap into them? Try bluff. Hope for the luck to cook
up a good story. They're pretty punctilious about the red cross. It
might work.'

'And if it does?'

He laughed. 'You're a devil for punishment. Well, then it's just
a piece of cake. Run due south for fifty miles—to be sure to keep
out of trouble, then turn east to the "wire", then north back to the
coast to find our unit. We'll send you straight on to Alex from
there.'

'I don't know much about it,' she said, 'but petrol, water, and
things like that?'

'It will be two-fifty miles at the outside. On what Tom says we
have, there's three-fifty miles' petrol—even over the worst going.
We've got ten days' water and a week's food. We should be there
in two days. What more could anyone want?'

Tom spoke for the first time. He said, 'We could break down.'

Anson stared at him. 'Then it would be the hell of a long walk.'
He turned to the girl again. 'Well—?'

'We'll go.'

'Let's get cracking then. Every hour will make it more tricky.
But stop at the supply depot on the way past, Tom, and we'll sling
on a bit more food.'

As Tom bent towards the starter button, he turned to look at the
girl. 'Can either of you drive, miss?'

She shook her head.

'Oh—' He stared at Anson. 'I was afraid of that. It means there
will only be one of us to do the man-handling. And there's some
awful soft sand south on the "wire".'

'Wait till it comes, Tom. The girls will have to push, that's all.'
Then he said, 'Sister, this is going to be rather bloody for you—but
the best way you can help at the moment is by keeping Norton

quiet and being out of sight. So don't come out of there until you get the word.'

'I'll do that.' She smiled at them both and got up and went in to the back of the car.

They moved off and soon they were in the main South African Laager area. And things were different. There was no doubt of it now, the look in the eyes of the troops they passed—open hostility, shading to something worse. They did not mention it to each other, but they both knew; Tom hunched a little closer to the wheel, holding it tighter, there was a little click as Anson opened the flap of the revolver holster that was hanging from his belt.

Now shouts were accompanying their passage, and then there was a man standing in the road with a raised rifle.

'Run him down—if he won't move.' It came through Anson's teeth.

As Tom accelerated and swerved, he saw for a moment the fear and hate in the eyes behind the sights, there was a stab of flame and then the bullet whammed high and wide behind them. His spirits soared as the captain leant back and inched open the door and said, 'Someone shooting sparrows,' in a cheerful voice.

'Four hours now,' he thought, 'and he's still right on top. It's going to work out all right.'

But round the next bend they came on the supply depot and the first cracks that led to the abyss were there in front of them. The looting . . .

They saw it just in time as they were slowing down to turn into the sweep before the tent of the main office. Anson had just said, 'I'll nip in and show them the brig's orders—that should be enough,' when they saw the crowd erupting from the trampled side wall of a swaying tent.

Four separate figures broke from the mass, running towards them, staggering under the weight of the rum jars they were carrying; one tripped and fell and there was the moment's sight of the bloody mask of his face as he lifted it from the fragments, the brown ooze of the rum as it spilled and soaked into the sand. An officer was running, revolver drawn, and then a pick-handle flashed and the whole dissolved into a dark heaving mess that flashed away into the dust behind them. Tom had not needed Anson's shout of 'Keep moving', to put his foot down hard. The Austin's engine had snarled as the tyres spurted the soft sand and they were out through the other end of the turn-in and back on the road.

'My God!' said Anson.

He slowed down as they moved on down the boundary of the
depot. There were gaps in the barbed wire, but no crowds milling
among the low stacks of rations that were covered with tarpaulins.
No one wanted to loot hard tack.

'Drive in the next gap, Tom. Go from stack to stack. I'll try and
find what we want, and sling a case of each on quickly.'

Like a great bee drifting from flower to flower, they drove a
zigzag course between the stacks, stopping only long enough for
Anson to jump down, lift the sheet to identify and heave a case on
to the cabin floor. They had sugar and bully and milk before there
was a crackle of sound from the corner of the enclosure behind
them. The biggest tent was dissolving in thin tongues of flame under
a pall of smoke, ant-like figures spilling out of it, running across the
open space.

'Get moving, Tom.'

Before he could start, the door opened and the girl's head came
out; she was white, and her hair had come down at one side. 'I
must have a hand for a moment—she's so strong. I can't control
her.' For the first time they were aware of the thin screams and the
banging behind her.

'You go.' Anson was running round to the driving seat. There
was nothing to do except slide from under the wheel and follow the
girl into the back, slamming the door behind him.

It was dim in there and full of noise and there was a faint sour
smell in the air. He had been out there long enough to know exactly
what it was—fear . . .

The girl on the bunk was crouching up on it, her fingers making
a scrabbling noice on the plywood wall as she tried to tear it away;
as the other jumped over and started to pull her back, one shoulder
showed white where the shirt had split away, then the head, arching
back towards him, the eyes tight shut, the mouth a round 'O' from
which the screams came in one long high sound that seemed to hit
the inside of his head.

'I'll hold her—if you've got a shot of something. It's the only
way.' It was small comfort to feel the car swaying under them and
know they were moving.

The girl was panting. 'Yes . . . in my haversack . . . Hold tight
. . . she's so strong . . .'

He took a grip and at his touch she seemed to redouble her
struggles, then, suddenly, the noise stopped as she jerked her head

sideways and sharp teeth bit deep into his forearm. The strain was too much for the shirt and it ripped down the front with a dry brittle sound, a smooth pink-tipped breast was straining up through the gap towards him. He almost let go, not from the pain of the bite, but a feeling of revulsion. It was the first time he had seen or touched a woman . . . since . . .

Now the other was back, ripping the cover from the orange capsule, leaning over him to slide the needle into the exposed shoulder. The teeth left his arm and slowly the fight went out of her, in spasms, like a dying fish.

'No more trouble—for a bit,' said the girl.

They were standing close in the narrow space between the bunks. Now there was only heavy breath beside them and the roar of the tyres on the tarmac beneath that showed that the captain was back on the road. He saw how tired, how desperate she was. He reached forward and gripped both her arms at the elbows.

'Listen, miss. We're going to be all right. We've taken on extra food. There's plenty of water and petrol. Captain Anson will get us through that minefield—I know he can. We won't meet any Jerries. And you'll both be in Alex in three days.'

'Sorry—'

She was steadying herself against him now and he could feel the touch of her forearms on his—both soft and firm—but it did not worry him as the other had done. Slowly, the trembling stopped, she gave him the ghost of a smile and then sat down suddenly on the other bunk.

'I could do with a drink,' she said. 'There's a flask in my haversack. Would you like one?'

'I think we've earned it.'

He sat beside her, sucking the pin-pricks of blood from the purple bruise, watching her fumble for the flask, then the rattle of the neck against her teeth. 'You wanted that badly,' he thought, 'but you wouldn't scream—whatever happened.'

When he had had his turn, he said, 'I'd best get back to the cab with the captain.'

She held out the flask. 'What about him?'

'No, miss. Please don't give him one—don't even let him see it.'

'Why ever not—?'

He stared at the shining brown linoleum on the floor, swaying to the movement of the car, feeling a traitor as he searched desperately for the right words. 'He's had a bad time lately—been on the bottle.

But he hasn't had a chance to have one since we met this morning.
All his own stuff—was on that car. He's over the worst of it now
and he'll be all right if he thinks there's nothing. If he knows there
is, he'll start all over again. And then—' He spread his hands in a
gesture that implied a finish to everything, then he looked at her
desperately. 'I couldn't take you through that minefield—my navigation isn't good enough to risk lives on—so far south.'

She said, very quietly, 'I'm sorry. I didn't know.' The flask went
back, deep down in her haversack. There was silence for a moment,
and then the noise of the tyres deepened as they started to brake.
'Hell,' he said, 'what's up now?' He pushed open the door and went
out into the cab.

The road was empty, a little ahead was a pull-in with a single
tent surrounded with stacks and stacks of white water tins and
jerricans. Anson said, without looking round, 'All right in there?'

'Yes.'

'I'm going to pull in, Tom. That water point seems deserted. It's
worth a few moments to sling on extra petrol and water—to be
sure.'

They were coasting in to the track that led up to the tent. It was
then he had his first sight of Captain Zimmerman.

He was standing in front of the tent, a big, square pack slung from
each shoulder. The first impression was the size of the man, broad
and tall, like an oak. Tom saw the orange bands of the UDF below
the badges of rank on the shoulder straps, the short wide shorts,
the calf-high desert boots. As they slid by, he gripped the pillar of
the windscreen with one hand and swung himself up on the step,
then sat down on the floor of the cab, facing them. He looked up
at Anson. 'Good morning, Captain,' It was the clipped guttural
English of the Afrikander.

Anson had stopped now. 'Good morning. In trouble?'

'Yes. Can you tell me where there's a chance of getting a
truck—to get to hell out of here?'

'A truck?'

'Yes—mine's down the road—' he jerked his head in the direction
in which they would be going—'big end gone.'

'Where do you want to go to?'

'The Delta.'

He had got down from the step and stood facing them, the packs
still swinging from each shoulder. It was then that Tom decided he

didn't like the shape of that square neck that ran in a straight line
into the back of the shaven head, or those deep-set, very blue eyes.

The South African went on speaking, rocking back and forward
on his heels. 'Yes, the Delta—where I belong—at my own HQ.
Out of this bloody shower. I wouldn't have believed some of the
things I've heard today.'

Anson said, carefully, 'Such as—?'

'That there'll be no fight for it.'

'No fight?'

'Just that. They'll surrender. At least, that's my lot—the 2nd
Div. I don't know about the English. But I shouldn't imagine there's
much difference.'

'I don't believe it.'

The South African shrugged. 'Man, I heard it. They were always
a lousy lot. The general's a notorious OB.'

'I'm not interested in your bloody general. I take it you're 1st
Div. What are you doing up here, then?'

'R/T specialist—attached. But they don't need me any
longer—and I'd be wasted in a prison camp. So I thought it would
be a good idea to get back where I'd be more use.'

Anson said, 'I've got two nursing sisters in the back here. Got to
deliver them to Alex. They got left behind. We were just too late
to get out to the east—and one of them is bomb-happy already.'
He looked at Tom. 'Is everything really under control in there?'

'Yes, sir. For a bit. The other sister's given her a shot.'

The South African said, 'What are you going to do now?'

'Try and get through the minefield—I know an old path—and
then feel our way round to the coast behind our own lines. We'll
have to keep pretty far south.'

'I'd like to come with you.'

There was no one near the water point, no sound from the back
of the car. They were in a little world of their own. From the south
came only a dull mutter of guns and there was nothing in the sky.
It seemed so peaceful.

Anson broke the silence. 'It's the extra weight, the drain on water
and rations—I don't know—'

The big man lowered his packs to the step. 'There's one point I
don't understand. If you get through this minefield, how are you
going to get through the German troops outside?'

'How do you know they are there—?'

He shrugged. 'It's common talk in the 2nd Div—and why could you not get out from the east this morning? Be your age, man.'

Anson's voice was sharp. 'We'll bluff it—I don't know your experience of German troops here—but they usually respect the red cross.'

'You speak German—either of you?'

'No.' They said it in turn.

'Well—I do. Worked for years in South-West Africa. That might be useful. And—if we dealt with that one—I could push. I know the going down there. You'll need a strong man.' He flexed his great shoulders, then patted one of his packs. 'And last—just plain bribery—I've got a thousand cigarettes and three bottles of gin in there.'

As Tom's head jerked round to Anson, he was in time to see the pitiful reaction, the jerk of his Adam's apple and the flicker of the tongue over the lips. In a second the eyes were glittering in their agony and the sweat was shining through the stubble of his chin. Breaking point had been nearer than he had feared.

'You stupid, clumsy bastard,' he thought. 'You weren't to know—but now you've done for us all.'

Anson said, 'All right—you don't mind if I check your papers?' He turned to Tom. 'While I'm doing that, slip on six cans of each, will you?'

Sick at heart, he trudged off to the stacks, bringing back two tins at a time, humping them on to the cabin floor, then into the back, stacking them against the back doors. He did not speak to the girl until he had to; she was sitting on the bunk opposite the form under the blanket, head tilted back, eyes closed. The desperation of his thoughts scarcely allowed room for pity that surged up in him at the sight of the drained, defeated face. But, at the fifth trip, the gin bottle was out in front and they were holding mugs; after the last cans were stacked, he closed the door and leaned against it, looking down at her.

'Miss—there's a South African captain outside. I think the captain is going to take him with us. He's got some booze—and they have started to drink already. I can't do much. Please help me.'

She opened her eyes. 'I don't see I can do much, either. But I'll try. And don't call me "miss" all the time. The name is Murdoch—Diana Murdoch. What's yours besides Pugh? I can't mouth through "sergeant-major" all the time.'

'Tom.'

'All right, Tom. I'll come out with you and see what I can do.'

She came through behind him and Anson put his mug down quickly. He said, 'Sister, this is Captain Zimmerman, of the UDF, who is coming with us to push. And this is my sergeant-major, Mr Pugh.'

They both shook hands and then the girl looked down at the bottle and mug on the floor of the cab. 'What's this—a party?'

'Sort of "One for the road",' said Anson.

She looked at him steadily. 'I thought the first part of the "road"—was through a minefield. Is that the usual kind of training?'

There was a faint sound as Zimmerman banged the cork back into the bottle. 'The lady's right,' he said. Tom watched Anson tilt the mug to drain the last dregs.

The girl said, 'Then we go—now?'

'Yes.' Anson turned to Zimmerman. 'I should warn you. This track, it's old, we don't know if the tapes are still there to mark it—it may have been re-mined—'

'What are the chances?'

'About even money, I should think.'

'Fair enough.' He looked round at them for a moment. 'After that—the chance of being stopped. If I may say so, we won't have a hope, however well I talk, if you wear that—' his hand pointed to Anson's holster—'or those cap badges. They know them all, and they never let any but medical personnel through.'

'But we aren't doctors—any of us.'

'We all must be—to them.'

'It would be—like going through as a spy. They would shoot us if they found out.' Anson's voice was a mixture of fear and revulsion.

'They'll put you in the bag if you don't. If it does happen—that we're stopped—the only chance is to let me do all the talking. But I won't be able to do anything if you have those.'

Anson took off his cap and looked at it for a moment, then unstrapped the holster. With a quick jerk, he sent them both spinning to the side of the road. 'We'll have to, Tom.' Then he turned to the girl. 'We'll have to rely on you to look after the back. Keep on the bunks—as far forward as you can—in case a back wheel hits something the front ones miss. And don't come out at all until I tell you.'

She said, 'All right, Captain Anson,' and went into the back.

'You drive, Tom.' Then Anson gave a last hard look at the South African. 'It's understood, of course, that I command this party?'

'Of course.'

Tom let in the clutch and they moved off from the water point, making for the winding road that led up the ridge that guarded the inside of the minefield.

He drove fast and the noise of their movement and the fact they were on the lee of the hill seemed to blank out all other sound. The three of them sat in a row, Anson in the passenger seat, Zimmerman on the floor against the door listening to the snarl of the tyres on the black road, eyes flicking at the scattered transport that was all they were passing now. Tom thought of the silence in a concert hall after the conductor had raised his baton and before the orchestra crashed into sound. It was just like that.

Anson said, 'About two hundred yards ahead, Tom. You can see the marker cans on the track going up the hill.'

He slowed down and swung the car off the road, taking a line on the row of empty four-gallon cans that were strung out up the hill. It could hardly be called a track, for the going was far different from the soft sand at the other end of the perimeter; slab rock, with the space between covered in loose grey shale and flat stones, the lurking place of countless scorpions. The heavy box of the ambulance car lurched and swayed as they went up the slope, while the stones clattered from under the wheels. When they had reached the crest, a small shallow valley unfolded before them and then another, higher ridge that cut across the sky. Beyond that, Tom knew, was the descent into the minefield.

But there was something there that he had not counted on, the first pattern of any form of defence. Scattered there, hulled-down below the further ridge, were seven or eight tanks . . . Grants, he saw, by the big gun sticking from the side of each like a towel-rail. 'Poor sods,' he thought, 'there's only fifteen degrees traverse on those—and if they fight in retreat, they got to move in reverse, at five mph maximum to get them to bear at all.' His eyes were still searching as he followed the line of cans, then his spirits rose a little when he saw troops digging and the blunt muzzles of 25-pounders sticking out from the scars in the sand. If Jerry came over the top he'd catch a packet from that lot. He knew what HE would do to a tank at point-blank range.

They were all silent, eyes fixed now on the line of petrol cans stretching up the far hill; only the sway and the stones running from the wheels marked their progress. Then from the right there was the sound of another engine, revving, and the blare of a horn, short—long—short. He looked across, to see a scout car, driven fast, cutting diagonally towards them; there was a figure standing in the turret, waving its arms.

'Better stop,' said Anson.

The scout car circled them and then came up on the left; a tall fair lieutenant jumped down and walked over. He was a gunner.

'Good morning,' he said. 'And where the bloody hell do you think you're going to?'

Anson felt in his pocket and produced the message form. 'To Alex,' he said.

The lieutenant stared at them all in turn. 'You're crazy.' Then he unfolded the paper and read it. 'And the bloke that signed it is crazy too.' He stopped and peered at the signature. ' "Dangle-toes", I might have known it.' There were not many in the fortress who had not heard of the brigadier.

Anson spoke very patiently, 'Crazy—or not, I've got them. And I'm going to carry them out. And no one this side of hell is going to stop me.'

'That would be about the place—' the subaltern broke off and then grinned. 'The only thing that surprises me is that the brig isn't sitting on the bonnet, waving that bloody cap of his, and roaring at Jerry to clear a path through the minefield for him and have a hot bath ready by six. They'd probably do it, too.'

Anson said, 'He won't any more. He bought it this morning. Direct hit on a staff car. We saw it happen.'

The lieutenant said, 'God! I'm sorry,' and there was a silence. Then he looked at Anson again. 'These sisters—do they know the risk?'

'Yes. They've agreed. And I don't want them disturbed now. We know that path through the minefield, anyway. We've done it before.'

The gunner was scratching his chin, he looked at Zimmerman. 'What about you, Captain?'

Zimmerman, sitting there, legs straddled out on the floor of the cab, the two packs resting on his knees with his hands folded on top of them, said, 'It's all right with me.'

Tom had been staring at him through all this. He was wondering what could be in those packs, apart from that bloody gin . . .

especially in that big square one that had not been opened yet . . .
that looked so heavy . . . and was handled with such care. The first
dislike had gone—after all, he could not have known, be expected
to know, of the problem of booze. But he didn't want him . . . didn't
trust him . . . however good he might prove to be in the pushing in
soft sand.

He came back to the present to hear the gunner saying, 'Is there
anything we can do—? We're dug in all along the top of the ridge.'

'Nothing—except not to fire—even if they do.'

'Our OP says there's nothing on the far slope of the minefield,
although there's a lot of dust kicking up over the skyline. There's
no air report yet—but their R/T is very active.'

'Thanks.'

'If I were you I'd bear pretty sharpish south-east, if—when you
get through the field. Well, I'll get back to the blower and tell our
people you are coming.'

He turned on his heel and walked a few steps back towards the
scout car. Then he looked over his shoulder and said. 'But I still
think you're quite crazy.' Then he climbed in and the car jerked
forward to circle round and return in the direction from which it
had come.

When they reached the second crest, they almost ran over an old
embrasure that now housed a Bofors with its long barrel sticking
out through the camouflage netting. For a moment, Tom saw the
shine on steel helmets, the glint of field-glasses played on them,
then they were past and running down the steep slope towards the
minefield.

'When you get to the bottom, Tom, turn right along the wire. I
think I'll spot the old gap. We'll stop and check it on the bearings
I've got on the map.'

'OK, sir.' As he eased her down the slope, he looked across the
field and then up the ridge on the far side. There was nothing; no
movement, no sign of vehicles. No sound above the noise of their
own passing. They were alone.

The wadi, though broader, was the pattern of them all; the steep
rocky walls, shading grey to brown in contrast to the flat bottom
of softer yellow sand. It looked like a river against the sides, the
illusion heightened in this case by the ragged, rusting coils of wire
that gave the impression of banks. Between, the ground had the
look of weathered untidiness, a cross between a neglected garden
and a scrap yard; on the pocked sand and among the patches of

camel-thorn were rusting and blackened piles of metal, the burnt-out wrecks of lorry and tank that had been caught. Everything was still—and, somehow, the more menacing in its stillness. With nothing to see, there was a feeling of being seen.

They kicked up a cloud of dust as they ran fast down the slope and then skirted along the edge of the wire. One gap . . . two . . . and then Anson said, 'That's it, Tom. I'm sure. Stop and I'll take a bearing.'

He watched him get down and then move a few yards out of the ambulance's magnetic field before putting the compass to his eye and then taking a bearing right and left on landmarks on the opposite ridge. He came back to the car, sitting with map-board on knee, drawing with protractor and ruler.

'That's it.' He walked round to Tom's side. 'I'll walk in a bit and see if any old tracks are there—or any sign of re-laying.' He looked up at Tom and smiled and said, 'I'm sorry about that drink this morning—I could do with it now.' Then he turned and started to walk down to the gap in the wire. As Tom swung the car round in a half circle so that they were facing down towards him, his heart was sick with pride . . . and something more . . .

Zimmerman did not move, he did not speak. Both sat quite still watching the slight figure dwindle as it walked out into the field.

It was an odd sort of walk, slow, with one foot placed in front of the other like a tight-rope walker, head bent forward as if he were searching for a valuable lost at yesterday's picnic on the sands. When he had gone about twenty yards, he stopped suddenly, took a jump of a few feet, turned left again and came back towards them in the manner he had used going out.

Zimmerman shifted. 'What the hell's he doing?'

'Found an old track—walking along it to see if there were any signs of re-laying. Then he jumped to the opposite one—and he's doing the same thing back along that.' Tom spoke through gritting teeth.

'Man—he's got some guts!'

'Yes.' He wondered how long he would be able to say that.

When Anson reached them, he was almost cheerful. 'It's all right to the first sharp turn. The tracks are very faint, but there is no sign of re-laying. But I think we had better walk the whole thing, though.'

'But that will take hours, sir.'

Anson looked up at the ridge opposite. 'No one's objecting to us yet. And, with the girls, it would be better to be sure—than sorry.'

Zimmerman stirred. 'Look—if one was to walk the other track at the same time, it would halve the time, wouldn't it?'

'Yes. But—I can't ask you to do that. You're heavier than I am.'

Zimmerman put his packs down, then swung his legs down at the side of the cab and stood up. He grabbed the biggest pack, slinging it over his shoulder. 'A Springbok can go as far as any bloody Englishman,' he said. 'What do I look for?'

'Take the left-hand track, watch for any place where the ground has fallen in, or the marks of the tyre do not follow on. Go slow, and if you see anything you're not sure of, give a shout, and I'll hop over.' He turned to Tom. 'And don't you follow up closer than ten yards.'

'OK, sir.' Tom looked at Zimmerman. 'Wouldn't you like to leave that pack in the cab, Captain? It will make it easier for you and be quite safe.'

Zimmerman gave him an odd smile. 'No, they're my valuables. I'd rather they went with me than with your ambulance.'

The path through the minefield ran zigzag, always with the longer legs down the length of the field. The turns were the worst for him to follow on their path, but in a way it was relief to have them come back close and guide him round foot by foot. In the other time, there was nothing to do except watch the two figures as he crept along behind them, in bottom gear, intent on Anson's slim back, expecting any moment to see it disappear in a cloud of smoke and flame and shattered flesh. The sweat was pouring down his face now; salt, smarting in his eyes so that he could not see. He brushed it away with the back of his hand, but more came to take its place.

They were in the middle—at a turn—when the first intrusion came into their lonely battle. Droning high overhead in the wide bowl of sky came a single plane circling before it went away, then from the far side, the German side, came a faint crackle of automatic weapons and the soft sighing of something passing overhead. But he dare not turn to see. Then, the two in front stopped suddenly and looked back to the way from which they had come, lifting their heads and shading their eyes.

Zimmerman shouted, 'Three star shells—two white and a red between.'

'Good boys—' Anson's reply was fainter, '—they're trying. It's the best they can do to signal the red cross.'

There was no more firing and they went on, creeping, feeling for each step. It was on the last, longest leg, when the sweat was so blinding that he had to stop for a moment, that the door opened behind him and Diana came out of the cab. She came quietly and quickly, and he did not know she was there until she spoke. 'I just couldn't stand it any longer in there,' she said.

He could not look round. 'We're in the middle of the minefield. You get back.'

'I know we are. I've been trying to look out through that little side window. I couldn't stand it.'

'The captain will be livid. You get back, miss, like he said.'

'Not miss—Diana. Isn't there anything I can do?'

'The sweat in my eyes—I can't see. There's a handkerchief in my trouser pocket. Can you get it out and wipe my face?'

He felt her hand groping down against his leg and then the relief came of the mopping of his forehead. 'Thanks,' he said. 'I wouldn't like to muck the whole thing up—on account of a little sweat—after he's done so much—'

'I think both—are doing wonders.'

There was silence for a moment. 'Too good to last,' he said.

She was crouching beside him now, wiping gently, steadily. The sweat was still flowing, he could feel the trickle of it between his shoulder-blades, but it didn't matter any more.

'You love that man—don't you?' It was very soft. When he didn't answer, she said, 'Sorry—I'm putting you off.'

'No. I like you talking. If you don't mind me answering when I'm not at a tricky bit.' There was silence again before he said suddenly, 'It was at Sidi Rizegh—we were with ambulances then—and at one dawn we got overrun by Jerry tanks. I think it was a mistake—in that light they couldn't see what we were. We got shot to hell. In the confusion, I was left, without my truck.'

Another pause while he swung the wheel, staring intent on the slim figure walking in front, then he said, 'I was just standing there, the stuff cracking all round, wondering whether to dive in a slit-trench or run, when the captain swans up in his truck—as cool as a bloody cucumber. All he said was, "Morning, Mr Pugh. Want a lift?" And he hauls me in—about four hundred yards from the leading Mark IV—and we go lickety-spit after the rest, with bullets clanging into the back of us all the time. Then he said, "How

careless of you not to arrange transport, Sergeant-major,'' and a bit
later, when we had a bad burst from them, ''Do you think we are
showing them the most lady-like view of our arse?''—sorry, Miss
Diana—but that's the sort of man he is, really. I wish I had a son
like him—'

'And you have no son, Tom?'

Silence. Another turn and the last short leg of the path that
reached to a gap in the wire before the steep rock slope of the wadi.
The two figures had gone farther in front again, walking their tight-
rope, treading that dusty path of death.

'No. And it's too late now. I'm rather glad.'

'You're married?'

'Was. Plymouth blitz. She was only there for that one day, visiting
her sister—'

'Oh, I'm sorry.'

'No need,' he said, 'I don't mind talking about it now.'

There was a dream-like quality about their movement over those
last few yards—a feeling that something must happen, that they
could not be through. Then they were through the break in the
wire, on harder ground, with the walkers waiting for the car to pull
up to them. In silence, they all turned to look back at the silent
yellow river they had crossed.

Zimmerman leaned against the side of the cab, wiping his arm
across his face. 'Man—I'm sweating.' He looked back across the
field. 'But I don't believe there's a bloody mine in it, now.'

'There were,' said Anson, '—plenty.'

The girl got up. 'I'd better get back. She was showing the first
signs of coming to.' She went through and closed the door.

When she had gone, Anson gave one look up the silent empty
slope that stretched on towards the skyline in front of them. 'We
had better take it diagonal; south-east, like that gunner said. I don't
like it—too damned quiet.'

'You drive, sir?'

'No. My legs are too shaky. Carry on for a bit, will you, Tom?'

Zimmerman said, 'What about a drink, first?'

Tom, cursing silently, inwardly, watched the eyes light up and
one hand come forward, then hesitate and fall back to his side as
the expression on his face changed. 'No. Make it later—we must
get on.'

They piled into the front of the cab and started moving off up
the slope.

The diagonal course was long and fairly steep and there was no chance of seeing what lay beyond until they had reached the crest. They moved steadily, and were about halfway up when the noise came breaking over the sound of the engine and the rumble of the tyres on the rocks. It came from the air, the sound of aero engines that changed to the scream they had heard over the harbour.

'Dive-bombers—' Tom did not know who shouted it first, but the car was stopped and they were running away from it, scattering. Then he remembered the girls, turned on his elbow from where he had fallen to see what had happened. There was only Zimmerman, ten yards away, on the far side. The captain must have gone in the back, but it was too late to do anything about it now.

The noise was falling on them and above he could see the glint of the bombers: there were eight. Their dive steepened and in the moment of their release the bombs were plain, like clusters of black eggs. But they were not the target; in an instant he had rolled to his knees, looking down the wadi.

In a pattern, far down beyond where they had crossed, he saw the ochre fountains spew up across the minefield, the smaller blobs that rippled out in strings from their bases as the mines exploded by concussion. So that was the way they were going to get through.

The noise came, thunderous; the bombers climbed and turned, heading back to the east. Far away, there was a dry crackle of machine-gun fire and then one dark spiralling plummet staining the sky. There were no more sounds, no second wave coming for the moment. He got up, dusted himself and ran back to the car.

Anson was already in the driving seat, shouting, and the engine was running as he and Zimmerman climbed on board. 'Come on—for Christ's sake. You know what that means. They're going to attack.' Then they were bumping on, accelerating up the hill.

Zimmerman turned to him. 'So—it was live, after all?'

'Yes. It was nice of you both to leave me flat when those birds arrived. We could hardly hold that stupid bitch—had to tie her down.'

Nearly at the top now. Tom silent and ashamed. Then Zimmerman started to say, 'Man, that was a fine bit of navigation across—' when his voice died and they were all staring at the sight of the plain that was opening up to them over the crest.

The sun was high now and the mirage had started, but, whether they showed as thin black rods, far to the south, or sprawled like fat slugs on the nearer fringe, there was no mistaking what they were. Widely dispersed, but with the nearest squat, square turret showing plainly the white cross, they were running at an angle towards a laager of German tanks, ready to go into the attack and at a range of about a thousand yards.

Anson swore horribly, put his foot right down to the floor and the engines snarled as they turned a few more points to the east. The going was better now they were on top, hard gravel and clumps of camel-thorn replacing the rock. They ran diagonally, like a hare before the guns at a corner of a field, jinking and swaying as the captain cut in and out of the patches of green. Tom watched the speedometer needle hovering over the forty mark and even at this time the engineer came to the fore. 'For Christ's sake, sir, watch for holes—you'll bitch all the springs . . .'

Anson did not answer and beside him Zimmerman, crouching, peering past his shoulder, called, 'They're coming to cut us off.' Behind, in the back of the car, Tom could hear screaming, then he too, beyond the captain, could see the plumes of dust trailing out behind two trucks that had appeared from among the tanks and were heading directly towards them.

Something whined over their heads and then came the cracking of giant whips all around him and he knew that the fire was coming straight at them.

'Turn your stern towards them,' he shouted.

'No. The girls—' Anson swerved, but did not alter course.

Then another noise came—a deeper, angrier sound. It went 'wacker-wacker-wacker-wack' like a great stick being scraped along a paling. The body of the car jumped and shook and he knew they had been hit, and cried out to stop, but he knew that the captain would not heed him. Then the door behind pushed hard against his back and as he rolled to one side his heart turned over in terror as he saw the red stickiness on her hands. She was crying, 'Stop, stop—for pity's sake! It's Denise,' and for the first and last time he overrode the captain. He bent forward and cut the ignition switch and the engine choked to nothing, but Anson did not try to start it again. There was no more firing and in the silence as they coasted in a wide circle to face the oncoming trucks, her sobbing voice went on. 'She went mad . . . tore off those bandages we had tied round . . . I tried to hold her down . . . but I couldn't. Then the bullets came . . . she's been hit . . . in the stomach . . .'

They had stopped now and the two trucks were fanning out to close on each side. They were open and he could see the grey mushrooms of the steel helmets and the yellow dust rolling away behind. The girl said, 'I had better get back—and see if there's anything—'

Zimmerman was on the ground now, and his voice had a different tone; there was an authority when he spoke. 'I'll talk to them. Don't say a word—except to me.'

Without waiting for an answer, he shouldered the pack and walked round the ambulance, slow and unconcerned, towards the leading truck with his hands held high above his head.

Tom felt in his pocket. 'Cigarette, sir?'

'Thanks.' Just before they lit up, a puff of hot air brought the scent of crushed camel-thorn towards them. With it—that unforgettable, bitter-sweet smell—came back to Tom all the times, the good and the bad, that they had spent together in the desert. Perhaps the captain was thinking the same, for he said suddenly, 'Sorry, Tom. I've made a balls of it—as usual.'

'No—'

They lit their fags and drew on them, sitting quite still, side by side, watching the distant group of figures, one towering out of the mass of khaki and grey. Anson said suddenly, 'Where's that bloody pack of his?'

'Captain Zimmerman's?—he's got it on his shoulder.'

'No. I mean the other one. There's a bottle of gin in it, I know.'

'It's on the floor here, sir—but don't—'

'Give it to me.'

When Tom had handed it across, he ripped the flap open and pulled the bottle of spirit upright from among the medley of socks, shaving kit and cigarette cartons. Then he put it back on the floor beside him. His eyes drifted back to the group breaking up and coming over to them. Zimmerman, surrounded by the Afrika Korps. 'If we are going in the bag,' he said, 'I'm going to drink the whole of his bloody gin, now. If—' He stopped suddenly and gripped Tom's arm. 'Do you see the way they are holding their guns? Quite loose—they've dropped the muzzles. He may have pulled it off . . . it's just possible . . .'

They were close enough to see the faces now, and they were wary, not hostile.

Anson's voice went on, it was different, held a faraway, dream-like quality. 'If he has . . . I'm going to tell you something right now, Tom. It will be a sort of peace offering. Do you know the next drink I'm going to have—? A beer, Tom. A bloody great, tall, ice-cold glass of Rheingold in that little bar off Mahomet Ali Square in Alex . . . and I'll buy you one, all of you one, because I'm bloody well going to get you there . . .'

He could not bear it. He said, 'Shouldn't one of us go in there—to help?'

'You go, Tom.'

They were very close now, the Germans. He could hear the crunch of their boots on the gravel as he slipped through the door into the back of the ambulance.

CHAPTER 3

It was only in the middle of the minefield, when she could stand it no longer and she had come out into the cab to talk to Tom Pugh, that Diana had begun to try so desperately to remember those long-forgotten prayers.

Before that, the chain of events had been no more than alternate discomfort and annoyance. The trip to Tobruk had started as an adventure, spoilt only by being put in charge of that stupid little bitch by matron. When Denise had panicked in that raid on the harbour, it had been a sweat to go and find her, there had been the discomfort of being left with only a medical haversack and a handbag; having to sleep in her clothes. After that, the bore of having to stay in the back of the car, trying alternately to cajole or bully Denise into some form of self-respect, before being forced back on the last remedy of morphine. But now, for the first time, there was fear, not for herself, but for others.

She had thought a lot about her escorts—Zimmerman she classed as a passenger—and though she had liked both from the start, she understood one far better than the other.

Anson was the replica of hundreds she had danced with, dined with, and fought off with good-natured firmness in the backs of staff car or taxi; and the greatest tribute to her honesty in this was that none of the escorts ever bore her the slightest ill-will afterwards. Yes, Anson was the pattern—but with one great difference: they had been in the Delta, relaxed, with trouble behind them, or far in the dim future that did not matter; he, with too much sun, too much sand, too much of everything to bear. She thought of a band of rubber, stretched so tightly that it twanged transparent; now the cement of alcohol was taken away, it was liable to break any moment.

The warrant officer, Tom Pugh—? She could not quite under-stand herself there. She did not know many—none well —and there was therefore no yard-stick to judge by. Yet she knew he was far above the average of his kind and something of his withdrawn feeling had touched her from the very first. And now, as she came out and saw him there, crouching over the wheel, jaw clenched, sweat pouring down his face, the fixed agonized concentration on the slighter of the two figures ahead, there had been fear—for him, for all of them. And beneath it, something deeper, a stab of jealousy.

While she crouched beside him, mopping his face with that sodden handkerchief, while she had been listening and talking, her mind was groping back desperately into her childhood, trying to find the right words.

She couldn't remember. The ones that she did were no use ... 'Please, God, make me a good girl ...' but she didn't want anything for herself, only for the man walking ahead, and the one who steered behind in the cleared tracks. What else used she to say? 'Please keep Mummy and Daddy safe and well ...' But she had not heard—did not care if she did—of her mother for three years, and Daddy, dear inconsequential Daddy, was dead.

She smiled in the middle of wiping, as she thought of him; the little professor of the Midland university; his agnosticism —how he would laugh at her now—and his lapse.

Even as she listened to Tom Pugh, half her mind was remembering the day he left; suddenly, without a scene, with a lady snake-charmer he had met first through the gift of a complimentary ticket to a visiting circus. Happy ever after ... ? She remembered her mother's pursed lips and the sneering, 'He'll be back,' but he hadn't. She had visited the den of sin unknown to her mother, to find it clean and comfortable, the old man looked after and laughing for the first time in years; later, saw the girl's performance with the python, that she thought vaguely disgusting. But there were only four years between them, daughter and mistress, and a deep bond grew up, through common affection for the professor. The more she saw of them, the farther she drifted from her mother; at last a job away from her home—nursing—had been the only answer. And when the war came, and she had heard, in the North, of the bomb that had brought down the theatrical digs in a welter of brick and plaster to bury the snake-charmer and Daddy and the python for ever, she had dried her eyes and applied for overseas.

Now she was in the middle of a minefield, wiping the face of a strange warrant officer who would call her 'miss' with a fierce, unreasoning jealousy in her heart, searching for the things that Daddy had not believed and Mummy had had no time to teach ...

not for herself, but for them . . . not to save them from pain, but fear of their own fear . . .

It was easier when they were through the field and she had gone into the back again, to sit and watch Denise begin to come round, muttering and plucking at the blankets. It was when the bombs had come that she had started to struggle and scream and she did not think she would have been able to hold her if Anson had not been there. When they started off after, she had been quieter, still under the blanket and the bandages with which they lashed her down. It was only when the ambulance had begun to go very fast, bumping and swaying, that she started to go mad.

She broke free, screaming again, clawing at the walls as she tried to reach up them; Diana had her by the knees, gripping tight to bear her down, to get on the floor as she had been told, when it happened.

The noise had started—that awful 'whacking' noise—and Denise had jerked and gone limp against her as the red dripping stain had spread on the shirt above the waistband. The inside of the car was a dancing pattern of sunshine from the row of jagged holes that ran up and across the side above the bunk.

After she had put her down and run to the door and begged for the end of movements so that the slaughter might stop, it had become the numb concentration of routine. She had torn up the dressings from the medical box, making pads from shell dressings, bandaging round from the purple bruise hole above the navel to the worse torn mess of the back. There was so little there to satisfy those terrible demands and soon, as she worked, she knew it was to be no use. But it was her job, and she went on working on it methodically, not conscious of anything outside except that they had stopped. There was no thought of capture until Tom Pugh came through the door and closed it behind him.

Denise was lying flat now, covered by the blanket, eyes open, staring at the roof. She did not make a sound. Tom did not speak either, but stood looking down at her. Recognition came back in her eyes and she said suddenly, quite normally, 'I want a drink.'

His hand was on the screw top of one of the white water cans before Diana caught his sleeve. She turned so that her body shielded both of them from the bunk, then shook her head and pointed to her stomach.

'I'm thirsty.' The voice came clear from behind her and she

turned to look down. Denise was crying, soundlessly, the tears just running down her cheeks.

Tom did not look again. He just stared at Diana and said, 'We are in the bag. They're just coming over to us. That Zimmerman—he's been over to talk to them. The captain thinks he may have worked something—but I doubt it. So I came in to say—"sorry"—from us all. And see if there was anything I could do . . .'

They were standing close and perhaps the thing that made her feel better than anything was the way he had said, 'that Zimmerman'. She agreed. She said, 'Don't say, "sorry". You've all done so much—it makes me feel ashamed.' Then she let her eyes slide down to the bunk. 'But there's so little we can do for her,' she was almost whispering, 'she must not drink—just moisten her lips.'

He held the water can and tipped it over the wad of bandages she got ready; she knelt on the floor beside the bunk and started wiping her mouth. She said, 'Does it hurt, darling?' and the voice came back, faint but petulant, 'Who kicked me?'

They were still in the same position when the door opened quickly and a Hauptmann of the Afrika Korps came in with Zimmerman close behind.

She did not move, stayed kneeling, holding Denise's hand, feeling for the feather of the pulse, keeping her eyes fixed on the badge of palm broken by swastika that was in the front of that grey long-peaked cap. He did not look in the least like the blustering bully that was always depicted to her as a Hun. He was oldish, dark, very pale, the cheeks had a sucked-in look and there were dark rings beneath his eyes. She wondered how long it had been since he had had a good night's sleep.

He gave her a little bow and clicked his heels and there was nothing she could do in that position but give a silly bob in answer. He ignored Tom and turned back to Zimmerman. A stream of German passed between them. She thought, 'Perhaps it may have done the trick—I don't understand a word, but he certainly speaks it well.'

Zimmerman's voice was quite impersonal.

'The captain says that he bitterly regrets this accident, Sister. The Afrika Korps do not shoot women. If the red crosses had been more easily distinguishable, if we had asked for a safe conduct it would never have happened.'

There was nothing to do except nod again. More meaningless,

guttural words, then, 'He wishes to know if she is badly hurt—and if they can do anything.'

What was the use of telling him she would be dead in an hour or two—that nothing could be done? There were others, the ones that had the chance to go on living, to be considered. It might depend on what she said—whether they were allowed to go on.

'Tell him she has an abdominal wound—it's not too serious, but she should be taken to hospital as soon as possible.'

The Hauptmann nodded, then leant against the end of the bunk as a few more sentences passed between him and Zimmerman. She had found Denise's hand again, and suddenly, as they were talking, the cold fingers gripped hers, unbelievably strong; she looked down at the face and the eyes were open, filled with entreaty.

'What is it, Denise?' She soaked the pad in water again and started to moisten the mouth.

The Hauptmann had walked past her now, still ignoring Tom, to start a perfunctory search. He opened the medical lockers and lifted one or two of the cans stacked at the back. After kneeling to peer under the other bunk, he gave her another of those funny stiff bows and walked out of the door into the front of the cab.

Those open eyes, so sunken and ringed with purple now, lifted to look over Diana's head; she turned to see Tom bending forward, staring.

'What is it, miss?' The soft Devon burr sounded so persuasive. Now the lips were opening and shutting slowly. She was trying to talk.

Diana went on sponging, seeing in pity how that full mouth she had always admired was shrinking, cracking, some flecks of lipstick still hanging loose like flaking paint. She bent close and said, 'I know you're thirsty—but you mustn't have a drink yet.' The lips moved again, but even with her head right down there was only a faint rattling at the back of the throat. Fighting the instinct of years of training, she picked up the mug and let a trickle of water fall down into the open mouth. And then she knew she could not stand another moment of it without a break.

'Tom—I must have some more dressings. I'll go out and see if I can scrounge any.'

'I'll stay here, then. Is there anything to do?'

She shook her head gently. 'No. Not now. Just be near.'

When she had got up he slipped into her place. At the door, she turned to see him kneeling as she had done, chequered in sun and shadow from the gashes in the wall of the car, one big hand engulfing the little one, the other reaching up while the blunt fingers stroked up and down the forearm.

Her eyes were blinded by sudden hot tears as she went out into the still sunshine of the cab.

DENISE

Please, please don't let it happen.

I know that something has happened already ... after I got frightened ... and then I went to sleep ... and then the noise started all over again. I thought I was back in the nursery and started to try and get out of bed. Then someone hit me ... in the stomach. And now I'm thirsty ... but they won't give me a drink.

I'm not surprised that snooty bitch Murdoch won't—she would stop anything that I wanted, but that man, the big one with the grey hair and the blue eyes, he would. I'll ask him in a minute ... and tell him about that other thing ... He'll understand.

There's a great cold weight lying on my middle and I can't feel anything below that ... but when he comes closer, I'll tell him and he'll take it off and get me that drink. After that I'll tell him what I heard.

There's so much to be sorry about now ... but it's always too late to be sorry. I couldn't help having the body I was given ... and men liking it ... and I liking men. I know what everyone thought ... particularly the women ... but I couldn't help it. And then, after the last time, when matron said she was sending me home ... though I hated it ... I knew she was right to send me up here.

But why with Murdoch? She never tried to understand ... always looked down her nose. And when the noise started, she was bloody ... swore at me ... smacked my face. But she's gone now and there's only this man, closer, holding my hand. So it's the chance to tell him.

Can you hear me ... nice man with your grey hair and your crinkly eyes? ... You must, because I'm shouting at you. Those other two that came in ... did you hear what they said? ... but perhaps you don't understand German. I do, nice man ... and it was bad for you ... bad for all of us. Something about Cairo. That big one ... with the orange on his shoulders ... he's no good.

So watch out ... watch out for us all. That big one ... he's not what he pretends to be. He's a NAZI.

Did you hear? I think you did, for you're coming closer. There's a strange

*look in your eyes . . . all the understanding I always wanted . . . and never
had. Go on stroking my arm . . . I'm so tired . . . and so thirsty . . .*

After she had come out to the cab and brushed her sleeve across
her eyes, Diana jumped down on the sand beside Anson and Zimmerman, who were leaning against the side of the car, smoking.

The Hauptmann had disappeared, but they were surrounded by
a ring of the Afrika Korps, khaki and grey, with their automatic
weapons crooked loosely under their arms. She saw the ripple of
interest pass round the circle and wondered how long it was since
they had seen a woman; it would be something to talk about in the
canteen, something to write home about, if they were allowed to.
There was no enmity in their look, only a curiosity; she returned it
in the same spirit, wondering that they looked so young, so tired,
and why hadn't someone done something about those dreadful
desert sores. Then, deliberately she had turned her back and taken
a cigarette from the packet held out by Zimmerman.

Anson said, 'I think Zimmerman has fixed it.' He spoke very
softly. 'The Hauptmann has gone back to his truck to radio for
permission for a safe conduct.'

'What did you say, Captain Zimmerman?'

'The truth, dear lady, except that I implied the captain and the
sergeant-major were—medical officers.'

She did not speak again but stared past his head at the slanting
line of holes that ran across the canvas and the red and white paint.
Which one of them was Denise's? . . . Probably the third along . . .
They didn't look so spectacular from the outside.

She came back with a jerk. 'Captain Zimmerman, I must have
some more dressings. Do you think you can do anything?'

'I'll try, Sister.'

He moved past her and walked over to the nearest Feldwebel.
Anson looked round at her and said, 'How is she?' hopefully, but
she shook her head.

Zimmerman and the Feldwebel had gone over to the remaining
truck and presently came back with a square grey package. 'That's
all they can manage,' he said. The other truck was bumping back
towards them from the direction of the tank laager, and because
she could not bear to hear the verdict out there, she took the
package and said, 'I'd better get in,' and climbed back to the inside
of the car.

Tom was in the same position as when she had left him, kneeling,

holding the hand, but he was no longer stroking the arm. There
was trouble in his eyes as he said, 'She tried to get up—and she
said something. But she hasn't moved since.'

The sun was still low enough to throw a speckled pattern from
the ragged holes across the floor. There was plenty of light to make
the quick examination, even down to the formality of holding the
mirror from her handbag before the lips. There was nothing.

'She's dead, Tom.'

Quickly she got a hypodermic from the haversack and laid it on
the blanket, then folded the loose arm underneath and closed the
eyes. She turned and gripped Tom fiercely by the shoulder. 'But to
anyone else—until we know what's going to happen—she's asleep.
I've given her an injection.'

'If you want it that way.'

There were voices outside and then she said suddenly, 'What did
she say?'

'I couldn't really hear—it was only one word. It sounded like
"nasty".'

'Poor kid,' she said. 'But I don't think there was any pain.'

There was a soft tap on the door this time and then the
Hauptmann came in again, followed by Zimmerman. The South
African said, 'The captain has orders to escort us to a point south
of German operations. They are taking Captain Anson with them
in the truck to ensure we follow. You are to drive the ambulance,
Sergeant-major. They would like to move as soon as the sister is
ready.'

She said, 'Now, if you like,' and the Hauptmann looked down at
the bunk, his eyes expressionless, before he turned to Zimmerman
and spoke softly.

'He wants to know how she is.'

'Asleep. I gave her an injection.'

Her voice seemed to come quite naturally and the German
nodded and went out of the car. As Tom passed her she managed
to press his arm and whisper, 'Not yet.'

When they had started she did the few things that had to be
done and then sat on the opposite bunk, holding Denise's handbag,
watching the pattern of light from the bullet holes dancing on the
floor as the car swayed. She had bent over and pulled the blanket
up over the face opposite before she remembered that the German
might come in again. So she folded it back as before and then went
out to sit in the cab with the others.

They were almost at the far cliff that they had seen for a moment when they had first come over the escarpment. There were no tanks near them now, nor any transport that she could see except the one grey truck ahead of them, a cloud of dust trailing away sideways from behind it. She could just make out Anson's head, sandwiched between two grey caps in the back. In their own cab, Zimmerman was lounging in the passenger seat, the pack balanced on his knees; Tom, upright, hands loose but sure on the wheel, driving.

She shut the door and sat down with her back against it, feet stretched out straight in front of her across the floor. She shook her head, without speaking, at the cigarette offered by Zimmerman, then turned to watch Tom.

Though she did not drive, she knew in a moment that she was being driven by an expert. It was difficult to know how she knew, except that there were not any bumps. Everything was anticipated: a turn of the wheel, and the hole they would have jolted over passed harmlessly just to the side of their track; if there was a gully, he sensed it yards ahead. There would be a check on the brakes, a loosening of them at the critical moment to let her roll over easy, then the quiet pick-up in a lower gear. There was never a fault. 'And he's had six hours at it already,' she thought.

Now the truck ahead had reached the foot of the cliff and was nosing along it to the east. Presently it turned sharp right between the boulders and up the thin crack of a wadi.

They followed in and at once the going was rougher. She said, 'Take it slow, Tom—just as you would if—' She stopped remembering that Zimmerman did not know.

She turned to where he sat, still, staring straight ahead, with that heavy pack on his knees. She wondered what was in it.

She said, 'Sister Norton is dead. I didn't say anything, because I thought—well—it might prejudice—'

He didn't answer, but nodded, not looking at her, pulling at his bottom lip. The car crept on up the wadi behind the truck, the noise of the two engines echoing back from the steep rocky walls. Ahead now was the straight line of blue sky where they would gain the next level of plain. The Germans would be leaving soon and there was something else to say before they did—and Anson came back to them. And because she knew there was no time, she said it badly.

'Captain Zimmerman, I want to ask you a favour. Captain Anson had had a pretty bad time, before you met us. He—was drinking, quite a lot. He's probably screaming for one now. But we all depend on him, absolutely, for navigation. So please keep that gin of yours out of sight.'

He was silent for a moment. 'What do I do—if he asks me for one?' he said at last.

She searched the clipped English for sarcasm—and decided there was none, but before she could answer, Tom's voice cut in fiercely from the other side, 'He won't—he'd rather die than do that. But help him—don't let him see it, or offer him one.'

'I'll do my best,' said Zimmerman.

They were at the head of the wadi now, coming out on to another flat brown plain, with the same kind of low cliff far to the south of them. A hundred yards in front, the grey truck had stopped and the Hauptmann and Anson were standing beside it, waiting.

They pulled alongside and then Zimmerman jumped down and went over. Tom and Diana sat watching the group while Zimmerman and the Hauptmann talked.

Tom broke their silence suddenly. 'After we left the water point—where we picked him up—did we pass anything on the road?'

'I don't know, Tom—I was in the back.'

'Of course you were—I must ask the captain.'

'Why—?'

He did not answer and she saw the three men were walking back towards them.

Zimmerman looked at the Hauptmann, standing a little apart, then said, 'We are now well south of their operational axis—at least for the first part of their attack. The captain is leaving us here, but advises us to go farther south, in case of a chance meeting with one of their patrols. He is sorry he cannot help us with petrol or water, but they are short themselves.'

He stopped for a moment and stared straight at Diana, '—and he asks how the sister is.'

'Still asleep,' she said.

Zimmerman turned to the Hauptmann and there was one last exchange of words, there was a quick jerk of his head and then Anson and the South African came over to the ambulance and climbed on board.

The German stood close to them, stiff, with the background of his truck and the faces of the troops in it, all heads turned, staring curiously. He looked all round—at the dull brown and olive of the shimmering plain, the full blue bowl of the sky, the emptiness of both; when he looked back at them there was a flicker of expression on his face, and somehow Diana knew exactly what he was thinking. That it was one of the times when it didn't much matter whether you had the red desert rat or the broken palm painted on the front of your truck, because ahead of you were hundreds of miles of loneliness and soft sand and rock, the doubt of thirst, the danger of error in navigation, or the chance of a stray mine.

He drew himself up and gave a funny little military salute. As they passed by and he slid back out of their vision, he shouted something.

The ambulance gathered speed and there was only the open desert in front of them now, and silence among them for a few minutes. Then Anson said, 'What did he say, Zimmerman?' and the South African, looking straight ahead, answered, 'Good luck,' and after that no one spoke for a long time.

It was very crowded with four in the front and she thought that it might be a good idea for someone to go in the back and have a rest. There was no question of who it should be, for at close quarters Anson looked pitiable. The face was shiny and white and the sweat showed in little beads through the stubble of his chin. She had never seen anything so exhausted as those red, ringed eyes.

She said, 'Don't you think it would be a good idea to take turns to lie down for a spell? Why don't you start, Captain Anson?'

She saw the gratitude in his eyes, and then he said, 'But I'll disturb her,' and she remembered that he was the only one that did not know and had to tell him that Denise was dead.

He looked older, even more tired, when she had done and for a moment she was sorry she had ever thought of the idea. But Tom's voice came the other side, 'Yes—you go on, sir.' There was distaste in his face even then, so she said, 'I'll go first—and get things ready.' As she went through the door, she heard him say, 'All right. Another twenty miles on this bearing—and then stop for a brew up.'

There was only time to pull the blanket over the still white face and unstack those on the other bunk before he stumbled in after her. He almost fell across it and she had knelt and taken off his desert boots and swung his legs up before she realized that he was already asleep. She pulled a blanket over him and stood for a moment looking down, smoothing the dark hair away from the temples, thinking of all the lost and lonely little boys she had ever

seen, while the earlier jealousy drained away. Then, softly, she
closed the door on the living and the dead and went out to the cab.

There was more room now. They sat in the same order, silent
save for an occasional call from Zimmerman, who held the compass.
She moistened her mouth from the water can and passed the mug
in turn to the others. The tiredness was coming back, heavier, more
urgent. There was no sound but the hum of the engine and the
steady hiss of the tyres against the gravel, soothing. The ambulance
went on, a minute dot in the immensity of the desert. That far low
cliff seemed to hang at the same distance on the horizon. As the
sun climbed higher, the mirage grew and closed in on them. Sometimes they were running into a great shining lake that always moved
on; then chains of mountains or fairy castles would sweep in majestic
procession across the sky; once the gaunt timbers of a shipwreck
that melted when they drew near to the bleached ribs of a long-
dead camel.

Nothing was real—or lived. It was getting hot now and soon she
was tired of watching it and turned to look at Tom. The greying
hair, the firm jaw, the eyes shadowed by sunglasses. She noticed
the long white scar on the tan of his cheek and wondered how he
had got it . . .

KATY

*My official name is A1079654, ambulance, Austin K2. I have a six-cylinder,
overhead valve 29.8 hp engine, four gears, and I weigh about two and a half
tons. But I have always been called KATY.*

*Not KATY II, or KATY III . . . just KATY, which shows the measure
of care I have had from my one and only driver. He drew me from the depot
at Slough, brand new and drove me and maintained me until yesterday; he
painted the name on my bonnet in England, just before we set out on that
awful cross-country journey to Swansea in the winter of 1940; then I lost him
when we were loaded in the dark. I was deck cargo on a superannuated tramp
that took me round the Cape, smothered in salt spray in the Atlantic, grilled
across the Equator. But my driver was there for me at Suez and he took me
back to the camp and cursed and sweated until he had got the brine and the
rust off and had me back in good nick.*

*And then it was up into the blue. Up and down, up and down that strip
from Matruh to Benghazi; boulders and soft sand, shale, gravel and solid
rock—my wheels have hardly touched a road. And with it, the strain of the
banging and the twisting and the bumping, however careful he was.*

They say that machinery can't speak. But it can, through little subtle sounds that are different, or the flicker and fall of a needle on a dial. The ones that know these things—that think of us in terms of straining muscle and pumping artery—they understand. The one that's driving me now—he knows. I can tell by the way he lets me ride a bump. Brakes off at the last moment to let me roll; just half the strain on the springs.

Springs . . . that's one of the things I'd tell him if I could. I was never designed for this kind of war; on the drawing board, they were thinking in terms of the continents . . . roads. But for me it has been sand and rock all the way, and I've taken my fair share of punishment, and got through eight sets of springs to date. The trouble is that the replacements—they're not so good now, not from England, but tempered by Wogs in the Delta. And something has started to happen to mine, the rear ones, right at this very moment. In the main leaves, the important part that is the only connection of axle to body—and takes all the weight. Cracks are starting, hardly cracks yet, for only a microscope could find where the crystals are forming in the texture of the metal. But it will get worse with each jolt, however hard he tries, until they break. And then two tons comes straight down on the back axle.

There's another thing, but I think he'll see that in time. Just as my springs were not made for the desert, so my engine was not designed to run all the time in a temperature of 110°. I run too hot, but there's a water pump that circulates the stuff that keeps me cool, and it's as vital to me as a man's heart. In that pump there's a washer, made of carbon, to stop the water escaping past the spindle. It is starting to crumble . . . soon the water will leak past . . . the water that is essential to stop me seizing . . . and more precious here than petrol itself. But I think he'll spot the drips when they start. It's only an hour's work to strip the pump and put in a new washer . . . if he's got one . . .

There's nothing to be done about the springs, nothing to see, until they go. So take me easy, driver, and I'll do my best. Only, I hope you spot the first ooze of water from behind the fan . . .

CHAPTER 4

Zimmerman sat in the passenger seat, clasping his heavy pack on his knees, staring out over the shimmering desert, thinking. There was so much to think about, and as he was a methodical man, he divided the agenda into separate compartments of his mind. He would think of them one by one. There was plenty of time.

The past . . . but only as much of it as was safe to remember.

The directive had been explicit. The MUST of delivery to the Delta and the joining up with P9. Then the secondary—'if possible'—task of making trouble in Tobruk before he started on his way.

He had always known that the most dangerous part would be the getting there. Not in Tobruk, not inside the Delta, but the passing out of one security net, the blank between, and the getting through the other. It was curious that he had felt and would feel safest when he was surrounded by them; it was the emptiness between—the lone South African making for the Delta, the chance, casual meetings, the check posts on the way—that worried him most.

Afraid? . . . No, he had not been afraid before he jumped. But he had tried not to think about it too much, it would be better to trust to opportunity. Any thought-out plan always involved some consideration of failure, and he knew what had happened to the ones that had tried before . . . he was not going to follow Brünner and that other fellow—what was his name?—Schmidt, to their stone walls at dawn. He would not think about it, be very, very careful, and something would turn up. And it had—beyond his wildest dreams, just at the right time.

He gave a little secret smile as he thought of that swinging drop into blacked-out burning Tobruk the night before, hanging to the ropes of his harness as the flak and tracer came up to meet him in orange streams, the burying of the parachute and the shouldering of his packs. With his clipped English, the genuine South African uniform and identity card, it had been simple to get shelter for the night on the excuse of a ditched truck. He had moved on at first light, looking for a means to escape east and implementing the minor part of his mission.

But there was no need for the second, no point in wasting precious time in fomenting something that had burst into flower already. There was enough alarm and despondency in Tobruk without his bothering to work on it.

So he had gone from camp to camp, unchallenged, searching for the truck that was to carry him east, the sooner the better for him while that flood of transport was still streaming out along the Bardia road. In each place he had managed to slide in some little thing, a nasty remark about British to South African, or vice versa; some may have struck, done a bit more of the good work, but he had not borrowed a truck. He had waited by the water point as a likely place and within a few minutes all his difficulties were solved in one stroke by the arrival of this ambulance.

It was almost too good to be true. A party, with written orders to go straight to the Delta. The danger of their method had been no worry compared with the relief that all gates would be open to him now. Alone, his story and his papers might—probably would have—got by; as a passenger, with the others, genuine, to vouch for him, it was certain. He would be the passenger, sit tight, help where necessary to convince them. That was the most important, then they could do all the talking.

All of it? . . . He smiled again as he thought of the irony of that meeting with the Panzer Group: remembered with gratitude the quickness of the Hauptmann in spotting the sign and transmitting his code number to headquarters. It had worked, these English had swallowed it, but he would not care to have to do it again.

Zimmerman . . . his mind lingered over his new name, then jumped back over the time he must not remember to what had happened before. All those years in the Union and South-West Africa . . . so busy, so long . . . the fluency of his English and Afrikaans making him almost forget his native tongue. The homesickness and then his return to the Fatherland just before the war.

That was the time he must not think about, the war; not until the day the real Zimmerman, dying, was brought in to their lines after a skirmish near Bir Hakeim. There had been no likeness between them except in size, but someone must have said something, and then Intelligence were on it. His papers were vetted and he had had to admit his knowledge of the Union, his English and his Afrikaans.

And now he was Zimmerman . . . in dead Zimmerman's clothes. They had asked him to volunteer—he smiled again—for one was not usually asked to volunteer in the Wehrmacht, and of course he had said, 'Yes.' Not for love of the Fuehrer—he despised him, though he was always careful to say the right things at the right time—but the simple calculation of the war being nearly over and won. When it was, there would be the reward, the pickings for such as him back in Africa.

And all he had to do was to complete the job and stay out of trouble. It was dangerous, but he was better equipped than most. The part he liked least was the heavy pack that lay across his knees.

Just keep out of trouble . . . that brought him to the present . . . and his companions. He glanced sideways for a moment at the girl and the sergeant-major, then stared out over the desert again, trying to weigh it all up.

So far, so good. The captain had hardly glanced at his identity card, had accepted him, it seemed. But had the others? It was too early to judge yet, but they might be more difficult. It was lucky they were all British, though. When in difficulty, he could always fall back on talk of the Union. He doubted if their combined experience would add up to more than a few days at Durban or Cape Town.

He looked across again. That girl . . . he thought he understood her. She should have been a German, that type; strong, capable, attractive. *Ein kamarad*...No, he must not do that—even think in anything but English. 'A pal'—that was the right phrase. He went on thinking about her, grudgingly, liking her. He must make her like him.

The one that was driving. He could not see the face, only the arms resting on the wheel, the brass coat-of-arms on the leather strap on one wrist. The Unteroffizier—no, sergeant-major. There was a different one, he could not fathom him, he was so totally different from his German counterpart. He and the captain were friends, in an easy natural way that would be impossible in the Afrika Korps . . . Yet, all the time, he was—correct. Be careful there, Zimmerman, that one says little but sees a lot.

Last, the captain. He made a contemptuous noise in the back of his throat. Those lectures they had had were right. There, in the back now, was the living example of the decadence, the morale propped up with gin. He hadn't believed it, but it was true. He would admit he had courage of a kind—he had shown it in the minefield—but that was different. The moral fibre had gone, and now the captain was deprived of his drink, he would crack altogether. But not before he had finished his usefulness. He was the only one to navigate—then let him take them back to the coast the other side of the frontier. Then let him sign the movement order that would send him and the girl back to the Delta. After that, he would not think of them . . . or care. But he had the means with this captain, it had been stupid of the others to mention the gin . . . a carrot to any donkey was better than a stick . . . he would feed it to him, in secret, in small doses, as long as there was the need. He knew that type. They couldn't hold out against it.

Yes, that was the way to play it. Feed the captain, make up to the girl, watch the sergeant-major. It would be simple. There was nothing else to worry about for at least two days.

Or was there? A little frown crossed his face . . . were they quite so simple, so easy to bluff. He remembered the one disturbing thing . . . when he had come back with the Hauptmann to the ambulance and found his other pack opened and disturbed. Had they been searching? His hand tightened on the big square pack on his knees. At all costs, they must not get at that, it must never leave him. It would not be a question of not getting to the Delta then, but being up against the same wall as Brünner and Schmidt. Be careful, all the time, don't underestimate them. Especially at night . . . when he had to carry out those special orders . . .

He eased the pack on his knees and stared out over the heaving plain, brooding.

CHAPTER 5

Tom said, 'What's the reading on the bottom row of figures on the speedometer, Miss Diana?'

She leaned forward and read them back, 'Five . . . seven . . . eight, on the yellow one—no, that's just coming up to nine.'

'Good enough.' She watched his hand come forward to cut the ignition and then the car crunched on across the desert until it came to a halt. There was no particular point in the place he had chosen to stop, just a patch of pinky-brown gravel, bounded on three sides by low coarse sage-green scrub.

'That's the captain's twenty miles,' he said, 'now we brew up.' He turned in the driving seat and started rummaging behind it. 'And if I know anything about Driver Grimes, there'll be enough tea somewhere here to start a café. Ah—' He tugged and strained and then his hands came away with a square biscuit tin. He pulled off the top and looked inside. 'Half full,' he said.

When he had jumped down, he looked over at Zimmerman. 'You'll find the tins under your seat, I think, sir.'

She looked at Tom and said, 'What can I do?'

'I don't want to go blundering into the back, waking the captain yet. Do you think you could slide out another tin of water—and a jerrican? Mind that one, it's rather heavy.'

She turned with her hand on the door. 'I'm pretty strong,' she said.

Anson was still asleep, so dead to the world that she stopped by him for a moment to listen to his breathing. When she came out with the cans, Zimmerman was just walking round the front of the car with two cut-down petrol tins, both blackened on the outside. Tom was ripping the wood from one of the cases he had lifted out from under the dash.

'Thank you,' he said. 'Could you put the sand in, sir?'

'Sand—?' Zimmerman stood quite still, a tin in each hand, staring at him.

'Yes.' Tom had a puzzled look on his face. 'Sorry—I thought all the Union troops brewed-up in the same way as we do. Don't worry, I'll do it.'

He took the tins, smelt them, and then turned one over on its side to scrape sand in from the ground. When he had got enough to cover the bottom for about three inches, he righted it and walked over to stand it well away from the ambulance. 'Always down-wind,' he said. Picking up the jerrican and a splintered stick from the packing case, he poured petrol on the sand, stirring it until there was a consistency of porridge. Then he moved the remaining petrol away, struck a match and threw it at the tin.

It ignited, almost exploded, with a soft 'woosshh'; the first flare had died down as he filled the other tin with water and placed it on top, leaving a little gap at one side. He handed the stick to Diana. 'Now you watch it. If the flame gets low, just stir the sand, and more petrol will come up to the top.'

Zimmerman was standing, watching them. 'Anything else I can do, Sergeant-major?'

'Open up the biscuits, sir. And find the sugar. It should be in another biscuit tin, behind the driver's seat.'

She sat by the fire, absorbed in her job, poking the sand as the flames died, watching them flicker and rise again. Once she turned, to see Tom at the front of the ambulance with the bonnet open and the tool kit strewn out beside him. The fire had just been tended, so she got up and went over.

It all looked so terribly complicated, those copper tubes and the wires and the thing that looked like a teapot with warts on that she believed, vaguely, was the carburettor. The thing that surprised her most was that it was all so clean.

She leaned over, watching him. 'I wish I understood it all.'

Her eyes stayed fixed and intent, but he smiled. 'Not so difficult, or different from your job. They're like humans really. If you give them the right food and drink—a dose occasionally —and don't overwork them, they obey all the rules.' He was moving the fan blades to and fro, feeling with the other hand behind it. 'The only trouble—and difference—is they can't talk. So that by the time you know they have a pain, it's usually too late.'

She ran her hand down the hot, smooth olive of the bonnet to where the name was painted, so beautifully, in white.

'Has KATY got a pain?'

'I don't think so—yet. But she's got what your docs would call a "constitutional weakness"—and I've got to watch it.'

He was whistling through his teeth now, as he manoeuvred his hand under the fan while he moved the blades left and right. Then the hand underneath, cupped, came out and there was a small drop of red water in the palm. The whistle died suddenly as he stared at it. 'You had better go and watch that fire,' he said.

When the tea was made, it was hot and very sweet and the best drink she had ever had. There were only three mugs that they could find, and Tom said, 'One for you—I'll share with Captain Zimmerman—and one to go in to the captain.'

She could see from his eyes that he didn't want to go in there, so she said, 'Can't we leave him in peace?' But he shook his head: 'No, he must eat.' So she took the mug, and a cigarette that she lit and put in between her lips, and climbed into the back of the car.

Anson was deep, deep down in exhaustion still, so that she had to shake him. When he had opened his eyes and remembered her, she put an arm behind him just like a patient and helped him to sit up and gave him the tea. When he had swallowed, she took the cigarette from her mouth and passed that over as well.

'Tom's done your twenty miles,' she said, 'he's getting some grub now.'

He had another drink from the mug and then drew hard on the fag, letting the smoke trail out through his nose. 'I feel better,' he said, and she thought that he looked it. He moved a little sideways and patted the empty space on the edge of the bunk. 'Sit down for a minute, Sister.'

She said, 'Please call me Diana—the others do.'

'—All right, Diana. I wanted a word with you, before I talk to the others—' He looked across to the other bunk and his eyes clouded; she thought how she had forgotten for the moment what was there—and felt ashamed.

He said, 'First—I don't want you to think we are—unfeeling —in not doing anything about that, yet, but it will be hard work, and we're all very tired. I would rather get on as far as we can today. So, last thing tonight, or first thing tomorrow morning—will that be all right with you?'

'Of course.'

'Then, when that's done—I want you to have the back of the car, for your own, for the rest of the trip.'

She said, 'I wouldn't dream of it. I want us all to share. I'll come in with any of you—all of you—except Zimmerman.'

He blew out another long trail of smoke. 'You don't like him?'

'No. Do you?'

He ignored the question; he said, 'He's useful. He got us right out of the last mess—and, I realize now, we wouldn't have had a hope on our own. And he's strong. We may need that.'

Both were silent for a moment. 'Anyway, Diana, I'll work out some sort of rota—two sleeping, two awake—and fix it so that you're never paired off with him.'

'That's nice of you. Now come and have your grub. You must be starving.' But he held her arm. 'There's one more thing—and I must say it. I've had a pretty bloody time lately, and I'm afraid—'

She put a hand to his mouth. 'You don't have to say anything.'

There was gratitude in his eyes. 'I won't, then. But I have told Tom, so I must tell you. The next drink I have—is going to be in a certain bar in Alex. I don't suppose you know it—just a little place off Mahomet Ali Square. There's a marble-topped counter, and high stools, and they serve the best and coldest Yankee beer in the Delta. And when we've got this lot sorted out, I'm going to take you and Tom there, and buy you one. And it will be my first. So don't tempt me before that.'

She said, 'I won't—and I'll dream about that bar.'

They went out and ate their bully and biscuit. The bully wasn't like any she had had before, it came out of the tins almost liquid, greasy, like a half set jelly. It was nauseating to have to push it on to the biscuit and swallow it like that, but no one made any comment, so she kept quiet, assuming that it was always that way.

When they had cleared up and were ready to move off, Anson said, 'Your turn for a kip in the back, Tom.' But his eyes had moved away and he said, 'I'm all right, sir.' There was a long silence before Zimmerman said, '—if no one else wants to, I will,' and he went through the door into the back, taking his two packs with him.

Anson took over the driving, Tom in the passenger seat, Diana on the floor between them. In a moment the atmosphere had changed and she leaned back, eyes closed, listening to the flow of talk that passed over her head. She heard calculations of food and water and petrol; gathered they had plenty of all for their trip to the 'wire' and then back to the road. There was only one time when their voices held a serious tone, something about, '—if that bloody pump holds—'

Tom said suddenly, 'I meant to ask you, Mr Anson. Do you

remember that drive along the road in Tobruk—after we had picked up—' he jerked his head backwards—'*him,* at the water point?'

'Yes. Why?'

'Did we pass any truck—that was abandoned?'

'No, not that I remember.'

'No. Nor can I—but *he* said he had run a big end there.'

'It could have been farther on, you know, beyond where we turned on to the track.'

'He must have had a long walk, then,' said Tom.

The talk turned to other, more comfortable things. Of the 'hay-box' that had been found in the back and speculation as to whether it worked. She opened her eyes to ask what it was and was told it was a sort of giant vacuum flask. She looked at Anson. 'Do you mind me asking questions? There's so much I don't know—and want to. I don't want you to think of me as anything different—a woman—a liability.'

Anson smiled, swerved to avoid a gully, and said, 'Ask away.'

'Well, when we brewed up. There was no one keeping a lookout for other vehicles. Wasn't that risky—when we're still so close?'

'We were listening all the time. It gets automatic. You can hear a truck long before you can see it in a mirage. And the next—?'

'Where are we going now?'

'I was going to talk to you about that. I'm turning slowly east—running diagonally towards the escarpment, that cliff you saw before the mirage came down. Then we'll skirt along the base until about six. Run into one of the wadis then—snug for the night and we can have a good rest. Then—' he hesitated, '—see about Sister Norton.'

His voice was very gentle as he went on. 'You see—out here in the open, we can't be absolutely accurate as to position. It might be very difficult to find afterwards. A wadi on the edge of the escarpment is much easier—we can mark the edge of the cliff above with a cairn of stones.'

There was silence for a moment and then he went on, 'Then tomorrow, head for the "wire", and when we hit it, turn north-east straight for Sidi Barrani. That's about the drill—what do you think, Tom?'

There was no answer and she turned to see that he was fast asleep, his head nodding on his chest, swaying in his seat to the movement of the ambulance.

'He's asleep,' she said.

'Good. But for God's sake see he doesn't fall out if I have to swerve. Hang on to his belt.'

She slid a hand up between it and the top of his slacks and was conforted, strangely, by the warmth of him and the easy rise and fall of his side in the slow breathing. They went on steadily with the engine monotonous in its even beat. The sun had fallen away behind them now and the square shadow of the ambulance was creeping farther and farther away ahead on the sand. The mirage had quite gone, there was a luminous purple staining the brown of the sand, and on their right the cliff was close and clear, with the dark jagged cuts of the wadis showing like valleys on a coastline. Nothing else but their tiny moving speck on all that broad horizon. They talked in spasms, of the Delta, of home—that other life. Tom slept on.

The shadows were long when they reached the foot of the cliff, and after they had nosed their way along it for about a mile, Anson said, 'I think this will do.' He swung the car in towards a narrow cleft, twisting round boulders and bumping over rock slab. Tom woke up with a start and apologized and she was sorry to have to leave off holding his belt. They were cut off from the plain behind them now, going up the twisting channel of the wadi bed with the rock walls rising steeply to each side. The going became easier again, the flat bottom of hard-baked clay covered with tinder-dry camel-thorn. They went on until it widened into a sort of dell and then Anson turned the ambulance sideways and cut the engine. A deep compelling silence fell over everything.

They got down, stretching and rubbing their eyes. Anson said, 'I'll wake Zimmerman and start the brew. Tom—to save time—will you go up the side of the wadi and back to the edge of the cliff? Have a look round, and then put up a little cairn. It needn't be big—just a marker.'

She said, 'I'll come with you.'

The climb looked steep, but she was past that sort of tiredness now, light-headed, almost floating.

When they had made the slope, the top was hard and level, another flat brown plain stretching away to the southern horizon without a break. There were plenty of loose flat limestone slabs about and soon they had made a pile about four feet high on the edge of the drop to the level below. As they finished, a breath of wind came suddenly from the north, infinitely refreshing. Tom eased his back and then turned through the full circle of the compass, staring at the desert and the sky.

He said, softly, 'I've lived in green hills all my life. But here—at this time—it always gets me . . .'

The ambulance was hidden by the angle of the wadi, there was nothing but the two of them standing under the wide bowl of heaven that ran through every shade from pink to lilac, with the blue curtain of night sliding up from the east. The red tip of the sun was going and the plain below a moving, changing sea of orange and slate-blue. They were the only two people in the world. She moved closer to him. Then he said, 'We'd better get down.'

The petrol fire was flickering pale in the shadows of the wadi, with Zimmerman squatting in front of it, stirring. When they came closer, a delicious, unbelievable smell wafted towards them and then Anson walked round to them from the back of the ambulance. Though his voice was steady when he spoke, she saw his face was deathly pale.

He said, 'Driver Grimes will either go on a charge—or get an extra week's leave—when we get together again. I've never seen such a scrounging b—. He's got everything except the kitchen stove on this car. I found a sack of spuds and onions under the stretchers. Most of them are in that stew now.' It was ordinary, but breathless, and she knew he was talking because he had to.

'Anything else happened?' she said.

As he looked at her, his face changed. 'No—except I've cleared out the cans at the back and opened the doors. I thought it might be a good thing to get her on a stretcher and take her out of there now.' Then he added, very slowly, 'Unless you want to scrounge a drink first.'

'A drink—?'

'Yes. A drink. Zimmerman's been flashing that bloody bottle of his. I expect he would spare you a little one.'

'Did he give you any—' It was Tom, the voice very low.

'Why should he—if I didn't bother to ask him?' There was a sort of smile there and the voice sounded brittle. Then he turned away. Faintly, she heard Tom's breath go out in a long hissing sigh.

They went to work without another word and it was easy to lift her down on to the stretcher they had put between the bunks because she was so light, almost impossible to avoid the dark stain that was left on the mattress beneath her. When the two men had run out the stretcher and carried it over to the far side of the wadi,

Anson said, 'Fix the back up, will you, Tom?' and they were left alone together.

She said, 'I'm terribly sorry—'

'About what—?'

It was so difficult to put into the right words. '—That Captain Zimmerman upset you—'

'Upset me—why should that fat bastard swigging gin upset me? I'm tired, that's all.' Then his voice changed completely, 'Sorry to have to talk about these things, but have you got her identity-discs?'

'I've got one in my bag—and I put the green one round her neck. Is that right?'

'Yes.' He was staring down at the long dark shape on the stretcher. 'Would you think it awful—if we postponed this till first thing tomorrow? I don't feel too good—I don't suppose any of us do.'

She said, 'I was wondering—couldn't we take her with us—to Sidi Barrani?'

He shook his head. 'We can't be certain how long that will take. It's the top of the summer now—might be grim, and then we would have to do it anyway . . .' His voice trailed off to nothing.

'Tea's up, sir.' Tom's voice came from behind them.

'Tomorrow morning, then,' she said, and they all walked back to the ambulance.

The stew was very good, and though they could only find one plate and two spoons, they finished it to the last drop. She sat back with the plate, watching the three of them sitting cross-legged round the tin, bending forward to fish in turn, just like those men with hammers who hit crowbars into roads. She should have been revolted by the sight of the poking and balancing with fingers of bits of stew on biscuits, but somehow it seemed quite natural.

Then came the tea, sharing mugs, and she saw the rest of it being poured into the big cylinder with the bolt-on top that she now knew to be the hay-box. After they had sipped their tea in silence for a time, Anson said, 'Now, orders. It's eight o'clock and Diana has agreed to my decision to do the digging at first light. So we'll divide into two shifts. You, Tom, and Zimmerman and I will carry on till five. That gives us four hours each. Then we'll be fresher to get cracking with it—and then for the dash to Barrani.'

Tom said, 'Do you think we'll do it—in a day?'

'If all goes well—yes. We should hit that old ambulance track near Piccadilly by sundown, and it's a cakewalk to the road on that, dark or no.'

Zimmerman spoke for the first time. 'Wouldn't it be as well to wait for the light—and make sure who is in Barrani?'

Anson stared at him. 'Do you mean Jerry? Hell, man, Barrani is halfway to the Delta.'

Zimmerman shrugged. 'It's your party.' Then he said, 'If Sister doesn't mind us coming in the back with her—why don't we rack up the top bunks, and all get a good night's rest?'

The last of the light had gone so quickly that it was impossible to see their faces now, but she knew that Tom and Anson were looking at each other. Then Anson's voice came quietly: 'Someone must watch—there might be wild dogs—and Denise—'

Zimmerman broke the silence. He got up, swinging the bigger of his packs on his shoulder. 'It's OK by me. See you later.' He went over to the ambulance and she heard the scrape of the spade as he lifted it from the retaining straps; it showed in silhouette against the night sky as he walked off up the wadi with it tilted over his shoulder. The grate of his boots faded in the darkness.

'What on earth is he doing?' she asked.

There was a pause before Anson answered and then a hint of laughter in his voice. 'Lavatory. In the desert, you never ask anyone where they are going with a spade.'

'Common to both sides—' It was Tom's voice coming from the direction of the fire; she heard the rustle of scattered sand and then the last flicker of flame died.

The silence fell on them again, heavy and foreboding. No one seemed inclined to move. She thought, '—if I offer to sleep on the bunk she was on, Tom will be offended. He'll insist he does—and I know that he won't like the idea any more than I.'

Anson solved the problem for both of them. He said, 'Before you two buzz off to bed, I want to tell you a story, Diana. And remind you of one, Tom. It won't take long, and I want to—because, when you go in there, you'll be thinking of things . . . and I want to tell you of something else that happened in this very car . . .' She could only see the change of shape in the pale oval of his face as he turned towards Tom. 'Have you forgotten the piano?'

There was a faint chuckle from the darkness. 'Of course. It was this one—and Driver Grimes. I'd forgotten.'

Anson's voice went on, 'It was a year ago. The first time we took Benghazi. This car was attached to—I think it was, the Royals—when they went in as striking force. There wasn't any fighting, the Ities had gone, so the driver, Master Grimes, was told to come back and report to us in the desert at first light.

'In the meantime, there was some pretty terrific looting going on in the town, so, human nature being what it is, Grimes and his medical orderly helped themselves. After they had collected a silver teaset and some nice lace tablecloths, they came on a very fine upright piano in an empty house. Then Grimes thought of his poor commanding officer—me.'

He paused for a moment. 'I try and think I can play the thing,' he said.

'He does—very well,' came Tom's soft voice.

'Well—somehow, and I didn't probe too deeply, naturally, they managed to get it down the stairs and into the back of the ambulance. It just fitted between the bunks. Then they pulled out of the town to have a few hours' sleep before starting off to where we were, right in the middle of the bulge of desert that's east of the town. Everything was fine when they started off down the ten miles of road before they had to turn off into the blue, but when they had done about three of them, they saw, to their horror, that an MP checkpost had sprung up in the night, swarming with red-caps, searching all the transport going out, on account of the looting. They couldn't turn back, they couldn't dump it in sight on the open road. The only chance was to bluff their way through.

'They coasted up to the post very crafty and slow. When the red-cap sergeant came out, the orderly—who was just as bad—put his fingers to his lips and said, "We've got a bad case for the field ambulance in the back, Sarge. It's urgent." When Grimes told me afterwards, he said there was only one lie in that. Really it was a good case—rosewood.'

Another chuckle from the darkness; she could sense the flow of warm intimate feeling between those two, the bond of so many things seen and done.

'The sergeant said,' Anson went on, ' "All right, boys. Just pull to the side for a moment, while I look at your paybooks." Grimes said afterwards that it was sheer bad driving, but, as he eased her over, the back wheel went over a rock, and there was a bloody great *dooiinngg* from the strings.

'The sergeant said, "Christ—what's that?" and the orderly said, very quick, "He's groaning, Sarge. He's terrible bad. *Tussis alcoholica*—we've got to get him to the doc pretty sharp."

'The sergeant fairly threw their paybooks back at them and then

he said, "Just one second, boys," and went running back into his
tent. He came out with a young corporal and he said, "Corporal,
there's a very sick man in the back there—get up on that ambulance
and see they have absolute priority down the road." And off they
went. Grimes said he nearly wet himself laughing: there was the
copper sitting on the bonnet, waving his red hat and blowing his
whistle, shouting to all the stuff coming up to get out of the way,
and all the time behind them, the old joanna bouncing on the
bumps, doing *dooiinngg, dooiinngg, dooiinngg*. They made the end of
the road in record time and dropped their escort and thanked him,
saying that they would be sure to tell the patient all the MPs had
done.'

Now she was laughing too. 'I shouldn't approve—but it's very
funny. Did you get your present?'

'Tell her what happened, sir,' said Tom.

'Well, they cut straight across the desert, and when they were
right in the middle of sweet nothing, they had a puncture. It was
a place just like where we were this afternoon—a brown plain
stretching in every direction to the horizon, with just one ambulance
stuck in the middle. Only, being winter, there was no mirage.

'The ground was a bit soft, and Grimes didn't fancy all that
weight on his jack, so they got out some bits of plank they had in
the back, and ran the piano down on to the desert. Grimes got
under to change the wheel and while he was doing it he said, "Let's
have a tune, Charlie," because he knew that the orderly could
play—one of those arpeggio boys. Grimes said he never saw
anything so funny as that bloke, sitting on a pile of jerricans, with
nothing round him but sand and sky and a piano, playing "I dreamt
I dwelt in marble halls" with all the twiddly bits.

'The trouble started when he had finished the wheel and they
tried to get it up the ramp again. It was too heavy for them. They
cursed and sweated, but it was no good. Then, to cap everything,
there was a cloud of dust coming up on the beam, a big convoy
from the east that would pass close. They couldn't do anything
except wait until they had gone past, pretending that nothing was
there. But a truck and a three-tonner broke away from the formation
and raced over. There was an officer and he said, "What the hell
are you doing with that bloody piano?" and Grimes said, "Found
it here, sir. We were trying to salvage it—to save deterioration."
The officer said, "I'll stop that right now—I'll give you ten pounds
for it." Grimes said that they had their work-shop lorry over and

had it up on the crane and he was left holding the money before he realized properly what was happening.'

'So you never got your piano?' She found herself resenting the soft laughter that was coming through the darkness, and was ashamed at once of resenting it.

Anson said, 'No. I'm sorry to have kept you up with a silly story. But when you are in there—instead of thinking of other things—remember a piano going *dooiinngg* beside you.'

She got to her feet and said, 'Thank you. I thought it was a lovely story—and I won't forget.'

Tom was standing too, she could see the dark height of him against the sky. 'Time to turn in, then.'

Anson said, 'Sleep well, you two,' then, petulantly. 'Where the hell has Zimmerman got to?' and the two of them groped their way to the square bulk of the ambulance looming against the stars. Then they had climbed into the back and she had flopped down on *that* bunk and pulled the blanket up over her before she realized—and then didn't care any more.

In the darkness, Tom said, 'Would you like a last cigarette?' and she had said, 'No, but I'll have a drag at yours.' They lay there, separated by the narrow gap of the alley, with the glowing tip of the cigarette passing to and fro; each time she took it, she felt the touch of his fingers. When it was smoked right down and he had said, 'I'm stubbing it out now,' her hand had strayed back again and found his still there.

It was nice to go to sleep like that, surrendering to the waves of tiredness she had been fighting for hours, touching him—and with the ghost of a piano going *dooiinngg, dooiinngg* beside her.

CHAPTER 6

When Zimmerman walked off up the wadi, he had gone straight along the bed for about fifty yards and then turned sharp left to start the scramble up the steep wall. Slowly, carefully, with his desert boots making only the slightest noise with the loose stones they dislodged, he made the top in a matter of minutes. Then he moved away from the edge, ten yards on the hard, level ground, dropped the spade and lowered his big pack to the ground. He turned it on end, looking at his watch before he started to fumble with the straps.

It was the worst, most dangerous thing of all—the part that he hated; to make it worse, in his opinion the most futile as well.

He knew that they had to be got to the Delta—that they were too new, too advanced, to risk being dropped by parachute; he could understand the necessity of the orders, 'Singly —by safe hand,' but not the added danger of testing them on the way. If they wanted strength and range data, they had the whole of Tripolitania to do it in; why add to the risk in ordering him to do this, when they must know he would be in the position he was now—watched or in close contact, all of the time? But those were the orders. He wondered bitterly if the same sort of thing happened on the other side . . .

Well, he had better do it. They had been explicit. Each night, between eight and nine—only call-sign unless there was anything vital. He looked at his watch again as the flap fell open . . . only eleven minutes left. He had better hurry.

Now the shirt had been pulled aside from the mouth. No need to see anything. Feel was enough. He grunted as his fingers touched the little knob, twisted and pulled, and then the thin rod of the telescopic aerial jerked its way up into the dark. He felt along the panel and there was a click and a tiny light glowed. Another inch to the left, and he found the key. It made a faint clicking noise as he started to transmit.

GMX . . . GMX . . . GMX . . . Over and over again, the thin

crackle of his call-sign went out into the black aether, the faint
ghost fingers of it reaching out over the desert, groping for his
headquarters, hoping they would detect, get the strength and make
a fix. There was nothing else to transmit, nothing to tell them. They
would know he was on the way, would not be interested in details
of dead English nurses.

GMX ... GMX ... GMX ... He went on steadily until the
luminous hands of his watch showed nine exactly. Then he switched
off, lowered the aerial, replaced his shirt and strapped up the pack.
Slinging the spade over his shoulder, he scrambled down the side
of the wadi and made his way back towards the ambulance.

To Tom, it only seemed a second before he was being shaken by
the shoulder and Anson was standing over him, holding a mug of
tea. From the other bunk there was a faint blur of movement as
the girl slipped out of her blanket, the open square of the door at
the back showed only a difference in the texture of the darkness.
The moon must have gone down.

They changed places in silence, there was only Anson's quiet,
'Call us at first light and then we'll get on with it,' before the bulk
of Zimmerman slid in behind them and the door of the ambulance
closed. They walked round to the front of the car, drawing the
blankets they had kept tight round their shoulders, and then leaned
back against KATY's bonnet, sipping the tea in turn, silent, looking
up at the sky.

The night was so still, so beautiful. The strip of sky that showed
between the banks of the wadi was like a glittering river with the
stars so bright and close that it seemed you had only to reach up
your hand and pull them down. The sides of the wadi came down
dark and uneven in contrast with the pale grey of the scrub. He
tried hard to avoid looking at the long dark shape that broke the
smoothness of it on the far side. The girl was still looking up. She
said, 'I never dreamed there could be anything like that.'

'No. When we get home, we'll be missing it—longing to be back
here again.'

'I suppose so. As now we long for those other things—that seem
so remote and past.'

'Just a few of them,' he said. 'Not many—with me.'

'What do you miss most, Tom?'

He said, 'Haddock,' quite seriously and without hesitation and
when she had stopped laughing went on in the same tone, 'Do you

know, often when I wake up out here—and think of that bully again for breakfast—my mouth starts to water, I almost sweat, when I remember a great wedge of golden haddock, properly done in milk, with a poached egg on top.'

Her voice was still full of laughter as she said, '—But you can have the eggs—'

'Eggs? Do you call those things eggs? The size of marbles and no taste at all. Do you know the official rate of exchange for them with the Bedouin? It's in general orders—a handful of tea for each one. I call it encouraging robbery—'

He broke off suddenly, running over to the far side of the wadi, circling round the stretcher, kicking the scrub. As she joined him, she said, 'What was it?'

'I thought I saw a dog.'

'I didn't believe that was true—would they—?'

'Not if there was anyone around. They're very timid.'

They were standing close to the stretcher now and he did not think that she liked it, so he made a move to go back to the car.

'No. Wait a minute, Tom.' She stood looking down at it and the starlight was so bright now that it shone on her hair. She was quite still and he could not see any expression on her face. She said, 'Don't think me silly—but I can't bear to think of her—covered up, on a night like this.' And without waiting for him to reply, knelt down and folded the blanket back off the face. Then she got up and took his hand and walked back to the ambulance without looking behind her.

They sat down close, their backs against the front wheel, and she said, 'Will it take long—tomorrow?'

'It depends—some places are easy, at others you hit solid rock two feet down. It's all trial and error. But I'll find a likely spot as soon as we can see and start right in.'

'Cover her up before the others come,' she said.

There was a long silence after that. He tried to ease it by pulling a couple of cigarettes from his packet, lighting them and passing one over. She drew on it eagerly, staring out into the shadow of the far side of the wadi; she said suddenly, 'She wasn't a friend of mine. I hardly knew her. I was just put in charge of her for this trip. She was a silly, man-mad little bitch—and useless as a nurse. But I feel worse about it than anything else that has ever happened.'

'You weren't to blame. Our fault—if anyone's.'

She said, 'I wonder what she was trying to say to you—'

'I don't know. Nothing to me, really, I expect. She may have
thought I was someone quite different.' They were quiet again, each
locked with their own thoughts, then he said, 'Captain
Zimmerman—he shouldn't have done that.'

'No. Not after we had asked him not to. But we weren't there,
Tom, we don't know what happened. And—perhaps he may have
taken notice already. He took the pack with him when he went
off—with the spade. And I saw it slung over his shoulder when he
went in to bed, just now.'

Tom snorted. 'It isn't in there—it's in the other one.'

'How do you know?'

'We looked—when he was over talking to the Germans, and you
were in the back—' He got up and moved back to the cab, there
was a fumbling and a faint scraping. Then he came back swinging
a pack by its straps. 'He's not so careful about this one,' he said.
'It was lying on the floor.'

He stood swinging it, listening. There was no sound from the
back of the car. Then he said, 'I'm a very careless man, Diana.
Clumsy. After I had to get up in the cab, when I jumped down, I
tripped on Captain Zimmerman's pack and knocked it off—' He
shortened his grip of the strap and brought it down hard on a rock
that was by his feet, there was a faint brittle sound above the thump
and then he lifted the pack again, feeling the underside carefully.
'I'm afraid I broke his bottle of gin,' he said as he put it down again,
'so you must remind me to apologize first thing in the morning.'

When he came back and sat down beside her, he added, almost
defensively, 'The captain's got over it now—but perhaps it will
make things easier.'

She said, 'He's probably got some more—in that other pack.'

'Then I'll drop that too—or run over it—if I get a chance—' He
stopped suddenly, jerking his head round. 'Hush . . . Listen!'

The sound came to them, suddenly and very clear, perhaps
because they were fully conscious of it for the first time. 'Plop . . .'
A little sound, a cross between a ping and a splash. It came from
directly behind them, underneath the bonnet. She started to say
something, but he said, 'Hush', again.

It came a second time at an interval of about ten seconds. 'Plop
. . .' He cursed and turned, burrowing his head and shoulders
underneath the car; when he came out, he dragged a shallow tin
after him.

'That bloody pump,' he said. 'I thought it had begun to leak at lunchtime. So I put this tin underneath tonight to check. Look—it's half full already.'

'KATY's constitutional weakness,' she said.

'Yes—and it might be serious. It's the washer that's gone. I haven't got a replacement—and if you try to tighten this one to stop it, it might break up altogether.'

'What would happen then, Tom?'

He tried to explain a little of it, but gave up as soon as he realized she hadn't got a clue. He put the tin back and, to stop thinking of the wound that dripped behind—that could use up their water so fast that there might not be any left to drink, started talking of other things, far-away things.

Of the garage, of the village and what his life had been like so long ago; in turn, he heard of her father, the snake-charmer, what had happened in the blitz.

Quite suddenly the stars were gone and a faint luminous greyness was creeping into the dark of the night. He said, 'First light,' and got up stiffly and went to the other side of the wadi and pulled the blanket back in place. When he came back he said, 'If I light the fire, will you watch it while I find a place to start?'

He left her crouching in front of the tin, stirring the sand, then went and got the pick and shovel from their clips and cast round in the bed of the wadi until he found what he thought was a likely place. He started with the pick, swinging slowly and rhythmically until he had broken the surface in a space two feet by six. As he stooped to lift the spade to clear away, he stopped and stared for a moment at the bright, clean blade. Captain Zimmerman must be very particular to have cleaned it after use in the dark last night ... or perhaps he had not used it at all. He went on with the shovelling.

It was when he had got down about two feet that he came on trouble. The point of the pick started bouncing back with a hollow sound, the shock jarring up the handle to his hands. Rock. He tried all along the narrow trench, but it was all the same.

It was clear grey light now. He straightened as the girl came over with a mug of tea in her hand. 'I've wakened the others,' she said, '—and broken the news of the accident to Zimmerman. They're just coming over.'

'What did he say?'

'Nothing.'

He stayed, leaning on the pick, until they walked over. He said,

'I'm terribly sorry, sir. Knocking that off the step in the night, I'm afraid I've spoilt everything.'

Zimmerman shrugged. 'An accident, Sergeant-major, it can't be helped. Most of the cigarettes are all right—and my socks will dry.' He looked down into the trench. 'How are you getting on?'

'I'm not. I think we'll have to start all over again. I've hit rock.'

Anson said, 'Solid—or a layer?'

Tom let the pick bounce of it once again. 'It sounds hollow,' he said.

Zimmerman stripped off his bush-shirt and spat on his hands. 'Give me that thing.'

Tom watched him, standing in the trench, the rippling play of the muscles of that great back as he swung the pick high and brought it down with terrific force . . . 'About twice as hard as either of us could hit,' he thought. Zimmerman was hitting always in the same spot and now little sparks were beginning to fly, then there was a sharp crack and the pick point went on through. He grunted as he levered up a slab. 'The rest should come up easy,' he said. He went on lifting and shovelling, while Tom watched the swing of his arms, the red and green identity discs hanging against the matted black hair on the chest. He wondered if he had been wrong in all those half-formed thoughts, was ashamed of what he had done last night. There was only one thing certain, neither he nor Anson would have had the strength to break that rock.

When the captain had taken over for a spell he went back to the lee of the ambulance where the girl was opening tins of bully and a second batch of water was near the boil. He talked at random, trying to keep her mind off other things, but the chink of the pick and the dry scrape of the shovel kept on breaking in through their words. Then the noises stopped and he looked over the bonnet to see that they were walking over towards the stretcher.

He said, 'Look—I must try and fix the pump. Will you help me while we're waiting for them?'

'Of course. What do you want me to do?'

He spread a blanket beside the car and tipped out the entire contents of the tool-kit box on it. 'Look through all those little bits—the nuts and bolts—and see if you can find a black washer, it will feel sort of soapy.' He had looked earlier and knew there wasn't one.

Then he wriggled under the sump. 'And pass me the tools as I want them.'

He lay on his back, fumbling, listening to the shovelling noise that had started again, delaying as long as possible to keep her on the ground beside him where she could not see. Only when the sounds from the far side of the wadi had stopped and she had reported that there was no washer there, did he wriggle out, pulling the tin after him. 'Over a pint gone,' he said, 'and I've tightened as much as I dare.'

As he straightened, to pour the water from the tin back in the radiator, he saw the two men walking towards them from the far side of the wadi, carrying a folded stretcher.

They all tried to be terribly normal while they ate, the conversation ranged on anything except the last thing that had to be done. The words got steadily more stilted, more brittle, and at last he could stand it no longer. He looked at Anson and said, 'Shall I try and make something up, sir?'

Anson nodded, so he got up and ripped two strips of wood from the top of the case that held the tinned milk. He took a bit of the binding wire and got it red hot in the fire and bored holes through each and then bound them together in the form of a cross. He searched his pockets but he only had a pen and that wouldn't take on the wood. None of their pencils were indelible and they could not think how to do it until Diana said, 'My lipstick's supposed to be waterproof—and I don't want it any more.'

So he printed with that—her name, her number—which Diana got from the other identity disc—and the date. Then Anson got up and said, 'We'd better get it over. We must get on our way.'

As they walked over to the long mound, the sun came over the lip of the wadi and it was hot already, with the first dust-devil spiralling along the edge of the cliff, the scrub at the bottom beginning to shimmer in waves. Zimmerman had put on his bush-jacket but had not buttoned it up. Tom thought, 'He might have'—but at least he had left that bloody pack behind.

They stood two on each side while he pushed the wooden upright hard down in the sand and banked some stones up round it. Then Anson had said, 'I'm sorry—I don't know the service. Does anyone?' But Zimmerman shook his head and Diana turned away.

And not because he was in any way a religious man, not for the dead Denise, but for the living Diana, he felt he must do something. Slowly, the soft Devon voice stumbled out in the words . . . 'The Lord is my shepherd . . .' He got half of it wrong and dried up after a few verses because no one else had joined in. Then he said, 'I'm sorry—that's all I know,' and they all stood silent, looking at the ground, before the noise came to them for the first time.

It started as if someone was shaking a chain, softly and a long way off. It went away for a moment and then came back louder, more clanking. He looked up at Anson and the knowledge passed between them, then they were all running back towards the ambulance.

The noise got louder as they began to throw the kit on, but then Anson said, 'No good. If we move, they'll spot the dust. Douse that fire quick, Tom. And stay still.' As he shovelled sand on the fire, he looked across at Diana and said, 'Tanks —probably theirs.'

The clanking came up the wadi to them in gusts, but there was nothing to be seen because of the bend towards the mouth. It stopped for a moment and then started again, coming closer. Anson whispered, 'Christ!—they've seen our tracks.'

It was very loud now, echoing off the rocky walls, sounding like a scaly dragon crawling up to meet them. They stayed together, quite still. Then round the corner came the long grey shape of a German half-track and Zimmerman had cursed and started to run down the wadi towards it with Anson close behind.

He stayed where he was, leaning against the car. Diana was very close to him, and somehow his arm had gone round her. The haze jumped and shimmered over the tangle of scrub and the grave.

CHAPTER 7

Anson could feel the sweat running down between his shoulder-blades as he pounded after Zimmerman. There was no question of catching up, as the big man had had a couple of seconds start and was running very fast. All he could hope was to be at that meeting as soon as he could . . . he wanted that very badly.

The half-track had stopped and the troops in it had jumped out to form a semi-circle in front, their automatic weapons crooked under their arms; between them, leaning back against the radiator, arms crossed, with a big Luger held loosely in the right hand, was an officer, a lieutenant. He looked young and tough and arrogant. 'Not a hope in hell, this time,' thought Anson as he came level with Zimmerman's shoulder.

It all happened so quickly that, afterwards, it was difficult to sort out the order in which he noticed things. Perhaps, first, the way the lieutenant was looking, not at Zimmerman's face, but his chest, his eyes not hostile, but wary—just as they had been the time before. Then, Zimmerman's hands, the way they were up on his chest, just as if he was buttoning his jacket, the speed with which they cut away as he realized Anson was at his shoulder. Last, the tone of his voice.

There was no diffident explanation there, it was intense, almost commanding, as question and answer went to and fro; wishing desperately that he spoke the language, he watched the circle of hard eyes under the steel helmets.

At last Zimmerman turned to him. 'Twice is bad luck. They were on patrol. They saw our tracks and followed them. I have told him we have a safe conduct from 15 Panzer Group but—' he spread his hands, '—there is nothing written and I do not think he believes me. He says he cannot check our story as there is wireless silence. I think he suspects a trap—for he says he will search and question us all before he decides what to do.' He stopped for a moment and looked very straight at Anson. 'He tells me that they entered Tobruk at certain points last night—and that the whole fortress surrendered this morning without a fight.'

It made him feel sick—physically sick. He said, 'I don't believe it,' but in his heart he knew that it was true and if that had gone there was nothing much left. Matruh? . . . he remembered that sham fortress, how its minefield looked so impressive on paper, how, only last year, he had led a convoy over the fringe of it by mistake . . . and not a single mine had exploded. Someone had said they had been filled by a civvy contractor in the Delta . . . probably with sand.

Zimmerman's voice cut through his thoughts. 'He says to go back to the ambulance.'

As they walked back to the car, he heard the crunch of the steps behind of the soldier who was covering him; watched others climbing the walls of the wadi, slipping and scrambling up the sides like grey beetles, then standing at the top to sweep the horizon with binoculars. Then he heard the faint call of, '*Nein, nicht*—' float down from one side and the other. At the ambulance Tom and Diana were standing close together. Even in this moment he envied them, thought for a fleeting second of Ariadne . . . then Paul. Where was he now . . . ?

The questions, passed on by Zimmerman, were confined to the simple name, rank, number and the details of the shooting up and Denise's death. It was when the Germans made the search of the ambulance that he saw the other small thing.

It was only because he was watching—intent on every little movement now, that he spotted it. The lieutenant was rummaging in the clutter on the floor of the cab when his hand moved towards the square pack that Zimmerman had rested on while he leaned against the windscreen pillar. It never got there, that hand, because in that instant the South African's eyes and the German's caught and held and something sparked between them. The hand hesitated, and moved on to another object. No one else saw, he would not have seen if he had not been watching for it. Perhaps it was imagination. But now he was so nearly sure . . . and being sure would make it all the more difficult.

After he had finished, the German gave a jerk of his head to Zimmerman and they went over to the grave together and they saw him copying the inscription into his field pocketbook. Then Zimmerman came back alone.

'He says we may go. That the Afrika Korps do not bring women

into fighting areas—and we should not either—but he cannot be
bothered with her. But we must go farther south. Their armour is
already through the "wire" as far down as Maddalena. They will
have cut off Matruh in two days. He says we must start now.'

They threw the rest of their gear on, watched by the stiff circle
of grey figures in the shimmering heat. When it was done, the
lieutenant gave a signal with his arm and the circle drew back.
They moved off, passing close to him as he stood, stony-faced, by
the grave. They climbed on up the slope of the wadi bottom and
the walls fell away to nothing and then they were on the last stretch
of endless brown plain, heading south.

Anson was driving, Zimmerman in the passenger seat, still hugging
that pack, the other two had gone into the back of the car for a
rest.

Anson felt in his pocket and pulled out the compass, he passed
it over without looking round. 'Keep her on 170°, Zimmerman.'

'OK, man.'

Except for his clipped directions to keep them on the course, they
did not speak for the first half hour. Once or twice Anson glanced
at him, sitting there, hunched over the compass he had balanced
on top of the pack. Then his eyes went back to the way ahead.

It was brown and dead. No camel-thorn here to make any form
of pattern, only coarse gravel like Demarara sugar, and as the sun
got higher, the mirage took on a new form. It was as if the edges
of the horizon were drawn up into the sky all round and they were
floating in the bottom of a brown bowl, with only a small circle of
blue sky directly overhead. The going was good, so smooth that
they did not seem to be moving at all, they were stationary at the
bottom of this dun sea and the gravel was sliding by them in a
quiet dry crackle.

At last he said, 'So you got us out of another jam.'

The voice came back, tight and clipped. 'Man, I don't know. He
was a bastard. But with Tobruk gone—they had more important
things to do than to round us up.'

'You believe that—about Tobruk?'

'Yes.'

Another fifteen minutes . . . another 7.2 miles on the clock. But
they were still at the bottom of that brown bowl, did not seem to
have moved at all.

Zimmerman said suddenly, 'What's the plan, Captain?'

'I was going to talk about that when we stop to brew up. But do you know the lie of the land this far south?'

'No. Only what I've read.'

'Well, if it is true they are through the "wire"—and I don't believe a word of that cock about outflanking Matruh—it won't be wise to try and make the coast road west of there. That means we'll have to keep on bearing south-ish, to give the coast as wide a berth as possible, until we hit the Masrab that runs along the top of the Depressions, when we can turn north up the Garawla track to the sea.' There was a pause and then he said, '—But it means another hundred and fifty miles.'

Zimmerman did not say that he understood the geography; only, 'There's plenty of petrol, isn't there?'

'Yes. That's not the trouble. It's the bloody water pump. Did you hear the sergeant-major swearing at it? We lost a quart of water last night, though of course we can save that. But we can't when we're running.'

'Can't it be tightened—or disconnected?'

'No. There's a carbon washer—it's wearing. If you tighten too much, it will crumble altogether—and then we're done. I don't think you could disconnect the pump anyway—and if you did, she'd boil like a bitch in this heat.'

'So—?'

'So there will be an increasing drain on the water—and always the chance of a bloody long walk.'

Silence again, floating on the bottom of the brown sea, with the gravel rushing under them in its quiet sound.

Anson said, 'I was attached to your div for a bit.'

'When?' There was a hint of sharpness in the question.

'Oh—let me see—about nine months ago. When they first came up. I was with supply services. They were a bloody good lot.'

'I wasn't up with them then. I only came up from the Union last January. I'm afraid I haven't had much to do with the supply side.'

Nothing could have been more negative. He said, 'But you must have heard of some of them—old Kramer, the colonel—he was a character.'

'Kramer—Yes. I did meet him once. I can remember him.'

'And the general—?'

'Dan Piennaar?—Yes.'

'Do you remember . . . ?' Anson embarked on one of many tales that surrounded the legendary figure of the commander of the 1st

SA Division. While he was talking, his voice seemed to come from outside him, from someone else. He could even listen to it while he was thinking . . . 'You managed to get one name right, Zimmerman. But anyone would know about Dan Piennaar. Kramer, though . . . you have met him . . . the colonel of supply services. There's only been one head of supply services, and his name was not Kramer . . . it was Maggs . . . Eugene Maggs. And he was such a well-known and loved type . . . you must have heard . . .'

His own voice finished, '—And he put it in orders, that any gun troop that fired at a range of more than eight hundred yards would be court martialled, or castrated, on the spot—whichever was the most convenient.'

Zimmerman did not laugh. He was pointing through the screen. 'What's that ahead?'

Something was showing on the edge of the bowl ahead of them. At first it looked like a row of thin black columns, then the mirage cleared and it was a low rusting barbed-wire fence that stretched across their path from horizon to horizon.

'The "wire",' he said, and leaned back and pushed open the door to the back and shouted, 'Wake up, Tom, it's the "wire".' They were quite close to it when Tom came out from the back, rubbing his eyes. 'That's pretty good, Captain Anson. Where are we on it?'

'Unless we're a lot adrift—about two miles north of El Washka—you know, where there are those two palms, and a gap. I'm going to turn south and find it.'

It was four miles to the south of them in fact, but still he was very pleased. They ran that distance down the edge of the fifteen-foot-thick fence. Diana was peering out through the door now and Anson told her how it had been put up for the 180 miles from Sollum to Siwa by the Italians, to keep the Senussi in Libya for not too pleasant purposes. Then there were two stunted palms, the gap, and they were bumping over the flattened coils. The brown plain looked exactly the same as before. Only now it was Egypt.

As if to welcome them home, the going altered within ten miles. It was rougher, with flat grey stones jutting from the ground, the smaller ones rattling away from under the wheels, but ahead the flatness had gone, weird mountains and terraces were floating now in the mirage, that resolved to low flat-topped hills at closer range.

'Where to now, sir?' Tom was still looking out from the back.

'I'm going 15.2 miles on 152°. That should hit Bir Bayley. We'll brew up there—and see if the well is worth digging out. We can't drink it—even if there is any—but it will help for the radiator.' He looked across at Zimmerman. 'It's a well we dug out two years ago—but God knows what happened to it since.'

The desert was as empty as it had been all day, the going got steadily worse. Now there was bare rock on the ridges and in the hollows between patches of cracked mud. The sand was taking on a reddish tinge.

He drove on until Zimmerman said, 'Fifteen up,' and then stopped and climbed up on the bonnet with the glasses. The mirage was bad, but nothing like that of the morning. He swept the lenses round the dancing hills that seemed to come towards him and then curtsy away; at last he found the little yellow pimple that jutted out from the side of a ridge. 'There it is—half left. We'll go over and brew up there.'

Diana had never seen anything that looked less like a well. After they had come through the 'wire', and she had got up from the bunk to tidy up, Tom had told her about Bir Bayley. She knew that 'Bir' meant 'well'—in this case having, presumably, refreshed or been discovered by a Mr Bayley—and even if her imagination did not reach as far as lush grass and bubbling springs, at least she thought she was in for a few palms.

There was nothing. Just a mound of yellow sand on the lee of a hill, and in the bare rock beside it a small square pit with more sand drifting up to one lip. She stood in the cab looking at it while the others jumped down. 'Where's the water?' she said.

Anson turned from unstrapping the spade. 'Five . . . ten . . . fifteen feet under that lot. We've got to dig to find out.' He turned to Tom. 'It looks a lot worse than last time, but go down a bit in that corner and see if there's any dampness. Then we'll decide. I'm going to do a bit of thinking—and plot the next course. Diana, will you start up the brew?'

She put out the tins and the water and the petrol, was proud and grateful that he sat in the driver's seat, the map-board propped up on the steering wheel, without attempting to help or interfere. When it was going, she looked over towards the well and there was nothing but Zimmerman sitting on the edge smoking and the bright blade of the spade flashing out of the hole at regular intervals, each time dropping off a gout of sand. She walked over to it.

Tom was still digging. He was stripped to the waist and it was the first time she had seen him like that. She watched with pride and it was a personal, possessive thing.

He had not the spread of Zimmerman, but he was brown and supple and smooth, the sunlight flickered over the play of muscles each time the arms swung up and winked on the brass badge strapped to one wrist. Then she looked at the other man, sitting there, watching lazily, smoking. And she was full of a hot resentment.

Tom threw the spade down suddenly and knelt in the bottom of the hole, feeling with his hands. He turned and looked up at them. 'It may be wishful thinking—but it feels dampish to me. Will you take a spell, Captain Zimmerman?'

'Sure.' He stood up and stripped off his shirt and laid it carefully on top of the pack that was by his side. Then he jumped down to Tom. 'What do I do?'

'Just dig, sir. Until you hit real wet sand.' Then he said, 'My God! I've forgotten that bloody pump—it's been dripping all this time. Must put a tin under it.' He climbed out of the hole, grabbed his shirt and almost ran back to the car.

She stayed for a moment, looking down at the great shoulders that were making the sand fly. Then she bent down to reach for his bush shirt. 'Shall I take these back to the ambulance for you?'

He stopped in mid-stroke, with a jerk that spilled the sand from the side of the spade. His whole body went rigid.

'No, thanks. I'll bring them myself.'

'Very well.' She turned on her heel and walked back to the car.

Tom was standing beside the captain, who was still fiddling with ruler and protractor. She said, 'Captain Anson, I want to talk to you.'

He looked up from his board and she saw that through his tiredness his eyes were wary. 'So does Mr Pugh, Sister. I imagine, on the same subject. Don't you think it can keep? I may think the same—but listen . . .'

He held up his hand and in the silence there was that little sound they had heard the night before. *Plop . . . plop . . . plop . . . plop.* Water dripping into the tin. Only now it was coming five times as fast.

He said, 'I don't want to frighten you, but that is far more important.' He looked towards the well, where the flash of the spade still came regularly. 'Whatever we think—let's keep it as thoughts. Until we can do something about it. He's strong. We're going to need him.'

Then he turned back to Tom. 'What happened to his haversack last night?'

Tom, wooden-faced, looking straight back at him, said, 'I had an accident—I dropped it.'

'All right—you dropped it. But we don't want any more—accidents like that.'

The tea was made and the bully opened by the time Zimmerman came back to them from the well. He lowered the spade and opened the other hand; on the palm was a pile of sand, darker than they had seen before. 'That's from the bottom,' he said. 'I've gone down another three feet.'

Anson took it and crumbled it and put a fragment to his lips. He spat. 'Hardly damp—and salt as hell. We might go on for hours, and then get nothing. Let's eat, and talk about it after.'

The bully was tepid and almost poured out of the tin. It made her feel sick but she knew that she must eat it. The sun beat straight down on them now, very hot, and they crouched in the little strip of shade at the side of the car. The mirage heaved and swirled outside the narrow circle round them. They were alone in the middle of it and they talked because they had to—of anything that would shut out that background noise that was in their minds all the time now. The steady, fast dripping of water into the tin under the pump.

She said, 'Flies—I've only just noticed. There aren't any. But there were clouds at Tobruk. Why?'

Anson spooned another gob of bully out of his tin with a wedge of biscuit. 'No human beings, Diana. Flies only go with man and his filth. This desert—no one ever comes to it—for nothing has, or ever could, live here. So there are no flies.' He munched for a moment. 'How many times have we been up and down between Matruh and Benghazi, Tom?'

'Five—no, six, counting this swan.'

'It was different there,' said Anson, 'though we always tried to keep it clean. It's funny—though all the desert looks the same you get a fondness for certain spots, and always go back to them if you can.' He took another bite of biscuit. 'We had a notice made—Tom did it beautifully—a lovely big board painted in the correct German. When he had to retire, we stuck it in the ground. It said, *We are coming back—leave the desert as you found it*. Twice when we came forward again, we found it turned round the other way, and they had written, *We have—and so will we*.'

Tom said, 'And they did—always left it like a new pin. The Ities, that was different.' He looked at Zimmerman. 'Did you find the same thing, sir?'

Zimmerman didn't answer for a moment and then he said, 'I can't remember us—ever leaving messages for Jerry.'

While they were clearing up, Anson said, 'The water, Tom. Check every drop, and then we'll talk this out.' He sat on the step with his map-board on his knee, with the others beside him, waiting for Tom to come back. Then he cleared his throat.

'Well, how much?'

'Ten full tins—and a drain in the one we're using.'

'That's twenty gallons. And how fast is that thing leaking?'

Tom shrugged. 'It's difficult to say. Perhaps a gallon to every four hours' running. We can't save that.'

'Say, three gallons a day—at the top. We've been using four for cooking and other things. So there's three days water.'

'Can't you tighten it up at all?' It was Zimmerman.

'No. Tom tells me another quarter turn and the washer will break. All he can do is to keep it packed with grease—and we haven't much of that.

'Three days . . .' Anson repeated, '—and there are two—no, three alternatives. Have a crack at digging that out—' he jerked his head towards the well, '—in hopes of getting enough to fill some cans for the radiator only. It will be undrinkable —too brackish. But we might not find any, and waste the time and be consuming water ourselves, just the same.'

Diana said, 'What are the other two?'

'The first—to disregard what our German pal said, and go straight from here to Matruh. That's not more than 150 miles. Easy. But we would be converging on the coast all the time, and it would be awkward if he was right. The other way is to stick to my original plan and skirt round the longer, safer camel road at the top of the Depression and then up the Garawla track. 270 miles—all of three days and about our limit.'

He was silent for a moment. 'Of course—there is one other. Go south from here to Siwa or Qara Oasis, where we know there's water. Fill right up and then go straight across the Depression itself—'

It seemed as straightforward but equally as incomprehensible as the other plans. But there must be something different about it, for she saw Tom's face—and it was as if his CO had made rather an improper suggestion.

'You wouldn't do that, sir.'

'Why not? I've done it before. I know the distance is greater, but we would be filled up, and certain not to meet anyone.'

Tom said, 'I didn't mean that. The other time—it was training. You had light stuff—and there were planes to keep a check on you. But alone—in this crate, no.'

It was completely beyond her, so she said, 'What is this Depression?'

Anson got down from the driving seat and propped the map-board up against the bonnet. 'Come here, Diana—and you, Zimmerman. I'll try and show you.' She peered over his shoulder while his finger moved over the face of the map.

'From here, east, the desert proper funnels down until it's only forty miles wide at a place called Alamein. The sea is the boundary to the north and this Depression comes up to meet it from the south. It's a salt marsh—and to understand it, you must try to think of the lie of the land sideways. From the sea, the desert rises up in shelves—'

'I know—escarpments. Like those yesterday.'

'Yes. And the ground rises gradually between them, so that here we are at about six hundred feet. It goes on south of us to eight hundred or so, then drops a thousand in one big cliff to the Depression—which is below sea level. There is a track across—but the going is—very bad. That's what Tom meant.'

She was watching his pointing finger. It rested now on a great area that was coloured grey-green, a faint dotted line wandered along its length, almost uncertainly. There were words printed in places beside it . . . 'Bad going' . . . 'Soft sand'. In one place, just '???'.

Anson said, 'I think I could make it.' Then he looked round the group. 'Well—there you are. Direct to Matruh, or the Garawla track, or across the Depression.' No one said anything, so he looked straight at Tom and said, 'Then it will have to be like a court-martial, junior first. You, Tom?'

'The Garawla track, sir. And—somehow—I'll make that pump last.'

'Now two pips. Diana?'

'The same as Tom.'

'Zimmerman?'

He said. 'I've heard about that Depression. No, the same as the others.'

Anson did not make any comment. He just said, 'The ayes have it,' and then he looked across at the well. 'At least, we haven't wasted much time on that caper. Might dig for a week for nothing. One order before we start, though. No more washing or shaving—' he rubbed his beard, '—we've left part of it a bit late, anyway.'

He looked across at Diana. 'We'll try and spare you a drop. Not more than a pint a day, I'm afraid. We must keep the tea ration up if we can.'

She said, 'Put that in the tea. I don't want to be different. If you don't shave—then I don't wash.'

He said, 'Good girl,' and threw the map-board on the driver's seat. 'Well, let's get cracking. Nuts to you, Bir Bayley —some other b—can dig you out. I'm going to get a taste of that Rheingold soon. Tom, will you take over? Sixty miles on 115°. Then call me. I'm tired.' He went into the back of the car and Zimmerman, with his pack, followed him.

When Tom had emptied the tin back into the radiator and poured in a good deal of the cans besides, they set off into the emptiness ahead; the only living moving object in a thousand square miles. But they had made their decision. They were moving on a set course towards their destination . . . For four miles—to be exact 3.8. Then on a bit of level going, suddenly and without reason, the left rear spring went.

There was a sharp crack and the car lurched and seemed to sag backwards and sideways. Tom swore horribly and braked gently to a halt. As they jumped down, the other two piled out of the back.

She could only stand and watch, feeling useless. But there was one thing she noticed at once and it did not seem strange to her: without a word being spoken, Tom had taken over control. He had gone straight to the back, squatting, sucking his teeth as he looked at the bright, broken end of the main leaf of the spring where it jutted out beyond the shackle. Then he crawled underneath and came out dusting his hands and looking quite cheerful.

'Not too bad. We can fix it. Get a lot of flat stones.' Then he looked at her as if she was an orderly: 'You, Diana—put that tin under the radiator like you saw me do it last night. And make sure the drips are falling in it.'

Meekly she went, and when she had finished crawling under the sump and went back to the others, the wheel was off already and the jack supporting the chassis. While Anson was going out in the surrounding desert and bringing in flat slabs of rock, Zimmerman was underneath the car making a pile beside the jack. Tom looked up from his work on the axle, pausing to wipe his hands and smile at her.

'Best know what we're doing, Diana. It's got to be done in two stages with only one jack. We put her up—make a pile of stones under the chassis, then let her down on that—so that the jack is free to work the spring in.'

'Work the spring—?'

'Yes. You've seen the spare ones tied on the front. Well, when there's no load on them, there's too much camber—bend—to let them reach the shackles, the bolts that hold it to the car. So we fasten the front end, then press the spring up against the weight until it is flat enough to reach the back. Then we bolt up, put the wheel on, kick away the stones and let the whole lot down. Simple.'

'It all sounds as if it will take a long time.'

'All of two hours,' he said, 'but there's nothing we can do about it.' He went on with the task of unbolting the broken spring from the axle.

She wandered round, watching them; Anson was underneath with Zimmerman now, helping to pack the stones. At last he said, 'That seems firm enough. Let her down gently, Tom.'

She watched him leave his work on the spring and go round and twist the lever of the jack. Slowly, the body of the ambulance sank down on to the stones, there was a grating noise, a gentle rock, and then no movement. Tom slid the jack clear.

When it happened, it was so quick that she had not time to gauge the disaster before it was past. Anson was coming round from the front with the new spring. Tom was lifting the old one clear, Zimmerman, apparently resting, still underneath the back, when there was a brittle cracking and puffs of dust jetted out from underneath the chassis and the ambulance started to slide down while the stones slipped out of the pile in a rattle.

Tom shouted, 'Christ!—she's going. Captain Zimmerman —try and hold her—just for a second—'

While he was shouting, he moved, and she had never seen anyone move so fast in her life. He dived down, the jack in one hand, pumping at the lever with the other while he stuffed it into position. But, before the pile disintegrated entirely, before the jack took the strain, before even Anson was under there to help, Zimmerman took the strain. Zimmerman, on hands and knees, grunting, joints cracking, held the body on his own for five long seconds . . .

CHAPTER 8

He had not been resting underneath the car, only thinking. It was in the shade and as good a place as any, had the advantage that no one could see his face. He was beginning to wonder how much they were watching him . . .

So, when he had finished piling the stones and Captain Anson had gone out to get the spring, he had just stayed where he was, working the whole thing out.

It was not going as well as he had hoped . . . it had been damnable luck to run into his comrades twice . . . and that second one had been so aggressive, so slow, that the Englishman had almost seen. Or had he seen? . . . there was the accident to that other pack of his . . . but that was before. Had they been searching for something . . . or was it just to sabotage that gin? There was only one thing certain, that it was no accident. The bottle had been smashed to fragments.

He had looked out sideways, at the bottom half of their legs moving about as they worked, then on to the flat dun heaving plain of the desert. He supposed they must be 180 kilometres from the coast now . . . a long way. He thought for a moment about what it would be like, that 'long walk' the captain had spoken of . . . quickly turned his thoughts to what now lay ahead. He was glad they had not chosen the short way back to Matruh. It would be the certainty of walking into his own, having to start all over again. Equally relieved that the Depression had been ruled out. They had had lectures . . . he knew their General Staff had assessed it as impossible for transport in their plans for invasion of Egypt. So it was the middle way—three days, if they were lucky. Could he keep them satisfied for that time? He had to, they were his only chance of getting into the Delta.

Then the cracking started and he had turned on hands and knees before Tom shouted. He had locked his arms and his legs and heaved up, taking the intolerable strain while the cross-members of the chassis ground down into his spine, the terrible tearing moments, with the twisting pain in his guts and the thudding, red haze before his eyes. He had taken it, and there had been no thought of his mission, of the war, as he had done so. Only that long walk there would be for all of them if he failed, the unending waste of sand that would divide them from other humans, the thirst, the sunstroke. There was only one enemy in those seconds. The desert.

Then relief came and they pulled him out. He sat on the sand, unable to get up, drained of everything except that awful pain in his guts. When he could see properly, he looked up and they were grouped round him, staring down in a peculiar way. The girl said, 'Are you all right, Captain Zimmerman?' and he couldn't answer for a moment and when his voice did come it did not sound like his own. 'I've hurt my back—I think I'll lie down.'

She said, 'Let me help you into the car,' but the captain said, 'No, not until we've finished the job. There's some shade on the side now, put him there.' Then, louder, looking round the circle, 'That was one of the most bloody marvellous things you have ever seen. If she'd come down hard on the axle—we would have been done.'

They got him under the arms and walked him round and it hurt like hell. When they were in the strip of shade, the girl said, 'I can manage now. You get on with the job.' As the two of them had walked away, he heard the sergeant-major say, 'He must have stood up to all of a ton—perhaps more.' The tone was awed, but it didn't help him much ... didn't take away that pain ...

The girl had got a blanket and spread it out, then she helped him move on to it. 'My pack,' he said, 'it's still under the car—could you get it?'

'Of course.'

She came back at once holding it by the strap and he knew there had been no time to open it. She put it down beside him. 'Would you like a drink?'

'I would, but mine's broken.'

'Wait a minute.' She went to the front of the car and fumbled in her haversack, she came back with a flask he had not seen before and held his head while he tilted it back. It was Scotch whisky and made him feel better. She knelt beside him. 'Where does it hurt?' she said.

Something in her attitude irritated. 'Everywhere. I think I've twisted my guts. But if I've ruptured something—which is what you think—there's nothing to be done about it, is there?'

'Nothing,' she said.

'Then give me a cigarette—and go and help the others. We don't want to be here for ever.'

When she had gone, he lay quite still, flat on his back, watching the thin spiral of smoke twisting up into the hot air, regretting everything.

It took them three hours to complete the job. They worked slowly with a double check on each stage, and this time there were no accidents. Diana's part was the selection of the smoothest, flattest stones, and she thought afterwards that she must have walked at least five miles in her circling of the ambulance looking for them. They had made her loosen her hair to hang over her shoulders as protection against the sun. Secretly, she thought it silly, for it was not so hot now, a deathly stillness coming with the cool. The sun was sinking away behind them now, getting redder with each degree it dropped down the sky. The mirage had gone, the low flat-topped hills clear and steady on every side.

When she came back from one trip she went up to Anson and held out her hand. 'I thought you said nothing lived here?—where did this come from, then?' On her palm was a dry white empty snail shell.

He looked up from tightening the rear shackle. 'So we're getting near that part. Tomorrow you'll see millions of them —the ground is just covered. Don't ask me how they came. No one really knows, though there is a theory this desert was a sea bed once.' He gave another couple of turns with the spanner. 'How's Zimmerman?'

'I keep having a look at him. He's asleep—and a much better colour. I don't think there's anything—vital—hurt. He's just played out.'

When they had finished, they let KATY off the jack and stowed away the tools. Anson looked at the slanting rays of the sun and said, 'Not worth it—before dark. We'll brew up now and get Zimmerman in the back, then wait till the moon comes up and I'll have a crack at some night driving.' They got Zimmerman into the back without much difficulty, it was just as if he was rather stiff and tired. They brewed up and took his share into the back of the car and he seemed grateful, but uncommunicative. The sun vanished soon after they had finished clearing up, suddenly, twisting the purple shadows in a moment to blackness. Anson looked at her.

'Tired, Diana?'

'No, not particularly.'

'Well, take the first stretch with me and let Tom have a spell. We'll be off with the moon and drive while it lasts. Tom, I'll call you at midnight.'

After Tom had gone into the back and they waited for the moon to rise, Anson said, 'Sit down—or walkabout?'

'Walkabout.'

They wrapped the spare blankets round their shoulders and started a slow circle of the black square of the ambulance. They were out of earshot, but she spoke very softly: 'I picked up Zimmerman's big haversack this afternoon,' she said.

'So what—?'

'It was heavy—and it didn't feel like bottles. I thought you ought to know.'

He stopped in his tracks and swung round towards her. 'Do you know he saved us all—completely—this afternoon? If she'd come down on the axle, we'd have been bitched, had to walk a hundred miles—probably straight back into Jerry hands.'

'That's not the point,' she said.

'It IS the point, Diana. Look, I think I know what he's got in there—' he peered at his watch—'and if something happens soon—I'll have proved it.'

'If what happens?'

'—Regardless of his twisted guts, or his stiffness, Captain Zimmerman will continue his regular habits before nine.'

It was ten minutes to the hour before they heard the sounds coming from the cab; when they had circled to that side, it was Zimmerman, standing on the ground, unclipping the spade. They moved over to him.

'Are you all right, Zimmerman?'

He turned, leaning heavily on the spade. 'Yes. I won't be long.'

'Don't be. The moon will be up any moment, and I want to move off at once.'

'All right.' He turned away and shuffled off into the darkness.

She waited for Anson to speak, but he just resumed his leisurely pacing. She said, aghast, 'But aren't you—?'

'NO.' It was fierce. 'Whatever's wrong, he can't be doing any harm *yet*. And he's saved us three times already.'

He wasn't long. When he had come back out of the gloom with that slow shuffling gait, the tip of the moon was just beginning to show over the hills to the south. 'He just made it,' said Anson; 'now, let's get moving.'

He climbed into the driving seat and gave her the compass and showed her how to use it. There was deep satisfaction in being for once rather important, and she held the heavy roundness of it clasped tight on her knees, peering at the swing of the needle's luminous point against the pre-set mark of 95°, giving him the direction when he veered off course. As she got more used to it, she could relax and they talked in spasms. Once he said, 'That shell you brought in—it reminds me of a story about these parts.'

'Tell me—I love hearing of the desert.'

'Do you like it?'

'Yes.'

'Well, I hope you still do when you've finished with it.' There was a silence while he concentrated for a moment on the dim moonlit way ahead and then he said, 'It was two years ago. I had been sent down here from the coast—to dig out that bloody well we were at today, as a matter of fact—and in those days anywhere within twenty miles of the "wire" was the front line, and you had to be careful. We were a bit east of here—country you'll see tomorrow—even more desolate than this, just red sand spattered with gravel on top, and millions and millions of those white shells lying about—'

She cut in, 'Right a bit, George—a bit more. Now, steady as you go.'

He picked up the new course and then went on. 'We were trundling along quite happily—until we came on some other tyre tracks. Now, you learned to know all the patterns made by our vehicles and theirs, but these weren't like anything I had ever seen, thin and narrow. I was wary, but curious, because they looked so new; where they had broken the gravel crust, the edges were as sharp as a razor. Anyway, they were leading in the right direction, so we followed them. They led south to one of these flat-topped hills—they call them quarets—and then turned off to the west. But on the side of the hill, "they", whoever they were, had stopped and made a fire. And then I was even more wary, because the charred bits of wood left balanced on each other and the ashes looked so new that I expected them to be hot. But they weren't.'

The moon was sinking already, the faint grey light fading so rapidly that now there was no horizon for him to take a mark on any more. Anson said, 'Another couple of miles, and I'll have to stop.'

'All right—but go on telling me.'

'Well, having felt the ashes, I was happier—but not quite sure, so I thought I had better climb to the top of the hill for a look round. There were other footmarks going up the sides and I had the queer, rather frightening feeling that I was going to find something at the top. There was—but not in the least what I expected. Laid out in a pattern of the shells like the one you had today was a message and a date. It said, "LONG-RANGE DESERT CAR PATROL. 21st NOVEMBER 1916".

'That was why we had not recognized those tracks—they were "T" Model Fords, and they and the fire had been made almost exactly twenty-five years before. But there's no wind here, it never rains, and so they had stayed as sharp and new as the day they were made. We were the next people to chance that way.'

'What did you do?'

He laughed. 'Just put our unit and the new date underneath. But I don't suppose anyone will ever see it—unless they start another war in about 1970, and some other poor bloody fools have to come mucking about in these parts.' He bent forward and threw out the gear lever. 'That's the lot—my eyes are getting sore.'

When they had coasted to a halt he struck a match, shielding the flame as he looked at the speedometer. 'Twenty-one miles farther east—that's good. Anything should be behind us now.'

'Behind us?'

'I didn't like to say anything before, but if that Jerry was right and they're through the "wire" and striking at Matruh, they must come south and occupy Giarabub and Siwa—or be outflanked. But now, they'll pass well behind us.'

'Giarabub, Siwa—they are just names to me. Tell me, I want to know.'

He jumped down from the driving seat. 'Come out from under there—and I'll do my best.'

After they had gone through the routine of putting the tin under the bonnet and wrapped the spare blankets round them, they sat on the sand with their backs against the front wheel. For the first time, she saw the full sweep of the night sky and it was even more beautiful than the night before. Wistful, almost angry, she wished that Tom was beside her to share it.

There was the dome of black velvet, so riddled with stars that there seemed to be more light than dark; they did not twinkle like the pinpoints of a northern sky, but glowed, each enormous, hanging just over their heads.

'Oh . . . !' she whispered.

'Yes.' His voice was just as soft. 'The deeper you get in the desert, the better it is. They'll look so pale when you get back to Alex. Look—there's Cassiopeia . . . and the Plough, over there to the west. Those two stars—the pointers—follow them through—' his finger moved dark against the blaze of light, '—and the next bright one is the Pole Star. That's got me home, many a night.'

She said, 'I think I could watch for ever.'

'Yes—if you had the right kind of things to go with it.'

'Such as—?'

'Oh, the right kind of music—Beethoven, and the right kind of girl.' Then he said quickly, 'Sorry—that wasn't meant to be rude.'

'I'll forgive you, George.' She was laughing. 'Tell me—have you got a girl?'

He made an uneasy movement with his shoulders. 'I don't know. Sort of—but it's all rather complicated.'

There was a silence and then he said, 'But you wanted to know about the desert. Well, you see the Pole Star? Keep that over your left eyebrow and walk about a hundred miles, and you'd hit the coast at Sidi Barrani, going downhill over the escarpments all the way.'

'Yes, you told us about that this afternoon.'

'The other way—south—you'd climb a bit more, and then break your neck over the thousand-foot drop to the Depression. Siwa and Giarabub are on it, at the western end. Oases—real ones, lush, plenty of trees and water.'

'This Depression,' she said. 'What's it like—? Why was Tom so dead against crossing it this afternoon?'

'It's a salt marsh—a bog, if you like. It's shaped rather like a pear, stalk up and tilted over to the right. It's two hundred miles from end to end and a hundred across the broadest part. It's all below sea level and water seeps through the deep rock strata of the desert and comes up from underneath it. But it never rains, so the sun dries out the top in a sort of crust, thickest in the summer, of course. But the whole issue is floating, really, and if you break through the crust, you've had it.'

He was silent for a moment. 'There's one track down the middle—I suppose the ground may be a foot higher than all the rest and dries out quicker and thicker. It's marked "safe for vehicles", but it's difficult to follow. If you don't—'

There was another pause and then he said, suddenly, 'I did it once. There were two blokes in a jeep with the convoy. They started fooling around, wouldn't keep to the track—went arsing off on the mud at the side. And it went through—God!—it was like a bloody submarine diving. We got the blokes out with a rope. But the jeep—it had gone—completely —in a minute.'

She said, 'That's why Tom didn't fancy crossing it?'

'Yes. And he's right. This ambulance is far heavier than the trucks we had.'

'Could we go round to the south of it?'

'No. The Great Sand Sea is there.'

'What's that?'

He turned his head towards her and the starlight showed he was smiling. 'You're a devil for punishment,' he said. 'I'll try to describe it. But it's difficult—I've never been there—only seen it once.

'Can you imagine rows and rows of sand dunes, all running due north and south, each about five hundred feet high and a mile from crest to crest? Bright yellow sand, soft—and the length of them—no one really knows, but at least six hundred miles. You can't cross them, only run down the troughs. It would be all right if we had enough petrol and wanted to get to the Cape.'

'So we must keep to the top of the cliff?'

'Yes. It's wisest.'

He pulled out his cigarettes and lit two carefully, turning towards the ambulance to shield the flare of the match with his body. 'Half an hour—and then I'll wake Tom.'

She said, 'You're very careful about lights.'

'Better be safe than sorry. They might try a night dash for Siwa—and you can see a match the hell of a distance.'

'They . . .' Her thoughts turned abruptly to other things, 'Zimmerman,' she said, 'he—'

'Skip it, Diana. I'll talk to you and Tom about that later.' Then his voice changed and became very casual, so casual that she knew the question was important, 'Can I—talk to you about something completely different? Ask your advice—as my big sister, if you like?'

'You're not very flattering, are you, George? But if that's the only way I qualify, I suppose I'll have to.'

'I've got eyes in my head,' he said; she blushed and hoped the starlight was not bright enough to show it.

'Go on, little brother.'

'It's a question of the woman's angle, and it's rather complicated. You asked about girl friends. That's the trouble. I don't know what to do.'

'About what?'

He said, 'Paul Crosbie—my best friend—he's with the company, and he was left in Tobruk. We've always done everything together—leaves, and things like that. We always used to go to Beirut. And we met a girl there, always went about together as a trio—' It was coming out in a rush now, but he would not look at her.

'What's her name—and which of you does she like best?'

'Her name's Ariadne—and I don't know. That's the trouble.'

'So—?' she prompted.

'I am terribly fond of her—but I was never sure about Paul. It was the one thing we never discussed. But things seemed different after we came back from the last leave—and then I had to take over the CO's job, and I started hitting the bottle—'

For the first time, he looked at her. 'It seems so stupid—but I was so bloody tired—all the time.'

'That's finished,' she said, 'and anyone who thinks at all can understand. But go on with this problem.'

'An officer had to be left in Tobruk. I had no say—the brig detailed him personally. But I know Paul thought—because it was him—that I was ratting.'

'And now—?'

'Paul's in the bag—I'm certain of that. At the moment, I'm outside. If I stay out, and get a chance to write to her—or go and see her, what do I do?'

She said, 'You don't understand women, George.'

'How do you mean?'

'You think that because you're free, there might be an unfair advantage—that your nearness might tip the scales?'

'That's the rough idea.'

'Well, all I can tell you is that if your Ariadne's a real woman, she will know already just what she wants—if anything. If it's neither of you—there's no harm done. If it's Paul—nothing you can do will make the slightest difference. So I would write to her, George. Tell her what's happened. If there's no answer, tip your cap and walk in another direction.'

'Do you always know what you want?'

'Always.'

'Right now?'

'Yes.'

He said, 'Let's talk about something else . . . Beer.'

'But I thought that was out.'

'It is until that date in Alex. Do you know—I've been thinking about that one particular drink all day. I've told you about the bar, haven't I? But that Rheingold—it's so bloody cold that there's a sort of dew on the outside of the glass. I always run my finger up and down—to make a sort of trail—before I have my first swallow.'

'And what will you do then?'

'Oh, have a bath and pull the lavatory chain about six times—to hear running water. Then take your advice, I think.'

She said, 'After the desert—the oasis.'

'Not any oasis,' he answered softly, 'but Zerzura.'

'What's that?'

He did not speak for a long time. Then he said, 'I'd better call Tom.'

'No. Give him a few minutes more. Tell me.'

He looked up at the slow turn of the blazing lights round the Pole Star, then he said, 'I've never talked about it before—though I've read all there is to read. It's the lost oasis. The name means, "The Place of the Little Birds".'

'Please tell me.'

'There's not much to tell. The story goes back seven hundred years—an oasis, somewhere down there—' he jerked his head back towards the south—'that's never been properly discovered. It comes up again and again in the old chronicles—with always the same detail: palms, a white city in the middle, a wall and a door with its handle carved like a bird. Inside there is a treasure, and a king and queen, sleeping.'

'How lovely—go on.'

'There's not much else. Up to thirty years ago, there were old men that remembered seeing it, but that's all gone now. But the point always was, it was only ever found by someone who was lost themselves—or looking for something that had been lost, like a straying camel. And afterwards, they could never find it again.'

'Did it really ever exist?'

'I don't know—I'd like to think so. Some Europeans still believe in it, passionately. They've spent most of their lives trying to find it. Personally, I think Ralph Bagnold has the truest idea. It's the wish-oasis. That when you are in danger—desperate—there's always something left to discover a little farther on, something difficult, but nice, if one has the guts to carry on and look for it. Perhaps, not even a physical thing . . . an idea . . .'

His voice drifted in silence. Then he said, 'You must think I talk an awful lot of drivel.'

'I don't—and nothing has ever been discovered?'

'Not a thing. And with planes—and the war—the possible area has shrunk to nothing. I'm afraid it is just the echo of that idea started by the Bedouin long, long ago.'

She looked up at the stars for a minute. 'Still—I hope you find your Zerzura, George.'

'And yours—' he said.

'I will.'

As if in answer, there was a bumping and a scuffling behind them and Tom Pugh came out of the cab to jump down on the sand.

'I woke up, sir.' The voice was reproachful. 'It's an hour past your time.'

'Sorry, Tom. We were nattering. How's Captain Zimmerman?'

'Still asleep. I didn't like to wake him.'

'No. Let him go through.' He looked at Diana. 'Would you like a spell?'

'I don't have to drive. I can sleep any time. I'll keep Tom company.'

Anson got to his feet stiffly. 'Well, I could do with it.' He stretched. 'Don't do anything I wouldn't.' Then he started to climb up into the cab, stopped and looked down at them. 'Are you sure he's asleep, Tom?'

'Yes. Snoring.'

Anson got down again. 'Then we had better get it sorted out—once and for all.' He came and squatted close to them. 'Both of you—at one time or another—have come to me to complain, or comment, on Captain Zimmerman. I wouldn't listen to you. Now's the chance to get all of it off your chests. You first, Tom.'

Tom looked down at his feet. 'Well, sir, he just appeared from nowhere—said his truck had broken down up the road, but we didn't see it. Then, when we went through the minefield, and they fired on us, he was swearing—and I'm certain it wasn't Afrikaans. He hadn't a clue as to how to make the fire—yet all Union troops brew up the same way as we do. And—excuse me, Diana—why does he always go out to the lavatory—at exactly the same time—and what's in that other pack—the one he keeps so close, and never lets anyone touch?' He ran down.

'Diana?'

'The same as Tom—I've never liked him, but it's more than that, there is something phoney. I haven't told anyone before—but after he had been over to the Germans, had been talking to them, he came back and called me "dear lady". Isn't that rather near German—not South African form of a address? That pack, too. I'm the only one that's touched it. It's heavy, solid, as if it was just one thing, not a collection.' Then she said, 'And why should he snap at me when I tried to pick up his bush shirt?'

Anson answered them very softly, 'I know all of that. But, for the last time, whatever it is that's wrong, he can't do any harm—now. The most important thing is that he shouldn't know. We want his help—there's enough on our plates without having trouble with him as well. We need him. So, ignore it, try not to think about it. I don't want any more "accidents". But if you see anything, just let me know on the quiet.'

Then he said, 'That's an order. Understand?'

Tom said, 'Yes, sir,' and as she did not quite know what to say, she said nothing. Anson swung himself up on the step again and melted into the shadow of the cab. The door to the back of the car shut with a click.

They sat on under the silent, circling stars, they talked of many little things but afterwards she could not remember any of them. The only jarring note was the noise of the pump dripping into the tin behind them. It was faster, and she hoped that Tom had not noticed. She did not want to spoil a moment of it, she was still thinking of Zerzura.

CHAPTER 9

It was the most wonderful thing in the world . . . this soft warm feather bed of sleep, and it was infuriating to be dragged back from it, to be shaken and see Tom Pugh standing there, a mug of tea in one hand.

'First light, sir. That pump—it's much worse. Almost running out now.'

It all came back to him and he turned, propped on one elbow as he took the tea, looking back over his shoulder out of the open door, seeing that the darkness had changed to pale grey.

He said, 'Damn the bloody thing!' and then swung his legs down and rubbed a hand over the stubble on his face and into his hot eyes before he leant over to the other bunk, looking at Zimmerman.

The big man stirred and muttered in his sleep, but Anson could not hear what he said; he reached forward and shook the big shoulder and then Zimmerman rolled on his back and opened his eyes.

'How do you feel, Zimmerman?'

'Rested, man.' Then he groaned as he tried to sit up. 'But stiff—bloody stiff.'

'Take this tea. I'll get some more outside. We must get going as soon as we can.'

Zimmerman sipped. 'I'll be all right. When I've had a walk round and limbered up.'

Despite himself, Anson was listening to every word now, trying to weigh up the clipped English, trying to remember if the Afrikander did speak like that.

They were away by seven, with Diana going into the back for her sleep, Anson driving, Tom in the passenger seat and Zimmerman sitting on the floor between them, which he said was the most comfortable. They took a course a little south of east and soon were in the shell country. They were littered everywhere, stretching to the horizons, covering the dark gravel like white flowers on a black field. They heard the crunch of them under the wheels, the softer hiss of the gravel flowing on in between.

By noon they had made sixty miles, with three stops to top up the radiator with water, and it was taking nearly a pint at a time now. Their course wound in and out of the flat-topped hills, with nothing to see but the red sand, the black gravel and the white shells; as the sun rose in the sky above them, the curtain of the mirage started its weird writhing dance.

As he drove, he kept on glancing down at Zimmerman. The long hairy legs in their brief shorts were straight in front of him, the square pack balanced on the thighs. It looked so square, that pack, almost like a box, and at one corner the canvas had started to fray. Was it wishful thinking—or was that a gleam of metal beginning to show through? His eyes strayed farther to the left and he found that Tom Pugh, from the passenger seat, was looking at it in exactly the same way. Their eyes met for a second and then flicked away. Tom's voice came quick and guilty. 'Two points to the left, sir.' He kept his eyes fixed on the plain ahead after that.

The desert was opening out in front of them now, the hills falling behind; far to the south, through the mirage, a yellow tinge stained the sky. He pointed. 'Reflection of the Sand Sea—we're getting close to the cliff now.' Then there was a thin column dancing in front of them, so that they were afraid for a moment it was a vehicle, but it cleared to a single conical hill.

He said, 'That's Qur el Laban—we should cut the Masrab just beyond it bearing north-east. We might as well stop there and eat, then crack on hard for the rest of the day.' All the time now, his mind was reaching out in calculations—water lost, time spent, miles to be done.

The hill was only about fifty feet high but it looked greater because of its loneliness. Behind it, the ground went on level to the horizon, only it was a nearer, clearer one than they had seen before, without mirage. They stopped on the east side of the hill and he unhooked the glasses from the back of the door and said, 'I'm going up to have a look.' He had scrambled halfway up the slope when he heard a shout from behind him. It was Diana. 'Can I come up with you?'

Soon they were standing on the hard level top, about the size of a tennis court, littered with the white shells even on this older level of the desert. He swept the glasses to the north, but there was nothing but the mirage; south, about a mile away, was a faint wavy line running across in front of them; scattered near in several places were lumps of white, far larger than the shells.

He handed over the glasses. 'There you are—straight ahead. Do you see those faint lines, with the white things beside?'

'Yes.'

'That's our track.'

'What are those white things?'

'Camel bones—probably hundreds of years old. It's a Masrab, an old caravan route. There will be bones marking our path all the way now.'

He saw that she had lifted the glasses farther towards the horizon. 'What can you see now?' he said.

'It looks like the edge of something—the cliff, I suppose. Then a haze—the most wonderful colours, blues and greens. Then far, far off, something yellow and knobbly, like the backbone of an animal.'

'The colours are the reflection of the Depression—and you, lady, have joined the select band who have seen the Sand Sea. That's the dunes, end-on to us.'

She said, 'This Depression—I wish I could see it.'

He looked at her gravely. 'I don't think you'll miss much.'

A faint call came up from below and they both turned to see the ambulance the size of a matchbox, the pigmy figure of Zimmerman, crouching by the fire, Tom standing by the open bonnet, waving his arms. 'It's that damned pump, I suppose,' he said, 'I had better get down.'

'Can I stay for a bit? I'll never see it again.'

'Not too long—without anything on your head. The sun's right on top now.'

'What about you lot? You walk about in it all day without a hat—even a shirt.'

'We've had two years of it,' he said, 'we're kippered.' Then he started to scramble back down the slope.

It was the pump, and now the leak was so bad that Tom had wanted his permission to risk another tightening. The two of them became absorbed, Anson holding his breath as Tom coaxed with the spanner, only relaxing when he said it would be all right, but could not be touched again. Only when they were wiping their hands, and Zimmerman came over to say that grub was ready, did he realize that the girl had not come down.

They all shouted and it was some time before she appeared at the edge of the slope; she was waving her arms and shouting back but they could not catch what she said. Then she came down the hill in a sliding run towards them.

'I heard a plane,' she gasped.

'A plane . . . ? Hush . . .'

They all stood quite still: only the sound of the occasional crack from the cooling engine and the steady dribble of water into the tin. Outside their own world, nothing.

'I heard it—I swear I did,' she said. 'Very faint. It went away—and then came back, louder.'

He said, 'You've had too much sun. I told you not to stay up there. Get into the shade of the cab at once.'

She went without a word and he was sorry in the instant that he had spoken to her like that. When food was dished out, he said, 'Let me do that, Tom,' and went over himself to the cab with the plate of stew and the spoon. 'What else did you do up there, Diana?'

She looked a little better now, not so white. 'I hope you don't mind—but I was thinking of your story of the shells, and I arranged some as our names—and KATY's—and the date. I hope someone sees it . . . one day.'

He said, 'I doubt it—but if you want to tell your grandchildren, the name of the hill is—'

Behind them, Tom said, suddenly, 'Listen.'

They all heard the drone now. It got louder every second, coming from high up and the north-east. Diana made a move to lift the glasses that were still slung round her neck, but he pushed her hands down. 'No. The sun might catch the lenses.'

They stayed frozen, looking at each other, not the sky, while the noise got louder and louder. Then, with the tight roar of a power dive, the plane came straight down at them from out of the sun.

In the last seconds they scattered a yard or so, crouching. There was that awful split-second of shattering sound and the dark shadow flicked over them like a bird of prey. Anson turned on his elbow to see the plane banking to climb away, and his whole being filled with relief at the sight of those stubby wings with the curved tips, the roundels.

'Spitfire—' he yelled and was running out into the desert. 'What's the bloody ground to air recognition sign?' They were running after him and through it all he heard Tom—'a "Y" in white strips, I think.'

'We haven't got any strips—we'll make one ourselves. You,

Zimmerman, go out about ten yards, Tom, thirty beyond him. I'll
get out between and behind them—Diana, you get back directly
behind me.' As he ran out to his position, he shouted, 'And wave
like b—'

The pilot was very careful, he came past low in long runs four
times before he climbed and headed away to the west. The noise
faded.

Anson looked back from where he was standing to Diana. 'Good
boy, that. Didn't stay stooging around for too long—in case he
attracted attention to us. But it means—' He stopped suddenly.

'Means what—?' She had walked close up to him now.

He looked at her for a moment. 'That something, he doesn't like,
could be very close.'

They had only just picked up their food when the sound came
in from the west and he was coming in again low, flaps down.
Before he got to them, there was a flash from the cockpit and a
bundle of coloured streamers tossed behind in the slipstream, to
float down behind their metal container and bounce on the desert.
Tom ran out for it and unscrewed the top and pulled out the
message before he got back to them. The writing was uneven, in
places almost indecipherable, but Anson remembered with gratitude the difficulty of writing on your knee while trying to watch
your plane, the ground, and the sky all round you at one and the
same time.

The message was brief and to the point.

MATRUH BYPASSED. JERRY ARMOUR STRIKING TWO-PRONGED DABA
AND BAGUSH. NOTHING YET SOUTH OF LAT 31° 2', EXCEPT COLUMN
RUNNING DOWN WIRE NOW AT EL WASHKA. OUR TROOPS FALLING
BACK TO ALAMEIN. DO NOT REPEAT NOT ATTEMPT COAST WEST OF
THERE. IF UNDERSTOOD CIRCLE VEHICLE CLOCKWISE.

They heard him coming back, high this time, directly overhead.
Anson said, 'Tom, get in her quick, circle wide, right hand down.'
When he had done it they waited again and the Spit came back for
the last time, so low that he seemed to be touching the desert. For
a second they saw the open cockpit hood, the helmet, the goggles
and one bare arm raised in salute. Then he was gone, spiralling in
a victory roll, while another bunch of streamers fluttered down
towards them. The message was very short this time. WILL INFORM
ALL GOOD LUCK.

The plane was high again now, dwindling to a speck in the blue of the north-east. The noise thinned and faded to nothing. They were alone again and no one spoke for a long time.

Tom tidied up and refilled the radiator automatically, but all the time he was watching the captain, sitting there, hunched in the driving seat, scribbling furiously on the corner of the map-board. He knew what that message meant to them; that hard look had come back into Anson's eyes and he did not like it.

At last Anson laid the map down and said, 'Conference, chaps. And then we'll be off.'

When they had gathered round, he said, 'I'm not going to muck about with this. It's come down to a simple time and motion study. We are here—' his finger pointed at the map—'this column on the "wire" is there, and to the north, Jerry has reached there.' Then he smiled, '—At least, according to that birdman. They tend to exaggerate, but as we're grateful to him, we'll take it as truth. So you see—on the coast, Jerry is a hundred miles ahead of us already, and because of the lie of the land, the farther we move east the nearer we must get to him. Within forty miles, near Alamein, we must be right in it.'

He paused and looked towards the north; Tom looked after him, over the flat dun plain, knowing that they were both thinking the same thing, that somewhere out there, unseen and incalculable, was a grey stream, flowing east. Like a tide on the shore, it might check for a moment, but a thin feeler would move out, turning to find another way. Then the whole would move on.

Zimmerman broke the silence. 'So—?'

'The cliff route is out—the odds are too great. Even if we don't meet anything, we could not last to Alamein on our water.'

'Then—'

'Yes. It must be the Depression—the whole bloody way.'

No one spoke.

'I'll have a crack at it—if you want me to.' He said it very quietly and again no one answered.

'We know we can leave Qara Oasis full up with water—probably food and petrol as well. Now the only danger there will come from this column moving down the "wire"—and that's where time and motion come in. El Washka to Siwa, which they must occupy first, is a hundred miles. Give them twenty miles in the hour—that's top going—and they would get there in seven hours—' he looked at his watch—'that's nine tonight. Now we are only twenty miles from Qara here. Say two hours, because we've got to get down the cliff—which makes them five hours behind—apart from the seventy miles they still have to do between Siwa and Qara. A fair start.'

'What do we do then?' It was Diana, speaking for the first time.

'Pull out ten miles from Qara tonight—that's to the edge of the soft stuff—and get cracking as soon as it's light.'

'Couldn't we push on tonight—supposing they follow us?'

He gave a short laugh. 'Even for a prize like you, dear, they wouldn't risk their vehicles on that stuff—and I wouldn't move an inch on it at night.'

Zimmerman said, 'I don't like it—supposing—'

Anson stared at him. 'Yes. Suppose that. It would mean we'd had it. But there is a chance of getting through. The other way—' he jerked his head to the north, '—is a certainty of walking into the bag. Do you want that?'

Zimmerman didn't answer.

'Well,' said Anson, 'there it is. In my humble opinion, a certainty with Jerry—or a chance against the marsh. There's only one other thing I must tell you before you decide. You won't be able to change your minds. Once we're down that cliff, it's too high and steep for KATY to climb out until the far end.'

Tom saw the eyes fix on his and he stared at the ground because he did not want to let the captain down, let him see the doubt in his face. He heard the voice go on quietly, 'Diana? . . . Zimmerman . . . ?' but no one answered. He understood for the first time in full measure how they would be lost without the captain, and that he knew it, realized the loneliness—the responsibility of leadership.

'So I have to decide . . .' Anson was staring at the board, skin glistening tight on his cheekbones. 'Well, it's the marsh. And tomorrow—or the day after—when we're bogged down to the axles, and the water's gone, and we're a hundred miles from anywhere—you can spit in my eye.'

It was a silent party that started to pack up to move; while they were doing it, Tom saw that Diana had gone quiet and was very pale. 'All right, Diana?' he said as he poured the precious water back in the radiator.

'No—I feel sick. Got a bit of a headache.'

His eyes met Anson's behind her back and he touched his head and looked up at the sun. 'You silly girl,' he said, 'you have got a touch of the sun. Go and lie down.'

When they were ready to move, he said to Anson, 'Why don't you go in the back with her for a bit, sir? You'll want all the rest you can get before tomorrow.' He knew who was the only person to do the driving then. But the captain smiled and said, 'It wouldn't be quite the same thing, would it?' So he went and sat on the edge of the bunk and made a compress with bandages and the tepid water, bathing her face and neck, not caring how much he wasted; sat on, wiping gently, holding her hand between whiles, not talking, not wanting to. Soon he felt the first jolt as the car hit the furrows of the track, the rocking as they turned south along them. She was asleep now, and he went to the door for a moment, looking out at the grooves worn by generations of plodding camels, the white bones of the fallen gliding by on either side. Then he went back to his watch.

He was drowsing, nodding over her, when a jerk told him that the car had stopped. He went out into the cab, but there was no one there, and ahead on the desert, where the track dipped out of sight between two spurs of rock, he saw the little figures. It must be the edge of the cliff and they had gone on to spy out the land.

He went back into the car and she was still asleep. He shook her shoulder gently and said, 'Diana—we're at the top of the cliff, I think. The others have gone on to have a look with the glasses to see if the coast is clear. Do you mind if I go and join them?'

She didn't open her eyes, just said, 'Tom, darling—' and took hold of his hand and turned over on her side with it against her cheek. Then she made a little soft noise and went to sleep again. So he did not go, but stayed, watching her through the still, hot afternoon.

The two captains were sweating but cheerful when they came back. The report was that they had had a good view of the oasis and that there was no sign of transport there. Anson said they must move down as soon as possible.

'It's a rough track, Tom. Steep slab stuff. Will you take her down—dead slow, in bottom? I'll walk ahead and try and find the best path.' Then he looked towards the back and said, 'How is she?'

'Asleep. I don't think she's got it bad. Be all right tomorrow.'

Zimmerman was unslinging his haversack. 'God, I'm thirsty. Can I have a swig of water, Captain?'

Anson said, 'Only a mouthful—until we're sure. Don't forget the water we take on will be bitter—not too good for tea.'

Tom was looking at the square pack. It lay on the cab floor where Zimmerman had put it while he tilted the water can. That split in the canvas was bigger, he could see the gleam of metal quite plainly now. How long could they possibly go on without a showdown?

They entered the rocky defile and were soon creeping, almost hanging, to the steepness of the tilted slabs of white limestone that fell away in a giant staircase over the thousand-foot cliff.

Tom took it dead slow, with eyes only for the figure walking in front, ready to twist or stop according to his signals. Zimmerman was in the passenger seat, silent as usual, and then the door opened behind him and he knew it was Diana coming to join them.

He said, 'Better?' without looking round, and was relieved by the answer of, 'Yes.' Then she said, 'Oh, Tom—it's beautiful.'

'I can't look—tell me.'

As they banged and bumped their way down she tried to describe it all, the magnificent sweep to the bottom of the Depression, with the evening shadows coming up to smother the blues and greens of it, the Sand Sea behind, the humping backs of the dunes already slanting orange and purple; then Qara itself, over on the right, the palms in a hollow with the curious white rock rising from the centre that swelled out from its base like a mushroom and had the mud village sitting on top of it.

As they went lower, the air seemed heavier, sticky. Then the smell of the oasis came, dank, like moist rotting grass.

They drove straight to the outside fringe of palms and it was a strange feeling to be under the shade of anything again.

Anson said, 'I'll go off and scout round—see what I can fix. Zimmerman, will you come with me? You had better keep quiet, Diana, and in the shade, with Tom.' Zimmerman slung his pack over his shoulder and the two of them walked off into the trees.

Tom made her sit quietly as he put the tin under the radiator and lit the fire for their tea. When it was going, because she said she felt, and looked, a great deal better, he agreed to go for a little walk, circling the car. There was no one in sight; underfoot, a coarse grass, and everywhere, between the tufts of it, flakes of encrusted salt gleamed; over them, the palms rustled dryly, secretly as the sunlight slanted through the fronds. There was no other sound—except when they were close to the ambulance, and then there was the reminder of that constant dribble of water into a tin.

Once, through a gap in the trees, they had a glimpse of the white rock, and she said, 'It's like a dwarf's house on top of a toadstool in a picture book.'

'The captain was telling me. It's the wind that's worn it like that. They live on the top for fear of raids by the nomad tribes.'

'But why build so high?'

'They can't expand sideways—they're up to the edges already. So if another house is wanted, they just slap some more mud on top. Siwa's the same—only bigger, and really fertile. There's real gardens, and wells. One built by the Romans—about twenty feet across—and you can bathe in it. The water bubbles up from the bottom like a fizzy drink.'

'Have you been there, Tom?'

'No. But the captain told me. He has.'

It seemed a long time before the others came back, but they were accompanied by a silent, ragged Siwan, riding a skeleton donkey.

Anson said, 'They are pretty scared here. A British convoy came through from Siwa early this morning, probably the garrison. They went east very fast along the edge of the Depression. Must have been making for the one track up the cliff that leads to Daba. Probably sorry they tried it now.'

Tom was thinking of two things: first, this news—and Zimmerman standing there listening—what price was his potential harm now?—then Anson, having made the hardest decision, was so much more like the old captain, treating even the most serious things with a sharp flippancy.

He was speaking again. 'We can have all the water we want—free, as is the oasis custom. But he'll charge for his moke to bring it here—and make us pay through the nose for our own petrol that was left in a dump. And some dates—and perhaps a few eggs.'

They loaded the empty water cans on the donkey and, while they were waiting for the man to come back, had their tea and food. At last the donkey appeared, laden high and followed by a procession of the curious from the village. They stood at a distance, silent, staring, while the water cans were counted, the four-gallon tins of petrol laid out beside them with a slab of dried dates and a cloth containing twelve tiny eggs.

'Will they take money?' said Diana.

'I doubt it—we can try. But it will have to be reinforced with tea and sugar, I'm afraid.'

The Siwan squatted opposite Anson, wrapping his robe close, eyes dark and watchful. 'Come on. Divvy up your cash—' the captain was looking round at them, '—we can't hurry this, but we must be away as soon as possible.' They felt in their pockets and Diana emptied her bag and the piles of notes and coin grew beside Anson. Tom noticed that when he thumbed through his own money, he pulled off three green pound notes and put them back in his pocket.

He looked up and smiled. 'Rheingolds are fifteen ackers each, Tom. That's sixty a round. Three rounds, with tip—two pounds. The other one for luck. We'll be drinking them the day after tomorrow.'

The Siwan looked at the money that was pushed over to him and shook his head. Anson sighed. 'Get out the tea and sugar—and a few tins of milk.'

They put out handfuls of the first two on the cloth beside the eggs, the tins of milk near the dates. The Siwan watched carefully. All the time the sun was slanting lower through the palms above their heads. At last, without a change of expression, he made a gesture to indicate his side of the collection was theirs. Then he scraped the tea and sugar into bits of rag that he produced from odd parts of his person, stowed the money, and collected the tins of milk. He got up and turned on his heel without a word, leading the donkey off through the palms, while the sightseers faded away behind him. They were alone again.

Anson looked at his watch. 'Six. They can be no nearer than forty miles to Siwa. That gives us a hundred start. Don't let's waste it.'

Zimmerman said, 'What are you going to do now?'

'Push off for the first ten miles—to the last ridge before the marsh. Then on again at first light, without waiting to eat.'

'Wouldn't it be better—to push on a bit farther tonight?'

Anson just looked at him. 'In the dark? I wouldn't move an inch on that stuff then—with all the hounds of hell after me.'

They topped up the radiator and moved off, out from the shade of the palms. As they went east, skirting the edge of the cliff on a faint wandering track, the air seemed to get even more breathless. At Tom's suggestion, they clipped back the rear doors of the car, so getting a little relief from the wind of their passing.

Anson's voice came back through the open front door suddenly, as Tom sat opposite Diana on a bunk in the back.

'Ladies—and gentlemen. We are about to begin the passage of the Masrab Mahashash. The old camel road by which all bloody fools—since Alexander the Great—have returned from Siwa.'

Diana looked across at him and smiled. 'He seems so cheerful—so different.'

He leaned forward and took her hands. 'Yes,' he said, 'we're going to be all right now.'

When they reached the last slope of the hard ground, it was in the grace of the last few moments before the sun went down behind the cliff and night descended like a curtain. In that little time, there was nothing to see ahead but a mysterious purple flatness that stretched to the horizon, flanked on their left by the diminishing perspective of the cliff buttress.

Anson made no bones about the next move. 'As I have done it once before—and as I made the choice, I propose to do all the driving while we're on this lot. So I'm going to have a proper night's rest. I think Diana ought to have a full spell too—make certain that head of hers is right. You blokes can sleep all day tomorrow.' Then he looked straight at Tom, 'Let's have a shufti at that pump before I lay me down.'

There was no point, there was nothing to be done to it, only look, but he opened the bonnet and waited till Anson came round on the other side. 'I don't know there's anything we can do—'

'No, Tom—I just wanted a private word with you. I must get some rest before tomorrow—I'm not feeling too good,' he was almost whispering it as they bent, heads together inside the bonnet—'but I rely on you—Zimmerman must NOT take one of those walks tonight. Whatever happens.'

'But how can I—'

'Use your loaf, man. Do the same thing at the same time.'

Then he had straightened and said, in that mocking, half serious voice of his, 'The curfew must not ring tonight—' and they had walked back to the cab; there had been a few directions, a watch to be kept for lights and noise, the eggs they had bought to be hard-boiled at the first brew, and then he had gone into the back of the car with Diana.

It was a difficult, uneasy watch. They had agreed to sit on the back of the ambulance facing the direction of Qara, so that it would be easier to watch for lights, listen for sounds. The darkness was complete now, a blanket round them, the only noise came when a breath of wind bore back the noise of the dripping water from the front. But he didn't care any more, there was plenty of water now . . . plenty of everything. And he didn't mind that his captain was just behind him, asleep there in the dark, close to his girl.

He thought of her like that now, had done since the moment she had whispered in her sleep and rubbed her cheek against his hand. But he didn't know what she really thought . . . for a moment his mind jumped forward beyond their lonely battle . . . to what would happen afterwards. A warrant officer . . . and a nursing sister. Too difficult . . . there was nothing he could say.

They sat there huddled in blankets, silent. Suddenly, Zimmerman said, 'What's that?' sharply. He got to his feet and peered round his side of the car.

'What, sir?'

'A noise—listen . . .'

'It's only that water dripping.'

'No, it was louder than that. You have a look your side—I'll take this. It came from the front of the car, I'm sure.'

He walked down his side and up past the radiator, stopping to listen, but hearing nothing but the monotone of the dripping water. When he got back to the rear of the car Zimmerman had disappeared.

He cursed softly, ran a few yards out from the car and went flat on his stomach, swinging his eyes round the level of the skyline, it was an old desert trick: there was always a little difference in the dark of ground and sky, and anything on the first would show up against the latter.

Over to the left . . . yes . . . there was something, a vague humped bulk jutting from the ground. He stared until his eyes smarted. Was it imagination—or was that thing beside it real, a thin dark line that was jerking up against the stars? . . .

'So that's it,' he breathed and, regardless of noise, got up and ran towards it.

Zimmerman was standing up again when he reached him and it was too dark to see his face, or note anything more than that the pack was slung loosely over one shoulder.

The big man was peering about him. 'I heard something—I swear it. Out near here.'

Tom played for time. 'Would you like to scout round a bit and see, sir? As long as we don't get too far from the car.'

He looked at his watch as he walked, never more than a few yards from the captain. Nine o'clock—so it must have been about 8.55. He must tell Anson that. They made a wide aimless circle and then went back to the car. They sat on the step, huddled in their blankets, leaning back against the door, waiting. Soon there was a soft sound beside Tom and he turned to see the big head nodding forward on the chest, the hands falling limp from where they had been folded across the pack. Captain Zimmerman was going to sleep.

He waited, almost holding his breath, for a minute, then reached out gently towards the dark square on the other's lap. In the same instant, there was a grunt, the head jerked up and the body stiffened, just as he pulled his hand back in time. Zimmerman, yawning, said, 'Mustn't do that, must I? Supposed to be on watch.'

Tom said, 'Yes, sir,' and laughed.

'What's the matter?'

'Nothing, I was only thinking of something.'

He couldn't tell him that it was about the certainty that neither could go to sleep for the fear of what the other might do. Only, it was going to be an awful long time before the dawn.

Zimmerman lay on his back, staring at the white ceiling above the bunk, feeling the gentle sway of the ambulance as it moved, hearing the creak of the body, the steady soft snores from the sergeant-major opposite. He was lucky to be able to sleep—Zimmerman could not. They had been two hours on the road, it was starting to heat up already, but there was no let-up, no peace for him. He lay there, dead tired, yet wide awake, sweating . . . and thinking.

Were they very clever . . . or complete stupid fools? His mind dodged back over every incident . . . how they had reacted . . . how his own varying moods of contempt and wariness had pulled him this way and that like a straw in the wind.

Last night . . . had that been deliberate or an accident . . . when the sergeant-major had come blundering at him out of the dark, before he had even got the aerial right up and had had no chance to transmit? Was it coincidence that it was the only time there had been anything to transmit—that Siwa was undefended. And what had he been thinking . . . the rest of the night, as they both struggled to keep awake, so correct, only speaking when spoken to, but even then with a barrier of reserve he could never penetrate?

There was something else that made it all the more difficult. Increasingly, he liked them—and it was dangerous to like those you had been taught to despise.

The girl. He thought of her for a moment, she had not cried or argued, done all she had been told—as much as any of them. And she had been kind to him when he had hurt his back. Anson?—there was only increasing respect now. The decadent Englishman of those lectures had gone, he had risen to the occasion, shown himself the leader not only by knowledge, but by authority. There was no question of taking orders from a vacillating drunkard now. He had seen a new man born.

It was an alliance, he supposed—a subconscious, growing challenge between them all against the worst the desert could do. He remembered the first time he had realized that, accepted it in those tearing seconds when he had held up the car. It had not been for them, or his mission, only against the thought of a long, cruel walk. And so—he had been committed, would keep it that way: help, and not think of his job until he had been brought safely through the net. Well perhaps not quite . . . this was a personal thing, because he had been foiled last night. This evening, to show he could do it, though he doubted if the strength would reach them, he would send his call-sign only out for the last time.

He smiled. But he would remember them . . . and all they had done. He would keep their names, numbers, if he could get them. And when the Afrika Korps was victorious in Cairo, he would do what he could . . .

No use trying to sleep now. He swung his legs to the floor, pulled on his boots and went out softly to the front of the cab.

The girl was in the passenger seat and she turned and smiled at him. 'Sleep well? And how's the back?'

'Better, thank you—still just a little sore.' He crouched down between them and stared out over the plain ahead.

There were no purple and brown shadows like those that had masked the Depression the night before; in their place, a dead flat mottled expanse, smooth, shading from patches of brown to yellow, grey to almost blue. Everywhere, it twinkled with flaking salt. There was no rotting vegetable smell of the oasis now; something else hung in the hot sticky air—clinging to everything, sour, metallic, like brass polish.

He looked to the south and far, far off the yellow haze of the Sand Sea just broke the horizon. To the other side, the great cliff hung like a curtain in folds, shadowed light and dark with valley and headland.

'What a place,' he said.

The girl let her eyes follow it round, 'I've just told Captain Anson it reminds me of a mouldy rice pudding.' Anson, driving, laughed, and he joined in politely, although there seemed little point.

'Twelve miles in the last forty minutes,' said Anson. 'We're safe from behind now. Actually, I doubt if they would be halfway from Siwa to Qara yet.'

'How's the track?'

'Easy for the first ten miles—lots of new tyre marks, that lot of yesterday, I suppose. Then they branched off towards the cliff as I expected, but I managed to pick up the other way. It's faint—it would be after two years, but I can just see enough.'

'Is it straight all the way?'

'For the next forty miles—more or less. Then there's a fork, and we'll have to watch that. It's marked *?? White Stone??* on the map. Helpful—but if we turn the wrong way—to the right—we'll land up hundreds of miles to the south, in the Bahariya Oasis.'

While he was talking, Zimmerman had been looking at the ground ahead and to the sides of them. The track—and there were faint lines, like a road where the tram rails had been taken up—stretched straight on to the horizon. But that was not the only mark of the way they were following: there was a slight, subtle change in the appearance of the ground. For about the width of an ordinary road, it curved up, lighter in colour, more gravel-strewn, the salt flakes closer, sometimes showing as solid blocks. On each side, the ground was smooth hard mud, cracked finely into an octagonal pattern, it went on unending, only changing in the shade of colour. It looked so firm and safe. He wondered if Anson, or his own General Staff, knew what they were talking about.

The air was getting hotter, damper. He found that he was beginning to pant. He looked down at the girl beside him, and there were the dark stains of sweat spreading down her shirt from under the arms, then he felt the first trickle of his own running down between the shoulder-blades.

Anson jerked suddenly from his crouch over the wheel, sniffed, and bent forward, listening intently with his head cocked sideways though his eyes were still on the track.

'That engine's getting bloody hot,' he said. Then he bent forward and switched off and, as they coasted to a halt, another sound was coming above the noise of the tyres. A rumbling bubble from the front of KATY. When they had stopped, the front of the bonnet was wreathed in billowing steam.

'What is the matter, sir?' It was Tom, pushing past him from the back.

'Boiling like a bitch—but we topped up before we started. I can't understand it.'

'Must be something to do with no wind—and the density of the air. Don't forget we're below sea level.'

They jumped down and came round the bonnet as Tom opened it, showing no longer a clean engine, but caked sand and oil and spattered rust. While they were waiting for her to cool, Anson said, 'No walking sideways off the track—everything fore and aft from now on. Diana, you take the back stretch—we'll keep in front.'

It took a long time for her to get cool and when they topped her up, they found they had lost three pints.

They went on and this time it was only ten miles before she boiled, the next time seven, the next four. Hotter . . . hotter . . . the sweat pouring off them now, the plain heaving in steady waves, the northern cliff fading and then shooting forward again in the mirage. There was nothing else but the brassy sky that seemed almost filled by an ever-growing sun.

They hardly spoke. He did not ask, could not ask, if they felt as he did, that raging thirst, the lack of any desire for food, the feeling of being pressed down into their own little world as they crept across hell. Hotter . . . the cliff had gone now. Nothing but that heaving mottled plain.

In turns they went to the back to lie on the bunks, panting at the stream of hot air that drifted by in the speed of their passing. All except Anson. Zimmerman wondered how long Anson would stand it—sitting there mile after mile, hunched over the wheel, hands slipping in their own sweat as they clenched the rim, all through that endless morning. He felt an odd surge of pride—in what he did not understand—when, after the sergeant-major had said once, diffidently, 'Let me take a spell, sir,' he was turned on with a savage, 'Jesus Christ, Tom! I got you into this—and if anyone is going to make a final balls of it, I will.'

At last something came out of the mirage in front of them and did not fade away as they approached. It was a single patch of colour that cleared to a flat white rock, just to the left of the track. 'White stone,' said Anson, and cut the motor and when they stopped leaned forward over the wheel as the clouds of steam billowed up in front of them. Stiff-legged, he got down from the driving seat and walked round to the back of the car. 'Brew up if you want to,' he jerked over his shoulder as he went.

They left him for a time, but they were too exhausted to do more than make tea and hard-boil the eggs in the water; as all the cans were hot, it did not take long. When they had managed to swallow an egg each and chewed at the sweet stickiness of the dates, Zimmerman looked across at Tom Pugh and said, 'He, must eat something—otherwise—'

But Tom looked down at his feet. 'I'd rather not do it—after this morning—'

Zimmerman had looked across at Diana. 'Will you come?'

They put a mug of tea and some dates and an egg they had shelled and broken on the back of his map-board and took it into the back of the car. Anson was flat on a bunk, eyes open, bare chest jerking in convulsive pants.

The girl said, 'Here's your grub, George.'

'Grub,' he said, 'I don't want any.'

'But you must—'

He turned his head slowly. 'Is that an order, Sister? Yes, Sister, if you say so.' Then his eyes slewed round to Zimmerman. 'What's he—the matron? You would make a bloody good matron, Zimmerman.' And he started to laugh—or tried to, but no sound came, only a quicker shaking of the throat and chest.

Zimmerman pushed past the girl. He shouted, 'Eat it,' in a parade-ground voice and between them they managed to lift him up and hold him while he swallowed the pieces of egg. He whispered, 'I feel bloody,' and Zimmerman picked him up as if he were a baby, carrying him through the open door at the back to sit him on the step. He held him with one hand and said, 'A can of water, Sister,' and when she had passed it he tilted the whole of the two gallons over the head and the neck and the body, so that it ran down off the step and was sucked into the salt like a sponge. Then he scooped up the wet limp body in his arms again and carried him back inside; he saw that he was asleep before he had put him down. All the time the girl had been watching without a word.

He looked at her now, shame-faced almost, as he muttered, 'A

can of water—so little—for a brave man.' Then he went round to
the front of the car before she had time to answer.

The sergeant-major was there, head pillowed on his arms against
the steering wheel as he slumped in the driving seat. He touched
his shoulder and said, 'Sergeant-major, the captain is asleep. But I
think he would like you to go on. Would it be of any help if I went
and sat out in front to help guide you?'

Tom's head had jerked up. 'Not out there—in this heat. You
would fry, sir. No. Come and sit here by me—and we'll manage
somehow.'

Perhaps because they had eaten, things seemed a little easier in
the afternoon. By six they were forty miles farther on, ten halts for
the boiling behind them, three more gallons of precious water gone.
Anson was still asleep in the back, reported Diana, who had stayed
with him. He had woken twice and asked for a drink, had not
displayed the slightest interest in the fact that they were moving.

It was Tom who called a halt. There was no reason for it from
any consideration of geography. It was the eleventh boiling. He
said, 'We can't go on overheating her like this. Let's call it a day
now—it will give us a better chance for tomorrow.'

They just stopped. No turning off, no looking for shelter in that
emptiness. The faint thread of the track went on and on in front,
the firmer mark of their own tyres thinned to nothing behind them.

The sun was lower now, the mirage gone. No northern cliff was
there to keep them company, only to the south the faint yellow,
jagged line of Sand Sea, with the hazy plumes blowing sideways
from the points like smoke from a row of factory chimneys.

'There must be a wind up there—to blow the sand off like that,'
said Tom.

Zimmerman grunted. 'I wish the bloody thing was down here.'

Slowly, drained of all energy, they fumbled over the making of
the brew, and it was nearly finished when Anson came out of the
back, followed by the girl. He did not remark on what had happened
except to say, 'Sorry to have been so long.' He sat on the sand,
sipping his tea, looking at the map-board. 'Did you take the speedo
reading?' he said.

'Yes. Forty-two from the white stone.'

They all watched while he measured. 'That's good. Only—' he
turned to look down at the wheels of the ambulance '—only I wish
we had got a bit farther. This part is the lowest of the whole issue.
We're sitting on top of a bloody jelly here. We'll have to watch out

she doesn't bog down in the night.' He looked better, Zimmerman thought, the eyes were really taking in what they saw, the fallen-in look gone from the face in all he could see through the beard. But then he stared sideways at the smooth, flat mud, stretching unending on and on. It looked so firm, so safe. For the second time he thought, 'He doesn't know what he is talking about . . .'

When they had finished, Anson said, 'Tom—do the headlights work on this crate?'

'Should do, sir. But of course, we had them all disconnected.'

'Well, in case of anything—' he looked at the wheels again, 'wire them up. And have the sand-mats out ready.'

The heavy air was cooling now. They sat on, smoking, basking in the blessed relief. They watched the sun go down, blood-red, behind them and the purple shadows flood out once more over the flats. Just before it was dark, Anson got up and went to the back of the car; he came out with two of the white water cans, walked ten yards back and put one down, then forward past the radiator to leave the other the same distance in front.

Then he came back to them. 'Your territory behind, Diana, we'll take in front. You can sight on the gleam of the can going out, the bulk of the car coming back. But don't go a step sideways.' He looked over his shoulder to where the sergeant-major was bending over the bonnet, fixing the wiring of the lights. 'Did you hear that, Tom?'

'Yes, sir.'

Zimmerman wanted to smile. Already there was a twinge of regret at his earlier feelings. They were not worth it. But . . . why this business about the lights . . . the detailing of the only path he could take . . . right in their range? Did Anson believe in these fantastic preparations . . . or was it a trap?

The other side of his thinking surged up stronger within him. Did they think him that much of a fool? . . . Then he would transmit tonight, even though no one might hear him. Just to show these clever English. It would be amusing when they saw his footprints on the mud in the morning . . .

He waited, smoking and listening to the snatches of dying talk until it was quite dark. Eight-thirty . . . just right. The girl had gone to bed and the sergeant-major had said he was soon following. He and Anson were taking first watch to see that the wheels did not sink. A waste of time.

He got to his feet, stretched, and moved towards the cab to unclip the spade. 'I won't be long.' No one answered. He slung it over his shoulder and with the pack bumping on his back, started to stroll away down the track ahead.

When the gleam of the water can came up to meet him, he turned sideways and took six quick steps to the right. His boots felt the gentle fall-away of the ground and then he was on the smooth mud, as firm and solid as he had expected.

Crouching, he fumbled with the straps and soon the flap was open in front of him. He was just feeling for the knob to extend the aerial, when the darkness was rent by the searing white light of the twin headlamps. The suddenness was a physical shock as they fanned out to miss him by a yard.

As he went flat, he swore. So that was it. Anger welled up in him at the charity he had wasted. Crouching again, bending double over the pack clutched to his chest, he started running farther sideways, away from the light.

The first steps were normal . . . but then something happened. The foot on which he had his weight would not come forward in the next stride, and for a moment he was left like that with the other one pawing the air. To regain balance, he dropped it quickly, hard.

There was a soft, shivering sigh . . . a crackling that spread away from him in every direction over the mud. Now the back leg was up to the calf in tepid treacle that pulled . . . and pulled. He twisted, falling on his side, and the crust crumbled beneath him. The comfort of those headlamps seemed so far away now.

A horrible sour smell was coming up all around, and with it a noise . . . slow, heavy bubbling, like washing on the boil. But that steady downward tugging was the worst.

He started to scream.

CHAPTER 10

Diana was getting ready to slide under her blanket when she heard the first of the chain of events that led to those screams.

After she had been out behind the car, she had come in through the back door and switched on the interior light—for Anson had said it didn't matter now they were so far out. Then she had got mirror and comb from her handbag and started to try and do something with her face and hair.

The door to the front had been ajar, and she could hear the soft murmur of the two men's voices. Then Anson had said, sharply. '*Now*' and in the same moment the white reflection of the headlights had flooded back through the crack in the doorway. She dropped her bag and pushed through to see what was happening.

After so long, the twin beams, so white, so straight, seemed almost indecent. They slashed the track ahead, etching the faint marks of the old tracks, magnifying the height of the stones in the gravel, but there was no sign of anything else.

'What are you doing?'

Anson said softly, 'Trying to catch our friend with his pants down,' and Tom laughed.

She had started to say, 'Well, you haven't,' when the screams started; they came from ahead and to the right of them.

Tom shouted, 'God! the bastard's gone in—' before Anson's voice cut in, tense and quiet.

'Start her up, Tom. Drive on slowly. Swing over a bit to the left of the track and come round to the right. But, for God's sake, don't go too far.'

The headlights wavered a little to the left and then came round in a slow arc to the right. Anson was standing in the cab, ripping off his shirt, then boots and stockings. As his hand reached for the buckle of his shorts, he said, 'Sorry, Diana—but this stuff stinks.' Then, pale and slim in the headlight reflection, he was at the front wings, uncoiling the long, bamboo-stiffened strips of canvas that were the sandmats.

At the edge of the light, something low and dark showed . . .
another few degrees and it was in the centre of them. Tom stopped
the car.

The mud looked grey and ten yards out on it there was a darker
patch, jagged, with cracks running away from it like a hole in a
frozen pond. In the middle, something that moved . . . a black slug
that raised an arm at slow intervals to paw the air. The screaming
was coming from it.

All was confused after that. There were vague memories of a
naked Anson stepping out gingerly towards the hole as he unrolled
a sand-mat in front of him; Tom wrenching off his clothes and
following with the second one from a slightly different angle;
shouting, being told to stay where she was. Then they were both
lying flat, reaching out to that black thing that had stopped moving,
crawling backwards, dragging it after them, foot by foot, until they
were safe at the edge of the track. The smell came back to her in
great waves . . . the soft puffing of the bubbles. She was not looking
at them now—only at that dark patch centred in the glare of the
lights. On it, rocking, was a square pack. Slowly, it tilted to one
side and disappeared.

Anson's voice was the first thing that came back to her, panting,
as they dragged Zimmerman to the car. 'A can of water—quick.
Then look at the wheels and see if they're sinking. I wish to God
we had a drink.'

When she came back, she had the water and her flask. She said,
'The wheels look all right.' They were kneeling beside him, stripping
off the stinking, sodden bush-shirt and she saw that it was split
right down the back. Then Tom took the water from her and started
to dash it over Zimmerman's face while Anson tried to clean out
his mouth and nose and ears. She held the flask without speaking
and he took it and opened it unblinking and poured the spirit back
into the mouth so that it spilt down his chin and on to his chest.
Zimmerman choked and spluttered and the breath came out of him
in long uneven shudders.

'He'll be all right now—' Anson had got to his feet and was
holding out the flask. 'But we must move on a bit before we try to
clean him up. Once that's happened, the whole strata's disturbed
and the track might collapse.'

They got Zimmerman on the step and Anson held him there
while Tom backed the car to the centre of the track, very gently.
When they were straight, Anson said, 'Wait a minute.'

While Tom held the sagging body, he got down and went to the side of the track where the bush-shirt lay in a dark heap. He lifted it, holding it at arm's length, walking into the glare of the headlights to turn it round, looking carefully. Then, going to the edge of the mud, swung it to gain momentum and then threw it out so that it landed with a dull splash in the middle of the hole. He came back wiping his hands against his naked flanks. 'He won't be needing that any more,' he said.

When they had moved on fifty yards, they set about the task of cleaning both themselves and Zimmerman. Water was too precious and they used petrol. The smell of it was sweet beside that of the sour metallic mud. As she helped them soak and scrape and rub off with one of the blankets, it did not seem at all out of place. She thought, suddenly, of all the blanket baths she had done as a probationer—wondered if there had ever been another one like this.

They managed to get the silent, semi-conscious Zimmerman into the back and covered him up. When they had got outside again, she reached to the hip-pocket for the flask and held it out. 'It's mine—but I think you've earned it.'

Anson shook his head. 'Not me—I'm concentrating on that Rheingold. You—Tom?' And when Tom had said 'No' he went on, 'I should keep it for Zimmerman, Diana. He's still pretty rough.' Then he turned and switched off the headlights. 'That's enough of them—though even if a plane did see them here, they just wouldn't believe it.'

The darkness seemed intense after the headlights, she could hear them groping for their clothes. Anson's voice came, 'I'll see how he is—and get some blankets out. We'd all better kip down on the sand for tonight.'

She said, 'That pack—' and stopped.

'I know—I saw it. Closer than you did. Now it's gone—we need not discuss it.'

They showed her how to make a hole for her hip and then they all curled up in a row on the sand and it was quite comfortable. Sleep came very fast and it seemed only the next second that the scratching noise wakened her. It was daylight, Anson was squatting a few feet away from her with a tin of petrol beside him, scrubbing away at Zimmerman's shorts with a stone. He stopped to smile at her.

'Good morning. We let you lie in. Tom's making breakfast and I'll bring it to you in bed.' He held up the shorts. 'That's the best

I can get them. I've done the boots, but the stockings are impossible. I'll take them in to his lordship and tell him the rest of his stuff has gone down in the drink.'

When he came back out of the car, she looked at him enquiringly. 'He's OK. Tried to make a speech, but I told him to forget it.'

Both of them were beside her, eating eggs and dates, sipping tea, when Zimmerman came out of the back to join them. He had a blanket draped round his shoulders and she thought he looked so much older—as old as he had after the time he had held the ambulance on his back. A surge of pity went through her. 'When there are other things . . . that is what I must remember,' she thought.

Zimmerman came and squatted down beside them, he took the food offered him and ate it in silence. Then he put his tea down and cleared his throat.

'I wish to speak of last night—I—' She was looking at the streaks of blue-grey mud that still mottled his neck. But there was something else different . . . the voice seemed to have changed, deeper, more guttural, the accent not so clipped . . .

No one said anything, Zimmerman took another date, chewed it, and spat out the stone. Then he looked at Anson. 'It was madness—to disobey your orders, Captain.'

'Well, it turned out all right, Zimmerman, Except that you've lost your pack and your shirt. But you'll have a tale to tell your pals—won't he, Tom?'

'He will indeed, sir.'

Anson went on quickly before the big man could speak, 'Now—today. It should be easier. Only sixty-five miles to the end of this rice pudding. With halts, I should say, five hours. We should be there at three, but it may take a time to find a good place to get up the cliff, even though they are much lower there. We can't be at the top much before dusk—and that last run to the coast, it's about sixty on one bearing, and I don't want to do that in the dark. I think the thing is to find the best place, lie up there, and then do the climb and the last leg in one crack tomorrow.'

It was not as bad as the day before. The air seemed cooler and not so sticky, the view not quite so desolate as the ground rose and fell in slow waves that always gained a little in height. The track had edged close to the southern side of the Depression now and sometimes they had to cross thin tongues of hard ground that reached out into the mud flats. Beyond this, the dunes were still there, but they had not the massive structure of the Sand Sea, they were lower, in colour a paler yellow, and they could see the thin crests, ragged as a horse's mane, where the sand had blown sideways. 'Ramak Dunes,' said Anson, '—impassable.'

On their other flank, the cliff was closing fast. It was lower too, more broken and in places there were what looked to be smooth, easy slopes. They still had to make their halts for the boiling radiator, but the gap between was creeping up . . . from six miles . . . to eight . . . to ten. At one halt while she stood by the bonnet, waiting for the engine to cool, a few puffs of wind came down from the north to ruffle her hair. It was hot and dry, but it was the first movement of air she had felt for days.

Soon the mud flats dwindled to isolated patches, there was a different sound to the movement of their tyres. Then the northern cliff curved round in front of them to block the way to the east.

They had made it. They were through the Depression. Tom, driving, gave a great shout, and Anson, sitting on the floor beside her, said, 'Take her in at a gallop.' She turned from the passenger seat and stepped over him to go into the back of the car. Zimmerman was lying there, quite still, naked but for his shorts.

She said, 'We're at the end of the Depression, Captain Zimmerman. We've made it.'

But he did not answer, did not even look at her. He lay there, hands clasped behind his head, staring up at the roof as he had done all day.

They turned towards the north end of the cliff, running close along it, looking for a likely place. She saw there were plenty of breaks in the rock wall now, all steep, covered with a smooth fall of sand that seemed to pour down between the spurs of rock from the level above. At last, Anson said, 'That looks a good one,' and they stopped and walked over to where the end of the sand-fall met the desert floor.

He started to walk up it, slowly, carefully. When they began to follow, he looked back over his shoulder and called 'No. Stay where you are. We don't want to disturb the pattern more than we need.'

'Pattern—?' She turned to Tom.

'I forgot. On a slope the grains always lie in a certain way to each other. Once that's mucked up, they don't grip—start sliding. And our wheels wouldn't grip.'

They stood watching Anson climb on. After the first few yards, she saw his feet were digging in, slipping back a little at each step,

while the sand flowed down silent over the toes of his boots. When
he came down to them he seemed preoccupied.

'It's pretty dodgy, Tom. I don't remember it being anything like
as bad as that when we came last time.'

Tom just looked at him and said, 'You only had to come down
it—then.'

'Well, we had better look at one or two others.'

They tried six in all, but the sand was the same and they came
back to the first because it seemed the lowest. They camped a little
way from it and had started the tea going when Zimmerman came
out of the back of the car for the first time that day.

As they ate, between mouthfuls, Anson gave them details of
the remaining supplies. 'Thirty-two gallons of juice—that's ample,
fourteen gallons of water, four sweet, and the rest from Qara. Seven
days' vehicle rations untouched. And it's only a hundred miles to
Alex.' He looked over his shoulder to the sand slope behind them,
glowing red-gold in the setting sun. 'We'll go up like a dose of salts
in the morning—and you'll be drinking that Rheingold in Alex by
six, Zimmerman.'

Zimmerman did not answer.

Tom said, 'Couldn't we spare a couple of gallons of the bad water
now—to have a good clean up? I wouldn't like to be seen in a town
like this.'

Anson laughed. 'A wash and brush up? We haven't got the
razor—what about poor Zimmerman? He hasn't got a shirt.'

Zimmerman spoke suddenly, 'There's soap and a razor in that
small pack of mine. Help yourselves.'

'Well—' She could see Anson hesitating, '—it mightn't be a bad
idea at that.' He looked across at her. 'I'm sure you could do with
a swill, Diana. All right—a gallon for us, and a gallon for you.
Would you like it heated?'

'Just tepid,' she said, 'straight out of the can.'

They found her a tin and she went round to the back of the
ambulance and stripped off all her clothes. It was heaven to feel
the dry air flowing over her body and let the lukewarm water trickle
down the back of her neck to spread out over her spine and fall
down her thighs. With the dirty ball of her last handkerchief she
scrubbed away all the stains and sand; there was only a pint of
soupy, grey liquid left when she had finished, but she managed to
wash out her socks in it and then hung them on the back step to
dry. The clothes felt quite different when she put them on again,

and barefoot she went round to the front of the car to join the others.

Tom was just finishing his shave. As he wiped his face on a towel she had not seen before—presumably from the Zimmerman haversack—and smiled at her, she hardly recognized him.

He said, 'Captain Anson thought we might like to have the first shift. He's gone in the back with Zimmerman—he's still a bit worried about him.'

'Shift—? What are we supposed to watch for? There's nothing to watch, now.'

He looked at his feet. 'I don't think that was quite his idea. He said, "Stooge around if you want to—but don't get lost.".'

So it had come at last. She said, 'All right—if you like. As it's the last night, let's go for a bit of a stroll.'

He said, 'What about your feet—won't they get sore like that?'

'No, I like it. It makes me feel clean.'

They walked off along the hard flat bottom below the cliffs, towards the red ball of the sun that was dripping below the Depression, turning the rock walls into all the lovely shades of pink she had ever imagined. She thought of what had been said about it being the last night and where she would be that time tomorrow. She imagined for a moment the comfort, the tablecloths and the soft lights of the sisters' mess, the cutlery and china plates, and someone saying, 'What was it like?' But she knew that she could never tell them. Tom was very quiet and she thought again. 'It was just one of those things—you must have imagined it all. So save your dignity, Diana. There isn't much else left.'

Soon the night came down and the stars pricked out one by one. She looked back and the ambulance was a vague blur over to the east. Without a word being spoken, they sat down at the foot of one of the sand slopes and Tom pulled out his cigarettes. As they smoked, the talk strangled in shorter sentences, died. Suddenly he got to his feet, throwing away his cigarette. 'We'd best be going back.'

'Why, Tom—?'

'Because it's better.'

'But, why—?' She had got up to face him.

In the starlight she could see that he had turned his head away.

'Tomorrow,' he said, 'you'll be back in your hospital—a nursing sister—with two pips up. I'm a WO. It—everything—would be too difficult . . .' His voice trailed away.

'But would it be—?'

'It might—' his voice was rough, 'and it would spoil even this. I want to keep this—don't you understand . . . ?'

Time dripped out its slow seconds under the silent circling stars. She stood close, looking at him, eyes nearly level with his. 'Am I that stiff, snobbish nursing sister now?'

'No.'

'What am I, then?'

He did not answer, only turned his head away blindly, like something that is hurt. She said, very softly, 'I think I know what I am—to you—now. I'm going to put my pride in my pocket and say that I'm hoping, so hoping, that I'm right. And I want to be like that to you, always . . .'

There was only a dry sob and he was stumbling forward into her arms, and as she held him tight she knew that she was the last refuge for all the sorrow and loneliness of two barren years.

Afterwards, when they had finished the lovers' first bout of 'Do you remember', they lay back against the soft warm sand, heads pillowed on arms, looking up at the wonder of the heaven.

She said, suddenly, 'What was your wife's name?'

'Ann.'

'Tom—do you think she would mind?'

He did not answer for so long that she turned to look. The dark eyes beside her were staring up, fixed on Orion. 'Would she?' she said again.

He answered very softly, 'I've never believed in much. But if she's somewhere—outside all that, then she'd say OK. She was always so unselfish. I liked watching the cricket in the summer—and if she was tied up, with the teas, or the chickens, she would always make me go. It made her happy to see me happy—even if she couldn't join in.'

'That makes me feel sort of cheap—a pick up—'

'No.'

There was silence again, then she said, 'Are you, by any chance, working round to a proposal, Tom?'

'Sort of—'

'Then you needn't say any more. Because I accept, darling. But I'll always remind you that I—' The rest was lost as his big square hand was placed over her mouth.

'I've only been trying to think of all the complications—on your account.'

'I can look after myself,' she said.

When they got back the car was dark and silent and there was a neat pile of blankets stacked outside with the glimmer of a white piece of paper pinned to the top. Tom pulled it off and took it over to the dashboard light to read. She heard him chuckle and then he stuffed it in his pocket.

'What does it say?'

'Personal to me—from the captain—and it's rude.'

She was aghast. 'But he can't know—'

'Know? He's not a fool. And he's back in his old form again. That's what matters.'

'He's nice, Tom. One of the nicest blokes I've ever met.'

'They don't come any better than that,' he said.

They made their beds together, side by side, and when they were down, she spread the blankets over both of them and came close, pulling his head down on her shoulder. 'You sleep,' she whispered, 'I'll take the time from your watch—wake you before the others. You've got the worst of the driving tomorrow.'

He lay still for a while and then turned his head restlessly.

She said, 'What's the matter, darling?'

'I'm worried.'

'About us—?'

'No. That sand up there. It's going to be dodgy.'

'Leave it till tomorrow. You sleep now.'

He said drowsily, 'The captain said we'd go up like a dose of salts—I hope so.' He did not speak again and soon she felt the steady rise and fall of his side against her breast. She held him close, thinking of everything, not back, only forward—the village, the garage . . . children. A tender smile played on her mouth and then she stared across the Depression floor to that sand-fall on the cliff, pale in the starlight, silent and challenging. 'We'll go up you like a dose of salts, we will.'

But they didn't.

CHAPTER 11

The scheme was that the three of them should walk halfway up, leaving Tom to rush KATY up on her own, and run on behind, pushing if necessary.

The dawn was just coming when they made a start, she and Anson going up one side against the cliff wall, Zimmerman on the other. As she plodded up behind the captain, she looked across and back down the slope. It did not vary in angle from top to bottom, smooth, unbroken, the colour of clotted cream. She noticed that with every step her feet would sink in and slide back a little as the sand in front ran down, slithering over her ankle with a soft, persuasive sound. Like the others, she had gone barefoot.

About half way up Anson stopped and said, 'That's enough —he should be moving fairly well here. Just move across and get your shoulder to it and shove.' He called across to Zimmerman, and he halted too.

The ambulance was clear in the new light below them, and it looked small and square, like one of those miniature toys. The noise of the engine starting came up to them and they saw it circle off to the far side of the hard ground below before turning to come straight at them, accelerating. The sound of the motor rose to a high-pitched snarl, KATY was flat out in third gear when she hit the bottom of the sand.

She seemed to rise up towards them as if she was in a lift, there was a feeling as though the car was stationary and the sand and the slope were running down it. The engine got louder and louder; under it Anson shouted, 'I told you—like a bloody dose of salts.' Twenty yards separated them . . . fifteen . . . and then Diana noticed something different.

The car had another movement now, beside the forward one. The bonnet seemed to buck from side to side as if it were a fresh horse trying to get its head; great plumes of sand were spurting from behind now, the sound of the engine no longer constant, but rising and falling in a sobbing. Then the whole thing slewed sideways as KATY seemed to sit down on her haunches. The motor cut to silence. When they had run over, she saw that the back wheels were buried up to the axles.

Tom looked at them from behind the wheel. 'Too soft.'

'Give me that spade,' said Anson. 'You, Zimmerman, get the sand-mats out. We'll dig her out and run her on to them. Then, Tom, you take her down backwards and have another go.'

He tried twice more, and Anson three times, always making a fresh track, but they never got farther than the first mark. Always, just before that point, the wheels began to spin, the momentum went, and KATY would buck and bury her back wheels.

Minute by minute, the sun rose higher, hotter. Now that smooth slope was furrowed like a ploughed field. Then, at the sixth attempt, KATY started to boil.

Anson glowered at the steam billowing from the bottom of the rust-splashed radiator. 'We'll have to take her up on the sand-mats—six feet at a time.'

Two on each side, they took it in turns to clear a level trough in front of the back wheels and feed in the mats, holding them taut until the tyres had taken a grip. They made the whole length the first time and about half the second, before one wheel started spinning and sank in. The third time, nothing. Both mats ripped through to shoot out behind like two snakes while the tyres showered up sand as they bit their way down to axle level.

It was then that Anson seemed to go mad. He snatched the spade and threw himself down by the wheels, almost hacking at the sand in his fury.

'Get round the other side and dig,' he shouted at them. 'Don't just stand there—'

She said, 'But you've got the spade.'

'Well—use your bloody hands—but DIG. And when the mats are in, get round to the back—and push . . . PUSH.'

After that he did everything except hit them. He seemed to be everywhere, never stopping, pushing and swearing at them . . . at KATY, tearing at the sand with his fingers. Once, when Zimmerman, bare to the waist, had stopped for a moment to wipe off the sweat, he turned on him, snarling, 'Come on, man—you look like a Hyde Park whore—wondering how she's going to get through the winter.' When she sniggered, he turned on her. 'And if you'd stop grinning about your love-life, Diana, we might get this bitch nearer the top. Try pushing—instead of leaning against the bloody thing.'

It all became dream-like after that, a nightmare only pierced by the physical pain of her nails worn down to the quick from the scrabbling, the raw bruises on her shoulders from heaving at the back. But always beside her, pushing, cursing, there seemed to be Anson. Anson, with his yellow mask of a sweating sand-grimed face, the two holes in it that showed the insane eyes . . . 'It mustn't happen . . . it mustn't,' she thought, ' . . . he's going mad . . .'

Twice she had slipped at the back and fallen on her face, while a sand-mat had smacked across her and the spurting sand had filled her nose and mouth and ears. Only afterwards, she remembered his sobbing voice beside her as he heaved and strained, 'Get up—you bloody, sodding bitch—' and she did not know or care if he meant her or KATY. There was just one feeling now—that of a great resentment, they had all stripped off to the waist, they were cool. She felt the wet heavy weight of her shirt, the sweat trickling between her breasts. It wasn't fair . . . she'd show them . . . if he spoke to her like that again, she'd take it off.

Tom stopped it all. Suddenly, the engine cut, and as they sat down panting he came round to the back of the car. 'It's no good, sir.'

Anson, sitting on the sand with his head down between his knees, did not look up. 'What do you mean—no good? You're a bloody fine one to talk—riding all the way.'

The line of Tom's jaw hardened. 'You told me to drive. I was meaning the engine. She's boiling—overheating all the time. And a seized motor won't get us to Alex.'

'So what—? You want to walk do you?' He looked wildly round at each face. 'All right, b—off, the lot of you. Here's the compass—' there was a soft sound as it fell at Tom's feet—'help yourselves to all the water and food—keep on 30°—for two days. And I hope it keeps fine for you. Only leave me alone.'

He put his head between his knees and there was no sound but the sawing of the breath in his throat. At last he looked up again. 'I'm going to get this bitch to Alex—somehow. Do you understand—? I'm going to. It's a personal thing.'

Tom's voice was very gentle. 'No one wants to walk. I just thought we might try to wind her up.'

Anson stared at him. 'Wind her up—on the handle? With the plugs out, you mean?'

'Yes. We've only done it over a few feet before. But in reverse—the lowest gear—I don't see why it shouldn't work.'

'But how are you going to turn her round? She'll turn over on a slope like this.'

'I don't think so—not if everyone hangs on the inside when she's across the angle.'

Anson seemed to shrink. 'You carry on.' He got up and walked over to the strip of shade by the far cliff wall.

Tom stood looking after him, then he said, 'We'll dig her out first. Then I'll let her go back and lock over sideways. I shall do it right-hand down. So I want you two to come and hang on the right side when I do it. Lean out as far as you can—it may make just the difference to stop her going over.'

It took a long time to get her across the slope with Diana and Zimmerman hanging out backwards as far as they could. It seemed as if the angle was impossible, that any moment the inside wheels would lift up under them, and KATY would roll over down the hill. But Tom, from the driving seat, said, 'It's all right,' and then he put the steering hard over the other way and coaxed her with the engine until they were facing downwards. In doing it they had lost all the ground they had made in the last hour.

She said, 'What do we do now?'

'Wait—until the bloody plugs are cool enough for me to get out.'

She left him and went over to the boulder by the cliff where Anson had stayed all the time, sitting with his head down. He was still breathing like a man who has run a losing race. She said, 'He's turned her, George. He's waiting for the plugs to cool, he says. But I don't understand what he's trying to do.'

He didn't answer for a moment, then to the ground, between his legs, he said, 'Sorry—it's just that I counted so much—on getting there today.'

'But we will—please tell me what he's up to.'

He didn't seem particularly interested. 'If you take the plugs out of the engine—there's no resistance from the compression. You put her in the lowest gear, that's reverse, and just wind the handle in front—the starting handle. Because the gear is so low, the wheels move so gradually that they don't disturb the pattern of the sand grains, and grip. That's the theory.'

She looked up the yellow mound that went on ahead of them. It was only a hundred yards before it ended in the line of clear sky. For a moment she wondered why no one had bothered to trudge up and see if it was really the end of their troubles. Then she understood—no one had dared.

There was a noise from the ambulance and she saw that it was Tom shutting the bonnet and going round to the radiator with the starting handle. She held out both hands. 'Come and watch him, George. Please. He's trying so hard.'

By the time they had got over he had started turning slowly, winding in rhythm like a man with a barrel-organ. It did not seem to take any effort. He looked up at them and smiled; without stopping the winding, he said, 'I've just worked it out—thirty-two turns to every six feet up—that's if there's no slipping.'

They went round to the back wheels, silent, watching them. They were turning, but so slowly that they hardly seemed to move at all, but as each bar in the tyre tread dipped down to bite at the sand, though it sagged, there was a fresh clean surface waiting to take the next one . . .

'Look—!' It was Anson, crouching now behind one wheel. The firm pattern of the tread was beginning to show, moving away back from it. They were rolling up—no slipping.

'It's working, Tom!'

Tom, winding, not stopping, said, 'I thought it would.'

They took it in shifts after that, five hundred turns each. When it came to her, she was surprised at the little effort necessary to wind the great bulk of KATY backwards up the slope. It seemed that at any moment she must lunge forward, down at the one in the front, but they told her they had lashed the gear lever in position, so that it could not happen.

The sun was high now and Anson had ruled that the one winding should have Zimmerman's towel draped over their head and neck. But it was so slow . . . Each in turn they wound, watching in achievement the straight, firm tracks stretching out behind them. But in between the two, there was something else . . . and she knew it was not so good. At inches distance, dark blobs on the sand where the drops fell from the radiator. When Tom came round as she was winding, he stared and then scuffled the trail out with the toe of his boot. 'Don't let Captain Anson see,' he whispered, 'he's got enough—already.'

498 . . . 499 . . . 500. Each in turn reached the magical number and handed over to the next. Zimmerman was at it now, and there was only ten yards left to the unknown, beyond the barrier of sky. But no one made a move to find out if there was another ridge beyond.

Then Anson broke the tension. 'Hold it, Zimmerman. We may

as well look—and know the worst.' They all scrambled up the last few feet to the top.

It was the end. There was nothing but a flat, stony plain that stretched on towards the horizon, with a faint ridge showing to the north-west. There was something else, a wind, hot, dry, bearing down on them from the north. As she stood there, feeling it search inside her clothes, pulling at the strands of her hair, she felt cleaner, happier, in the first moment.

Anson looked at his watch and then back down the slope to KATY just below, then the long, long way to the bottom. 'Two and a half hours—for a quarter of a mile—' Then he gripped her arm and pointed. 'But—look—'

The sky had that brassy tinge that she knew so well that she hardly noticed it. Now, to the north, almost on the horizon, it shaded to a deeper, clearer blue.

'The reflection of the sea,' he said.

She sat between them, back to the door, feet straight out, listening to the singing.

Things had gone well since they had cranked KATY over the top. The radiator had been filled, she had heard the course—'Sixty miles on 68°, Tom. And if I can navigate at all, we'll finish slap in the middle of Burg el Arab railway station.' It had been funny to hear of an ordinary everyday thing like that.

The singing was of no quality, even though it came from her too. Zimmerman had disappeared to the back, Anson was driving, Tom in the passenger seat, while she, between them, listened; not caring if they were out of tune, only happy because they were. As they went steadily over the plain, their spurs went jingle jangle jingle as they went riding merrily along, Casey waltzed with his strawberry blonde, and then came the detailed recital of the peculiar misfortunes of one Samuel Hall.

She did not try and join in; for one thing, she was not sure if she should know the words. It was nicer to let it all flow over her head, to think about more important things—how long it would take to learn the rudiments of keeping chickens, if she would ever understand enough to be able to work in the garage . . . Without thinking, she put a hand sideways and took hold of Tom's.

'Oy, Oy.' It was Anson from the other side. 'Don't distract the navigator.' Then, 'I suppose I've got to do some congratulating.'

She turned and smiled at him, not letting go.

'What do you think?'

'Another good man gone. But I think I'll wait—for active blessing on you—until we're at Burg el Arab. And I'm sure there aren't gentlemen in coalscuttle helmets waiting to greet us.'

She wondered if he meant that, looked away to the left, towards that faint ridge. But there was nothing in sight.

Tom's voice came, 'We're counting on you—as best man, sir.'

'No, Tom. I started the job—I'm going to finish it properly—give the girl away.' Then he started singing, 'Sand in my Shoes' for no reason at all, and they all laughed because it didn't matter any more.

They went on steadily, there was no thought of stopping except to top up the radiator. The stages were getting shorter again, but at least KATY was not boiling the whole time. At one stop, Anson said, 'Have a look at Zimmerman, will you?' and she went into the back of the car.

He was lying on his back, just as before, arms clasped behind his head. She said, 'We're going well—half way to the road already.'

He did not seem to hear her the first time, so she said it again, and when he turned to look at her, there was something new, wary, in his eyes.

'What am I going to do about clothes,' he said, 'I can't go into the town with no shirt.'

'Why not?' she thought—but she said, 'We'll try and borrow one. Perhaps at the checkpost before Alex. We'll have to stop there and report.'

'The checkpost—? Ah, yes.'

They went on and twice they saw columns of vehicles to the north-west of them, but they were far off, running parallel, and impossible to identify. The ground was rolling now, with more sand in the bottom of the valleys and the first green things growing there—clumps of camel-thorn, once a stunted palm. The clear blue segment of the sky came farther and farther over their heads, the wind seemed cooler. At last, as they crested a rise, there was a row of thin wobbling rods in the mirage in front.

'Vehicles,' said Tom.

Anson laughed. 'No, you BF. It's the telegraph line along the railway.'

It cleared to that. Then they could see the tattered antheap that was the native village; beyond, the first proper building, the white walls and red roofs of Burg el Arab station. There was a train unloading, a swarm of khaki figures round it, but they were still too far away to be sure.

Anson leaned forward and peered at the speedometer. 'I'm slipping. A mile short—and too far to the south.' They changed course a point and went on slower, silent, searching for a sign. Then Tom said, 'The flag, sir—just to the right of the station, on that dump. Red and blue—it's Ordnance.' And then they knew they were right.

Across the railway track, bumping over the sleepers, with the troops working near-by turning to stare. Tom said, 'Do you want to know the griff?'

'Hell, no. Let's press on. Four Rheingolds come before any bloody war.'

They were on tarmac now—a real road at last—that led over the last ridge in a cutting. When they had reached the top the main road was below, crowded with traffic, all running west. Beyond, a thin line of palms and then the blue carpet of the sea. As they slowed down at the road junction to turn to the right, she saw the signpost.

It said, ALEXANDRIA 30 MILES.

CHAPTER 12

The checkpost was at the junction with the Cairo road; much larger than Tom remembered it before—a small village of tents now.

Anson said, 'Pull off in front of the office, Tom. I'll go in and grapple with officialdom.'

They had been driving down the road for half an hour, doing a steady thirty with nothing to pass, nothing to overtake them; the stream of traffic was all going the other way. His eyes had lit as he saw the stuff that was destined for the front, wherever that might be: 25-pounders, tanks on their transporters—even under the camouflage, he could see there was a new type with the big gun mounted in the turret. 'Much more like it,' he thought. As the endless flow slid past them, men in the cabs would lean out and stare, sometimes a shout would be whipped into the emptiness behind. They did not wave or answer. They had been out of the world so long that unspoken consent held them in their own isolation. They did not want to know.

The palm-lined road was broken in places by fig groves. The only time that anyone spoke was when Diana said, 'Oh, look—' and there, in a gap in the trees, was the sea again, so close, so cool, so inviting.

They were outside the tent with the flag now and Anson jumped down. 'This is going to give them a shock. Give me your paybook, Tom. Diana, have you got an identity card?' When they had handed them over, he looked towards the back of the car. 'I'll fix him—but watch the back.' He walked off into the office.

They stood waiting, leaning against the back of the car.

'Hadn't you better put that tin under, Tom?'

He looked at her. 'That tin—not ever again. You don't understand quite how I feel about that tin. One top up before we start and that will see us through.' Then he said, 'Stay here. I'd better see how he is—' and climbed into the back.

Zimmerman was lying quite still, the blanket up to his chin; Tom could see the steady rise and fall of the barrel chest under it. But

he also knew that he was not really asleep. He shut the door
softly and went back to Diana. He whispered, 'Keep nearer those
doors—he's pretending he's asleep.'

They waited and no one in the camp came near them, only
behind, the noise of the traffic on the road went on unabated. Then
Anson came walking out of the tent with a tall captain of the
Military Police and he watched her start to fuss with her hair,
and said, 'I shouldn't bother.' Anson said, 'Johnson—this is Sister
Murdoch and MSM Pugh,' and they were shaking hands.

The captain looked at them as if they were beings from another
world as he said, 'Captain Anson's told me all about your trip. I
think it's a bloody marvellous effort. I'll phone your hospital, Sister,
and let them know you're coming.' Then he looked at them again.
'What about some grub—and a wash?'

He wasn't hungry—but a real wash, that would be something.
Anson was shaking his head, though, saying, 'I'd rather get
on—unless you want to, Diana?'

'I'd love just five minutes, if I can.'

The policeman said, 'I'll show you my tent—and get that shirt
for your South African pal at the same time.' He looked towards
the back of the car. 'How is he—by the way?'

South African pal . . . ? He opened his mouth to speak but Diana's
fingers were biting into his arm. 'Still asleep,' she said.

The captain made to move off and then turned back. 'Are you
sure—you won't even have a drink?'

'No, thanks,' said Anson. 'We've got a date for that.'

When they had gone, he stared at Tom. 'Is he really asleep?'

'No—foxing. But, sir—aren't you going to turn him in?'

Anson gave him a strange look. 'In good time, Tom. All in good
time. There's our date before that. But we'll have to watch him.'

'But he'll rumble that—make a dash for it.'

'I don't think so—not yet.'

They had finished topping up the radiator when Diana and the
captain came back. She looked a clean, very different person and
Tom felt a surge of possessive pride in it. They climbed on board
and the shirt was handed up. 'The biggest I've got,' said the captain,
'I won't disturb him. Just see that he's handed over to his own
people.'

'I will—and see the shirt is sent back. Thanks for everything.'
Anson nodded at Tom and he let in the clutch and they were off
on the last lap.

Anson was sitting on the floor now, Diana in the seat. He glanced
down to where the captain was sitting cross-legged, with the shirt
in his lap. He was undoing the shoulder tabs and pulling off the
tubes of cloth that carried the three pips of a captain. 'He won't be
wanting those,' he said.

The outskirts of Alex were appearing now, the clusters of houses
perched on the side of the road, the Greek restaurants with their
shady verandahs, the sea running close on their other side. Anson
got to his feet. 'I'll take him his present—and stay and make polite
conversation for a bit. Those back doors open easily.'

When he had gone, Tom listened to Diana's chatter, excited as
she pointed out little ordinary things . . . half-listened to it, for there
was something else more important to hear. The trained ear that
always listened subconsciously to the beat of the engine had noticed
something different . . . a fast regular clicking. Perhaps it had started
on that last bitter slope—when she was overheating so badly. It
didn't matter when, really. But the bearings were beginning to
break up.

In instinct, he took his foot off the accelerator and let her coast,
then picked up the power, gingerly. Another quarter-mile and then
from the back, on the other side, came that sudden sharp crack
they had heard before. KATY sagged to the right and he swore
and let her ride to a gentle halt. Anson's head came round the door.
'What the hell, Tom?'

'It's that other—spring,' he said.

'Well, out of it—all of you.' He looked back into the car. 'And
you—Zimmerman.' They all got down in the road and walked
round to where the clean, bright break of the main leaf stuck out
behind them.

Tom scratched his head. 'We could stop a truck—scrounge a lift,
sir.'

Anson stared at him. 'A lift—? What the hell are you talking
about? I just worked out with Zimmerman—we've done nearly six
hundred miles, over every kind of stuff—and there's four left to do.
No, we'll take her in on blankets. We've done it before, and I'm
not leaving the old bitch now. Get the jack out.' He smacked
KATY's olive bonnet hard.

Tom, busy with showing the others how to roll the blankets from
the back into tight sausages, wondered why Anson had got out the
tool kit for a job when it would not be needed; understood, when

he saw him take the largest wrench, holding it loose in one hand
as he watched Zimmerman all the time.

On the other side of the road the traffic rushed by within feet of
them, at their backs the sea hushed softly against the beach. But
they did not notice either, nor the crowd of darting, chattering Arab
children that had ringed round, waiting to steal anything that
opportunity offered. They were back in their own special world.

The blankets were rolled in tight bundles and then wedged
between the spring and the jacked-up chassis. When the space was
filled, the jack was lowered, squeezing the two together. KATY
sagged, but not quite so much as before. Then Tom bound the
whole with rope, down the sides and along, to prevent slipping. All
the time, Anson stood to the side, swinging the spanner, watching
Zimmerman. A silent Zimmerman, who looked strangely smart in
the shirt that was two sizes too small for him.

Tom straightened. 'There's another thing, sir. A big end. Come
and listen.' He opened the bonnet, started her up and worked the
throttle. Anson frowned. 'Big end as well—sounds like number
four.'

'Shall I take the plug out, sir?'

'God—yes. We'll go in on five cylinders and a pile of blankets.'
He looked round them all, swinging the spanner gently. 'And we
want the weight as far forward as we can get it—so you can all get
in the cab. Take her in—in style.'

He did not see the beginnings of the city. He was too intent,
watching the road ahead, wary of the stray donkey—the children
darting ahead, deliberately, just under their wheels. The rumble of
the tyres told that they were on the cobbles now, and then the
stench of tannery, reminding him of that night on the Depression,
only two nights ago. There was something else to worry him, above
the whistling pump of the open number four plug—the clatter was
growing again. Other big ends were starting to go.

No one talked, there was no thought of singing now. Only an
unbearable rising tension. He was not hungry, nor thirsty—but
once when the captain said, 'I hope that beer's bloody cold,' his
mouth started watering uncontrollably.

The dim shapes of the warehouses drifted by, just out of his range
of vision, then there was the narrow cleft of Sister Street, with the
dark buildings towering high to the narrow strip of blue. At the
end of it, a patch of green.

Anson said, 'Mahomet Ali Square.' Diana said something
else—something he could not quite catch. It sounded like 'Zerzura.'

People shouted at them, a tram gong clanged, but they took not
the slightest notice, all their senses were strained in watching that
patch of green that slid nearer and nearer towards them . . . He
wondered what Zimmerman was thinking.

The clatter was rising, a vibration coming up through the
floorboards; for the first time a smell of hot oil, the well-known
clouds of steam billowing out from under the bonnet. He shouted,
'Shall I stop?' but Anson, sitting outside Zimmerman, still holding
that spanner, said, 'Christ, no! It's only the other side of the bloody
square. Keep her going.'

They limped out of the crack of Sister Street into the sunlight
and there was the wide square with the gardens in the middle and
the lines of tall palms streaming their crowns over in the sea breeze.
They crept round the square, he had to coax her now to move at
all, every instinct rebelling at the torture of machinery.

Then Anson said, 'Pull in. That's it.'

He cut the switch and coasted to the kerb and there was no
sound for a moment but the rumble of boiling water in the radiator
and the sounds of the traffic that seemed to come from a another
world.

Anson got down and threw the spanner on the floor with a clatter.
'Come on, you lot.' Then he ran his hand very slowly down the
length of the hot, rust-spattered bonnet. 'You bloody good old
bitch,' he said.

As they scrambled down to join him, each, even Zimmerman,
touched KATY's flank, although they did not speak. With Anson
leading, he and Diana falling in behind Zimmerman, they walked
across the pavement and into the narrow side street. At the corner,
he turned for a last look at her, lonely now, battered, with that strip
of bullet holes running down her side, propped up on blankets,
sizzling, but triumphant.

It was just six o'clock, too early for the usual drinking crowd and
the bar was quite empty. It was just as the captain had said it
would be; the high, marble-topped counter, the tall stools against
it, the clean light room, the few tables grouped round the walls.
After they had pushed through the swing door, they trooped up to
the bar in silence, pulled out four stools and perched on them in a

row. The barman yawned and got up from his seat to come forward and look at them without enthusiasm.

'Yes—?' A pause, and then, 'Sir.'

'Set 'em up,' said Anson.

'What up—?'

Anson turned to Tom. 'He thinks we're tramps. He thinks we can't pay. He's forgotten the order we put in six days ago.' He fumbled in his pocket and produced two crumpled pound notes that hc put on the counter.

'Get cracking, Joe. FOUR VERY, VERY COLD RHEINGOLDS.'

When they came up, again they were as he said they would be, pale amber, in tall thin glasses, and so cold, the dew had frosted on the outside before he put them down. They stood in a row now, but Tom waited, as he knew the others were waiting, for Anson to make the first move. He stared at his for a moment, looking all round it as if it were a rare specimen, then ran his finger up and down the side of the glass, leaving a clear trail in the dew. He said, 'That's that,' and lifted the glass and tilted it right back. Tom watched the ripple of the swallow in the lean throat, and there was a tight feeling inside him and his eyes were smarting and he knew that in a moment he would cry. So he lifted up his own glass and swallowed it fast.

When Anson put his glass down it was empty. 'I quite forgot to drink your healths,' he said. Then, to the barman, 'Set em up again.'

It was easier with the second one and they started talking on the 'do you remember' line, but not beyond that lonely grave in the wadi—and Zimmerman never said a word.

Tom said, 'What about KATY?'

'I'll phone the VRD and get them to pull her in. It's gharries for me from now on.' Then he turned to Zimmerman. 'You are our problem child. No clothes, no identity card, no money, no nothing. I'm afraid they'll take the hell of a long time to vet you. I'll have to come—and I don't feel like answering any of their bloody silly questions tonight.'

Zimmerman spoke for the first time. 'I hadn't thought of that. But must I bother you? Can't I just slip off to my own people.'

Anson shook his head. 'No. I've a better idea than that. Let's leave it all till tomorrow. Come with me tonight to where I usually stay. Mother Thompson's—she's got a boarding house on the front.

She's very good to me—she'll lend us cash—and clothes, even if they are only civvies. Then we can bath and eat and sleep. Face everything in the morning.'

All through this conversation, Tom had been watching Zimmerman. His face had shaded through every expression from indecision to resolve, brightened visibly at the mention of civilian clothes. 'Captain Anson', he thought, 'he's gone plumb crazy. Give that crafty—civvies, and he'll dodge out at the first chance—and they'll never find him.'

But Zimmerman was saying, 'Thanks, man. It seems the best idea. It's very kind of you.'

'Well, I'd better ring her now—she likes good notice.' He slipped off his stool and went over to the telephone-box that was in the corner. Tom went on watching. Something was flowing back into that big man. He looked younger, stronger every moment. Tom knew what hope looked like now.

Anson seemed a long time, and when he came back he did not climb on his stool. He stood behind them and said, 'That's fixed,' and there was a subtle change in his voice. Then, 'Will you bring your drinks over to a table for a minute. I've something private to say.'

They got down, wondering, and then Zimmerman said, 'I think I'll—wash my hands.' Anson standing between him and the door, said, 'That's an idea, so will I.' Tom saw his eyes flick at him, so he said, 'Will you excuse us, Diana?' and they marched out to the back of the room in procession.

All the time in the toilet, there was bright talk on how the war was going. Anson gave details of how the line had been steadied at Alamein, how lucky they had been to come out east of that. Tom wondered where he had got this information—he had spoken to no one except the MP at the checkpost, and surely, then, he would have mentioned it before. Perhaps Zimmerman spotted it too, for he tried to dry his hands rather quickly, and get out of the door in front of them, but, somehow, Anson was there first, and they walked back to the bar in their single file. He only had one glimpse of Zimmerman's face then—it was grey, and the broad shoulders seemed to be shrinking.

Diana was waiting, standing by the swing door out into the street, peering over the pane of frosted glass. She said, 'There is a truck just drawn up outside—it's full of—' She swung round and she saw Zimmerman and her face changed; behind her, they could all see

beyond the edge of the glass . . . the flat red hats of military policemen as they spilled out over the pavement.

Inside the bar it was so quiet, so still, he could hear the flies
buzzing. He looked once at Zimmerman's face and then at the
ground. He could only think of two things: that straining, cracking
back that had held KATY until he had got the jack
underneath—and the other thing to come, the grey cold of a dawn,
the wall, and the nervous firing squad. It seemed such a bloody
shame.

Anson's voice was tight. 'They've surrounded the place,
Zimmerman—but I've arranged they don't come in for another ten
minutes. So we must talk quickly. I'm sorry—but what else could
I do but ring Kom-el-Dick?' And he knew that last desperate question was addressed to him and Diana.

He looked across to the barman, shouted, 'Another round—over
here.' Then he pulled out a chair for Diana and sat down beside
her.

The Greek came over with the tray, put down the four tall glasses,
and departed, scratching. Anson leaned forward across the table.
'Zimmerman. What is your real name?'

There was no answer. The big man just looked at his glass,
rubbing his finger up and down the outside, just as Anson had
done.

'I'll tell you why,' Anson went on, 'I'll tell you just exactly what
I told our security people. That we came out of Tobruk; that, later,
we picked up a German officer, whose truck had broken down, who
had started walking, who had got a touch of the sun. That he
surrendered, gave his parole to me, and had behaved in a most
exemplary manner. And that I would deliver the body after we had
had a drink together.'

Still Zimmerman did not answer. The barman lifted a hand to
the radio on the wall behind him and fiddled with the knobs, a
bright, metallic voice started singing, 'Sand in my shoes . . .'

Anson said, 'You can get away with a hell of a lot when you're
moving round—but just with us three, so close, I don't think you
had a chance. And you had bad luck with your own people. To get
through once was a miracle—but twice, no. I was just in time to
see that fooling with the buttons in the wadi, but I don't know what
it was—I didn't look when I threw the bush-shirt away after I got
you out of that bog.' He looked across the table. 'You saw me,
Diana—say that it's true.'

Her voice came very low, 'I saw—he didn't touch it. Just threw it away.'

Anson's voice went on, 'I didn't look—because I didn't want to know. You see, there was no harm done till then—even with that precious pack of yours. I know it was a transmitter.'

Zimmerman looked at him and then down at his drink. He picked it up at last and took a long swallow. Still he did not speak. Anson's arm came out across the table, gripping him by the elbow.

'Christ, man—can't you see? There's no time. Tell me your name—stick to our story. I'll vouch for Tom and Diana, though we will be risking a court-martial. But there will be no more bother. Otherwise, I'll have to tell them a lot of funny things, give them the map reference where they can find a pack and a bush-shirt. They wouldn't take a lot of digging out. And then—?' He spread his hands. 'But we don't want it—any of us—because we know very well that we wouldn't be here if it hadn't been for you.'

The swing door at the front slammed open and a lieutenant of the Military Police came in. He was tall and thin and Tom saw that he had pale knees. He said, 'Captain Anson?' to the room at large.

'That's me.' Anson looked at his watch. 'You're early.'

The lieutenant slapped his can against his leg. 'That may be—but this fraternization—'

Anson tilted his chair back and said one short and very rude word. The lieutenant flushed. 'Must I remind you—there is a lady present?'

Anson looked at him. 'I know—and if she had thought of it, she would have said it herself. But it doesn't alter the fact that you are over-riding your CO's orders. Do you want me to phone and tell him?' Then he looked down to knee-level. 'Just off the boat,' he said to no one in particular, 'got to learn—thinks all that ironmongery is the answer.'

The red-cap flushed again as he fingered his revolver holster. 'Then I'll wait outside.'

Anson said, 'Do,' and when the door had closed he leaned over the table again. 'For God's sake—can't you see? It's the last chance.'

Zimmerman looked down at his drink, picked it up and drained it in one gulp. He said, quite simply, in a very different voice, 'Otto Lutz—Hauptmann Engineer—21st Panzer Group.'

There was a silence and then Anson's voice came again, urgent. 'Now listen. You lost your way—the truck broke down, Otto. You started to walk, then the sun got you. We picked you up after we'd buried Sister Norton—you only heard about that. From then on, just as it happened.'

He stopped for a moment to look at the others, 'Is that all right with you?' Hardly waiting for their quiet 'Yes', he went on, 'Quick—is there anything on you—or left in the ambulance —that might need explaining?'

Zimmerman . . . Lutz, it was easier to think of him like that, thought for a moment and said, 'Perhaps—in my pack, but I don't think so.'

'Well, I'll dump the lot—without looking—off the deep water quay, just in case.'

The door opened again, and pale-knees came in. 'Really—' he said.

Anson got up. 'Will you fraternize with us, Lieutenant—and have one?'

'No, thank you.'

Anson smiled at Lutz and said, 'That's that.' Then he stared at those knees again. 'He'll learn—one day.'

The Hauptmann was on his feet now. He looked at Anson and smiled and said, 'So you release me from my parole, Herr Captain?'

'Certainly.' Anson looked across at pale-knees. 'I've told your commandant that this officer has behaved in an exemplary manner. There's no need for a ball and chain. You'd better run along with nursie, Lutz.'

Lutz looked round the circle of them. 'It's been a great experience. Will you shake hands?'

They all murmured something, and while the lieutenant looked down his nose, he took their hands in turn across the table. For Diana, there was a special click of the heels and a quiet—'Fraulein'.

He walked to the door with the lieutenant, and then turned back to look at them once more. He said, 'It has been something. All against one—against the greater enemy. I have learned a lot.' Then he gave them that silly stiff bow again, the door flapped twice behind him and that was that.

They stayed quite still, looking at the blank door, until they heard the truck start up and the noise of the motor fade into the background of traffic. The radio was still playing softly on the wall, the barman appeared to have gone to sleep. Anson broke the silence, 'I'd better go and dump that bloody pack off the end of the quay before I get inquisitive.'

Diana said, 'And I must get to the hospital.'

Anson looked at both of them. 'I made another phone call. I took

the liberty of ringing them. I said that you would be escorted by a
WO who would need accommodation. You can beat me up in the
morning, Tom, and we'll find our precious unit.' Then his voice
went grave. 'Tell your matron, Diana, I'd like to call on her—about
Denise.'

She said, 'I would like that. And I want you to wade in on
something else. You can smooth out the marriage bother easier
than anyone. And we want it to be soon.'

The door opened and three customers came in, so they went out
of the bar, back into the noisy sunlight of the square, to KATY.
She was there still, cool and silent now, somehow, dejected. Anson
went into the back and came out with Zimmerman's pack. 'I don't
think there was anything else of his,' he said. 'Sorry I didn't have
time to ask you properly about this business—but you do agree,
don't you? And you'll stick to it?'

They both nodded.

He sat down on the step and looked up at them, drawn, dirty,
without a cap, but his eyes were back in the living again. 'I wish
I had a camera,' he said, '—two people, about to enter into holy
matrimony—entirely blinded by sand.'

Tom was holding her hand now, was surprised when she let go
with a whispered, 'Don't be cross.' He watched her walk over to
the step of the car and put both hands on Anson's shoulders as she
stooped to kiss him full on the mouth. He was near enough to hear
her say, 'Find your Zerzura, George—you're halfway there now,'
and wonder what the hell she was talking about.

Anson got up stiffly. He said, 'I'll try, Diana. See you both
tomorrow.' Then he smiled at them. '"Bye for now.'

They stood, holding hands again, watching the slim figure grow
smaller and smaller as it went down the square towards the sea.
She said, 'I do want it to be quick, darling. And then I want a
baby as soon as we can—so that I can get out of this, and home,
and start things up—for you to come back to.'

The little figure had almost vanished now. The tall palms looked
so green and stately as they bent their heads in rustling to the wind.
There was a red-cap standing on the pavement opposite, trying,
obviously, to make up his mind to come over and check them for
being improperly dressed and holding hands.

He tried to slip his hand loose, but she held on fast.

'Don't let go, darling. Everything—is going to be all right—for
all of us.'

Dead Men Rise Up Never

7

Contents

CHAPTER 1

I suppose there must always be that one moment of truth: the flash of pre-knowledge, whether in fear or in pleasure, that shows for a split second the chain of reaction that the future will unleash from one single act. The dictator must know, just for that time as he cuts the string of the innocent-looking parcel that contains the time bomb that will blow him to eternity; the peasant who looks at the wavering muzzles of a firing squad for a reason he does not understand and over which he has no control, in some dusty courtyard. Both have that moment entirely alone: neither can have had time to speak of it; but sometime, somewhere, it comes to all of us. Mine was given in the opening of a parcel.

It was nothing dramatic; just the manuscript copy of a short novel and a covering letter from the solicitors to say that since I had been named literary executor of the estate of the late Colin Headly they were passing his last work to me so that I could open negotiations with his publisher . . . nothing that could possibly tell me of the dark, shifting path ahead. But in the moment that I cut the string and laid the slim sheaf of pages at one side of my desk I think I knew. There was that single spine-chilling moment. Then it passed and I became immersed in the routine matters of the day of a junior partner in a big firm of city accountants.

It wasn't until lunch time that I picked up the manuscript again and flipped through the first few pages. Then, suddenly, from a paragraph of Colin's appalling typing, a phrase jumped out to hit me between the eyes. It didn't mean anything in itself except that it fitted with something that Colin and I had had in common. Something that only he and I could have known. I went on, skipping pages, and there was another of the same kind . . . then another. All afternoon, after I had thrown it into a drawer and sworn I would not look any further, those little phrases kept coming back to me. The poison was beginning to work. It was an effort to concentrate on ordinary things; through the columns of figures of a balance sheet I could see Colin. I understood what he was trying to tell me; the hidden message in the pages of his book. It was all disguised, every name and place changed, but it was *there*. I managed to hold out until I got home to my bachelor flat. I had a quick meal and sat down in the comfortable chair, with the whisky decanter beside me. Somehow it seemed a gesture, for you couldn't read Colin or talk to Colin without a drink in your hand. I read the whole thing through at one sitting; it was eleven o'clock and the decanter was half empty by the time I had finished. But I knew. There was no doubt about it at all. Only three people could have known ever. Colin; Lois, his wife; and me. And now Colin was dead. And what he was telling me, this echo from the grave, was a very terrible thing. That Lois had sent him there. She had poisoned him.

It will seem that this story begins in the middle, but I have to tell how everything started; I have to do it this way to tell the truth, as far as one person can ever see the real truth. And there is another reason—Lois. In fairness to her as well as to me I have to tell the whole story.

My name is Harry Andrews, and I am now a plump, balding, middle-aged, happy chartered accountant. But when this story really started I was thirteen, desperately frightened, and lonely on my first Sunday of the first term at a British public school.

It is possibly the worst day in your life, that Sunday. The loneliest, certainly, until the moment you die; the time, the very first time, that you are entirely on your own, with no past that matters, no present that you can control, and no foreseeable future. There is the vacuum after the rush of the first few days, which are filled in being drilled into a new routine; there is nothing to do after chapel for the whole day except to think, to fill the gap after the prefects have gone to their studies, the seniors for a nice frowst by the common-room fire; nothing for the new boy but to pace the draughty cloisters, hands out of pockets, as decreed for the first year, trying to sum up the rest of his fellow sufferers, whistling to keep his spirits up, or the last resort, trying to get away from it all for a few hours in a long walk over the downs.

I remember standing, debating which it was to be; watching out of the corner of my eye the rest of the forlorn group of 'new men'. I remember wondering if they all felt as dismal as they looked, as dismal as I felt. They did, all except one, the small fair boy with the girlish face and the very blue eyes. He was standing apart, as

he had through the few days we have been together; there was
something rather nice and defiant in the way he kept his hands
stuffed deep in his pockets, the purse of those red lips in a silent
whistle. He knew what it was all about; he knew where he was
going. And then the eyes met mine, twinkling; the mouth broke
into a smile . . . I knew I was going with him.

'Come for a walk with me, Andrews?' It wasn't an invitation;
more of a command.

'I'd like to.'

As I moved forward another of the lonely group took an uncertain
step to follow. The effect on Colin Headly was immediate and
remarkable: an arm came down on my shoulder, cutting the other
unfortunate off as if with a barrier. The voice that followed was
almost fierce. 'Not you, Smithson. I didn't ask you. I want to go
with Andrews. We want to talk.' And from the moment I followed
him meekly out of the house room to the bleak, wind-swept loneliness of the downs I was his slave.

We walked and we talked—the last is only a haze of memory
now—about the grievances of our new lot: the food, the cold, the
hard beds, and the general bloodiness of all in authority over us,
from masters down to prefects. But looking back afterwards, I
remembered one or two things that were significant in the forming
of the web.

'Where was your prep school, Colin?' He had asked me to call
him by his Christian name, perhaps a little too quickly, for I still can
think of the embarrassment of getting it out. But it was something to
hang on to in this hard new world.

He looked at me for a moment before answering; it was a look
that I was going to mark so well through the years that followed.
A slow, calculating look; charming in the way the mouth drooped,
the dark lashes falling slowly against the cheek. 'Where was yours?'
he said.

'At Horsham. It's where I live. I was a day boy. That's why I
hate this foul place so much.'

'I was in Dublin,' he said. 'Do you know Ireland at all?'

'No.'

At once the tone changed from the sharpness of the question to
a soft, flowing spate of memory. 'St. Saviour's, my school was called.
I was a boarder. We don't live in Dublin, you see, but in the wilds
of the country at the side of a big lake that is halfway down the
river Shannon. It's a big loch called Derg, Harry, and it's about

thirty miles long and eight miles broad at its widest. The castle
where we live—' He saw me looking at him in astonishment, then
added quickly, 'It isn't really a castle, but that's what they call any
big house out there. The name of it is Clonco, and it stands in its
own fifty acres beside the loch . . .' As I walked on, listening, the
springy turf of the downs faded and I was in a different world: the
grey stone of the house with its mile-long drive through the avenue
of trees; the view over loch Derg to the far mountains; the water,
sometimes angry brown, whipped by the wind into sudden storms,
mostly a placid, still blue; of the sailing on it; the fishing; the
shooting along its shores. It sounded such a wonderful life, so far
from my own.

'You must come and stay sometime,' Colin finished. 'The spring
is the best, I think, for the dapping . . .'

I did not know what 'dapping' was; it really didn't matter, for I
was thinking at the moment of something quite different.

'Have you lived there always, Colin?' I said.

'Oh, yes. My father inherited it from my granny.'

My peculiar analytical mind seemed to have fastened, against
my will almost, on the one weak link in the story. 'But you must
be a Catholic, and yet I saw you in chapel with us this morning.'

'Of course.' Again that look, that change of voice to something
approaching sharpness. 'There are Protestants in Ireland, you
know, Andrews, and we happen to be among them.'

'But—' I was still thinking of St. Saviour's, in Dublin. And that
didn't sound particularly Protestant to me.

'You tell me about your home, old man.' It was said a little too
quickly, but I fell for it, and my question was dropped. It would
have been such a come-down after all I had heard to have to relate
the dull doings of the only son of a chartered accountant in a small
Sussex town.

We turned back, and soon the grey loom of the school buildings
brought home the immediate thought of the shape of things to come.
I said gloomily, 'Fagging starts next week. That's all the grace they
give us.'

Once more he squeezed my arm; his voice had become smooth
and soothing again. 'Don't worry about that, Harry. You just work
damned hard to get into the middle school, and then you are free
of it.'

'But we've got a year to do for that, at least,' I grumbled.

'Oh, there are ways of getting out of the worst of it,' he said lightly. He looked so very appealing, so very attractive.

'What ways?'

'You'll see, Harry. You'll see.'

There was a moment's silence before he spoke again. 'Tell me something? You ought to be good at maths . . . being the son of an accountant?'

'That doesn't follow. But I rather like them.'

For the third time he squeezed my arm. 'I'm so glad, for I haven't the head for them at all. I knew I was right to pick you as a friend. I knew you were the best of the bunch.'

When we started it didn't take long to find out what he had meant by 'other ways' of making a fag's life easy. He got himself appointed, with no difficulty, as the personal slave to the head of the house. This apparently was a full-time job that exempted him from our communal chores of washing up, boot cleaning, and making tea for the rest of the prefects. What he did to deserve all this was a mystery. He seemed to spend his entire time closeted in the study of the gentleman, concerned with various tasks that were described to me vaguely as 'making toast' or 'tidying up.'

Of course I knew what was happening. Small boys are not the bloody fools and innocents that some people try to make them out to be. So much nonsense has been talked and written on the pseudo-homosexuality of the British public school—that it entails awful results of corruption, and that the younger concerned is always the victim. I had no practical experience; I was not one of the pretty ones. But watching, aware, I soon knew it was the inevitable result of treating men in body as boys and shutting them away without any contact with the other sex. For various reasons it became a form of prostitution. It was bound to happen, the results were seldom disastrous, and the younger partners rarely suffered. Indeed, some of them positively enjoyed it. Colin was among these. He revelled in his 'friendship' because it made life easy and gave him power above his station.

And I—left alone, with no one else to turn to, for the rest of the 'new men' had formed their little groups, which after that first snub were closed to me—I hated it. Perhaps, deep down, there were the same motives inside me, motives that I did not yet fully understand. But I was lonely, jealous, and unhappier than I had ever been before or have been since in my life. I hated every moment of the time Colin spent with Osborn, the head prefect. I hated the figure

itself: the long saturnine figure with the dark horn-rimmed glasses
and the baggiest of Oxford bags in the whole school. I hated the
way he looked only at Colin, never at me, as he gabbled his way
through roll call. He was taking something away, and I didn't quite
understand what. It came to a head one half holiday when Colin
had promised to go for a walk with me and didn't turn up.

I was hurt, so hurt it was impossible to be angry. I hung about
the cloisters like a dog, waiting for him to reappear. He was as late
as usual, and it was not until after prep that I had a chance to
speak to him alone.

'Colin, you promised me for this afternoon. What happened?'

'Oh'—he gave me that sidelong glance—'I couldn't help it.
Osborn took me up to the darkroom in the lab to develop some
photos. I had to go, Harry. I am his fag.'

'Were they good?' Anything to delay what I knew was coming.

'Good?' Again that rippling laugh. 'Good? There weren't any,
Harry.' I was given the whispered, detailed description of what
Osborn had said and done. It did not shock or surprise me; it only
made the hurt go deeper.

'Didn't you mind?'

'Mind? Why should I? And anyway, he gave me a shilling.' Then
Colin touched my arm. 'We'll go and spend it at the grub shop
tomorrow on ices.'

And of course, I went with him and ate them—and was deeper
in the mesh than ever.

There were other things. The question of signed chits from the
housemaster to be excused from games. 'Grits', as we called him,
would initial a piece of paper, after great searching into reasons,
and it was then passed to the prefect in charge of that particular
activity. I was never good at any game; hated most of all the ghastly
cross-country runs when I was always behind, with a stitch in my
side, barely avoiding the lash of the stick of the prefect who was
'whipper up.' It was a bleak November day when one of these
tortures was announced on the note board as compulsory. I sat,
miserable at the prospect, at a corner table in the common room,
next to Colin. 'I suppose you won't be going, as usual,' I said. I
knew now, by experience, that he would have found a way out of
it.

'No. I'm tidying up Osborn's room.'

I thought of him in the warmth and comfort of the study; felt

like saying something, but didn't. But he knew. He lowered his
voice.

'You needn't go, Harry, if you don't want to.'

'But I must!'

'Not if you fill in an excused games chit.'

'What's the use? You know what 'Grits' is like. He'd never sign
it. I'm not ill.'

'Grits won't see it. I'll sign for him.'

As I stared in astonishment he went on, 'Just write it out for a
bad ankle and I'll show you.'

When I had penned the application he snatched it quickly, gave
a quick look round to see if anyone was watching, then with a
sudden flourish signed the housemaster's initial in the corner.

It wan't a slow, clumsy forgery, something copied or written
backwards. It came like lightning . . . and it was exact. I doubt if
'Grits' himself would have known the difference from the genuine
article made with his own hand. 'Give that to Fosdick,' Colin said,
'and then put your feet up in comfort.'

I was still stunned as I put it away in my pocket. Colin gave me
a slow look of triumph. 'I don't do it too often, Harry. Might flood
the market or get caught. And that would finish it. You can have
one whenever you like, within reason. I charage the others sixpence
a time.' The cool, calculating eyes were fixed on mine again. 'But
you can have it for nothing . . . if you go on doing my algebra prep.'

Once again I was a coward, and I fell.

But there were times when he was not omnipotent—like the day
I found one of his letters in my locker.

They were all that we had for privacy, those lockers; they were
built in tiers, about two feet square each, and inside one had to
cram all one's worldy possessions—books, sweets, jam, photos from
home, and letters. At least they did have a lock. Colin's was directly
over mine, and there was a crack in the floor between. It happened
one evening when I went to get the books for prep, wrestling to get
out Godfrey and Siddons on algebra from the jumble of books that
crammed my locker to the roof. I got it out, and a letter that had
slipped through from the floor above came away, too. Without
thinking, I unfolded the sheet and looked at it.

It was written in a crabbed, ill-educated hand on cheap lined
paper. I just had time to take in the address—somewhere in
Streatham—the opening. 'My darling boy,' when I got a stunning
blow on the side of my head, and there was Colin; a Colin standing

with two pink spots flaming on his cheeks, the lips of that soft
mouth curling back in a snarl.

'You louse! You bloody, dirty, stinking louse! How dare you read
my letters?' For a moment I thought he was going to hit me again.

'I'm sorry.' I rubbed an ear that was already very painful. 'I
didn't really mean to look at it, Colin. But it must have fallen down
through the crack. I looked to make sure.'

I guess I showed at once that I was the one in the wrong;
immediately all the fire went out and there was a comforting hand
round my shoulder. 'Sorry, man. It's just that I don't like that sort
of thing, but with you, of course, it's different.' He took the letter
from me and put it in his pocket. 'Did you see who it was from?'

'Someone in Streatham who called you "darling boy," ' I
muttered.

'Oh, yes. That's my old nurse. She's retired back to England
now. She's rather a pet. You must meet her sometime.'

The bell rang for prep then, and that was that: not quite, though,
for it was the second small crack in the wall of trust. I was watching
from then on: watching his mail when it was handed out in hall
after breakfast; watching for any Irish stamp and postmark. But he
was too quick for me always; he had them stuffed in his pocket,
and in a way, that made it worse. I knew something, but I did not
know what I knew. I tried to press it further by offering to post his
letters. But he saw through the pretext and never let me: they were
either not quite finished or had already gone. That was the worst
of it; because I was so very fond of him, I would have died rather
than give away his most shameful secret, would have been honoured
and glad to share it.

The real break came on the day we went home, having finished
our year of servitude in the lower school. I went, deliberately, to
London instead of making the usual cross-country journey home. I
did not mind in the least that it cut a day off the holidays. It was
a carefully thought-out plan to give me a few hours alone with
Colin.

Those casual invitations to come and stay at Clonco Castle had
never become substantial, nor now did I think they ever would.
But this day was going to be mine with him alone. And I had
planned it as a surprise.

He was very gay going up in the train. He kept all the carriage
in fits of laughter with imitations of 'Grits' and the chaplain; the
fun died in the scramble of welcoming parents, the dive for taxis

and the underground; then Colin and I were left alone by the bookstall.

Now was the moment. 'Colin,' I said, 'let's go and have lunch some place together. I'll pay. What about the Criterion, a gin and ginger beer. Turkish coffee after?'

His face lit up with the usual charming smile. 'I'd like that, Harry.' But then I made the mistake of going on with my plans. 'We can go to a flick afterwards, and then I'll come and see you off on the train.'

The smile faded. 'I can't do that, man. I've promised to go and see Nanny—you know, my old nurse that lives in Streatham.'

Anything to keep him with me. 'Well, I'd like to come with you. You said I could meet her sometime.'

Now the smile changed to a frown. 'For God's sake, Slowboots'—he always called me that when he was angry—'I don't want you trailing round after me all the time. Can't a man have a bit of time on his own, ever?'

He must have seen the look on my face, for when he straightened from picking up his bag, his expression had softened a little.

'Bye for now, Harry. Have a good hol. See you next term.'

I watched with a stony heart as he walked away; noticed for the first time, in a wave of perception through my anger and disappointment, that the backs of his shoes were down at the heel, that his suit, though neat, was a size too small for him.

Next term came, but it was never quite the same again. Perhaps things had to change, for our ways in class parted in the middle school. He was doing classics, while I went on the modern side to do maths and follow in my father's footsteps. But there were other things to widen the gap. He was so good at games, playing all with an easy nonchalance when he wanted to; I was the duffer and I loathed them. He had twenty other friends by now; I had only two. We met in hall, we had tea together on rare occasions, but the old intimacy had gone. I was no longer the best of the bunch in his estimation.

But sometimes the closeness did come back. Like the time when I got kicked on the head at rugger and was in the sanatorium for a week with concussion and six stitches in my scalp. He was sweet and thoughtful then, coming up day after day to sit with me, bringing lemonade and cakes that I knew he could not possibly afford. He made me laugh when I felt grim, or sat in comfortable silence during the times the head was really bad. That was the sort

of patchwork that made up Colin: a mixture of light and shade.
But perhaps even then the two colours were beginning to fade.

In the last year, in the upper school, we were thrown together
again. Colin, a foregone conclusion, had been made head of the
house; I, to my own and everyone else's utter amazement, had been
appointed second prefect. He ran the house with the same easy,
carefree efficiency with which he played games, riding airily over
the fact that 'Grits' was getting grittier and older very fast, leaving
more and more of the routine to us. He ran it strictly and fairly for
everyone except himself ... and for him there were no rules.
Everyone knew that, and no one minded. He was so charming and
handsome.

I suppose I should have done something about it the time he had
two youngsters up to his study to take a glass of port, but I didn't.
I suppose I should not have consented to be his 'cover' when he
climbed out night after night to break bounds. But I fell for that,
too, waiting up for hours, willing myself to stay awake until there
was a scrape on the window and I had to haul him in. I never
knew where he went; I was never asked to join him. Often there
was a smear of lipstick, on his mouth when he came back, and once
he was very drunk and fell off the drainpipe in the act of shinning
up, making a horrible noise as he landed on the roof below. Even
'Grits' was awakened from his senile sleep by that, and there were
only a few awful moments to retrieve Colin, tuck him under the
sheets with all his clothes on, before the housemaster arrived in
person, looking even grittier than usual in his blue-striped pyjamas.
He retired grunting gloomily, vaguely suspicious of Colin's
theatrical snores that got mixed with giggles, on my assurance that
it must have been a cat.

And then in our last term, just three weeks before the end of it,
Colin went. It was very sudden and before the event, even after, I
had really no clue as to what it was all about. One evening a fag,
wide-eyed with suppressed excitement, simply came to tell me that
Colin wanted to see me in his room at once.

He was packing, throwing all his things into a bag with that easy
attitude of 'couldn't care less.'

'Hello, Harry.' He looked up and smiled. 'Glad you were about.
Grits wants to see you in a minute, but I thought I'd tell you myself.
I'm leaving.'

My first assumption was that of the receipt of bad news. 'Colin,
there's nothing wrong at home?'

'Oh, no, nothing like that.' Once more the smile was turned on like the sun breaking through a dark cloud, with all the warmth and intensity of days gone by. 'No, old man, it's just that Grits and the headmaster and I can't see eye to eye on a certain subject. As it's two to one against, I've lost. So I'm going.'

Then he leaned forward and ruffled my hair. 'Don't worry, Slow-boots'—and there wasn't the impatient tone that was usually there when he called me that—'don't worry. I shall be all right. All you have to do is to run the house for three weeks. You can manage. You'll get by. Now run along and get it officially from Grits. Don't keep the old bastard waiting. He's in a hell of a temper.'

He was, and after an embarrassing and unprofitable interview in which he only confirmed my appointment, growling at my 'But, sir,' he ended, 'It is sufficient for you to know, Andrews, that Headly *cannot* behave like a gentleman.'

I went back to ask Colin what it was all about, but Colin had gone.

CHAPTER 2

Oxford then for me; new faces, new interests, but I didn't forget him. Twice I wrote to Clonco Castle—knowing, I think, what the result would be—and each time the letter came back, marked in a crabbed hand, 'Not known.' But the thread joined again, by a million-to-one chance, during one of the long vacations.

I was making a bit of money on the side, helping out in the office of an accountant friend of my father's in London as a kind of super, half-paid office boy. I had been sent to Streatham to verify some figures of a gown shop whose audit we were doing. I had got them, and it was too early to catch the train home, not worth while going back to the office. It was a hot, golden summer afternoon, and I decided to go shopping.

Only a stroll and window-shopping; Streatham would not be my choice for the place to do it, but I had time on my hands. I walked slowly, stopping to stare at what was on sale, then suddenly at a road junction I looked up casually at the street name, and it seemed to jump at me . . . the same that had been on that letter which had fallen into my hands from the top locker at school so many years ago.

Abeline Road. It *was* the one. I could see that crabbed writing on the paper so clearly as if I had the letter in my hand that moment. But the number, I couldn't remember that. It was well in the two hundreds. Anyway, Colin's nanny lived there, and it was a chance to try. If I walked down that end someone might know. I might find her, and get some news of Colin.

Then I saw him. He was twenty yards off, walking down the right-hand side of the street. There was no mistaking the tall, slim figure, the fair hair almost glowing in the evening sunshine as he crossed the pavement in front of me. He was carrying some boxes piled high against his chest, and even at that distance I could see the tufts of some green vegetable sticking out from the top one. I checked my stride; somehow, by deep instinct, I did not want a meeting like that. I waited, watching him load the crates into the carrier of the bicycle that was propped up against the kerb. He didn't look round before he mounted the saddle and rode away. I knew what all the answers were before I walked on to face the shop front from which he had emerged.

It was a small greengrocer's; the usual tray of tired vegetables were stacked in tiers outside, the few flowers in small jam jars in the little window. Above there was a faded sign: HEADLY. FRUITERER & FLORIST. I knew it all now, but I had to go in.

An oldish man was sweeping the floor of the shop. He looked up and said, 'Yes, sir?'

I had to say it. It was horrible, but it was the point of no return. 'I'm looking for a Mr. Colin Headly. I think he lives here.'

'Colin? Our boy? You've just missed him, mister. He's gone out on a delivery, but he won't be long.' He looked at me enquiringly. 'Would you be a friend of his?'

I said, 'My name is Harry Andrews. I was at school with him.'

He dropped the broom, face wreathed in smiles. 'Why, Sir Harry! how very nice of you to call. Colin has spoken so often about you. How kind you were to him, asking him to stay so often at Littlestone Court and not minding that we could do nothing in return.' He was pumping my hand now. 'The boy won't be long before he's back, and I know Mother is just making a cup of tea. Come in the back and meet her.'

Slightly dazed by my sudden elevation to the knighthood, the acquisition of a country estate, I followed him into the parlour.

She was older than Colin's father: grey-haired and motherly. It made me terribly ashamed, the number of times I was addressed as 'Sir', despite my protestations to be called just plain 'Harry.' And all the times between, as I sipped my tea, I looked round the small, dingy room, with its horrible plum-coloured tablecloth, the photos of Colin that I knew so well, standing in a row on the imitation-oak sideboard, and I knew that this was—had always been—his home. This was Clonco Castle, the fairy tale that was acted all the time, just as in the mirror of his fantasy I had always been 'Sir Harry' to his parents. All I wanted to do was to get away . . . without being found out by them . . . without letting him down.

I looked at my watch. 'I really must be going. I'm so sorry to have missed Colin, but I can't wait much longer. I've got an appointment.'

'But you must stay, Sir Harry.' It was the old man, darting in

between intervals of serving in the shop. 'There's so much we want
to ask you.'

So I had to stay; had to listen, as I sipped my tea, to all that I
I gathered had taken place in my fabulous country house in Dorset;
had to be thanked for kindness that had never happened. But all
the time, there was the thought of the door opening behind me and
Colin coming in to shatter the dream that had been built up for
these two nice, decent old people over many years. I had to listen
and find out the truth. In between their talk, I managed to ask a
few questions.

'You lived in Ireland once?' I said.

'Oh, yes.' It was Mrs. Headly. 'That was when Colin was very
small. My husband was head gardener to Lord Mounteske, at
Clonco Castle, on the Shannon. It was a lovely place, though I
don't suppose that Colin would remember very much about it. We
were very happy there until his lordship died. He left us a nice little
nest egg, and as we didn't like the new heir we came back here and
started this little business.'

'And then you sent Colin to school?'

'Yes, you see, he had always been so well spoken. And he was
so lucky to spend all that time with his lordship's younger son—the
one that was killed in the war—that we felt we ought to give him
the chance of a proper education. Father always said that they
would be snobbish and stuck-up with the likes of him. But you
showed it wasn't so. It made no difference to you from where he
came.'

Another cup of tea; another dart to the front of the shop by the
old man when the bell rang. Still no Colin; still the reminiscences
went on. It was like a dream, a sort of nightmare where things are
happening but you are outside it all and have no control over them.
'Yes, we had always hoped to send him on to college, you know.
There was enough money put by, but then there was that awful
business at the school, that horrible woman.'

'What woman, Mrs. Headly?'

A plump arm was laid on my arm. 'You know, Sir Harry. Of
course you must. It's just nice of you to pretend not to. But how
could she say those terrible things about him in court? He may
have been a naughty boy, but it wasn't his baby, as she swore it
was. He's had to pay for it. He —we—are still paying.'

I had had enough. I swallowed the rest of my tea and then stood
up. 'I really must go.'

Mrs. Headly had risen at the same time. She gave me that half-frightened, appealing look I had seen before. 'Please stay for Colin.'

'Really, I can't wait any longer. Thank you very much for the tea.' I dashed out, muttering the same sort of apology to the old man in the shop, and ran straight into Colin on the pavement outside.

He was just getting off his bicycle, the basket now empty; the long white overall he was wearing didn't fit, but even in that he looked elegant. But his face—when he saw me and let the cycle fall with a crash on its side and came striding towards me—wasn't so pleasant. The mouth was a tight line, the eyes blazing; two pink spots showed up like stains on dead-white cheeks. He stopped a pace away, and for a moment I thought he was going to hit me. 'What the bloody hell are you doing here?'

What was there to say? Nothing except 'I was passing, Colin. I remembered this address. I just wanted to know how you were.'

He had always seemed taller than I, but now he seemed to tower over me as he gripped the lapels of my jacket. 'You snooping little bastard; you just wanted to pry into everything, that's all. Now don't you ever come here again, do you understand? Not ever again . . . because if you do I'll kill you.'

He let go and stormed into the shop. I lifted the bicycle and propped it against the kerb. I didn't try to go back into the shop. So many fairy castles had crashed to the ground on that summer day. And I had been the cause of it.

There was a long gap then, right up to 1939, with a mount of increasing work after I had qualified, other interests and worries to attend to. There was little time to think of Colin, and of course, I never went back to the shop again. My father had retired by then, and I had joined the firm I still work for in the city. I had my own flat; I was twenty-six, unmarried and unattached. It wasn't that I disliked women; I had enough girl friends to keep me quite happy. But I was shy, set in my ways, perhaps lazy and selfish. I didn't want to take the plunge. So it just went on with a steady round of golf, work, and motoring. There was one girl called Diedre, whom I cared for. But she was much more interested in someone else, and that is another story.

So that last summer went on; the hot, sunny summer when we all had our heads comfortably in the sand, ignoring, because we had to, such little details as the rape of Czechoslovakia. Then one evening Colin rang up.

It was so casual, just as if we had talked to each other the day before, but I knew at once the effort of pride that it had cost him to make the call. 'I got your number from the phone book, Slow-boots, and I wondered if it would be all right if I came round to see you.' It was five years since we last met, but there was no hate in his voice, like the last time. And as usual, I fell for his charm.

He looked a little older than I would have felt the five years warranted; he came in the evening with an old battered suitcase that he dumped on the floor of my sitting room.

'This is a very nice, snug place you've got here, old man,' he said as he walked round on a slow tour of inspection. Now he was close, I could see the lines in his face, the puffiness at the eyes that were the signs of dissipation far beyond his age. I noticed that his suit was shiny at elbows and seat, with one pocket torn, and the cuffs of his shirt were frayed.

He said, 'God! I could do with a drink,' and when I had poured him a stiff whisky and soda from the sideboard he drank it in one gulp.

'That's better.' Once more he made a slow progress round the room, looking at my sporting prints. 'Yes, a very nice, snug place, Slow-boots. Can you put me up for the night?'

'Of course, Colin.' Something of the old warmth had returned and I grabbed at it. Then I said, 'But what about your people? Won't they expect you?'

He didn't look round. 'They're both dead, Harry. And I'm just in the position of changing jobs, so I've nowhere to go.'

I said, 'Of course,' again, then suggested there was something cold in the fridge and I could rustle up quite a decent bottle of Burgandy, or would he rather go out.

'No, it would be nicer here with you. We can talk. I won't be a nuisance. It's only for tonight.'

We sat and ate, and drank and talked, through the long dying twilight, and for once he was rather vague about everything. The old people had died, I gathered, within a few weeks of each other; he had sold the business and gone into 'journalism.' What he wrote for, and when, was rather more difficult to get a grip on, but after his third glass of Burgundy he started to get back into the old form, waxing big on the conversations he had had with various press lords, the things he had told them, and their appreciative answers. It went on until well into the night, and when at last he went to

bed he stood for a moment with his hand on the doorknob of the
spare bedroom and one of those old smiles came that took me right
back to the days of loneliness and interdependence.

'I won't be a nuisance, Slow-boots. It's only for tonight.' He
stayed a month.

I didn't mind, even though my liquor bill trebled and the bottles
of spirits on the sideboard went down at an alarming rate. I didn't
mind even when I started missing small things: a pair of gold cuff
links and a rather nice first edition of Kipling that had been left
me by my grandmother. I had to be out most of the time, and I
didn't know what he was doing; he said he was working, but I
never found out quite where, or at what. The showdown came
partly because of the time he had stayed and partly because of the
way he was drinking.

It was early August; a still, hot morning in those last golden days
of 1939. I had come out of the bedroom in the very early hours to
cross to the front door to see if the morning papers were there, and
if their headlines were blacker, more ominous, than the day before.
It wasn't funny being a reservist in those days with every second
hanging on the phone call that would come to report for duty. I
walked softly, bare feet making no sound on the pile carpet, and as
I passed the sitting-room door, which was half open, there was the
slightest sound from inside. A cork being pulled out of a bottle.

I swung the door open quickly, and he was at the sideboard with
a bottle of whisky tilted halfway to his mouth. It had been there,
for I could see the dribble of spirit down his chin from where he
had jerked it down. He was in a dressing gown, and he did not
look the slightest bit embarrassed.

'For God's sake,' I said.

'For God's sake, what? I'm only topping up the bottles for you
after last night.

'By pouring them down your gullet, you mean.' I was really
angry.

There was a heavy silence before he put the bottle down with a
crash. 'What are you trying to tell me?'

'Exactly what I say, Colin. I can see it dribbling off your chin.
You can drink as much as you like in my house, but not neat,
behind my back, and at seven-thirty in the morning.

'Then I had better go.'

'Yes. I think you had.'

'All right, Slow-boots. I will. I'll be away by the time you get home tonight.' There was another of those looks that made me feel entirely in the wrong. I turned and went out to collect the papers; even the black news from Poland didn't seem to register very much. All through my bath, all through my solitary breakfast. I knew, though I did not see him once, that he was willing me to go and say I was sorry: 'I didn't mean it. Colin. Please stay.' But for the first time it had gone a little too far for that. I had written him off completely. I walked out of the flat without even saying 'Good-bye.'

When I got back in the evening he had gone. I think that the worst part was not the loneliness—for I had got used to him—but going over the place; the fearful, halfhearted way I had to go round looking for anything damaged, anything missing. But there was nothing at first sight; the bed was made, the washing up from breakfast done, the kitchen tidy and spotless. I crept off to bed, feeling rather ashamed of myself. It was only the next morning when his 'bread-and-butter' letter arrived that I missed my binoculars. It wasn't really a thank-you letter at all; it contained a pawn ticket and a scrawled note. 'Sorry about this. I could only get ten pounds on them, but I had to have some cash.' That only hurt; it was the last thing that was unforgivable.

I walked home the next evening, having visited the pawnbrokers and redeemed the glasses. They felt heavy on my shoulder; heavier even than the bad news that screamed from every newspaper banner I passed; the shadowed, secret look on the face of everyone I passed; the knowledge of the shape of things to come.

I stopped outside the pub at the corner of the mews where I lived. I was lonely as well as fearful; I wanted a drink, and I wanted to talk to some other human being. I had a scotch with the landlord and we talked brightly about the paper strength of the Polish Army and the impregnability of the Maginot line. I don't think either of us believed a word of it, but it was the sort of thing that helped. I finished my drink and paid for the bottle I was taking away. 'Well, Joe, I'll be seeing you.'

'Yes, Mr. Andrews.' He looked at me rather doubtfully for a moment before reaching for a clip of papers that hung behind the till. 'You're a Territorial, aren't you?'

'Yes.'

He leaned forward confidentially. 'Well, I wouldn't worry you in times like this, but everything's so uncertain. I guess we all get a bit absent-minded now, with so much to think about. But that cheque of yours—you postdated it a month and you might be called up. Anything might happen.'

'Cheque?' I turned to stare at him.

'Yes. The one your friend brought in to cash for you the other day.' He slid the oblong of pink paper over the counter towards me. 'I only spotted the wrong month after he had gone. You made it for the twenty-seventh of September, not August. I wouldn't have worried you, but—' A gesture of the shoulders summed up how we all felt those days before the war.

I put down the bottle carefully on the counter and picked up the cheque; it was one of mine, but I had not written it. It was a good forgery, good enough to get by the bank; anyone but me. I suppose Colin had postdated it deliberately to avoid the immediate chance of any slip-up.

I tried to keep my voice steady as I said, 'Sorry. I can't think how that could have happened. I'll alter it now.' I changed the month and initialled it, then went back to the flat and sat through the growing darkness, finished half the bottle of whisky and listened to the radio. The news was worse, but it didn't matter any more. It was Colin that I was thinking about; not the twenty pounds that he had taken off me, but the fact that he would go on doing it to other people. It was a complete write-off as far as I was concerned, but it would be better to nip it right in the bud. It was my duty to go to the police. But somehow on the other side, I just couldn't do it. I compromised by saying I would sleep on the problem, which was a mistake, for at two in the morning the phone jangled, and half awake, I listened to the adjutant of my Territorial Headquarters telling me to put on my uniform at once, go down the Edgeware Road, where I would find the sergeant major proceeding on his bicycle in the opposite direction, pick him up, and go to the drill hall for soldiering for an indefinite period.

If this were fiction there would have been some dramatic meeting of the two of us, with me as a struggling company commander and Colin as a suave, comfortable colonel on the staff. It didn't happen. He just disappeared into the melting pot of war with so many of my friends. Funnily, I heard of him twice, indirectly. And the first time, I really didn't know about it until after it had happened.

It was in the base camp at Mersa Matruh. I had come down from the 'Blue' to collect the men's pay. I had to stay overnight, and there was no poker game on in the mess that evening; nothing to do but sit in the stuffy tent that served as the anteroom to the mess, turning over the tattered copies of paper-backed novels so thoughtfully supplied by the Red Cross, while the flies and other insects flared and spluttered their lives away in the hissing glare of the paraffin lamp.

It jumped at me suddenly, the name on the title page: COLIN HEADLY. For a moment I stared at it stupidly, thinking, It must be a coincidence. There must be hundreds of Colin Headlys; probably only a *nom de plume*. But I started to read the book, and went on back to my tent and stayed until I had finished the whole thing.

It wasn't really good; it didn't really qualify for that irritating phrase of reviewers, 'I couldn't put the book down,' but it wasn't that bad, either. It was a 'cloak-and-dagger' job, set in London at the beginning of the war, with some pretty lurid scenes between the hero and a female Nazi spy. I don't think I am a prude, especially in my reading, but there was a little too much of the breast and buttock in it; most unnecessary to the story, and planted deliberately for just that effect. I don't think I had read the first chapter before I *knew* it was Colin. Apart from the somewhat forced sex, there were little phrases, little turns of expression that were his. No direct proof, for there was no 'blurb' on the jacket, and the dedication was to 'Nancy,' which meant nothing. I remember thinking that at least he had found something he could do, and I was glad of it. The next morning, I went back to my unit, and the bloody battle of Sidi Rezegh was on, and there were other things to think about.

Only after Alamein, when we had been pulled out, exhausted, and I was on my first leave in Cairo, did it register again. I saw his name on the dust jacket of a book in a shop in the Malika Farida. I bought it, and the mixture was the same as before. But this time there was no doubt, for his photo and a highly improbable biography were on the back. When I read it I wrote a brief note of congratulation to him in care of his publishers. Perhaps it was a casualty in the wartime mails; perhaps he never got it; perhaps he couldn't be bothered. At any rate, there was no answer. I was away after that on one of those sudden, unwanted army travels, and so forgot.

The end of the war, and plenty of other things to keep my thoughts busy. There was the reality of getting back to work; two years of hard slogging and very little play. I saw Colin's name in the press from time to time, the intervals between short stories and articles getting shorter. Then one day, going down to see a client in Brighton, I read the first part of a serial of his in one of the better national magazines. It was good, really exciting, far better than anything he had done before. I saw that it was going to be made into a film, and I suppose that old possessive snobbism came to the top of my subconscious once again. I wrote to him that night when I got home. This time in care of the paper. I never expected to get an answer, but I did, within a week. And that was one of the turning points of my life.

Well, there is Colin. Dead now . . . liar, forger, cheat . . . but my first friend. And what of the other side? Lois, his wife? That started when I got his letter.

CHAPTER 3

It came with an Irish stamp and postmark. It was written on very good quality paper with the heading 'Clonco Castle.'

Dear old Slow-boots,

How very nice to hear from you again, and thank you so much for your kind remarks, which I don't deserve. I feel so guilty in not having tried to get in touch with you before, but you can gather that these days I am kept pretty busy, and living out here tends to cut you off. By the greatest good fortune, I am coming to London next week (the usual round of agent, publisher, and editors) and *insist* you lunch with me at Rule's on Friday, the 25th. One o'clock, then, and if I don't hear by return, I'll take it as set. All news then.

Yours, as ever,
Colin

I got to Rule's on the dot of one, and even after all the years that had gone between there was not a second's hesitation in spotting him as he leaned against the corner wall of the crowded bar. The hair was still that sleek golden cap; perhaps a little silver in it now, but the contrast with those blue, blue eyes made it all the more striking. He was dressed as a properous country gentleman: loose collar, club tie, checked waistcoat, and a beautifully cut fawn tweed suit. I could just glimpse one foot propped up on the bar rail, and the brown shoe was polished like a mirror. I put my hat and umbrella on the rack and edged through the crowd to join him.

'Harry, my dear old man!' He was holding both my hands as we stood very close. The charming smile was just the same as years before, but I could smell a lot of whisky on his breath, and his eyes were bloodshot; the glass at his elbow was almost empty, and I wondered how many he had had already.

'Harry, this is wonderful! You haven't changed a bit. Except—' He prodded my waistline. 'You're putting on a bit of weight.'

'That's sitting at a desk five and a half days a week,' I said. 'I haven't had a holiday or any proper exercise for two years. But tell me about—'

'No. We celebrate first.' He called the barman. 'What are you having, Harry?'

'A sherry, please.'

'Don't be a bloody fool. This is a celebration. A large pink gin is what you want. Thank God I can afford it now.'

Always he made me sound priggish and pompous. 'No, thank you, Colin.' I was watching the barman pour him a very large whisky. 'I have got to work this afternoon—on some rather tricky stuff. Big drinks at lunch time always make me sleepy.'

'Well, have a small one then.' There was petulance, almost anger, in his voice.

After I had given in he made me talk first; all through the time it took me to drink the second half, while he had another double, I told him what had happened in the years between. When I had finished, he said, 'And what did you get out of it all, Slow-boots?'

'A few desert sores and a bullet wound in the calf. But it's all right now.'

'No gongs?'

'No gongs.'

'They gave me an O.B.E.—for nothing. I'm not particularly proud of it.'

While we had lunch, and I settled for a hesitant beer with it, against his third double scotch, he told me something about himself. He had not been able to do any real active service, having been discovered, surprisingly, to have a gastric ulcer. But he had managed to get into the Ministry of Information. His time had mostly been at home, during the blitz, but later he had been sent to the Middle East, where he had picked up a lot of colour and copy for his books. He had started writing almost as soon as he left me, and it had gone steadily better and better; his last had broken the twenty-thousand barrier of sales in hard covers, and it was also going to be filmed. But the taxman had no pity for poor authors, so he had gone to live in the Irish Free State. It was a little easier there. But—

I had been watching his face all the time he was talking, watching the break-up of it with alarm and pity. It wasn't the soft boy's face I had known any more. Character showed there, but it was being smeared away by too good living, too much drink. Apart from the puffy eyes, there were those tell-tale veins mottling each cheek. But as he talked something else was happening. he was changing colour, going grey, with beads of sweat pricking out on his forehead. 'But—' he said again, and then leaned forward with a half groan, half grunt, hands clasped to his stomach against the edge of the table. 'Sorry, excuse me,' he said after a moment, and then got up quickly and vanished towards the gentleman's cloakroom.

When he came back he looked a little better; there was a trace of colour coming back into his face. 'Sorry, Harry', he said as he sat down. 'I forgot to tell you that I, too, have some scars of war. I got amoebic dysentery when I was in Baghdad, and it never seems to go. Sometimes, like this, it plays me up like hell.'

The subject changed, and now, with two pink gins and a beer singing in my head, things were coming out easily that I had been wanting to say for a long time. 'Clonco ... Colin. Clonco Castle? Has that dreamboat really come home?'

He didn't answer for a moment. Then he said, 'So you knew. Or did the old people tell you?'

'Both.'

'I'm not going to make excuses, Harry. I lived a great lie. I wanted to be someone, someone I wasn't. I loved that place, but it wasn't mine, never could be mine. I dreamed all sorts of things that could never come true, to try to make them come alive. Do understand.'

'I do. We've both grown up now.'

He took a long draw at his cigarette. 'Well, it's true, at last. When I started to get into the money I made enquiries, and found that the last of the old owners was dying, broke and the whole place was falling down. I made him an offer, and like a wise man, he took it. Now it is all mine.'

There was a pause while he stirred his coffee. 'I always loved it, even when Father worked there. They were always so kind to me. His lordship and herself. There was always sixpence for any errand that I did, always a sweet for me whenever I met her in the garden. But I wasn't allowed to walk in the front door. Harry, have you ever thought what it must be like to trespass when you walk through a front door? When you can only use the back?'

'I think I can understand that.'

'So can I now. Because it is mine.'

He broke off suddenly, and he was staring over my shoulder with a strange, faraway look in his eyes. It was only when I turned to glance behind me that I realized what it implied. There was a girl lunching at the next table, a young girl who had thrown her coat off and was leaning towards her companion, so that it was easy to see the soft curves of her breasts shadowed in the opening of her light summer frock. I remember the look that Colin had then; the same as that of a lecherous brigadier I had once the misfortune to have had to accompany to Madame Bardia's cabaret in Cairo. It was exactly the same. Colin was undressing that girl, in his mind, garment by garment, to the bare flesh. It wasn't very pleasant.

I picked up my cigarettes and matches and put them in my pocket. 'I must be going, Colin.'

'No, don't for a minute.' He came back to me with a jerk. 'Not for a minute,' he repeated, pulling an envelope out of his breast pocket and pushing it towards me across the table. 'That's yours.'

'What is it?' I picked it up and looked at it blankly.

'Fifteen pounds, Slow-boots. It's been on my conscience for the last ten years. Those binoculars of yours. The tenner plus 5 per cent interest. I'm sorry, it was a bloody thing to do. But I hadn't got a job, as I told you. I was desperate.'

'Don't worry. All that's gone under the bridge now. I'd forgotten.'

'I hadn't. Please take it. Then I shall feel clean again.'

I waited for him to say something about that cheque, but he didn't. 'Now I really must go,' I said as I stuffed the envelope in my pocket.

'No, there's one more thing.' His hand gripped mine across the table; his eyes were fixed on mine; eager, almost pleading.

'Come and stay, Harry. It's the least I can ask. You look tired out. You said you hadn't had a holiday in two years. Look, man, there's all the shooting, fishing, and sailing to be had in the world there; the place is a bit broken down still, but we'll make you comfortable, and if you get bored with us you can go off by yourself for a few days at a time. We've got two cars, and all Kerry and Connemara are within two hundred miles of us.'

I said, 'I'd love it, Colin. But I've only just taken on an assistant, and it wouldn't be really fair to leave him.'

'Why not? If he's any good—and I can't imagine you taking on anyone who wasn't—the best thing would be to leave him on his own for a bit. This must be a slack time for you, and the best time for us. Do come.'

'Us? I said. 'Who is "us"?'

A faint shadow crossed his face. 'God! We've been talking so much about ourselves that I forgot to tell you that one. I got myself married, just after the war. You'll like Lois, Harry, I know you will.'

I left him with a promise that I would try to fly over to Dublin for a few days the next week, and that he would meet me in the car. In case anyone thinks I am a complete, sentimental fool, when I got home that night I did a little medical research in my encyclopaedia. I wanted to find out a bit more about Colin's symptoms at lunch. I looked at amoebic dysentery, and then at cirrhosis of the liver. The symptoms of both were practically identical.

Curiosity really made me go; there was the urge of a good holiday, and as Colin had said, my new assistant, young Johns, had settled down very nicely and was quite capable of looking after everything. But the strongest reason was the urge to meet his wife, this Lois of his; the one thing he had forgotton to talk about until the end of our conversation. I wondered what kind of woman could stand Colin for any length of time. So I wired him I would fly over on the following Monday, got together a suitcase of old clothes, and with that and my golf clubs boarded a plane for Dublin.

We had a good tail wind all the way, and arrived at least ten minutes before schedule. There was no one waiting to meet me in the entrance hall, which was understandable in the circumstances, so I picked up my gear and went out to the car park to await Colin's arrival.

There were quite a few cars there, and I walked down the lines of them, wondering if he was there. Then, three cars away, I saw him, though he didn't see me. I stopped dead, watching . . . the fair, almost silver hair bent towards the mop of dark curls; the completeness in which he and the girl with him were engrossed with each other. I remember thinking, It's good, he's found one who cares and he loves her very much too. I couldn't stand there and watch; I had to go and make myself known. Another car was parked too close to Colin's, the driver's, side for me to squeeze in, so the only thing to do was to go and wrap on the passenger-side window.

I don't think they had any clue that anyone was near until I did it; there was a sort of intensity locking them together that one could feel even from the other side of the glass. When they did hear me knock they jerked apart with an uncanny suddenness; a look of anger crossed Colin's face as he stared over the girl's shoulder and

saw me. It was gone in a flash, and then he leaned across and
wound down the window on her side.

'Hello, Harry. You're early—as usual. Must you creep up like
that and give us a fright?'

I was looking at the girl. The dark curls fitted her head closely,
like a snaking cap; the eyes were big, wide, and nearly as blue as
Colin's; the face, with a creamy complexion and soft curling mouth,
was made to be kissed. For a brief second I envied Colin, then was
glad for his sake. I held out my hand through the window. 'I'm
sorry, I didn't mean to startle you. We had a tail wind; that's why
I'm early. Anyway, it's very nice to meet you, Mrs. Headly.'

She did not take my hand, and on Colin's face there was an
instant flicker of the expression I had seen the moment I surprised
them. Then he laughed, but there was no laughter in his eyes. 'You
would get it wrong, wouldn't you, Slow-boots? This isn't Lois. This
is my secretary, Sally Macgrath. You can call her Sal.' It was
typical of him to make the invitation on her behalf. 'Sling your bags
in the back, old man, and get in front with us. Move over, Sal.
There's plenty of room for three.'

I didn't know what to say. There was not much anyone could
say in such a situation. As I loaded my clubs and suitcase into the
back I could feel the hot flush of embarrassment spreading over my
face. I got in the front and we drove off in silence. I looked across
at Colin and the set of his mouth was one thin line. There was a
faint smear of lipstick in one corner of it. I knew I had started my
holiday with one very black mark against me.

Colin relaxed and started to talk; casually, about my journey, the
weather, and its future outlook. He was not the smart Colin I had
seen in London, being dressed now in a pair of corduroy slacks and
a great hairy polo sweater. Sal did not say a word, yet I was far
more aware of her presence than that of the pleasant, rumbling
voice farther to my right. Usually I hated sitting three in the front
seat of a car; no one is quite comfortable, and the man away from
the driver always suffers most. There is no place to put his legs,
and the discomfort of bony, interlocking hips usually makes it a
torture. This time there was something different. The length of her
hip and thigh was clinging, close-fitting to mine; warm, sensuous,
and rather disturbing. I thought at once of some of the passages in
Colin's books.

She did not speak until we were out on the road to Naas, well in the suburbs. When the voice came it was soft, with a pleasant Irish brogue.

'Pull up at the next chemist's, Colin. I've got to get your medicine and that hair stuff for Lois.'

Colin grunted, and after a few hundred yards pulled up outside a chemist's shop. I opened the door and got out. 'Can I get it for you?'

'No, thanks. I'd better go. This stuff for Lois is tricky, and it usually takes a bit of time.' As she slipped past me there was again that intense nearness of something very desirable. I got back in the car to sit with Colin.

'I'm sorry. I didn't know you were ill.'

'It's my guts, Harry. I told you in London.' I could see he was going that grey colour again.

'I'm terribly upset that I made that dreadful *faux pas* at the airport.'

'That's O.K. Not to worry. You weren't to know.' He wasn't really with me as he answered; he was staring across the other side of the street. 'That looks like a nice clean bar over there, and the sun's nearly over the yard-arm. I'll go and set the drinks up. You wait for Sal and bring her over.' The sweat was starting to prick out on his forehead.

'It's bloody, is it?'

'Bloody.' He got out from his side without another word and walked over the road.

I had to wait another three minutes before Sally came back. 'Where has Colin got to?' she said abruptly.

'He's over the road. Setting us up a drink.'

'Setting himself up a couple of stiff ones before we get there, you mean.'

I had got out of the car and was standing beside her now. She was taller than I had thought, and our eyes were nearly level. 'You are very fond of Colin, aren't you, Mr. Andrews?' It was said very softly.

'Yes, I am, indeed. But please call me Harry. And I'm so very sorry about that stupid mistake of mine at the—'

She stopped me by laying a hand quickly on my arm. 'We were just engrossed in talking about one of his plots. I don't blame you for getting the wrong idea. But I'm very fond of him, too.'

'I'm glad.'

'So one of your jobs in life while you are here is to try to help stop him destroying himself. He's drinking himself to death.'

'But Mrs. Headly . . . Lois? Can't she help?'

She gave me a slow sidelong glance. 'You haven't met her yet, have you?'

'No.'

'Then I'd be a bitch if I said anything to influence you. Come on. Let's get over there quick, before he's put himself under the counter.' I followed her across the street, wondering again just what sort of woman Colin had married.

The bar was behind a little grocer's shop, and when we got in it was fairly obvious that Colin had had those two quick ones. The colour was back in his face and his eyes were bright; he was talking hard, too, to the girl behind the counter. Sally didn't say a word, but I knew how closely she was watching. I was thirsty, made more so by the presence of someone who had already been drinking. I had just reached for my gin and tonic when a church bell started a slow, steady chime from somewhere nearby. I was left, my glass in my hand, the one black Protestant. Colin and Sally put theirs down, and with the girl behind the bar bent their heads reverently and crossed themselves while the Angelus rang. No one said anything about it, we had the other half for the road, but I knew I had made my second stupid gaffe.

I didn't dare talk about it until we were well on the road to Tullamore. Then a little gin on top of a lot of nerve made me say, 'I didn't know you were a Catholic, Colin.'

He didn't answer for a moment; then he said, 'I don't think I'm a very good one. I did it to keep the peace with Lois and Sal. At least, I'm lucky in having a broad-minded priest. It's nice when you've done something particularly bad to be able to get it off your chest completely. And you, Slow-boots, what are your leanings?'

'I'm nothing, really. But I've often wondered about your faith. Someone told me it only appeals to the very stupid or the very intelligent. I'm neither, so I don't think it would help.'

Sally's one contribution to the conversation was a short, explosive laugh which effectively cut off any more of my theories.

We drove on with long silences between snatches of talk about his work and future plans. I felt very out of it. Once when there was some private joke between them and they laughed, I caught the look of their eyes as they met in the driving mirror. Then I was absolutely certain. There is one look you can never disguise; one

look between two people that, caught by a third party, is unmistakable. Those two, Colin and Sally, knew each other entirely: both
physically and spiritually. And in a way, it didn't shock me; it only
made me feel that the wife I had never met was somehow at fault.

The country was getting more interesting now; rolling, wooded,
park land as I was told we were nearing the banks of the Shannon.
Colin had gradually grown quieter, and then suddenly gave one of
those half-grunting groans that I had heard before. I looked across,
and his face had gone that awful shade of grey again.

'Are you all right, old man?'

He grunted again, then said through his teeth, 'I can last to Birr.
But don't talk to me, either of you, for Christ's sake, until we get
there.'

When we drove into the little square of the country town, he
slammed the car hard up against the pavement outside the door of
the hotel, wrenched open his door, and disappeared inside at a run.

I looked at Sally. 'Shall we . . . ?'

'No.' She sat quite still, looking straight ahead. 'No, he'll just go
to the cloakroom, be sick and everything else you can think of, then
go to the bar and have a couple of quick doubles to pull himself
together. He's best left alone, I know.'

I said, 'These attacks . . . they're bad. Has he seen a doctor?'

Again there was that short explosive laugh. 'He doesn't hold with
doctors. And if you had seen ours you wouldn't, either. He knows
nothing, and is sober slightly less of the time than Colin.'

I didn't like that. 'Colin sick!' I said angrily.

'Yes, he's sick. And you don't like me for facing facts. You said
you'd try to help. But you can't until you know everything.'

'Such as?'

'You'll soon see. Lois—' She broke off quickly, slid away the
hand she had placed impulsively on my knee. There were steps on
the pavement outside the car, and then Colin wrenched open the
driving-side door. A better-looking Colin, with colour in his cheeks
again; there was also an aroma of whisky.

'God! that was a near thing,' he said as he let the car into gear.
'It's the worst of these damned attacks, you never know when they
are going to hit you.'

'Why don't you see a doctor, Colin?'

He laughed. 'Wait till you've met O'Hara, and you'll know why.
He's drunk most of the time. All he can think about is hunting and
booze.'

'I didn't mean a local man. I meant some specialist in Dublin, or London.'

'Look, Harry. I know what I've got. If you go and see one of those clever Joes all he does is to pass you on to another pal, then on and on, round the silver ring. They all say something different, and you finish up two hundred guineas in the red, with not a bloody thing done. I know what I've got'—he repeated the words softly softly—'and I know the cure for it. Whisky, Slow-boots; lots and lots of whisky; as frequently as possible.'

The girl beside me made a faint movement; Colin looked across at her. 'Sal doesn't approve of the treatment. Do you Sal?'

'No!' The sudden sharpness of the one word made me jump. 'You know what I think, Colin. Do you want me to tell Harry here?'

'You can if you want to.' He sounded completely disinterested. 'Then it need not be discussed again. But it's such a bore, and I don't want to frighten Harry off. I want him to stay for a long time.'

'I don't think he will. When he sees the way you're getting through the stuff, how it's ruining your work; not only in quantity, but in quality. And Lois—'

'Oh, for God's sake! Leave Lois out of it!' There was an angry tension between them now. 'If you've been trying to slide in a sly word to Harry about us when my back was turned, he knows it already; if you added that Lois encourages me to drink, it just isn't true. She doesn't try to preach at me, which is a point in her favour. Let him decide for himself when he's had a chance to see a bit of my lovely household.'

It was horribly embarrassing. I turned away to look out of the window as we crossed the long bridge over the broad, winding, shining Shannon, flanked by its banks of reeds. It was very beautiful, but all I could think of at that moment was why I had ever said I would come; just how long it would take me to get in touch with my firm, asking them to fake a telegram to call me back to London at once.

Colin started talking again softly. It was almost as if he had read my thoughts and Sally wasn't there. He said, 'Look, Slow-boots, I asked you to come because I wanted you to enjoy yourself. I owe you a very great deal from the past, and it was the least I could do. I don't want it spoilt by a lot of bloody stupid talk. I told you you'd like Lois before you came. You will. Both of you have a lot in common. You would be good for her. You can take her out for some fishing and sailing, and leave Sal and me to get on with the work.'

So that was it; I was being made use of again, and what made me even angrier was that Colin could still smile and talk me into doing what he wanted.

We did not speak any more while we swung off the main road into a long leafy lane, arched over with twisted trees. Through them, to one side, was a tempting gleam of water. Then suddenly the road turned to skirt a long crumbling stone wall. 'The property,' said Colin suddenly, without looking at it.

It went on for a long time, that wall, but at last there was a break in it, flanked by two lodge gates. As we slowed down to turn in, I couldn't help noticing that there was no glass in either of the facing windows, that the gates themselves had gone, and not even the gateposts were in the position they should have been. One tilted away to the left; the other, broken in half, was lying right on its side. I didn't say anything, but for the second time Colin seemed to guess my thoughts. 'I've given up even the thought of letting the lodges for nothing. The types that take them only steal our chickens and prefer to live in a bog. As for the gates, they're a sign of great affluence in these parts. It means that you've got a combine harvester which has been driven through not quite accurately.'

As he said this we were going down the long, straight drive; the trees, the same as those in the lane, old, arched, and twisted. All the time, Sally had not said a word.

Suddenly the trees parted and there was the house sprawling in front of us. I hadn't really expected a castle—Colin, even in his dream days, had said it was not really one; but still there was a vague sense of disappointment. There was a high grey façade, with huge Corinthian pillars supporting the arch over the front door; mid-nineteenth century, out of place here, and anywhere not in very good taste. As we swung round in front on the sweep of the drive to draw up outside, the tires of the car hissed on the rough, weed-strewn gravel; I looked up and saw the front close for the first time. There was an immediate memory of something I had seen in a film once. *Gone with the Wind*. Tara in its worst days. Everything was flaking and falling down.

As we pulled up, the high front door opened and a flood of red spewed out from it. Not scarlet, but the deeper, richer tone of thoroughbred Irish setters—there must have been six at least. They bounded round the car, barking, while Colin bellowed at them to

keep quiet. Then behind them, framed in the doorway, was a girl.
I saw Lois for the first time. Like the castle itself, she was not what
I expected.

It seems to be an accepted rule that very tall men always marry
short girls; fair mates with dark. I'm sure it doesn't really match
up that way, but that is what one usually thinks. With Colin's
hair and colouring, I had always imagined his wife would be very
dark—indeed, the sight of Sally's black curls at the airport had
been one reason for the stupid mistake. I was certain Lois would
be the same that this first sight of her was almost a shock.

She was very small; I think that was the first thing I noticed
about her. Then the stillness of her as she stood framed in the
doorway, as if all the time she were listening and waiting for something. Then there was the hair; shoulder length, a titian shade
matching exactly the coats of the setters. It flamed red in the last
rays of the setting sun, as red as the dogs that had gone back to
surround her. It seemed to me to be a piece of monstrous affectation.
I had not liked the picture that had been built up for me in words;
now this first sight made my distrust grow even deeper.

There was an uncertain pause after I had got out of the car and
stood waiting for Colin to finish rummaging for my bags in the
back. Sally had slipped out past me, holding the package she had
bought at the chemist's, and walked over towards the door. She
gave it to Lois, who made no attempt to come forward. I did not
hear a word pass between them. Then Sally slipped out of sight,
into the darkness of the hall. A kind of sudden, brittle tension hung
over everything. Behind me Colin was cursing as he tried to free
the end of my golf bag from the back seat. Whether his delay was
deliberate or accidental I did not know, nor care. But I couldn't
just stand there, waiting. I walked towards Lois at the door, holding
out my hand.

She did not move an inch forward to meet me.

'Hello, Mrs. Headly.'

'Hello, Harry—may I call you that? I've heard so much about
the linchpin of Colin's life, the sober, reliable, refuge that he can
always fly to when he needs help. I feel I know you that well
already.'

Her hand was smooth and cool; the voice deep, slightly husky.
She did not look at me when she spoke, but over my shoulder at
something far beyond. I saw the colour of her eyes. They were

amber; as clear as those of her dogs. The feeling that she was deliberately posing recurred, strengthening my dislike.

I said that I hoped she would use my first name, and I could call her Lois. I tried to put the warmth of a gratified guest into the words, but it just did not work. It sounded false and stiff even to me. She did not seem to notice. 'Come on in' was all she said.

She turned and led the way into the hall, Colin coming up just behind with the bags, the dogs sniffing and fussing round my legs. Colin dumped the luggage in a heap and came over to stand between us. Neither he nor Lois attempted to touch or speak to the other, and I sensed again that brittle tension hanging close, all round us in the air. Colin said, 'Well, here it is, the ancestral home, old man, though, God knows, it's all falling down. Let's all go and have a bloody stiff drink. I need it.'

I managed to get up to my room about an hour later. I had to ask if I could, for no one seemed to have thought of asking me if I wanted to. Colin made it a heavy session, with frequent visits to the massive mahogany sideboard, the top of which was almost entirely covered with bottles. He seemed to have switched in favour of gin, and Lois and I had the same; the only difference was that I had two doubles thrust on me while Lois insisted on pouring her own, which consisted of one very small single.

We were, apparently, in what was the dining room, and between trying to cope with the drinks and Colin's small talk, I had plenty of time to take everything in. The rest of the furniture and fittings were in the same class as the sideboard: old, solid, good, but ruined by neglect. The top of the long table had once been a lovely piece of wood, but now had lost all its former sheen, and was pitted and scarred as if someone had tried to skate on it; two of the matching set of chairs were propped up against the wall, and I could not help but notice that one of them had a leg missing. Colin saw the direction in which I was looking.

'Admiring the heirlooms, Slow-boots? You know, they all used to belong to my wife's family. They owned the place.' I started, realizing how like Colin it was to have kept this information from me until now.

'When her father died,' Colin continued, 'her uncle went through what was left of the fortune in a few years. He was glad enough of the opportunity to sell the furniture along with everything else.' He glanced quickly at Lois, but she seemed absorbed in one of the pictures. 'Most of the pieces would have been too big and heavy for him to move, anyway. They were pretty ropey then, but God knows, they're far worse now. All anyone does in this house is to wander round, looking at things to be done and muttering "Time enough," It's a national motto, worse than the Spanish "*Mañana.*" The story of the way the table got like it is, is funny, though. It seems one of the aunts was a bit soft in the head for quite a time before they finally put her away. She used to persist in creeping down here first thing in the morning, before anyone was up to stop her, and polish it with Brasso!'

'I don't think it's funny. I think it's rather sad.' It was the first time Lois had spoken to him directly. She had been wandering round the room, glass in hand, fiddling with things. Now she was fingering the fringe of one of the huge velvet draperies that hung at the long windows. They were just like all the rest; faded, with tears just held together by safety pins. With no pelmet to hide the top, it was easy to see that several of the rings were missing.

She turned round. 'Colin, I've got to have some new draperies.'

He laughed. 'What, for something the size of a tennis court, and we never draw them? Don't you remember, darling, we measured them up once, and it came to over sixty yards? No, thank you, I've better things to spend my money on—at least that little the taxman leave me.' Somehow the 'darling' made it sound all the worse.

It was then that I made my bid to get out of the room and upstairs. Lois had not answered him, but she had turned her back again and I could see a pink flush spreading up her neck. I said, 'I'm a bit tired, and feel awfully scruffy. Do you mind if I go up to my room and do something about it?'

Colin was over at the sideboard, again, helping himself to another drink. Lois turned and said, 'I'll take you.' When we got out in the hall, my bag was just where Colin had left it. I picked it up and followed her upstairs.

'Mind the banister rail,' she said over her shoulder as we reached the first turn. 'It's a bit rocky here; I nearly went over once.'

The room was spotlessly clean, the bed looked comfortable, but about everything there was that same rickety, forgotten appearance. I put my bag down and looked around slowly, trying not to notice the great bulging crack in the plaster of the ceiling that was directly above where my head would lie. Lois stood in the door, hands on hips. 'All right?' she said.

'Fine.' I waited for her to say what time dinner would be, but the information was apparently not forthcoming. 'Is there anything else you want, Harry?'

I looked at the pitcher of water standing on the marble wash-stand. 'If you could show me where the bathroom is?'

She stood there and roared with laughter. 'Do you mean the bathroom or the loo? If it's the first, there isn't one. We take our baths in the loch. If it's the second, there's only one in the house and that's down in a passage past Colin's study. If you want to go through you have to knock if the master is at his work and get permission' She spoke in a cruel, hard voice, and Sally's comments about her making Colin unhappy came back to me.

'I just wondered if I could have some hot water for a shave. But it doesn't matter.'

'Oh, that. It's easy.' She walked across to a corner where the boards were not covered by carpet, prised up a loose length, and shouted into the depths below. 'Mary! The gentleman would like some hot water for shaving. Bring it up at once!'

There was a muffled reply, and then she let the board fall back into place. 'It goes straight through into the kitchen,' she said, 'and there's always Mary or me around there. Just shout. It saves all the bother of walking downstairs.'

'I'll remember.'

Those amber eyes were fixed on mine mockingly. 'Then I'll leave you now.'

The door closed behind her softly.

After Mary, a dark, buxom girl with rosy cheeks, had brought me a can of hot water and I had had my wash and shave, I got out my writing things and wrote a letter to my assistant. I was to be wired not later than Friday that the income tax appeal case was coming up before the High Court, and I must come back at once. I wondered how soon in the morning I would be able to slip down to the village and post it.

The dull booming of a gong from somewhere down below woke me from my reverie. No one had told in what degree of state they dined at Clonco Castle, so I was relieved to see Sally standing waiting for me in the hall wearing the same frock she had worn at the airport. 'Colin insists you are to be treated as one of the family while you are here,' she said. 'I agreed heartily, as it would have meant me getting out and cleaning most of the silver. It hasn't been touched for months. We eat in the kitchen. Come on.'

The kitchen was stone-flagged, long, with great beams in the

ceiling that sprouted their rows of hooks to carry the bacon. Along
one wall was a huge Aga stove; down the centre of the room a large
deal table, now covered with a cheap plastic tablecloth and set with
plastic plates and cups. In the master's chair at one end, tilting it
back, was Colin, reading a newspaper. He gave me one of his smiles
as I came in, but when he spoke his voice was thick and I could
see his eyes were very bloodshot.

'Sit down, Slow-boots. Lois and I have had a row about you. I
said you would much rather eat *"en famille"*; she said that we should
get everything pansied up for the distinguished guest. I won, but
what do you think?'

'It's fine with me. I take it as a great compliment.'

'Are you sure?' It was Lois, standing over the stove, so much in
the shadow from the light of the single naked bulb that hung
somewhere crookedly from the ceiling that I had not realized she
was there.

'Quite sure, Lois, thank you.' Colin had gone back to reading
the sporting page.

The meal she served was excellent. Even the plastic plates could
not take away anything from the quality of the pork chops, the
sauté potatoes, and the fresh green peas. It was when we got to the
coffee stage that I found a chance to remark on another aspect of
this Alice in Wonderland world. I know a bit about silver, and as
I picked up the wafer-thin spoon to stir my coffee I knew that it
was old Irish, as the knives and forks had been, and priceless; a
strange contrast to the plastic dishes.

'What lovely silver,' I said, looking at Lois.

'Yes. It belonged to my grandmother. I tell Colin it's a shame to
use it all the time like this, but he says what was it made for but
to use, and as we haven't anything else, it would be a waste of time
to buy another set of everything from Woolworth's.'

She did not look back at me; every word was glanced and spoken
towards Colin. I could see her point. It was unreasonable, when he
was, as my professional guess, making at least five thousand pounds
a year. There was an underlying anger in her voice that was
unnerving. He scraped his chair back and got to his feet rather
unsteadily. I could see his face draining of colour, starting to go
that awful shade of grey that I had seen before. 'I think I'll go . . .
and do a bit of work . . . Harry . . . if you don't mind. I may be
late . . . so I'll say good night now, and see you in the morning.'

It was said in jerks. He lurched rather than walked out of the room; Sally followed him with a muttered 'Good night' to me. No one said anything to Lois. And I was left alone with her.

A long silence; she stood by the stove, looking at the door that Sally had cloed quietly behind her. Then, 'Like some more coffee, Harry?'

'No, thank you. I'll get to bed myself soon, if you don't mind. I've had a long day.'

'Of course. I—' She was going to say something else, then changed her mind quickly.

'Can I help you with the washing up first?' I said.

'No. I just stack for the girl in the morning.'

'Then I'll say good night.'

'Good night, Harry.'

I left her standing there, watching the door with the same peculiar sense of expectancy that I had noticed when I first arrived.

It was true I was dog-tired. When I had turned off the light switch and padded back across the bare boards to my island of furniture in the middle of the room, found the bed surprisingly comfortable, even forgotten about that bulging crack in the plaster just above my head, I thought I would doze off in a few minutes. But somehow I could not relax: the house seemed quiet, too quiet, as I lay there, listening. There was no sound of work, the expected clatter of a typewriter that I hoped to hear. There was no movement of any kind. Only once, just before I drifted off, I thought I heard someone groaning.

CHAPTER 4

A soft, bright morning, the birds waking me with their dawn chorus outside the window, the loch, glittering in the sun beyond the trees, looking so inviting. The house was still quite silent, and as I looked towards the corner of the room I wondered if it was too early to pull the board and shout to Mary for hot water for shaving, decided against it, and did the job in cold. After I had dressed and made my bed a delicious smell started seeping into the room; I traced it to the kitchen via the loose board. It was a final prod to an empty stomach. I went down to see what was happening.

Lois was bending over the stove, frying eggs and bacon. 'Morning Harry,' she said over her shoulder. 'Do you want some hot water for shaving while I finish this lot?'

'I've done it already.'

'What? In cold? I told you all you had to do was to lift the board and shout. Sit down, then. This won't be a moment.'

She sat down beside me with a portion about half the size of mine. We ate in silence for a little. Then Colin appeared at the door.

'I thought Lois and I would show you round the neighbourhood today. I want Sally to catch up on my dictation.' If Lois was surprised by this suggestion she gave no sign, just murmuring that she would fix a picnic lunch.

It was a pleasant morning. Colin gay, talkative, pointing out the local sights with an almost proprietary air; Lois quiet, and for the first time since my arrival, smiling and relaxed. We visited the church and two old Anglo-Irish battle sites, then drove out into the country. When we stopped to eat, Lois shook off her dreamy silence and began chatting about her childhood at Clonco. She and her brother used to ride out to this picnic spot when he was home from school. They had been quite close. Then the war. She missed him. There was a softness about her face now, a new warmth, and I found myself describing my own school holidays. Those first long lazy days away from exams and required athletics. Bicycling, fishing, just doing nothing. I was just describing my clumsy attempts to learn how to ride when Colin's voice broke in, harsh and jarring.

'Quite different from a summer delivering groceries.'

It was such an unexpected remark—Colin was always so much in control of himself, so much the gentleman even in his most questionable dealings—that Lois and I exchanged an embarrassed glance. Suddenly it was as though a line had been drawn. Lois and I were the old friends and Colin the outsider looking in. I turned to include him in the circle, but he stood up and began collecting the sandwich papers as if nothing had happened.

We drove back to the house in silence. Colin stopped at two pubs, but was gone only enough time to swallow a straight whisky. Although he did not ask us to join him, each time he got back into the car, he put his hand on Lois's knee—a quick gesture, but one of familiarity and ownership. When we reached the house he excused himself, saying that Sally could bring his dinner to his room. As he reached the top of the stairs he looked back, saying, 'Not to worry, Slow-boots. I want you to have a good time.'

Later that evening when I went up to my room the first thing I saw was my unmailed letter to Johns.

The next morning, it was Lois who woke me up, coming in quietly with a bowl of hot water.

'Here,' she said, 'since you're too shy to call down.' She turned to go, but paused at the door. 'Colin will be working today. He suggested we go sailing on the loch.' It was said in a flat final way and she did not look up. I hesitated, remembering yesterday's awkwardness. Perhaps this was Colin's way of smoothing things over.

'I'd like to. But I want to post some letters.'

'You can do that while I'm packing up the food. Take the car.' The eager, half-pathetic way she said it touched off a wave of pity. Again I felt a curious sense of alignment with her. A feeling that we were both perhaps being manipulated by Colin.

I went to the village after breakfast and spent a quarter of an hour persuading the postmaster that all he needed to do with the letters was stamp and send them.

When I got back Lois was waiting for me in the hall, a wicker basket at her feet. 'All set,' she said. 'We'll go out through the garden—it's quicker.'

'Hadn't I better just go in and say hello to Colin?'

'No. Don't disturb him. He's hard at it.' There was a sudden sharpness in her voice. But as we passed the study door I could hear no sounds of industry. The typewriter was not working.

The dinghy, moored at the little quay beyond the far end of the lawn, was new-painted and in better condition than anything I had seen in the house. I watched with envy the quickness, the quiet efficiency with which she got the anchor up, hoisted the sail, the speed and sureness with which we headed out into the loch. It was a fine morning, with just the right amount of breeze coming down from the mountains, dim blue, far across the sheet of shining water. There was nothing to do but sit and listen to the hiss of water past the hull, feel the living surge of the boat and think of the unknown weight of conflict and trouble that lay behind us in the house.

'It isn't always like this,' she said suddenly.

'Sorry. I—' I jerked back from my daydream.

'The loch, I mean. You can get some very nasty squalls coming down off the hills. I know; my father was drowned in one. He was coming back from church.' She swung around and faced me.

'If he hadn't died Clonco would be mine. But his younger brother inherited, Uncle Willie, and he was . . . hopeless. The place fell into ruin. Colin bought it for a song.'

There was a pause as she swung the tiller over hard and the boom cracked across, just skimming my head. Then she said in the same bitter voice, 'If you stay here long enough you'll hear all about me. The locals seem to do nothing but drink and gossip. They say I married Colin to get Clonco back into the family. But sometimes I think that Colin married me to get the pedigree along with the house.'

I said nothing, looking into the water, trying to avoid the pleading look of her eyes.

Suddenly—everything she did seemed to be sudden—she pointed to a little patch of green that was showing larger each moment in the waste of water around us.

'Let's go in to that island and anchor and have some lunch,' she said.

It was only about a quarter of a mile long; covered with low stunted trees. On one side there was a little horseshoe bay that was completely screened from the mainland. The breeze dropped when we came into its shelter. As we glided across the still water she said, 'I always call this *my* island. It hasn't got a name. I've tried to buy it . . . something of my very own . . . but the owner won't sell.' Again I felt that twinge of pity.

'I think it's lovely,' I said.

'Yes.' She was up in the bow, letting go the anchor. Then she turned and smiled and the easiness we had felt the other morning returned. We talked for a long time, always carefully avoiding mention of Colin or Clonco.

Finally she stretched and said, 'What about a dip before eating?'

I put my hand over the side. The water was icy. 'But I haven't a suit with me.'

'Go in your shorts, then. Don't be shy.'

'It's too cold, anyway.'

That seemed to satisfy. She said, 'Well, I'm going in, anyway. I'm dressed for it already. Just steady the boat while I go over the stern.'

She came aft and peeled her frock over her head; underneath it there was only the briefest of bikinis. I remember she looked very smooth, very white, as she stood there, her slim figure a perfect contrast to the red-gold of her hair. As I watched, in a moment all the feelings of pity went; there was something else in its place. I wished she were standing there with nothing, not even that bikini, on.

Her eyes widened for a moment with a knowledge of what I was thinking. Then she turned without a word, stood on the stern thwart and dived. She was gone with scarcely a ripple. When she broke surface she swam slowly round the boat, a slim white fish, the copper hair draggled now, but still strangely attractive.

'Come on in!' she shouted, turning over on her back. 'It isn't that cold, Harry. Really, it's lovely.'

'No, not the first day,' I said. Suddenly I felt a twinge of regret at having posted that letter to London earlier in the day.

She did not press me again, and soon was swimming under the stern. 'Help me out, then. This is always the most difficult part on your own.'

I leaned over and caught her under the arms; as I hoisted her up I could feel the soft swell of her breasts. Then, wet, smooth, surprisingly light, she was in the boat beside me, her wet body pressing up against me. My arms tensed and went round her. For a long moment I held her, my mouth on hers. Then with a cold swiftness the thought came that this was what she had wanted all along, that the warmth and camaraderie had been a pose. The

antagonism I had experienced at our first meeting returned and I
gently pushed her away from me.

'You're Colin's wife.'

Her face crumpled, but she didn't cry. Slowly, almost painfully,
she moved to the front of the boat and began drying herself with a
towel.

After a few minutes she said, 'Are you hungry, Harry? I'd like a
sandwich after that swim.' She was desperately trying to be friends.

There was beer, and there was coffee; cheese and chicken sand-
wiches. When we had finished she tidied the crumbs and sat back,
still in the bikini, with the towel round her shoulders, and looked
me straight in the eye.

'Harry, why don't you like me?'

I muttered, 'I do,' but it wasn't convincing and she went straight
on. 'I know you don't. I can feel it. And I want you to.'

'Nonsense.'

'It isn't nonsense.' She was looking at me steadily, half smiling.
'Have you been filled up with the poison so soon?'

'What poison?'

'The usual stuff that is dished out to everyone who comes here.
That I encourage Colin to drink . . . impede him in his work . . .'

There was no use in trying to avoid it any more. I said, 'My only
interest here is Colin, my old friend. I know he's trying to destroy
himself, but you might try to fight. Keep him away from it a bit
more.'

She gave a short, sharp laugh. 'Have you ever tried to keep drink
away from an alcoholic, Harry? You don't know what you're saying!
If I tried to ban it from the house he'd just go down to the local
pub and get all he wanted . . . probably hide reserve supplies in
the hedges on the way home. If I try to hide it in the house he
always thinks of a better place to hide it from me. You have just
no idea of the places you can find bottles . . . behind books . . . in
the dirty laundry basket . . . I've given up. It's hopeless. It's too
wearing. Now I just try to keep the tap turned off as much as
possible. I certainly don't encourage him, whatever that bitch says.'

'That bitch being Sally?'

'Who else? And I don't give a damn to say so. She's the one who
encourages. And everywhere she goes she spreads these bloody lies
about me. I hate her guts!'

'Then why keep her?'

For the first time the fire died out of those amber eyes. Then she looked away. 'You don't understand,' she said. 'I can't. I don't give orders any more. She—'

Suddenly she stopped. 'Let's change the subject, Harry. Sorry, I didn't mean to make a fool of myself.'

'You haven't. But I still just don't understand the whole thing.'

'You will later. Now, for God's sake, let's leave it alone.'

We made the trip back in silence. The sunshine had gone out of the day. I kept on looking at her, trying to stifle the pity, yes attraction, that I could not help feel, but wondering at the same time if she was just not putting on a very good act.

Nothing happened when we got back. There was work going on in the study, for the clacking of the typewriter stopped suddenly as I knocked on the door. Inside, asking permission to go to the bathroom, I saw Sally sitting at the machine, Colin, feet up on a sofa, dictating. They both smiled at me in a most friendly way. 'Help yourself,' said Colin, 'and did you have a good time out?'

'Very.'

On my return journey Sally looked up. 'Dinner is at seven-thirty tonight, sharp, Harry. The priest is coming.'

Father O'Neill was red, rotund, and could put away his liquor nearly as fast as Colin. I don't know how much they got through between them in the course of the meal, but they both seemed completely sober at the end of it. The food—cooked, I gathered, as a joint effort by Lois and Sally—was excellent. The conversation was on a pleasant level of banter, marred for me only by the occasional oblique remark from Lois that referred to Colin's frequent visits to the sideboard. For the first time I began to understand the full meaning of double talk.

After dinner we played cards. It was poker, and I soon realized that Father O'Neill was a very good player. I can hold my own in most games, but in an hour on small stakes he had taken two pounds off me and about the same from Colin and Lois. Then an odd thing happened—at least, it seemed so to me at the time.

It was about ten-thirty, and I was getting a bit sleepy after my day in the open air. Suddenly Colin, who was gathering the used cards, put them to one side without attempting to deal again.

'I think that's about enough,' he said quietly. 'Would you be ready now, Father?'

The priest said he was, and there was an awkward pause while the three looked at each other and then at me. At last Lois said,

'Would you mind going to the kitchen for a little while, Harry? The Father says prayers for us now, and then hears our confessions.'

After all that drink and the cards it did seem a little odd. But it was really the cue that I wanted. 'Of course, but I think I'll go straight to bed, if you don't mind. I'm very sleepy.'

I shook hands all round, then made for the door. Colin followed me into the hall. 'Something I forgot, Slow-boots,' he said casually, then turned into his study. I really was tired. Unlike the night before, I went straight to sleep. I didn't even hear the rest of them come up.

I woke suddenly. It was a close, still night and through the open window the moonlight streamed to make a long, slanting pool of radiance across the floor. But there was something else—an instant awareness that someone, or something, else was in the room. The light switch was 'way off, beyond the bare boards, by the door. I turned over in that direction; an instinctive glance at my watch told me by the luminous hands it was half-past two; then beyond, towards the door and just outside the beam of moonlight, something ... a pale, tall column that was motionless. From stupid instinct I called out, 'Who's there?' And then the column seemed to move and glide into the centre of the pool of light. It was Lois.

She was wearing only a nightgown, and for a moment I thought she must be sleepwalking. 'Lois! What on earth ... ?'

She didn't answer for a moment. She just stood there, trembling slightly, and I knew it wasn't from cold. Then she said in a sort of rough whisper, 'Please, help me, Harry, please. I just want to be with you ... just for a little while. I've been so lonely. You don't know what these two days have meant to me. There's no one to talk to here, no one who cares. You're the first person who's been kind. Please, Harry, you do want me. You do even if you don't like me.'

Want you? I thought. God, yes. I remembered how her mouth had felt when I kissed her that morning. There was nothing I wanted more than to draw her into bed beside me; to feel all the warmth and closeness that I had missed for so many years. Even though she was my friend's wife, I think I would have taken her anywhere, except in his own house. Anywhere else in the world, but not under Colin's roof.

I scrambled out of bed, grabbing my dressing gown. 'No, Lois. Colin ... We can't.'

She swayed against me, but made no protest as I began to help her to the door. I could feel the faint softness of her, the faint muskiness of her body that was the essence of desire. All I wanted to do was say 'Yes,' but I kept walking to the door. As I opened it softly and looked furtively down the corridor the very fact that I wanted her so badly stirred a slight resentment. As she continued motionless, I shook her a little, and she looked up, her eyes filled with tears. There was a sound from the next room.

'Hurry,' I said, 'for God's sake, hurry.'

Someone was awake. The sound of his movements jolted her into action. She took three quick steps and banged into the hall table. I saw the vase on it sway, but I couldn't move. It tilted, tilted and went over. A light snapped on at the other end of the landing, and Colin was facing us.

'Colin, she's been walking in her sleep. I . . . was just helping her back to her room.' I did not expect him to believe me; still, what with Sally and all, I was not prepared for his reaction. His face was death-white, with ugly dark hollows under eye and cheek. A nerve was twitching at the corner of his mouth. He walked towards us and grabbed Lois's arm.

'Bitch,' he said, 'bitch.'

CHAPTER 5

In the morning the house was even quieter than it had been on the day of my arrival. Now there was no question of lifting the board in the corner and shouting for hot water; I shaved in cold, packed my bag, and stealthily crept down the stairs to the safety of Colin's study. I found the local taxi-man in the telephone directory and told him in an almost whispered conversation that I wanted him at once to drive me to the nearest railway station. He said he would be with me in a quarter of an hour, and that would give nice time to make the connection at Birr for the express to Dublin. I scribbled a note to Colin, saying it was better that I go. I began pacing the room, the best in the house—panelled, cool, and restful. On the big desk was the typewriter, with a page of typescript still in it; beside it, a tape recorder. A very normal thing for any author to possess—except for one small difference. I wouldn't have noticed it if I hadn't had to wait there, listening for the taxi. A thin wire led from the machine, not to a desk microphone, but up the wall, almost invisible against the panels, up to the ceiling, and then out of sight. Even in my anger and misery I wondered what on earth Colin was up to.

The house was silent, too silent. The first noise that came was a relief. At last there was a crunch of tires on the gravel of the drive outside, announcing the arrival of my taxi. I shouldered my golf clubs, picked up my bag, and went out to meet him. Still no sound, no movement. The windows of the peeling front looked at me like blind eyes as we drove away.

In the train I had time to think it all over. The first awkward meeting with Colin and Sally. My initial prejudice against his wife. Then the strange rapport that had sprung up between Lois and me. The unexpected attraction of her red hair and startling white skin, ending as it did with her visit to my room and the ugly scene on the landing. As I looked back, Colin's outburst seemed all the more disturbing because it was so out of character. A glib retort, a

clever quip would have been more his line. He had, after all, made
no attempt to hide his affair with Sally. Perhaps the truth was, as
Lois said, that Colin had married her because she was a part of
Clonco, and having finally acquired his dream, he could not bear
to share it with anyone else. Lois, if nothing else, was still the
mistress of his house.

Lois ... Her name throbbed in my head. How much of her
feeling toward me was genuine, how much a pose, I would never
know. The only thing I could do now was try to forget.

At least in London there were no reminders. Work and a full daily
routine helped ease the first painful weeks; and in time even the
image of her figure, poised to dive against a background of trees
and sky, blurred and faded. A year or two later, when articles about
Colin began appearing in the papers, I was able to read them with
equanimity.

Sometimes they weren't so lighthearted; the bit about his having
to go into hospital for treatment for 'a nervous breakdown,' I knew
what that meant. Three books of his in a row were put on the
INDEX—banned publicly by the Church in Ireland. The ban
didn't mean much—probably put his sales up 30 per cent—but
with the next book a real scandal blew up, and it was serious. No
longer just the question of offending beliefs of a certain faith, but
something official. The word *pornography* was mentioned for the first
time, and then both London and Dublin courts found that certain
passages in this latest work were obscene; the publishers and prin-
ters were fined ... and Colin? In the words of the London report
of the proceedings, 'We regret we have not been able to trace
the other defendant, M'Lud. We believe he is somewhere on the
Continent, possibly in Spain.' I read the expurgated edition and
found it rather dull; the sales, of course, soared with the free
publicity.

Then out of the blue one day a letter came from him. There was
a Spanish stamp, and the postmark of Gerona. It was short, and
like most things to do with Colin, completely unexpected. The thing
that worried me most was the writing—shaky, wandering, like that
of an old, half-blind man.

Dear old Slow-boots,
     I expect you will be surprised to hear from me after all this time
     and our last disastrous meeting. The only thing I'm going to say

about that is that it's all forgotten. Lois is away for the month in Madrid. She does not know that I'm writing, but I am in *desperate* trouble now and I *must* see you. This isn't a 'touch,' Harry. I've all the money I want, and more than I want. But it's terribly important I see you as *soon as possible,* and I enclose a cheque that will cover all expenses to fly to Barcelona. Wire ETA, and you will be met. Don't fail me. I know I've always asked too much of you, but *please* don't fail me this last time.

Yours ever,
Colin

Lois is away for the month. For a moment that was the only phrase that stayed in my mind. Then I looked down at the letter and remembered Colin. My best friend and worst enemy. Liar, opportunist, drunk. Still his note reawakened some of my old feeling towards him. In the end it was the handwriting that decided me. I took a week off and flew out to Barcelona.

For the second time there was nobody there to greet me. I stood in the heat and bustle of the airport terminal, tossed into a completely strange world, angry, a little bewildered, thinking that once again he had forgotten. Then suddenly from out of the bedlam of noise and bright colour a slight figure came into focus as she ran towards me. For a moment I did not recognize her. She looked like a rather broken-down Spanish gypsy. Then she spoke, and I knew it was Sally.

She was very brown; her hair was cut short, like a boy's. Her teeth showed dead-white when she smiled and held out her hand. The faded blue jeans, the red-and-white-striped jersey, the rope sandals, made her completely different from the way I had remembered her. Only the voice and the eyes were the same, and behind the last, even in that first moment I could sense something . . . a terrible strain.

'Oh, Harry! How nice to see you again! I've got the car outside. Let's get going. We've got a longish drive.'

'How are you, Sally?'

'I'm fine.'

'And Colin?'

She stood quite still for a moment, holding my hand, looking down at the floor. 'He's dying,' she said.

I don't remember much of that drive, my first view of a strange country; the wide, fast road, the contrast of Cadillacs hissing by

our battered old Ford and the bullock carts with great wheels that
trundled along on the verges, creaking out of another century; the
grey-green of the olive groves that dotted the rocky plain, with the
red-roofed white houses nestling in clusters among them; the darker
spires of cypress reaching to the pale blue sky. It should have all
been memorable, but it wasn't. I spent most of the time staring at
the dashboard in front of me, trying not to think of Lois, listening
to the story that Sally told me in snatches. It was much as I had
expected. And it didn't make me feel one bit happier.

They had survived the sudden exit from Ireland quite well,
though it had been a bit of a rush job in the end. Colin had been
persuaded to go only when they had convinced him that a warrant
was about to be issued for his arrest. Then it had been a devious
flight from Wexford to Gibraltar in a coaster, with all the money
they could lay their hands on in cash; the opening of an account
there, and by some strange oversight in Spanish fiscal law, the
opportunity to telegraph the lot to another bank account in Barcelona, this time in pesetas. Even in my worry of hearing the story
the accountant side of my mind marvelled at the way people could
get around things.

So they had their money in Spain; enough to rent a place for six
months, also get their permit of residence. They had settled down
like that in peace, cheapness, and comparative security. Colin went
on with his writing—the books were selling better than ever—it
looked like a new start, but . . .

He was drinking more heavily than ever—'It's brandy now,' said
Sally, skirting a bullock cart. 'The trouble is it's so cheap; only six
shillings a bottle'—but those attacks of his were getting worse and
worse. Before, they had seemed to follow a definite pattern. Now
they were irregular, more frequent and violent. He was dying. She
knew it.

'But the doctors, Sal?'

'He won't see any of them. He says that brandy is the only
medicine. I've tried and tried to make him go and see someone,
but he only works himself into a state and shouts and swears if I
suggest it.' It wasn't just the dreadful possessiveness of the way she
said it—as if she owned him—but something that was left out that
made me realize the 'they' that had been mentioned all through
her story did not refer to a duet, but a trio. Well, someone would
eventually have to refer to Lois by name and it seemed a good idea
to pass this hurdle before seeing Colin.

'And Lois?' I asked.

'Oh, she's around. But she won't be here for the next few days.' A careful pause, it could have been while she concentrated on steering round the next bend; it could have been something different. 'Colin waited until she left before writing to you. It seemed best after what happened at Clonco. . . .' It was the only time that was mentioned.

There was another long silence. Then I said, 'But how can I help, Sally? You know there's nothing I wouldn't do. But it all seems so useless.'

'I don't know what you can do except see him. He wants to see you, desperately. I can only tell you he's getting a bit queer . . . sort of secretive. This last book of his, for example, he's doing the whole thing himself for the first time—typing it and locking what he's done away each night. I've always helped in everything before, but now I don't even know what the plot is. So just try to humour him, Harry; be kind, as kind and understanding as you can be.'

We stopped after that for a beer in a little café, and while we talked of ordinary things the strange beauty of the whole scene suddenly struck me. Only when I had paid the bill and we were walking back to the car did she say the last thing, the dreadful thing that shattered me.

'Harry . . . it isn't only the drinking, and this dysentery of his that has got him. He's being given something . . .'

'Given something? What on earth do you mean?'

'Poison.'

I stared at her, appalled, my hand on the door of the car.

'Sally! You must be joking! You can't mean it. But who . . . ? And how . . . ?'

'I don't know. I wish to God I did. But listen, I know I've been accused in the past of trying to poison your mind against one person. Well, I'm just going to ask you one thing. Why is he always a *little* better every time *she* goes away?'

'You can't mean that. You're saying something terrible!'

'I do mean it. You ask him. He knows.'

'Then you must go to the police.'

She gave a short, sharp laugh. 'The police? You don't know the Spanish police, Harry. About one man in ten throughout the whole country is a policeman of some kind. And they are all interested in only one thing—your politics. If there is a matter of real police business all you get is a lot of talk about "*mañana, mañana.*" It makes

me want to scream sometimes, and then it's so Irish I just feel right
at home. "Time enough" at Clonco was just the same thing, I
suppose.'

'But if you went to them, they would have to do something.'

'The first thing they would do would be to denounce Colin or
me as a Communist—that's the major part of their job—and then?'
She went round to her side of the car and slammed the door as she
slid in under the steering wheel. 'I've never seen the inside of a
Spanish jail, Harry, and I don't want to. I've heard a bit about
them, and that is quite enough. They don't feed you on principle
the first day—the idea being that you must have enough fat to last
on—and then it's bread and water, and you're lucky if you see your
own consul within a month. No, thank you, Harry. I wouldn't like
to risk it. I've no definite proof about a damned thing, and Colin
isn't that popular with the high-ups here, anyway. He's been on
one or two considerable binges since we came to stay.'

She swung the car out on the road in a vicious burst of acceler-
ation. I knew enough of when to talk and when to think.

It was blazing-hot in the afternoon sun when we arrived. We
came down through a long, straight road, arched over with trees—in
some ways like the drive to Clonco—but at the end, instead of the
loch, was the sapphire sweep of the sea in the Gulf of Rosas, and
the little fishing village almost pressed into the water by the barren
ring of hills that surrounded it. Far off, as always, was the faint
hanging curtain of the high Pyrenees, still capped with snow.

Everything seemed asleep as we drove along the quay; it was the
same when we turned up one of the straight, narrow streets; only
the blinding white light beating on one side of the walls; the purple
shadows on the other; the dogs dozing in the gutters, turning their
heads lazily as we passed. At last she stopped beside a high gate
in a blank wall. 'This is home,' she said.

Inside, it was like being in another world—a broad courtyard,
paved in black and white squares like a chessboard; an old, twisted
tree with gnarled trunk that writhed its way out of the centre,
spreading shade; two white kittens, one with a blue ribbon, the
other with pink, playing tag; the shuttered house, cool and silent.

I put my bag down and looked around in appreciation.

'There'll be something to eat in about an hour,' said Sally. 'Then
we all lie down for a bit. It's wisest here in the heat of the afternoon.
Have a wash now, and then come and see Colin for a moment.
He'll have heard the car, and I don't want him to start fretting.

He's been counting the minutes until you arrived, you know.' She laid a hand on my arm. 'And don't be shocked when you see him. You'll find a big change.'

The room was high and white and cool. The shutters were closed, and in the striped half-light it was difficult to make out much of the long, still shape under the single sheet on the single bed. But other things are noticed first when you walk into a sickroom: the faint sour smell of vomit that hangs in the air; and something else which once known is never forgotten . . . the smell of death.

I went over and sat on the chair by the side of the bed. I took one of the limp hands. 'I'm here, Colin,' I said.

'Good old Slow-boots.' He stirred slightly and turned slowly towards me. 'I knew you'd come. I should have come to you, but I just couldn't make it.' I hardly recognized the voice; it was weak, slow and tired, like that of an old man.

'We're going to get you well, Colin.' There was a soft click of the door as Sally closed it behind her.

'Open the shutters, for God's sake,' Colin muttered. 'They all try to keep me in the dark here . . . just to get used to it, I suppose. They know it will be for good very soon.'

'Don't be a bloody fool!' I turned from swinging open the heavy slatted windows. Now, with the full light, the first thing I saw was a bottle of brandy and a syphon of soda on the table beside the bed; then, clearly, the view of that face on the pillow. Something—deep and heart-wrenching—turned over inside of me.

It was like a skull, that face. Sucked in at the cheeks, the bones of forehead and jaw jutting out through tight skin, like rocks in the sea. He appeared very brown from the sun, the hair bleached almost white, but underneath you could see the basic colour was a dirty grey. And the eyes, ringed with great purple stains, lay deep within their sockets. I knew, just as Sally knew, just as he knew, that he hadn't long.

'Don't be a bloody fool,' I said again as I went towards him. A thin arm had come out to clutch the brandy from the table. 'It's the only thing that does any good, and you can't blame me for wanting that.' He heaved himself up slowly and poured a drink.

'You must see a doctor, Colin.'

He looked at me with dull eyes. 'You know what I thought about the profession at Clonco. They're a bloody sight worse here. I want to hang on as long as I can, not be sped on my way.'

'I'm not talking about local men, Colin. There must be blokes in Barcelona—specialists—as good as anywhere else in Europe. Get one of them in.'

For the first time the faintest interest showed itself.

'Too late, Slow-boots. It's done already. She's doing it slowly . . .'

'*Who* is doing *what?*'

At once he seemed to lose interest. 'You must be damned tired, Harry. Go and get something to eat with Sal. Then come back and talk this evening after you've had a sleep. It's too damned hot to talk now.' He lay back with a sigh, then turned over on his side. It was a dismissal.

I went downstairs, and there was a table laid for two in the shade of the old tree. Sally and I ate without talking much, served by a pretty blonde girl called Lolita. She spoke no English, but there was something I could not fail to notice: a sort of reserve, an instinctive drawing back when she put the platter with the omelette and the salad in front of Sally.

Sally knew that I had seen. When Lolita had finished serving and walked with lithe grace across the pavement to the shadow of the house she said, 'Lolita adores Colin, Harry. He is her God, and she'll do anything for him. She doesn't think we take enough care of him, and is full of silent disapproval. My only consolation is that she is worse with Lois than with me.'

'Now tell me all the other—' I leaned forward to light her cigarette.

'No, rest for a bit, like Colin said. Then we can all talk this evening.'

In truth, I was glad to get to my room. I was hot, tired, and very depressed.

CHAPTER 6

It was nearly six when I woke to the sound of voices outside my room in the passage: Sally's, low-toned and angry; that of Colin answering back almost unbelievably. They must have heard me stirring, for there was a knock on the door, and then they both came in.

I think that Colin looked worse in his clothes than he had in bed. They hung on him, showing sharp edges, just as if they were suspended on a cheap coat hanger. He walked stiffly, in jerks, without bending his knees, then sat down heavily on the edge of my bed. 'It's no use creating, sweetie,' he said over his shoulder. 'I'm going with Harry. And that's that!'

Sally was standing just inside the door, hands on hips, face flushed. She said, 'You admit you've been feeling better for the last few days? And I took all the trouble to make that broth for you for lunch, and you kept it all down?'

Colin nodded slowly.

'Well, why spoil the whole thing by going out on a bloody great pub crawl tonight, boozing with all your low friends?'

He didn't answer her, but looked at me. 'I'd forgotten, Harry. Tonight is the feast of San Pedro Pescador, St. Peter the Fisherman. It's the most important thing that ever happens in a little fishing village like this. They make a grand fiesta on the quay, with dancing to the band. Everyone goes. And as they have sort of adopted me as local squire, I must put in an appearance.'

'But you're not fit to go out, Colin.'

'I'll be all right when it's cooler. At seven, when it's cooler.'

Sally tossed her head. 'Well, I'm not coming!'

For the first time he looked at her, and for a second the old smile flickered across that gaunt face. 'That's going to save me a lot of trouble. You see, sweetie, I want to make the promenade with Harry alone. I happen to want to talk to him.'

I was weak and went. We made the promenade, starting at about eight. I don't know how many drinks he had had out of that bottle

before we started, but he looked a lot better, and there were plenty
to follow after. Sal did not appear, and we walked out of the
courtyard unopposed. We went down the narrow street, and the
first thing I heard was the band playing in the distance; then we
were crammed in by the people; all walking arm in arm . . . the
men in their best trousers and fresh-washed white shirts; the girls
in bright frocks, with stiff swirling petticoats; all walking, laughing,
in one direction. Towards the quay.

For us there was a lot of stopping, introducing, handshaking.
Estaban and Paquita; Pepito and Maria; Tio Pepet, Margarita.
They all knew one another by their Christian names: everyone was
glad to see Colin. Trying to follow the quick Spanish, I could
understand that the question was always the same. 'Was Señor's
malady better? . . . That was good. And it was nice to see him come
with his friend to watch the *sardana*...He was going to try and dance
also? . . . That was better still.'

In the intervals between all this as we strolled towards the quay,
with Colin leaning a little on my arm, he gave me a running
commentary on all these friends.

'They're like kids in lots of ways, really. They don't worry about
money or tomorrow. They look at you for a long time, and then if
they like you they accept you completely. They're very poor, but
very proud.'

The groups of people trickled in from the side streets that led
into the one main road to the quay. Along each side now from every
balcony the girls, the old people, the children leaned over, shouting
greetings to their friends below; from every shop doorway music
blared from gramophone or radio. The whole was a scene of vital
pulsating life: the great womb of happy people, with no care of the
scraping and semi-starvation of tomorrow. Today was fiesta, and
that was all that mattered.

It was infectious; a sudden shout from the doorway of the café
and a blue-jeaned fisherman, his face the colour of burnt oak,
dashed out to thrust a glass of brandy into Colin's hand, with
another one for me. I should have tried to stop him, I know. But
I didn't. Like wine, the atmosphere had already gone to my head.

Another café, another drink, and then we were on the broad
quay, the band getting louder and louder. I could see the *sardanas*,
big circles of people holding hands, with the grownups on the
outside and the children in a smaller ring in the middle.

They danced in a slow, shuffling step, joined hands held high above their heads. Everywhere there was a riot of colour, sound, and movement. The circles swayed one way, then the other, stopping suddenly as the music died and starting again a few seconds later, faster and more vigorous than before. As I watched, Colin's running commentary went on in soft English. And there was something else which, though perhaps it should have been a danger sign, I was glad at that moment to see. There was a little colour coming back into those gaunt cheeks.

'They're not Spaniards, you know, Harry. They are Catalan. They have their own language, both written and spoken, and they're terribly proud of it and incredibly jealous of their traditions. They hate Franco's guts. Did you know that that bastard banned this dance until about ten years ago? Even now you can't buy a book in their language that hasn't been printed and sold under the counter. The excuse has always been they're Communists. Communists, hell—they are just patriots!'

Next to us was a civil guard whom I had noticed from the heavy smell of garlic. He was a solid, sombre character with gun on hip, watching the proceedings with hostile eyes. I got a little frightened.

I nudged Colin quickly. 'For God's sake, be careful what you're saying. He might understand.'

Colin snorted. 'Understand English? He probably can't even talk his own language properly, let alone read or write it. And if you're going to take notice of every policeman you see, you may as well give up before you start. About one man in ten—'

'I've already heard all about that,' I said.

'Oh . . . ? But perhaps your informant didn't tell you how damned cunning they can be in Madrid. All the civil guards up here come right from the south so they are antagonistic and do their job properly.'

Suddenly he changed the subject. 'Just watch the steps of the dance for a minute, Slow-boots. They're really quite easy. Then we can join in.'

He took my hand and started putting me through the slow, shuffling steps. Though I had always been shy and a bad dancer, this time it didn't worry me a bit.

Suddenly a complete stranger took my other hand and three more joined in to make a circle. Steadily it grew until we were about fifty strong, the children dodging under our arms to form their little inner circle. It went on and on. It must have been nearly an hour before the band gave up, and by then the sun was sinking in a purple haze, drenching the snow peaks of the far Pyrenees in blood. The groups broke up in laughter, and Colin and I walked back to the middle of the town. He looked almost well.

'The fun really starts now,' he said. 'We've been invited to a party, and I'm going to make it my business to see that you can use the *porrón* before we've finished.'

I hadn't the slightest idea what a *porrón* was, and though it was nearly nine o'clock I didn't feel hungry, or even tired, only thirsty; the idea of a party seemed to me to be a very good thing. I'm afraid I just forgot all that I should have done in the other way about Colin. I remember he looked fine.

I did, at least, make one halfhearted excuse. 'What about Sally?' I said as we walked on. 'Won't she be worrying back at the house all alone?'

He stopped short in his stride. 'Sal can damn well look after herself and cool her heels for once. It's years since you and I had a night out together. She's getting too bloody bossy. Just because I happen to go to bed with her sometimes, it doesn't give her license to put the mother act over all the time.' He broke off suddenly and said, 'Sorry, I shouldn't have said that, but I expect you knew. Come on, let's have a laugh for once!'

'What's a *porrón?*' I was glad to change the subject as he turned me by the arm down one of the narrow streets.

'A wine-pourer. They use glass ones up here, usually, but they can be made of hide. It's like a sort of giant teapot. You hold it high away from your mouth and the wine comes out of the spout in a fine spray. It's quite easy when you get the knack of it.'

'I shall get drenched in the process.'

'That's part of the fun. The Catalans love it. I only hope my old friend José—he's a free-lance photographer—turns up. He goes all round the bars later on, taking flashlight pictures. It would be nice to have you in the act. It might ginger up some of your more sober clients.'

The café was almost empty: only one table with about ten Spaniards laughing and joking round it was occupied. Colin made no attempt to join them, but sat quietly at a table a little way off.

'Manners are a very important part of this business, old man,' he murmured to me. 'We don't go and sit with them—although I know them all very well—until we are asked. But one of them will be over in a moment to offer us a squirt from their *porrón*.' I looked

quickly over my shoulder and saw being passed from hand to hand
a great glass teapot filled with wine.

'We can't sit here and drink their wine,' I said, 'if we're not in
on the party.'

'We can, you know. Because when the *porrón* is finished we ask,
with permission, to refill it for all. Don't worry—it's only forty-
seven pesetas a bottle. Just wait and see.'

He was right. We waited, and I watched the *porrón* being handed
round from hand to hand; the high tilt of it, the fine spray coming
from a foot away straight into the open mouth, and the upright jerk
when the drinker had finished so that not a drop was spilled.

A few moments later the oldest man at the next table got up and
came over. He offered the *porrón* to Colin, who managed it with
ease. Then came my turn; there was no way without offense to
refuse.

'Aim the spout at the tip of your nose, Harry. Keep your mouth
wide open and don't close the throat. Keep swallowing all the time,
then jerk the *porrón* back quickly to finish.'

It sounded easy, but I got very wet. Everyone at the next table
roared with laughter, but a kind laughter that I did not mind. The
porrón was returned to the big table, and Colin watched the level of
the wine sinking in it with a calculating eye. 'Now's the time, Slow-
boots,' he said, scraping back his chair. There was a bow to the
señor, a request that we might be allowed to refill the *porrón* for the
party, and we were welcomed into the circle with cheer and much
backslapping.

I don't remember how many times it went round after that, or
how many times it was refilled. Everything had become so friendly
and easy. Nothing seemed surprising, not even one of the young
girls at the table suddenly producing a pair of castanets from her
bag and starting the swirling rhythm of the flamenco all round us.
Then there was a loud shout and Colin was nearly shot out of his
chair by a terrific clap on the back. A gentleman with a Leica and
flashlight slung round his neck who looked rather like Lloyd George
was standing behind him, shouting '*Hola!*' at frequent intervals.

'José!' Colin pulled another chair into the circle. 'Sit down and
have a drink, and stop making such a bloody noise.'

José sat down, introductions were made, and by this time I
realized that Colin was fluent in Spanish. 'José is delighted to meet
you. He is fed up with taking photos of the tourists, and now he

wants to get drunk. He will take us, though, at any time we like, but not for money.'

We were taken . . . many times. I put another bottle in the *porrón*, and was snapped by flashlight using it. I was taken trying to repeat the performance of dancing the *sardana*. At four in the morning the owner of the joint threw us out. Not because he wanted to close the place on account of the noise, but because, as he announced with many regrets, he just had to get some sleep.

We stood outside in the small square, looking at the waning moon for a little while before we split up into small groups. Ours consisted of Colin, myself and José. Colin looked ten years younger and ten times better; except for some unaccountable reason there were sometimes two of him quite close together. 'There are other bars, Harry,' said one image. 'Let's make a round of it.'

I was only too eager, and so was José. Suddenly I found myself sitting in the middle of one of the narrow streets, singing the 'Volga Boat Song' at the top of my voice; José was beside me, taking photographs all the time. There were still plenty of people about, but no one thought it was anything out of the ordinary; one or two passers-by patted me on the back. Then Colin slipped and fell. For a moment I was frightened, but he seemed to have taken no harm, just lay roaring with laughter in the gutter. We righted him, and then José fell down; a rugged character this one, for he lay flat on his back, steadily clicking his camera as he took flashlight shots of the moon. It had all been grand fun up to then, but we overdid it, I suppose. At our last port of call everything changed.

It was the last café left open. Dawn was just beginning to pale the sky, and even in that bad light I could see that we looked a little scruffy. I hesitated on the doorstep. 'I think we ought to go home,' I said.

Colin was pushing me from behind. 'One last one for the road, Slow-boots, and then we do just that.'

The shabby counter had a dented zinc-covered top. Behind it a sallow Spaniard with a cast in one eye was washing glasses in a sad, disinterested way. Two fly-blown bulbs that lit the place left the corners almost in darkness. There was just enough light to see six Spaniards sitting at a table at the far end. They looked to be rather unattractive characters. I wondered how soon we could finish this last brandy and go.

Trouble started when we were only halfway through it. As we three stood at the bar, suddenly from behind us out of the darkness

a loud remark came in Spanish. Colin swung round and shouted
something back in Catalan. In a second the temperature of the
room seemed to fall about twenty degrees.

There was the scrape of a chair and one of the Spaniards came
forward into the light. He was a tall black-haired man with the
easy catlike grace that usually goes with a smaller build. Next to
Colin's wasted frame his powerful shoulders seemed immense, his
high colour a sharp reminder of the other's ill-health. Sensing the
tension, I put a hand on Colin's arm.

'What's the matter?'

'Catalan bastard.' Colin spat it out. 'Catalan bastard!'

The Spaniard walked slowly towards us and hissed another single
word. The café was very still, the muffled early-morning noises from
the street echoing strangely in the quiet room. Then the unbelievable happened: the Spaniard pulled a knife.

It came out quickly. One second both arms were hanging free at
his sides; the next, a switch knife was in his hand. It flicked open
with a sharp click, gleaming evilly in the dim light. I tried to pull
Colin out of the way, but he shrugged me off and stepped forward,
his body taut and shaking. For the second time since I had known
him he lost his self-control.

'You can't wait,' he shouted, his voice rising shrilly. 'No one can
wait. Not you, Miguel, nor anyone else.' He took a deep breath
and made a visible effort to pull himself together. Then he turned
to face me, his mouth twitching. 'Not even you, my good friend.' I
stared at him.

'Why so surprised?' he asked softly. 'Lois is quite a woman. I
wasn't quite sure you'd come if I told you she'd be away. But then
I remembered your lofty morals, your staid and stodgy background.
Well, cheer up old boy. I guarantee you'll be seeing plenty of her
in the future. More, in fact, than you may find entirely comfortable.'
And he began to laugh . . . on and on, his eyes glazed and unseeing.
It was the most horrible sound I had ever heard. Miguel, who
had been standing half posed in shocked attention, looked back
uncertainly at his companions. For a moment there was silence.
Then as the Spaniard turned away Colin slumped forward against
the bar. When I bent to help him up I realized it wasn't just drink
that had knocked him out.

José came up trumps after that. He did all the work. In some
miraculous way he pacified the Spaniards, and by even more
remarkable methods he found a wheelbarrow at that time of the

morning. We got Colin in it and trundled him back to the house through the silent streets.

The patio was empty. Dawn was drifting in patches of silver and bronze through the leaves of the old tree. Across the chequered pavement stalked one of the kittens. Everything else was silence and shadow.

José seemed to know what to do, and I followed his directions without thinking. Without a word of a common language he made it quite clear that I was to take the feet and he the shoulders; that he knew where Colin's bedroom was, but that we must be *very quiet*. Colin was dead-out; his mouth was open and he was breathing in short gasps, a bubble of froth hanging from the side of his mouth. We humped him up the stairs, José steering with accuracy at each turn towards his room. I assumed it had all happened before.

We nearly made it. We were on the landing outside his bedroom when a door suddenly opened, a light snapped on, and there was Sally in a housecoat. If ever murder sparked from anyone's eyes it was there in hers.

She dealt with José first. I couldn't understand the actual words in that hissing flow of Spanish, but I got the rough idea. José got it exactly, for he dropped his end of Colin with a thump and fled. Then it was my turn.

'You dirty, rotten, stinking bastard! You call yourself a friend of his? You know the state he's in and yet you take him out all night and get him plastered. You've probably killed him!' In her rage the Irish brogue was back, thick and full.

'I'm sorry, Sally. But—' I was still holding Colin's ankles, though his back was now flat on the floor. The ugly scene at the café was still vivid in my mind, and it didn't help that the last thing she said might be true.

'But—to hell! You've probably killed him.' She bent down and got hold of his shoulders, lifting them with ease. It was difficult to realize that someone so slim could be so strong. 'If you want to do something useful help me get him to bed. And then get out!'

He was still unconscious as we lifted him through the door and onto the bed. After that I don't know what happened, for she pushed me out.

It was nearly eleven o'clock when I woke. The sun was slanting down high through the slats of the shutters. I had a mouth like the bottom of a parrot's cage and a splitting headache. When I managed

to totter to the washbasin and pour a pitcher of water over my
head, I saw a sheet of paper had been stuffed under the door.

Have gone out shopping—also to try to contact Lois, in Madrid. If
she thinks the same of your capers as I do, I should get to hell out
of here as quick as possible. I've told the girl to get you some
breakfast. Colin insists on seeing you before you go.

It wasn't even signed.

I got myself down to the patio, and a smiling, silent Lolita served
me with black coffee and rolls. It was very obvious that she was
delighted Sally wasn't there. All the time, I was wondering about
Colin . . . if I dared go up and see him. Lolita solved the problem
when she came to clear away. With a little curtsy she made me
understand that Señor Colin was awake and wanted me to go up.

He was lying on his back under one sheet, his face the same
sucked-in grey that I had seen the day before. He opened his eyes
and tried to smile, but it didn't quite come off.

'We're in the doghouse with Sal, Slow-boots.' The voice sounded
far away and very tired.

'I know. I'm sorry. I shouldn't have let you—'

'Oh, it wasn't the grog. It was the other thing . . .' His voice
trailed away for a moment, and then he whispered, 'I'm so bloody
tired.' He had apparently forgotten that he had ever been angry,
and after a night's sleep the whole scene had lost much of its horror,
had been rationalized into the meaningless belligerent outburst of
a drunk. I relaxed a little.

'You rest,' I said. 'Would you like me to get a doctor?'

'No, I want to talk to you.'

Another silence, and then: 'Don't think me inhospitable, Harry,
but I think you should get back home. I've had a verbal lashing
from Sal already, and she's gone out to try to get Lois back. If they
both corner you together it will be pure hell.'

'Of course I'll go if you want me to.' I was ashamed at my feeling
of relief. 'But I can't leave you here on your own.'

He sighed gently. 'Lolita will look after me. I've told her to call
a taxi to take you to Figueras, and you can catch the evening train
from there to Barcelona.' A hint of laughter came into his voice. 'It
will be rather funny because you will pass Lois on the way. I don't
know how you are off for cash, but—'

'I've got plenty left.'

'Good.' He stopped suddenly. Turning over on his side, he reached blindly for the basin at the side of the bed. He was trying to vomit, but nothing came. I sat helpless and full of pity until the spasm had passed. Then I said, 'Colin, you haven't told me what you wanted me to come out here for, that very urgent matter.'

'Oh, I thought we would have plenty of time to talk, so I didn't bother last night. We were having too much fun. But I want you to promise you'll do something for me.'

'If it's possible, you know I will.'

'Just be my literary executor . . . if anything happens. I've got a novel in there.' He pointed to the locked drawer in the bedside table. 'It just wants a little polishing and then I'll get my lawyers to send it straight to you. I think it's rather good. Better than anything else I've done, anyway. Will you?'

'But why me? Surely Lois or Sally?'

'I want you to do it.'

'All right. I promise.'

'Good. I think I'll have a little sleep now. I'm so bloody tired.' He tried to smile again. 'Look after yourself, Slow-boots. It was nice to have one night out with you, anyway. Just one fiesta.' He turned over towards the wall.

When I had packed my bag I went back to say good-bye. Lolita was sitting in a small chair by the window, watching him. He was flat on his back, breathing in short gasps that became faster and faster, to die away to nothing. I went over and stood beside her, looking down at him. Gently she took hold of my wrist and pointed to the hands of my watch. Then there was the pantomime of a taxi, indicating that it was time to go. I looked at him once more and then at her. She smiled gently, put a finger to her lips, and slowly shook her head. I left them alone, closing the door softly behind me.

There isn't much more to add to this part. I got home and four days later received a post card from Rosas. It showed the *sardana* being danced, and on the back in a very shaky hand Colin had written, 'Something to remind you of a fiesta and a promise. Book finished. God bless. Colin.' Another five days and a cable came: 'Colin died 25th buried Rosas Lois.'

Well, I had known it was coming. It was the end of a long chapter. I wrote the usual stilted letter of condolence to Lois, trying not to think, not to remember. There was no answer.

I swallowed my grief—not quite sure of its reasons—and life and work went on.

The package of the typescript arrived from the solicitors. The novel. And I read it, knowing exactly what I was being told. The scene was Tangier, not Clonco or Rosas. The characters were not the ones I knew, but every little bit of what I did know fitted in perfectly. As I sat there in the cold chill of dawn by the dead fire in my study I could hear Colin's voice: 'It's done already. She's doing it slowly.' The book even stated what poison.

I looked back at the title page: DEAD MEN RISE UP NEVER. And then, underneath, the quotation from Swinburne:

> We thank with brief thanksgiving
> Whatever gods may be
> That no life lives forever;
> That dead men rise up never;
> That even the weariest river
> Winds somewhere safe to sea.

Beautiful words, but in this case not quite true. Dead men do rise up sometimes. Colin had. To tell me exactly how he had died. At the hand of a slim red-haired nymph whose image, though blurred and faded, I had never quite been able to erase from my mind.

CHAPTER 7

It took me a week to make up my mind. I read the manuscript through again twice, and on each reading something new caught my eye, confirming my suspicions. I knew I had to take some action. Colin had entrusted me with his book, and as I now saw, with his terrible accusation. There were only two alternatives. I could go to the police—who might or might not believe my story—or I could have the manuscript published and leave the outcome to chance. In the end I realized that I had never really had a choice. Nothing ever could have made me personally try to initiate criminal proceedings against Lois. I would keep my promise, go through with the publication. If after the book came out someone else recognized Lois as the murderer, he could take the next step. It was not my responsibility. Firmly closing my mind to the hundred small excuses that kept relentlessly intruding, I rang up one of the directors of Colin's publishing house and asked him to lunch at my club.

The meal was less awkward than I had expected. The director, Wilton, talked about Colin most of the time, and it was not until we were drinking our coffee that I handed over the manuscript.

'Have you read it?' he said.

'Yes . . . twice.'

'And what do you think of it, honestly?'

I hesitated for a moment. 'I think it's very good. I . . . well, I never really cared for most of his stuff. It was a bit rough for me.'

'It sold,' he said. 'It sold like hot cakes.'

'Perhaps. But I feel this is different. It's sincere, far better written in my opinion. I'm glad it was his swan song.'

'It will probably be a flop, then.' He looked at me for a long time, shrewd and hard. 'Anything else?'

'No, I don't think so.' This was my last chance to withdraw, to give some reason why the manuscript was unpublishable. I said nothing.

He took another sip of his brandy. 'What I meant was, there

isn't too much breast and thigh, pornography, you know. It cost us a packet with him before.'

'There's nothing like that this time.'

He stared down at his drink. 'O.K., I'll read it. If what you say is right we'll publish as soon as possible. The public is so fickle. They forget so soon. There's only one thing I'm worried about, old man, and that's the contract.'

'Why?'

'Well, our normal agreement indemnifies us—under Clause 4, I think it is—against violation of any existing copyright, and anything that might be libelous or scandalous. In other words, if a suit is brought against a book the author rather than the publisher is held responsible. I'm not worried about either a copyright or libel suit here, but from past experience with Colin's work I am wary of scandal. It's not that I doubt your word, old chap, but my co-directors know Colin of old. And since you can't sue a dead man I think we would want some form of indemnity from you.

I paused for a minute. If publication resulted in a murder trial there certainly would be a scandal, but that obviously was not the sort of difficulty against which Wilton needed to protect his company. There seemed no reason to refuse.

'Get your solicitors to draw up something,' I said, 'and I'll sign it.'

He seemed satisfied. 'We'll do that thing, old man, and I'm sure everyone will be happy.'

Talk got easier then. He said as he finished his drink, 'By the way, did you hear about the will?'

'No. Only the part that concerned me. I got five hundred pounds. I thought it was very nice of him to remember.'

'Then you don't know the rest of it?'

'No. I never worried. It was nothing to do with me.'

'It's rather odd. His wife gets only his copyrights. The rest, apart from a few small bequests to people like you and friends in Spain, goes to that secretary . . . mistress of his.'

'What does Lois think about that?'

'Not much, I gather. She's going to fight it. But just in case things go wrong I want to make as much as I can for her out of this.' He patted the manuscript. 'I do think it's rather hard on her, don't you?'

'Very,' I said.

'Well, I must get back to the office.' He finished his brandy.

'Thank you for a very nice lunch. I'll get cracking on this and send you the contract and that form of indemnity.' He hesitated for a moment. 'It's not that I doubt your word in the least, old man, but there are the other directors.'

'Of course.'

Within a week the contract and a short indemnity form arrived. I signed them without reading, wanting to get my part in the affair over as quickly as possible. After that there was a long silence. They sent me galleys of the book, but I couldn't look at them. My own work was increasing, and I let it absorb most of my time.

Then publication day was fixed. I had heard nothing from Lois, but I did try to give her one word of oblique warning. I wrote and told her all I had done.

The answer was surprising. It came from a firm of solicitors in Lincoln's Inn, saying that Mrs. Headly was still abroad and that she had forwarded my letter to them. She approved of all I had done to date, but there were certain legal proceedings pending with regard to the late Mr. Colin Headly's estate and they would be obliged if I would inform them of any change of address as they intended to call me as a witness if and when the case came to court.

The sting was in the tail. They added that though they realized that as an old friend of the family I might find such an appearance distasteful, it was vital to the case and they hoped they would not have to serve a subpoena.

I wrote that it would be distasteful; that I was very unwilling to be a witness, but of course, I would bow to a subpoena.

For some reason, perhaps best known to Lois, they did not call me. I read what there was about it in *The Times*—just a small paragraph, for Colin wasn't news any more—and gathered that Lois had half won, half lost her case. Mr. Justice Payden said that the legacy of the copyrights would give Mrs. Headly a steady income from—here, I gathered, he must have sniffed—'her husband's numerous and popular, if not very savoury, novels.' A wise move. He was satisfied, there being no children, it would keep her in comfort for life. But, and it was a big 'but,' although he was certain that Miss Macgrath had been a constant help and solace to Mr. Headly and that Colin had been of clear mind and intention when he had made the will, he was not quite happy in the provision for Lois. She was to get five thousand pounds out of the estate. Sally could keep the rest.

Well, that was that. The case was over and I had not been called.

Shortly afterwards Colin's book came out. It received good reviews and a sizable advance sale, but caused no unusual stir. If Colin's friends read it, and it was a likely assumption that they did, none of them seemed to share my suspicions. When the book had been in the stores for more than a month without anything happening, I began to think the whole ugly affair could perhaps be forgotten. The final judgment was not, after all, up to me. For the first time since reading the manuscript I relaxed. But even if I had been expecting trouble I would not have been prepared for the manner in which it eventually came. The action was taken by Lois herself.

Notification came in the form of a letter from her solicitors.

Dear Sir,
re Colin Headly Esq. decd.
We have been instructed by Mrs. Lois Headly, the widow of the deceased.

You will know that the deceased was the author of a book which we understand you, as his literary executor, have recently authorized to be published under the title of *Dead Men Rise Up Never*.

We are instructed that Amanda Fane, one of the principal characters in this book, was intended to be a libellous reference to our client, and that notwithstanding such knowledge, you have falsely and maliciously caused the same to be published, as a result of which our client has been injured in her credit and reputation, and thereby suffered substantial damage.

In these circumstances, we are instructed to demand of you the withdrawal from publication forthwith of all unsold copies of this work, and to commence proceedings for damages so far permitted. Will you please let us hear from you as soon as possible what steps you are prepared to take to mitigate this damage.

Yours faithfully,

I wondered if Lois realized what dangerous ground she was treading. I read the letter again carefully. Mine was the original copy, but carbons must have been made, one certainly for the publishers. I began pacing the room. In a little while they would call, asking whether or not I had been aware of the book's implications when I handed it over. A denial would mean breaking Colin's trust, but if I admitted recognizing Amanda Fane I would be deliberately tightening the noose about Lois's neck. If I only knew what she was thinking! Why had she decided to press the suit when, at best, she would be surrounding herself for life with suspicious glances and whispered insinuations? Suddenly I couldn't wait a minute longer, watching the phone and listening for the ring. I left the office and went around to see my solicitor, old Manners.

Manners had worked for my father on his legal problems and had known me ever since I was a boy. He was a tall man, spare, with thinning hair and sharp blue eyes. When I arrived at his office out of breath and without appointment he made no comment. He brushed some papers from one of his rather dusty chairs and motioned me to sit down.

He remained silent while I told him the whole story. The visit to Clonco. The visit to Spain. I omitted only the fight Colin and I had had over Lois and my strangely persistent feelings towards her.

When I finished, Manners leaned back and said softly, 'You've stuck your neck out, Harry, just as far as it will go. I've read the book. If you suspected that Colin intended his heroine to serve as an indictment against Lois why didn't you go to the police, or better yet, burn the manuscript and forget the whole thing? Colin doesn't seem exactly the type of friend worth making sacrifices for.'

'It was his last request. I had no choice. And when I signed that indemnity clause the last thought in my mind was that anyone would be suing for libel. Now, of course, I know I'm in for it. The publishers must be trying to reach me already.' It was impossible to point out the full complexity of my dilemma.

'Well,' he said, 'they are as involved in this as you are. That indemnity you signed doesn't really mean much. They'll have to join with you in any action.'

'Yes, but what action is there? I can't in all conscience claim to have been unaware of the book's implications.'

'It would be the safest way out.'

'And if Colin were murdered?' I couldn't force myself to mention the question of Lois's guilt.

'You're not certain he was.'

'But can I just ignore the possibility?' He leaned forward then, folding his hands like a bishop.

'That is a question only you can answer. There is one way to absolve both you and the publishers, but I would rather not go into it until you have made your decision. Do you really believe the girl is a murderess?'

We went over and over the story. The gossip that had existed at Clonco, Sally's accusations, Colin's own statement, 'She's doing it slowly.' Each time we went back Manners elicited more information, damning Lois and hardening my own mind against her.

Finally he looked down at his folded hands and said, 'In English law, under the Defamation Act, if a matter can be considered of public interest proof of truth may be accepted in defense of a libel charge.'

'You mean prove Lois guilty?'

'Well, isn't that what you've been doing all afternoon?'

Oh God. I closed my eyes. Manners was still speaking. 'I think the only thing for you to do is to go round to the publishers and let them make the decision, since in the long run they will have to share the major burden of expense.'

'Colin left me five hundred pounds,' I said dully.

'Well, that gives you a nice start.' He began cheerfully rummaging about for the phone book and looking up a number. 'I think we should give them a ring now and see if we can go over.' He got through quickly and learned that they had been trying to get in touch with me for several hours, that they were having a board meeting at five o'clock, and that they were very anxious I attend. Manners hung up the phone.

'I'll go with you,' he said.

There was a quorum of seven, excluding my friend Wilton, and they sat round an elegant mahogany table, looking like the minor relatives waiting for the reading of a rich uncle's will. We were introduced all round, then Wilton began.

'Heaven knows, old chap, we've had trouble with Colin's work before, but never anything like this. Libel. And on such an issue.'

'I'm glad you recognize your own responsibility here,' said Manners softly, always the lawyer, always with his eye on his client's interests.

'We do, old chap, we do,' said Wilton. That's the tragedy of it. You see, we've always sympathized with Mrs. Headly, and now she'll think . . . My God—' He broke off.

'Get to the point,' said another of the directors angrily. He was a ferret-faced man, pinched and thin. I could see him balancing publicity gains against court damages as he spoke. 'If Mrs. Headly wins she collects not only the full amount of the suit, but court costs

as well. A frightening expense. Frightening. I can't understand how
your client could have permitted us to publish.'

'How could he have known?' Wilton seemed eager to rush to my
defense, perhaps thinking that in doing so he was also excusing his
own gullibility.

There was a silence, and I remembered Colin's grey face, his
slow smile as he told me it was already too late.

'No,' I said. 'I knew Amanda Fane was meant to be Lois. I knew
Colin was murdered.'

'But you can't admit that. It wrecks our defense. Our only line
is to insist that we had no idea there was any resemblance between
Amanda and Lois. That the whole suit is a manifestation of Mrs.
Headly's warped imagination.' The ferret-faced one subsided, and
suddenly everyone began talking at once. Manners looked across
the table at me. He had been doodling, and I watched now as he
carefully added a final turret to an elaborate castle. Then he put
down his pencil and folded his hands.

'As I have already told my client,' he said, 'there is, since he
refuses to deny foreknowledge, only one defense possible. And that
is to prove the plaintiff guilty of the very crime on which she is
basing her suit.' The faces about the table blurred as I heard
Manners's dry, even voice droning on and on, quoting extracts from
the book and matching them to the story I had told him that
afternoon. The case was building. Slowly eight incredulous faces
took on a look of shocked horror. Manners's quick lawyer's brain
was turning my unhappy suspicions into a full-blown case against
Lois, protecting my position at a cost I wasn't sure I could bear to
pay.

'But why did he do it in this fantastic roundabout way?' asked
one of the directors. 'He could have gone to the police himself . . .
written to you. Why the need for this . . . this cryptogram?'

I realized they expected me to answer. 'He was my friend and a
drunk, a very sick alcoholic. It's the only explanation I can give.'
My voice seemed to be coming from a long way off. I looked round
the circle of faces, and they appeared pale oval blobs. Manners was
talking again, arguing convincingly.

Finally Wilton said, 'It appears to me an unbelievable piece of folly,
but it seems we have no other choice than to fight the case by
backing Mr. Andrews' story. I think if the rest of you agree with

me on this we must stop differing among ourselves and settle down to the building of a case. We will have to choose a barrister.'

'I thought Armitage.' Manners had the whole thing worked out in his mind, an unusual challenge, a fascinating brief. There was some more meaningless talk, and then a hesitant murmur of agreement.

I went back to my flat and got really drunk.

CHAPTER 8

After that it was only letters which I passed straight on to Manners. Each one piled up on top of the other—a three-cornered affair between solicitors—and I realized for the first time why the law costs so much. Only one small incident occurred that upset me. José sent me the pictures he had taken at the fiesta. There was no letter, no comment on Colin's death. Just a name scribbled on the back of one of the snaps. I flung them in the back of one of my bureau drawers.

It was just before Christmas that the little man in the shiny suit and battered bowler hat called on me. He rang the bell, and having established my identity, thrust the writ for appearance in the High Court into my hand. He was very polite, and I asked him in for a cup of tea. He had a shocking cold and badly needed a new pair of shoes. He sat and steamed and wheezed, saying over and over again that it was a pleasure to meet a gent who was so co-operative. 'Some of the things they say and do . . .' he said. I would have liked him to stay longer, but apparently there were other 'jobs.'

So I was left with two empty teacups . . . and a writ on the mantelpiece.

There were many meetings before the case was heard. Once they—the publishers—had decided they were in it they went after the crumbs wholeheartedly. It was well done, very subtle, and I don't think I would have known if I hadn't been watching for it. I would not have realized the ways in which a concerted attack can be made on the public mind.

There were 'puffs' in the gossip columns, the ones where the writer has a permanent cold in the eye from looking through other people's keyholes. There were hints of an impending action. A full-page review of the book appeared in one of the Sunday papers, along with an appraisal of Colin's work and character. The verdict was 'so fresh, so vivid, so different from all his other work. It makes

you feel you might have been there, that it might really have
happened.'

He was on a safe wicket, that reviewer. He hadn't been there.

The meetings with the directors grew more and more cheerful as
sales rose. They were reprinting, they told me, for the third time—a
large reprint—and several of Colin's books that hadn't gone too
well before were picking up remarkably. Everything was going fine.
True, they might lose something in damages, but the profits would
more than cover it. They almost rubbed their hands in anticipation.
They were going to get back into the fold ten times what they might
lose, and that was all they cared about. I didn't give a damn about
any of it.

At one of these meetings they made an appointment for me with
the private detective they had agreed to hire to do the spadework.
He came to the flat, and though I had never set eyes on a 'private
eye' before and was prejudiced against them from everything I had
seen on TV, I liked him from the start. There was none of the
toughie with the grey raincoat and turned-up collar, hat brim pulled
down, and bottle of whisky always at hand; I was certain he did
not spend most of his time up ladders, peering through bedroom
windows; also, that he had no predilection for blondes. He was
middle-aged, with greying hair and a keen, intelligent face, impecc-
ably dressed, and with the nicest of manners. His name was Proudfoot, and he told me that he was an ex-chief detective inspector.

'Well,' he said when I had settled him by the fire with a drink,
'I'm not going to bore you with all the legal side of this business.
I expect you've had a barrelful already.'

'You couldn't be more right.'

'Good. But you must realize that to win our case, as defense we
must rely on facts. The first is that you did your job as Mr. Headly's
literary agent, as he asked you, knowing nothing. Two, that you
thought you knew something which was fair comment and in the
public interest. But that thought has to be true—to be proved.
That's where I come in. To find the truth. Was he poisoned?'

'I'm certain of it.'

'Proof?'

'Nothing positive. Just a sum-up of all the things I know.'

'That won't help much unless we can be certain by whom he
was poisoned. Now just give me the setup of that *ménage*.'

I did so, at length, and his summing up was short and accurate.

'A lovable, irresponsible drunk; a strong-willed secretary who was probably his mistress; and a bitch of a wife. But it doesn't prove anything. It's just not good enough.' He was silent for a moment while he took a sip of his drink. 'Dicoumarol' was all he said.

'Dicoumarol?'

'Yes, that's the stuff he used in the novel. Do you know anything about it?'

'No.'

'Nor did I until I had mugged it up. Nor do many unless they are doctors.' He sighed as he picked up his drink again. 'You won't believe it, but I have a fatal fascination for detective stories, and the means used are all so old-fashioned they make me sick. Dear old arsenic—Marsh's test killed that from the time of Crippen—cyanide, which you can smell a mile off. And all that clever stuff about air embolism; you just can't prick with an ordinary syringe to get a bubble of air into a vein. It just doesn't work, Mr. Andrews. You need something the size of a bicycle pump to do any damage. It's all old stuff. I know.'

'Then this dicoumarol?'

'There your Mr. Headly has been very clever. He's found a new one, and it's very dangerous.'

'Why?'

He ignored my question. 'Tell me, Mr. Andrews, while you were in Spain did you notice the fields outside the town?'

'There were some all the way along the road.'

'Any clover?'

I tried to think. 'There must have been. They have to feed their cattle.'

'Was any of it spoilt?'

'Spoilt?'

'Mown and lying to dry in the sun.'

'I don't remember. They usually just tether a couple of beasts on the patch and let them eat it off.'

'Just as well for their economy,' he said quietly. 'If they had eaten the mown stuff they would have died.'

'Died?'

'Dicoumarol was first discovered in cattle that had eaten spoilt sweet clover. It's a decoagulant of the blood. The longer they eat it the longer it takes their blood to clot, and they become sort of haemophilic. There are no symptoms, no pain. All that happens is that they bump against each other or a fence, and the slightest internal bruise or cut, because there is no clotting, causes them to bleed to death.'

'But I don't see how that could happen to Colin. He didn't eat clover!'

He gave me a sharp look. 'No, he didn't eat it . . . but he probably drank it. She could have bought it or distilled it herself. It's soluble in alcohol, and I think you said his tipple was brandy?'

'But why? Just after I was there?'

'Just bad luck, I suppose. You also said that on the night of the fiesta he was pretty drunk, he took a bad fall. That, with a build-up, would be enough to finish him. You weren't to know then.'

'I see that now.'

He hesitated for a moment. 'You realize that apart from proving the truth of everything you have allowed to be printed, the other side will try to discredit you in every way possible?'

'I think I've got a pretty good record: socially, in my profession, and in the war. So what?'

'Just a few inspired stories are already in circulation about you.'

'Such as?'

He stared at the carpet. 'That you had an affair with Mrs. Headly, for a start.'

A chill settled over me, but while I was still wondering how to answer he continued. 'Another inference has also been made . . . that you were more interested in someone else.'

I drew a quick breath. So no one knew anything. It was just a lot of gossip. 'You mean Sally?' I said. 'That's nonsense.' I liked her, but I never even touched her except to shake hands.'

Now Proudfoot was examining his shoes with intensity. 'No, I don't mean Miss Macgrath. I mean Colin—Mr. Headly.'

It took a few seconds for the implication to sink in. I felt my cheeks burning. 'Do you think I'm a bloody queer? How dare you!'

He said, 'I don't think anything. It's just to warn you what the other side might try to drag up—to prepare you for what you might have to take when you're in the box. But we think we've got a nice piece of dirt on Mrs. Headly, too.' He sighed and got to his feet. 'But that's for the lawyers. I'm hired to produce facts. Any facts there are must be in Rosas. We've got a good man in Barcelona, but you know what Spanish officialdom can be like. I'm going out myself to do a little digging. There's only a month before the action is heard, so I may not be able to do too much. But I'll try my damnedest. Hope to have something good for you before the curtain goes up.'

He shook my hand and went out.

I can remember sitting on the top of a bus on my way to the law courts on the day of the hearing, staring out of the window at the crowds of workers streaming along the pavements, not really seeing them, just thinking of what lay ahead. I felt no fear, only determination. Win or lose, I didn't care. My problem was to forget all feeling I had ever had for Lois and accept her for what she was. A murderess.

I arrived early, as instructed, and the corridors of the law courts smelled of wet disinfectant. Manners was there, and Armitage and his junior, Green, the last two looking strangely different in their wigs, funny ties, and gowns. They walked me up and down, giving final instructions. There wasn't much I hadn't heard before except 'When you are asked a question, even by the opposition, you don't answer back directly to him, you look and talk to the judge. And you speak up.'

They stalked, one on each side, looking like two pelicans and just about as cheerful.

'We're up against old Rivers,' said Green, 'and he's a bastard.'

'Number One Court, and it's filling up already. I expect we'll get three full columns giving every detail in the *News of the World* next Sunday.' This was Armitage. Gloomy.

We talked a bit more, and then we went into court.

Lois was there already. It was the first time I had seen her in nearly three years. She was wearing a simple charcoal suit, a white blouse, and practically no make-up. Her lawyers had dressed her as the poor injured party and the effect was quite good, although her red hair was as startling as ever. She sat quite still, looking straight ahead, with never a glance at me. Armitage whispered, 'That's her counsel over there . . . Reeth . . . a very good man.' He sounded gloomier than ever.

The judge came in, and we all stood up. He had his wig cocked over his left eyebrow, and he looked like a man with a hang-over from the night before who had missed three trains on his way to work.

'In a bad temper,' said Green quite unnecessarily. We all sat down.

There was a lot of legal argument, as I had anticipated, but it was not quite as incomprehensible as it might have been, for I had studied up a bit after my first talk with old Manners. We were relying on the precedents set by *Alexander v. North Eastern Railway Co.* (1865), and *McQuire v. The Western Morning News,* (1903), and Sections 5 and 6 of the Defamation Act.

Reeth opened, throwing everything in the book at us. He skated over the subject of Colin with an innuendo, but didn't dare go too far. Lois denied everything. She made a very good witness, and I began to feel an odd stirring of pity, similar to that I had experienced at our first meetings.

Later I was called. I walked over to the witness box and was sworn in. As I repeated the words of the oath I looked round the well of the court; Lois's hair and face stood out in sharp contrast to the dull blur of faces all round. She did not look at me.

It wasn't as bad as I had expected. I remembered my lesson and looked towards the judge, bellowing at him whenever Counsel asked me a question. We started off quite well, for the book—Exhibit A, which was strewn all over the court—intrigued the judge as to the title, *Dead Men Rise Up Never.* Counsel suggested with due respect Tennyson and Stevenson, but the judge had the right answer himself. He quoted most of the poem of Swinburne and looked very pleased with himself when he had done so.

After that things didn't go so well. I was taking passages of the book and trying to marry them with the various incidents I had witnessed. The judge got more and more impatient as it went on. He kept on stabbing the top of his desk with a pencil, harder and harder, until at last he broke the point. Then he said, 'Mr. Armitage, I don't know if you have given your client a lesson on the laws of evidence, but does he know what *hearsay* means?'

'I think so, m'lud. He is giving an honest opinion of what he knows to be true.'

'I don't want opinions—I want facts. I shall adjourn for five minutes so that you can drum it into his head.'

We all stood up as he went, and with his going the court became an easier place. I slipped into a seat beside Armitage. 'I'm sorry,' I said, 'I seem to have made a complete mess of it.'

'It's not you,' said Armitage, as gloomy as ever. 'It's his piles.'

'But—'

'In a way, he's right. We've got to have facts. Look at Reeth over there, laughing his head off. He knows he's won. We can't without something solid to chew on.'

And at that moment we got our facts.

Proudfoot came into court. He looked tired and travel-stained, and he slumped down between Armitage and me, his brief case across his knees. 'No breakfast,' he said, 'but I've got it.'

I watched while he produced two stiff sheets of paper. All I could see was that one was in Spanish and covered with seals; the other was in English, with a consular seal at the bottom. Armitage read them quickly and passed them over to Green. 'I'll go over and show these to Reeth; he'll see there is no point in going on.'

Proudfoot was still sitting beside me. 'What have you got?' I said in a tight voice.

'The lot; boy, he was full of it . . . dicoumarol. It was the lime soil that saved us, boy. He was a pretty wild character, but they loved him, and they buried him in their own cemetery. The soil saved him—even after six months.'

Dicoumarol. I didn't hear anything after that. During the last few weeks, watching the case against Lois build, I had been moving in a dream. Now, confronted with the actual evidence of murder, I felt that I had been roughly pulled from a drugged sleep. This couldn't be real.

'What have you got?' I asked again.

'Wait and listen. It's going to rock everybody here.' He was so glib. 'That Sally . . . she's quite a dish. Did you ever meet a type called Miguel?'

'What?' He went right on.

'She's probably kept him away when you were around, but they're married now, and doing nicely out of the proceeds. He's just bought a new night fishing boat . . . must have cost over a million pesetas.'

'So?'

Before he could answer, Armitage slid back into his seat. 'Reeth is reading the papers. There's no point in his going on now.'

The judge came in and we all stood up.

'Mr. Armitage.'

'M'lud?'

'Have you had sufficient time to instruct your client in the difference between hearsay and evidence—fact?'

'I have, m'lud.' Armitage was being superobsequious. 'Mr. Andrews has convinced me he is telling the truth because he knows what is true. And that truth is now substantiated by facts that your lordship has been so anxious to obtain.'

'I will overlook the impertinence implied in that remark. What are these facts?'

'If your lordship pleases, I wish to hand in two documents, to be marked Exhibits B and C.' He handed them to the clerk of the court, who passed them up to the judge. 'You will see, m'lud, that one is in Spanish, signed and sealed by the appropriate authorities. If your lordship's Spanish is not too fluent'—he was purring now at his smoothest—'Exhibit C is a certified true copy in English by Her Majesty's consul in Barcelona. The documents are in three parts.' Armitage raised his voice slightly against the hum of excitement that stirred the court.

'The first is authority from the Governor of the Province of Catalonia, giving permission for the exhumation of the body of Colin Headly, a British subject, buried at Rosas. The second is an affidavit that this was done, signed by the parish priest and one Tio Pepet. The third'—and now the whole court was deadly silent—'the third is a report of an autopsy on the said body by Señor Juan Mendez, professor of forensic medicine at Barcelona University. He states that the body contained poison, dicoumarol, in such proportions to indicate frequent massive doses over a long period.'

The only sound was the crackle of the stiff paper of the documents as the judge looked at them carefully.

'Mr. Armitage, has your learned friend for the plaintiff perused these documents?'

'Well, Mr. Reeth?'

Reeth got rather wearily to his feet. 'Under the circumstances, m'lud, I have no alternative but to advise my client to drop this action.'

'So be it. I enter judgment accordingly.'

'With costs, m'lud?' Armitage was up on his feet like a rocket.

'With costs.'

Then a strange thing happened. The judge did not rise at once, as I had expected him to do. He gave a long, searching glance at Lois, who sat looking straight ahead of her; then he did the same thing to me. The papers crackled once more as he folded them carefully. Then he said slowly, 'I feel it my duty to send the papers of this case to the Director of Public Prosecutions.'

I didn't see Lois when we went out, and I was glad that I didn't. My thanks to Armitage and Green were mechanical, almost in a haze. I hated the backslapping of one of the directors from the publishers, his gleeful crowing over the fact they were going to run off another fifty thousand copies. All I wanted was to be alone. However, as I mused over the whole strange jumble of events one image kept returning to haunt me. The judge's cold, hard look at Lois when he announced what he felt it was his duty to do.

CHAPTER 9

It was nearly a month later that the detectives came, a pair of well-scrubbed gentlemen in plain clothes, one considerably older than the other. They were terribly polite and asked the most peculiar questions. It started with the information that they were enquiring into the death of Mr. Colin Headly, and that as a party to the libel action perhaps I could be of some assistance to them.

Of course, if there was anything I could do.

'Then you don't mind answering a few questions, Mr. Andrews?'

'No.'

'I believe you were very friendly with Mr. Headly?'

'Well, we have—had—been close friends since schooldays.'

'And Mrs. Headly?'

'I met her only twice before this action. Once at Clonco, in Eire, and then—' I checked myself. 'No, it was only that one time. When I went to Rosas she had gone to Madrid.'

'And Mr. Headly?'

'Since when?'

'Since after the war.' It was the senior, an Inspector Smithwaite his badge had said, asking all the questions. His boy was just looking about.

I thought for a moment. 'Three times, I think. Once when we had lunch together at Ruie's; then when I went to stay at Clonco; and then when he asked me to come out to Rosas, just before he died.'

'I see. Tell me, did you write often to Mrs. Headly?'

'I've written to her only once in my life, a formal letter of sympathy when I heard Colin was dead.'

'How do you write your letters, Mr. Andrews?'

'I type them. I've got foul handwriting.'

'But you sign them in pen?'

'Of course.'

'How would you have signed the one you wrote to Mrs. Headly?'

'Just "Harry." '

One of the new ball point pens and a piece of paper came out like magic. 'Would you mind giving me a sample?'

'Of course not.' I wrote it in exactly the same way as I would have ordinarily and handed it over. By this time red lights of danger were flashing in all directions.

'Mr. Andrews, do you type your personal letters in your office, or here?'

'Here. The machine is on the desk over there.'

'What make?'

'An Oliver Courier. You can see for yourself.'

'Then you have no objection to us examining it?'

'Not the slightest.'

Smithwaite coughed. 'We would like to take it away with us.'

I said with some natural irritation, 'That will be quite inconvenient for me, but I suppose there is nothing I can do to stop you.'

He shrugged and began closing up the typewriter. He had some trouble with the lid, and I let him struggle by himself. When the latch finally clicked into place I said, 'I don't know what this is all about, but I am beginning to have some suspicions. I think I'd better not answer any more questions until you tell me.'

Again it was Smithwaite who answered. 'Harry George Andrews, I am arresting you on a charge of being accessory before and after the murder of a British subject, Colin Headly, at Rosas, Gerona, Spain. *Offences Against the Person Act,* 1861, Section 9. I must warn you that anything you say . . .' The caution trailed on.

I said, 'I want to call my solicitor.'

Old Manners was quicker off the mark than I had expected, and he brought Armitage with him. But by that time I was safely housed in Wandsworth Jail. It had all been very polite and comfortable, and I think I was more aggrieved than frightened. 'It's all so bloody stupid,' I said to Armitage. 'Goddammit, I couldn't have poisoned him! I've seen him only three times in fifteen years. What do they think I did—send it to him by post?'

Armitage said softly, 'I think you ought to know that Mrs. Headly was arrested at about the same time as you—and on a much more serious charge . . . capital murder. In some way they're trying to tie you up together.'

'What do you mean? If they had anything that they thought might be evidence why didn't they tell me and give me a chance to refute it?'

'They don't have to, old man, when they make the arrest, but

they must at the preliminary hearing at the Magistrate's Court.
Then it's up to him to chuck the whole thing out or to commit you
for trial. It's as fair as that. I shall be there, and all you have to
do is to say "Yes" or "No." I shall ask for bail as a matter of form,
but I know I won't get it. Anyway, you'll be more peaceful in here
than at your own flat. There's been an awful lot of publicity over
this business. We know that all reporters are bastards, but they
have to earn their living. They can't get at you in here.'

I had the privacy he promised, and in a strange way, the restric-
tive measure of the prison brought me the first peace I had known
in months. Here at least I could take no action. My judgment and
opinions could neither harm nor help.

Then came the first appearance in the Magistrate's Court.
Armitage came down with me in the police car. He said, 'I don't
know what they've got up their sleeve, but it must be something
pretty damning. Normally I would just plead not guilty and reserve
defense, but this time I must put you in the box—to find out exactly
what it is. Do you mind?'

'No.'

'Then'—he pressed my knee in emphasis—'just confine yourself
to "Yes" and "No." I'll do the rest.'

The Magistrate's Court was crowded and small. The magistrate
was a national figure who looked at us all with kindly cynicism.
We were the star turn, but had to wait for the curtain raiser of the
row of prostitutes. They filed into the dock like something off an
assembly line, and were each dismissed with a fine of two pounds.
We came next. I stood quietly in the dock while the charge was
read out, and then a gentleman who represented the Crown got up
and went through all the stuff we had heard about before in the
libel action. When he had subsided Armitage shot to his feet—he
always seemed to me to be like a jack-in-the-box. 'Your worship, I
do not propose to waste the time of this Court in refuting every
word that learned Counsel for the Crown has said. I wish to call
two witnesses: Detective Inspector Smithwaite and the defendant.'

There was a slight stir in the court while Smithwaite detached
himself from the obscurity of a side wall and stepped into the
witness box. Armitage was very polite. 'Inspector Smithwaite . . . I
understand your evidence rests on a letter the defendant wrote to
Mrs. Headly?'

'No . . . there are other letters.'

'I don't wish to go into the contents at the moment, but I must ask you how you acquired them.'

Smithwaite was a nice type; he didn't like what he had to say. He shuffled his feet and looked at the floor. 'They were sent to the Director of Public Prosecutions six weeks ago.'

'And from where were they mailed?'

'From Barcelona, I think.'

'You *think*.' Armitage got all the emphasis possible into it. 'And do you know who sent them?'

'No, they were mailed anonymously.'

'Do you have these documents with you?'

'Yes.'

'Then will you kindly hand them in to the court. That's all I want, thank you.'

Smithwaite retired, looking rather baffled. The Crown had nothing to say. Armitage had plenty. 'I call the prisoner, Mr. Harry Andrews.'

When I was in the witness box and sworn in I think that for the first time, I really looked at Armitage. Before, he had been something omnipotent, far off; but now I could see him as an individual. He was about forty-five, with a shock of hair that was going grey in the right places and a craggy face that looked as if someone had been hitting it hard with a mallet for an entire afternoon. There were the most wonderful pair of eyebrows that sprouted in every direction; beneath them, two sunken humorous blue eyes.

He handed me a sheet of paper. 'Do you recognize that, Mr. Andrews?'

I looked at it carefully. 'Yes. It's the letter I wrote to Mrs. Headly after I heard of Colin's death.'

'And that is your signature?'

'Yes.'

'And it was written on your typewriter?'

'Yes.'

'This is Exhibit A, your worship. Now may we have Exhibit B.' He looked enquiringly towards the Crown, but there were no questions.

The clerk of the court handed over a sheaf of letters. Armitage handed them to me very slowly. 'Did you write these, Mr. Andrews? And are the signatures yours?'

They were written on flimsier paper, and they left nothing to the imagination. Each started 'Lois, my darling'; each was signed

'Harry' in my exact signature. 'Take your time and read them
through,' said Armitage gently. I did, and they made me feel sick.
It wasn't just the continuous passages of detailed love-making, with
fervent hopes of more to come; it was the continual urging to get
and administer more of 'it,' demands that became more and more
frequent and adamant towards the end of the batch, with reminders
that 'it' must be very easy to obtain in Spain.

I read them one by one, right through; and Armitage passed
them in order to the magistrate. At one point he said, 'What is
"it"?'

' "It" is presumed, your worship, from the Spanish depositions,
to be the poison found in the body, dicoumarol.'

'I see.' It was the only comment made until the reading was over.
Then for the first time the Crown had something to say.

'Mr. Andrews, you have read through all these letters very
carefully?'

'Yes.'

'And you wrote them?'

'Only the first, the one to Rosas after Mr. Headly had died.'

'Don't you think it rather odd that the signatures are identical
with the one on the letter you admit you wrote and signed?'

'All I can say is that I did not write or sign them.' But as I
looked at the letters again a cold chill swept over me. Although it
is much easier to prove that two letters have been typed on the
same machine than it is to show that they have been signed by the
same hand, no mention of my typewriter was made. As I realised
the reason the small hairs on the back of my neck prickled. My
typewriter was an old one. Over the years the letter heads had
become crooked and indistinct, and a few days after my return from
Spain I had finally got around to having it repaired. All the keys
had been straightened. With frightening certainty I knew that the
police had discovered this and that in their minds the renovation
was as positive an indication of my guilt as any proof that the letters
had been typed on my machine. One is brought up to believe
that innocence is its own defense. But now I was not so secure.
Mechanically I listened as Armitage came to my defense.

'I would submit, your worship, that there is no case to answer.
My client denies writing all these letters except one—he insists the
rest are clever forgeries made for obvious reasons.'

There was a long pause while the magistrate thought, doodling
with a pencil while he stared at his desk. When he looked up I

knew there was no hope. 'I feel, Mr. Armitage, that this is a very
tricky case. In fairness to Mr. Andrews, I think that it should be
tried before a jury. I therefore commit him for trial at the Central
Criminal Courts.'

'Bail, your worship?' Armitage was still on his feet.

The magistrate gave him a kindly, sorrowful look. 'On a charge
of this nature, Mr. Armitage, you must know that is impossible.'

So I went back to Wandsworth, and it wasn't so pleasant as
before. This time there was the possibility that the restrictions might
be permanent. There was a calendar on the wall, and I began
marking off the days until the trial.

Old Manners came twice. When I explained about the typewriter
he looked worried, but said only that Armitage was sure to pull
something out of the bag. Armitage himself did not appear until
the night before the trial. He sat, looking as craggy and confident
as ever. 'Are you a betting man, Andrews?'

'Sometimes.'

'Well, I'll lay you 85 to 40 you are sitting at home tomorrow
night.'

'Don't be silly. I haven't a hope in hell.'

'But I've got an ace, chum.'

'What is it?'

He said, 'I think it would be better if you didn't know beforehand.
It will look more natural. Now we'll have to go through all the old
guff again. You must know it by heart now, so just say "Yes" and
"No" in the right places. And . . .' He produced a bright blue
capsule. 'Take this with your breakfast. It's only a mild tranquil-
lizer. It might help a little. You'll be O.K.'

Old Bailey isn't the same as the law courts. Apart from the difference in architecture, there is the same smell of wet disinfectant; but
something additional lies on the surface—fear and tension. Also,
you don't just wander in to a seat next to your solicitor. I was down
below with two warders, and the message came bellowing down the
stairs, 'Call up Harry Andrews.' And I went up those long stairs
with the guard gripping one arm and whispering, 'You'll be all
right, mate.' Then I was in the dock.

It was terribly impressive and rather terrifying. The filled well of
the court, the wigs and gowns of the barristers; the empty chair
beneath the Royal Coat of Arms, looking even more formidable in
its vacancy. The jury looked the same as juries always look, bored

and rebellious. The only things that looked out of place were a table and chair in the centre of the court. On the table was my typewriter; I was almost sure by the cover. Perhaps this had something to do with Armitage's secret weapon. There was no time to find out before the judge appeared, splendid in his robes. I was arraigned, and the jury was sworn in.

There was one objection that held up proceedings: a juryman claimed exemption on the grounds that I had once done his income tax returns. I didn't remember ever seeing him in my life before, but he was released and hurried off with a look of triumphant satisfaction. Then we got down to business. I pleaded 'Not guilty' and waited until we had got through what Armitage called 'the guff.'

I watched it all with a certain detachment; I had taken that blue pill with my breakfast coffee, and it made me feel I just didn't care. Even the warder sitting on my left, whispering in a hoarse voice at frequent intervals, 'You'll be all right, mate,' did not worry me.

After the 'guff' was over, the prosecuting counsel, Kirkland, shot to his feet. Under his wig blue eyes glinted impressively, thin lips drew into an even thinner line. 'I don't propose to waste the time of this Court, m'lud,' he said. 'I would like to call as my first witness Detective Inspector Smithwaite.'

Smithwaite was called and sworn in. My typewriter was handed up to him in the box.

'You recognize this machine?'

'Yes.'

'When did you see it last?'

'On the day I arrested the accused.'

'And it was then delivered to Scotland Yard by you?'

'It was.'

'I would like to have this typewriter entered as Exhibit A,' said Kirkland. 'Now, Mr. Smithwaite, did you have this machine examined?'

'Yes.'

'Will you tell the Court the results of your examination?'

'I found the machine to be of the same make and year as the one on which the letters to Mrs. Headly were written.'

At this point the judge leaned forward and said, 'The letters in question have not yet been entered as evidence. Does the prosecution wish to enter them now?'

'Yes,' said Kirkland. 'I would like them listed as Exhibit B.' The letters were brought forward, and I shuddered, remembering their contents. 'I would also like the letter the accused admits writing to Mrs. Headly on the death of Colin Headly entered separately, as Exhibit C. The papers were duly examined by the Court and placed upon the table near the bench. 'Now, Mr. Smithwaite, would you wish to finish explaining the findings of the laboratory examination made at Scotland Yard.'

Smithwaite fumbled a bit with the bottom of his tie, and I could see that he did not enjoy speaking in public. Or perhaps he simply did not enjoy the thought of contributing to a hanging. Finally he said in a soft monotone, 'Examination revealed that while the letter sent upon Mr. Headly's death was written on the machine in question it was impossible to determine whether or not the letters included in Exhibit B had been typed on that machine or on some other.'

'The techniques employed by Scotland Yard are usually very thorough. Can you explain why in this case you were unable to reach any definite conclusion?'

'The accused had apparently had the keys of his typewriter renovated in the week preceding the writing of the letter listed as Exhibit C.' A hush fell over the court. I glanced nervously at Manners. We had both known this piece of information would come out during the trial, but as I looked over at the jury I felt we had neglected the effect its revelation would have.

Kirkland's voice pulled my attention back to the floor. 'You seem very positive of the time this renovation took place. How is that?'

'Because we traced the shop which made the repairs. They keep a record of all work done.'

'Can you tell us the name of this store?'

'Office Machines, Ltd.'

'Thank you, Inspector Smithwaite. That will be all.' Smithwaite moved quickly down from the witness chair. Kirkland was staring at the jury, seeming to gauge their reaction to the policeman's evidence. After a couple of minutes he straightened up and said, 'I would now like to call Mr. Robert Baker to the stand.'

Mr. Baker was duly installed, and I recognized the man from Office Machines, Ltd. who had taken care of my typewriter. Unlike the inspector, he obviously relished appearing in court and identified both my machine and myself with a frightened expression that indicated he expected me to rise from my chair at any moment and attack him. Kirkland played him to the hilt. After that things moved more quickly. The prosecution called a few more official witnesses to establish time of death, the poison, and where it was purchased, dismissing each with a short convincing summary of the information he had given against me. Armitage made no attempt to cross-examine, and by the end of the day the judge turned the floor over to the defense.

The next morning, following a brief statement of our position, Armitage called me to the stand. The judge looked at me. He had a kind face, wrinkled with all the knowledge of the crimes that could be committed in this world. He said, 'Mr. Armitage, have you informed your client of the consequences of going into the witness box on oath . . . that he may be cross-examined?'

'I have so instructed, m'lud. And my client will welcome the opportunity to answer any questions the prosecution may have.'

'So be it.' I was led to the box and sworn in, then led through the same preliminary questions that had been asked at the indictment. The only difference was that in answer to the Crown, Armitage produced my diaries and passport entries, showing that by these documents I had alibis for all the purchases of poison. He went on to say that these documents could be checked by the police and that if the Court desired he could supply witnesses. Kirkland, however, made it clear that since I might have easily have commissioned someone to make the purchases for me they were willing to concede that I had been guiltless of picking up the dicoumarol in person.

There was a general pause while the judge duly recorded the agreement on this point. Then Armitage did a surprising thing. He asked me to come down into the well of the court and sit at the centre table. I came down, and he walked over to the bench and requested that one of the letters in Exhibit B be handed to me. At this Kirkland leapt to his feet, protesting against the waste of time, but the judge hardly bothered to look at him. 'There is an axiom, Mr. Kirkland,' he said, 'of which I am sure you are well aware, that justice must not only be done, but *seen* to be done. Knowing the defense's next witness, I think I can guess what Mr. Armitage has in mind. If it turns out that the evidence has no bearing on the case, then it will be my place to decide upon its relevance.'

Armitage secured the letter and brought it over to me. He then handed me a ball point pen. 'To the right of the signature at the bottom of this letter I would like you to sign your name. Sign exactly the way it appears in the original.' I did so, and was dismissed from the stand. While I was walking back to the dock the surprise witness was being called. A Mr. Hautboy. He looked as unlikely as his name. Small, neatly dressed, with a pale oval face, rimless glasses, and a bald head with three streaks of obviously dyed hair combed back over it in exactly parallel lines. His head hardly appeared over the witness box. If this was Armitage's secret weapon . . . My heart sank.

Hautboy gave his occupation as an expert of type—and handwriting. He was then handed the letter I had just signed. He took a long time examining it peering through a high-powered magnifying glass. At last he said, 'Although both signatures on this letter belong to the same person they were not both *written* by him on this piece of paper.'

'That seems an unusual statement. Can you explain it more fully?' said Armitage.

Hautboy settled back in his chair. He seemed completely in command of the situation, the schoolmaster facing an interested class. 'Well,' he said, 'in the last year, since ball point pens have become popular, banks have requested that they not be used to sign checks. And for two very good reasons. The first is that a ball point not only makes a deep impression on the check itself, but also can leave a clear outline of the writer's signature on any sheet that may be lying underneath. On close examination of the letter in my hand, it may be seen that there is a very heavy indentation made where Mr. Andrews has just written his name. Looking at the back of the letter, one can see the raised lines.' He handed the sheet first to the judge and then to the prosecutor. When Kirkland passed it back Hautboy said very slowly, 'You will have noticed that when the letter was turned over there was just one set of raised lines. Just one. In other words, although both signatures were made in ball point ink, only one left an indentation in the paper.'

The judge asked for the letter back. Finally he said, 'But the signatures appear identical.'

'They are,' said Hautboy. 'That is exactly my point.' Then he did the most surprising thing of the whole morning. Sitting beside the judge, he produced from his pocket an egg.

'Hard-boiled, my lord,' he said half apologetically as he began to roll it along the judge's desk, cracking the shell.

For the first time the judge looked angry. 'Mr. Hautboy, I don't think this is the time or place to indulge in mid-morning snacks!'

'Oh, I'm not going to eat it, my lord. I wouldn't presume. I just want to show you something.'

Amid a stunned silence he finished his peeling, dropping the fragments into what was, presumably, the judge's wastepaper basket. Then he said to the clerk of the court, 'Could I have a blank piece of paper?'

The clerk handed it up to him. He took the shelled egg carefully, and between thumb and forefinger rolled it over the signature I had just made; then used it in the same way, like a rolling pin, on the blank sheet of paper. 'There you are, my lord. That is the second reason banks don't like ball points.'

The judge stared at the two pieces of paper. 'Amazing!' he said. 'They are exact.'

There was a hum of sudden interest in the public galleries, and I saw with complete detachment the jury whispering among themselves. Then the foreman stood up. 'My lord . . .'

'I take it that you want to examine these documents?' They were passed over, and as they circulated among the members of the jury it was obvious from their reactions that Armitage's secret weapon had done its job. The rest of the proceedings were strictly routine. On the following day when the jury retired to reach a verdict there was only a twenty-minute wait.

When asked to pronounce the decision the foreman faced the court and in a loud voice said, 'In a unanimous vote we have found the prisoner not guilty.'

For the first time the judge became human. 'I cannot agree with you more. Prisoner at the Bar, you are discharged.' Then he smiled. 'I'm sorry you've had this ordeal, Mr. Andrews, but we've both learned a lot about hard-boiled eggs.'

I bowed, and the guard beside me whispered, 'I told you you'd be all right, mate.'

CHAPTER 10

That night, Armitage, Proudfoot, and I downed a bottle of whisky; we had asked Hautboy, but he didn't drink, and anyway, he had to clean out his aquarium. So it was a quiet evening, with nothing to disturb the numbing effects of the liquor until the very end.

For a long time we talked over the mysterious forged letters. Who had written them? Why? They didn't make sense. I listened to the other two worry the problem round and round. They still saw it as just a legal puzzle. A loose piece of evidence. An annoying thread that couldn't be woven in. I closed my eyes. By this time I was pretty tight and nothing made too much difference. It was a pleasant feeling. I was beginning to understand Colin's perpetual thirst. Most things were easier to face with a pint of whisky under the belt. In fact, I had been drunk a good deal in the months since Colin's death. Or to be more exact, since that wild night at the fiesta.

'Fiesta?' said Armitage, and I realized I had spoken aloud.

'At Rosas,' I said. 'The last time I saw Colin. We got very drunk. Very wild. Very gay.' And then remembering, I added, 'Got some pictures somewhere here. Friend of Colin's sent them.' I rummaged about for a while and finally found them in the back of the drawer where I had flung them the day they arrived.

'Here.' I spread the photos out on the table. 'That's Colin. You never saw him, did you?' It was the first time I had looked at the pictures myself. Suddenly Proudfoot reached over and picked up one of the snaps.

'I thought you said you hadn't met Miguel,' he said.

'Miguel?'

Proudfoot pointed. In the corner of one of the photos, small but very clear, was the seated figure of the man who had drawn the knife. Miguel. Sally's Miguel. Colin had mentioned the name, but I had never thought of making the connection. Now in the back of my mind an idea was forming—hazy, but powerful. The alcohol helped. I conjured up a much vivider image of the Rosas café than

I could have when sober. The shabby counter. The six Spaniards
in the far corner. The tall, dark Catalan moving slowly towards us.
Miguel . . . who had married Colin's mistress less than three months
after his death.

I turned to Armitage. 'I told you about the fight, didn't I? Well,
that's the Spaniard. Looks like he had a reason for wishing Colin
dead, after all.'

'If it comes to that,' said Proudfoot, 'Sally herself may have been
impatient to switch from being the mistress of a sick man to the
wife of a healthy one.'

'I suppose we should pass the information on to Mrs. Headly's
counsel.' Armitage stood up. 'At least give them a line of defense.
Something to talk about.'

'Something to talk about. Oh my God.' I crossed my arms on
the table and rested my head on them. Proudfoot and Armitage
were getting ready to leave. I looked up, and they began struggling
into their coats with awkward, hurried movements. Their faces were
averted, and I suddenly realized that they were trying to avoid my
glance. I put my hand to my face and found it wet with tears. My
shoulders heaved painfully.

I tried to apologize, but Armitage shook his head, saying, 'It's
been a long day. Get some sleep.' He went towards the door. Just
before closing it he turned and said, 'You've been in love with her
all along, haven't you?'

I woke the next morning with a splitting headache. It was a few
minutes before I remembered exactly what was wrong. Then the
conversation of the previous night came flooding back. The
discovery that the man who had tried to knife Colin was now Sally's
husband. That both Miguel and Sally had a motive for murder.
That perhaps Colin was wrong and Lois was innocent.

As I drank my coffee I thought over the evidence brought out at
the trial. The letters certainly made more sense if they were forged
by Sally and Miguel in an attempt to frame Lois. I had never
believed that Lois had been responsible for implicating me. Driven
by jealousy or hatred, she might have killed Colin, but I could not
see her deliberately plotting to have me hanged. The letters at no
time would have served to mitigate the case against her. I wanted
to ring Armitage and ask him what could be done. *The Queen v.
Headly* was scheduled to come to court within the month, and if any
new evidence was to be unearthed action would have to be taken

quickly. I stared at my calendar, called my office. The trial had been an ordeal. I was sure they would understand my wishing to take a few more days off. They said I should take as much time as I wished and offered congratulations.

I wandered about the room for a few minutes after I hung up. The next step was inevitable. I was going to visit Lois.

I took a cab from my apartment to the prison. All the way I made up different apologies for what I had done. Over and over I muttered different variations of the same sentence until I arrived white-faced and tense in the outer court of the jail, only to be told she would not see me. The degree of responsibility I held for her position swept over me. It was small wonder she had turned me away.

Frantic with worry, the trial looming only short weeks away, I hurried to the Inns of Court and called on her solicitors. They, also, were not too cordial, but my hysterical repetition that I had some new evidence—I didn't care if this was stretching a point—finally got me an interview. I explained about the photograph, the fight, and Sally and Miguel. They said they would arrange for me to see Lois. I guess they were desperate themselves. The press was strongly against her. Each day new discoveries of dicoumarol purchased under her name were being announced. To believe the scandal sheets, she had bought enough poison to do away with an army, let alone a husband. By now the only problem facing the prosecution seemed to be an explanation of the attempt to implicate me, and public opinion was not concerning itself with such details. If I said I might be able to help, the defense was willing to give me the chance.

On my second trip to the jail some strange impulse made me stop and buy a huge bunch of chrysanthemums. God knows what was in my mind. Some shadowy memory of childhood courtship. Gripping the awkward bundle, I was conducted into a dull stone visiting room. Lois was ushered in. We sat opposite each other, a fine steel grille between us. A wardress stood watching in the corner.

It was three years since I had been close enough to Lois to speak to her. She was wearing no make-up and was dressed in a grey shapeless sack. Only her hair, even though it had been cut short, was the same, a vivid burning brush. I pulled back the paper from the flowers so that she could see them, but her eyes never wavered from my face.

'Why are you here?' Her voice was flat, devoid even of the anger I had expected.

'The photograph of Miguel. I didn't understand until then. Colin said . . . The book said . . .' I knew I was babbling. 'Lois, I never stopped loving you. It was just that Colin was my friend. He said that he needed me. That he was dying. It was wrong, but when I read the book . . . He always could make me believe what he wanted.'

For the first time her eyes softened.

'Lois, he was very persuasive.'

And finally she spoke. 'I know. It was his charm, for a while, anyway. He could build a picture in your mind and make you see it even if it destroyed everything else you believed in. Knowing that is the only thing which can help me forgive you.'

'And you do forgive me?'

'Not yet, but I think I will.'

Then more calmly I repeated my story about the knifing, Miguel, and Sally. 'Colin must have been blind.'

There was a pause.

'He had plenty of reason to hate me,' Lois said slowly. 'He knew I loved you. Once, in Ireland, he played a very vicious practical joke. For a month he secretly taped my confessions to Father O'Neill.' I had a sudden image of odd wires strung up across Colin's study. 'Not that he wouldn't have guessed how I felt, anyway,' she continued. 'But, Harry, if they ever find those tapes, no lawyer on earth will be able to get me off.'

'Maybe they were left in Ireland, destroyed.'

'I don't think so. He used to talk about them occasionally at Rosas. Gloat over my one abortive affair.'

'Well, can you think of any place he might have hidden them?'

'I caught him in the patio one morning. By the old twisted tree. Do you remember?'

'Very well.'

'And the old mill wheel that we had as a table beside it?'

'Yes, it was built up on bricks.'

'Well, he was pulling out one of the bricks.'

'I'll have a look.'

'In Spain? Harry, that's mad! And if you think Miguel killed Colin there's no reason to believe he won't kill you if he catches you poking about on the property. He and Sally live there now, you know.'

'I know. I want to see them. I told your lawyers about Miguel,
but it may not be enough. If I can speak to Sally perhaps I'll learn
something more definite. Enough to get you off. And while I'm
there I can look for the tapes. Destroy them.'

'You really believe the Spaniard's guilty?'

'I don't care.'

'I didn't do it.'

'It doesn't matter any more.'

'That's funny,' she said gently. 'Colin sent you his manuscript
because he knew you were the one person who would publish it no
matter what his personal feelings. Yet now you're eagerly going off
to destroy one piece of evidence and conjure up another.'

'Even if I believed you were guilty I would do the same,' I said.

'Would you, Harry?' Her smile held a genuine warmth. 'I don't
think so, but then that's why I'm sure you do believe me.'

The wardress now stood up. 'You have had more than your time.'

'I'm just going,' I said.

'Be careful,' warned Lois. 'Miguel is tough and Sally, well, I'd
be more inclined to place my money on her.' She was led away.

On the bench beside me still lay the chrysanthemums.

On the way home I tried to plan a course of action. I ruled out
Manners and Armitage, for they were hardly experts in detection
and I knew they would object to my going at all. Proudfoot was
the only answer, and without even stopping at my flat I went on
to his office. By luck he was not out on a job.

He listened very carefully to all I had to tell him and then said,
'I've been doing some thinking, too, since the other night. You may
have a point. Miguel is a nasty customer. And if you're right he's
sitting pretty at the moment, and he's not likely to let go easily.
You know, life is cheap in those parts of the world, I guarantee
that in less than twenty-four hours a hundred pounds could put
you in the harbor with a knife in your back.'

'I'm still going,' I said. 'I must find something.'

'When are you planning on leaving?'

'As soon as I can get a flight to Barcelona.'

'Let me go for you. At least with you.'

'No!' I had not, of course, told him about the tapes, and I tried
to think of a reason for my insistence on going alone. After what
seemed an uncomfortably long pause I said, 'It will look more
natural if I go myself. Just a friendly visit to Sally from an old

acquaintance. Besides, I feel a responsibility towards Lois for getting her into this mess.'

He thought for a minute. 'Well, don't leave for a couple of days. I want to get you some special equipment.'

He was back on the second evening with a small attaché case.

'Now before I give you what's in here,' he said, patting the case, 'I want you to listen carefully. If you find anything incriminating tell the police and get the hell out! But the chances of your discovering anything are slim. You have no experience at this sort of thing and the official investigators must have gone over the ground pretty carefully. My hunch is that you will have to trap either Sally or Miguel into giving themselves away, and this will be dangerous. I know Miguel and his type. He'll stop at nothing to keep you quiet. But he'll have one problem. I said the other day that a hundred pounds would put you at the bottom of the harbor. Well, it could if you were a Spaniard. With foreigners it's different. There is the bother of consular trouble—many people asking questions. So if you really are sure Miguel is your boy and are serious about going to any length to dig up fresh evidence, there are some odds in your favor. Not many, but enough to make an attempt at getting Miguel to spill the beans—if he knows them to spill—worth while. Sally would be a safer quarry, but she'll be a whole lot better at holding her tongue. Miguel, from my short acquaintance, definitely seems the bragging type. At any rate, that is the weakness on which you'll have to play. If you do get him to open up I've brought you something that will take it down.' He opened his brief case and took out a small plastic box about the size of a pack of cigarettes, with a thin wire ending in a disk the size of a sixpence extending from it.

'German tape recorder,' he said, 'new . . . and it runs for only about twenty minutes. The lead goes down your arm, and the microphone'—he held up the disk—'sticks under the back of your watch. It records on wire, not tape, so damp or pressure, even a spell in the sea, won't do it any harm.'

'Miguel drinks heavily. Maybe a night on the town would loosen his tongue.' I shuddered, remembering another night out at Rosas.

'It may,' said Proudfoot, 'but my concern is protecting you. Even a complete confession isn't going to do Lois any good if you end up at the bottom of the sea with it still taped to your wrist.' He opened his case again and took out a small gun. 'You can carry this and,' he said, bending once more, 'wear this.' He spread out what looked for all the world like a modified brassière with tapes hanging down on each side and a small bottle in one corner. 'A special sort of Mae West. It doesn't show under clothes, and you just press the button on the bottle and it inflates with CO_2. It can keep you afloat for hours. I want you to promise me to keep it on at all times if you think you're under suspicion.'

I nodded.

'Remember, drunk or otherwise, Miguel is a tough opponent.'

I nodded again. After all, I'd seen him in action.

'Well,' said Proudfoot, shutting the case, 'I've done my best. I think you may be right in suspecting the Spaniard, but I wouldn't count on it too much. In any case, I hope to hell she's worth it.'

He walked out quickly, as if anxious to free himself from the harebrained affair, and I wondered if he would have been so co-operative if he had known that I was going to Spain as much to destroy evidence as to dig it up.

CHAPTER 11

I had my flight to Barcelona the next day, but this time there was no one to meet me at the airport. I had to go the hard way by train to Figueras, then take the bus. It was evening when I arrived at the house, and the patio with it's old, gnarled tree, the mill wheel beside it, seemed deserted. Even the white cats weren't there. I just sat down and waited. Sally put in an appearance in about half an hour. She was very apologetic. 'Harry, how nice to see you! They are such idiots here . . . we got the cable that you were coming only two hours ago.' I had sent it two days before, and I thought she was lying; but it didn't really matter.

Sally . . . I looked at her dispassionately. She was darker, more like the gypsy I had seen before; but she was filling out. She wasn't Irish any more. It's difficult to describe, but she was . . . greasy.

I think I made a decision at that moment: to play it right to the end.

She said, 'Miguel's dying to meet you, but he's having a nap now before his evening meal. You know he owns a boat? Uses it at night for sardines. Maybe he'll take you out sometime.'

'That might be fun. Yes, I'd like that,' I said, thinking it might be a good opportunity to see Miguel alone.

A few minutes later the Spaniard himself appeared, yawning and stretching and still exuding the same feline power I had sensed the night of the fiesta. He made no mention of the incident, greeting me affably and then going into a long moan, in pretty fluent English, about the price of fuel for the boat, the lack of sardines in the gulf, and the impossible hours he had to work.

I sipped my drink and listened. The white cats—and they weren't kittens any more—slid from out of the shadows somewhere and started playing up and down the old tree. It all seemed so peaceful, so like a year before. But I remembered what I was certain I was sitting on, also the 'equipment' I had upstairs in my room. I thanked God that my travelling bag was made of tough hide with a real Yale lock, and that the key was in my pocket.

We had our meal outside, a pilau of fish, prawns, and octopus. It was not served by Lolita, but by a new, dark girl. At last Miguel arose, still grumbling at the iniquity of any man having to work from ten at night to five in the morning, six days a week.

As he was leaving, Sally said, 'Harry wants to come out and try it with you sometime, Miguel.'

'It's not very comfortable,' said Miguel. 'You can't sleep.'

'That's all right,' I assured him. 'You see, it would be a novelty for me.'

'Well, perhaps it can be arranged. Now I must go and see if the sardines are rising from the bottom of the Gulf of Rosas.' He gave Sally an affectionate pat on the bottom and trudged out of the door.

We sat sipping the last of the wine in silence while the dark girl cleared the plates away. Then I forced the issue deliberately.

'Where's Lolita?'

'Oh, she went, after Colin—' Her voice seemed to be cut off in mid-air, as if by a knife.

A long silence: then, 'Have you seen Lois?'

'Yes . . . once. I took her some flowers. That's about all they are allowed to have.'

'And you'll be going again?'

'I expect so.'

'Then will you please take her a big bunch of something really nice from me?'

'Why don't you go and see her yourself?'

'It's too far.' She was clasping her hands over her knees in an effort of concentration. 'And I can't leave Miguel—he depends on me so—he's such a baby in lots of ways.'

'All right, I'll deliver them. And your message.'

'I read all about it in the papers, Harry. I'm only sorry that you got involved the way you did. She had it coming to her, anyway.' Her voice had suddenly gone hard and brittle.

I got up. 'I'm a bit tired, Sally. Do you mind if I go to bed?'

'Me, too. Miguel won't be back until six by the time he's finished seeing to the nets.'

When I got to my room I opened the shutters wide and the moonlight was slanting on the leaves of the old trees, making them glow like silver. There wasn't a sound except the barking of a dog a long way off. It was all so peaceful.

My case had not been touched. For the moment, its contents seemed wildly melodramatic and implausible. I fell asleep quickly.

At nine o'clock the next morning I decided to start my search for the tapes. I had heard Miguel clump up the stairs at about a quarter to seven, and there was silence from their room. They must be busy; either asleep or making love. The girl, Maria, brought me coffee and rolls on the patio and put them on the mill wheel. I sat there eating, slowly shifting round after she had gone, feeling the brickwork underneath me.

It was a ludicrous position to have to shuffle round in a half circle, feeling each brick in turn. I was fairly well sheltered from the rooms of the house by the old tree. I worked round slowly, feeling every one, and at last I found it.

It was about a third of the way round; and it was loose; it came out easily with a little puff of dust when I prised it with the knife I had been using on my roll. A gust of cold, damp air came out when I put my hand in the gap, but there was something else. Two flat tins that rattled as I picked them up. They were sealed with tape, but I didn't wait to open them: I knew what was inside. One quick look towards the house. No movement, no sign of life. I slipped the brick back and walked out of the patio as fast as I could.

It was too risky to go back indoors. There was a chance Sally had not gone to sleep. She might come into my room, forcing me to hide the tapes there. Worse still, she might catch me destroying them. The one thing I had to do was to get as far from the house as possible. I began moving quickly up the street, forcing myself to walk, not run. Ahead a few dusty shops made colorful outlines against a background of jagged masts. Masts. The harbor. And then I knew where to go. Once wet, the tapes would be ruined. Even if they were found they would be harmless. Just two blank voiceless roles of plastic. My heartbeats slowed.

I was in the middle of town before the cheerful shout brought me up short. A thin line of sweat broke out between my shoulders and trickled slowly down my back. I turned and almost without surprise watched Miguel come steadily towards me.

'It's hard to sleep on such a fine day,' he said. 'That's one of the reasons I hate my working hours.' He fell into step beside me. 'Going to look at the boats? I'll keep you company, show you the *Santa Teresa*.' We continued down the street, Miguel taking long, easy strides while I tried to keep suddenly rubber-jointed legs from buckling. It was impossible to know why he was there, whether he had been watching all along from the house. I sensed his eyes on the packets in my left hand, but the glance might have been natural curiosity. There was a long silence while my mind, a feverish blank, uselessly totaled the gulls circling overhead. Then out of the corner of my eye I glimpsed a flash of orange and red. I twisted my head and looked straight into the folds of a gaily waving Spanish flag. We were in front of the post office. I stopped abruptly and opened the door. Miguel looked startled, but I motioned him inside.

'Took these with me in my brief case by mistake,' I said, pointing at the tapes. 'Have to send them back to the office. They'll be needed,' I started filling out a label, carefully noting my firm name, but listing my home address. I couldn't take the chance of having them opened by a well-meaning secretary. Miguel peered over my shoulder and I let him look, certain he was too unfamiliar with London to spot the residential location.

'They won't wrap them for you,' he said at last.

'What?'

'You'll have to go across the street and get some paper. The post office won't wrap them.'

Clammy perspiration was now working its way down my sides. As we crossed the street to the small general store the fine, sharp dust on the road pricked my nostrils and choked my throat. The shop itself was shuttered and stuffy, and a small Catalan behind the counter shrugged helplessly at my English. Miguel translated in natural enough tones, but when a crumpled piece of brown paper was finally found my hands were shaking so badly I could hardly fold it. After watching for a minute Miguel broke into another volley of Spanish. The shopkeeper vanished. I waited, wondering. Then the little Catalan reappeared with a piece of string, which I awkwardly tied around the parcel. At every moment I expected Miguel to whip out a knife, slash open the package, and turn on me. But when I was finished he just thanked the shopkeeper and walked me back across to the post office, where I bought stamps and saw the post office carelessly throw the tapes into a large bag marked VIA AERO.

Miguel left me after that saying it was getting late and he had better try to get a little sleep before lunch. I continued down to the bay and spent an unpleasant morning trying to convince myself that our meeting had been nothing but a coincidence, but the moment I returned to the patio and saw the two of them waiting I knew that it had been planned. It wasn't that they said anything or that they were any less cordial hosts. And I don't believe in hunches or extrasensory perception. But sitting in that quiet garden

beneath Colin's old room, I knew as surely as if they were shouting
their suspicions aloud. And I knew just as certainly what they
would have to do next.

The lead in was so obvious I might have guessed it.

'Miguel's arranged to take you fishing tonight if you want to go.'
Sally's voice was cheerful. If I sidestepped this they would only
think of something else, and perhaps it was best to have the attack
made where I expected it and could be prepared.

'That would be very nice, if you are sure I won't be a nuisance.'

'Oh, no fear of that,' said Sally.

'It should be a good night for the sardines.' Miguel looked at the
sky. I will have the *Santa Teresa* up at the quay, by the Nautico
Café, at nine. Don't be late, and wear warm clothing. It can be
cold in the gulf at night.' Again that look passed between them,
and I knew there was going to be a showdown.

I remembered Proudfoot's warnings and pocketed my gun. On
impulse I picked up the tape recorder and took that, too. I fitted
the recorder part of the machine in my hip pocket, making a little
hole so that I could run the wire up my back and down my sleeve;
the microphone fitted easily under my watch. The Mae West was
more difficult; it didn't show under my sweater, but the only possible place to stow the bottle of CO_2 was under my left armpit,
which wasn't very comfortable. I tested the switch on the recorder,
made sure I knew where the button was on that bloody bottle, and
then I went downstairs, ready for battle.

It was about half-past eight, and I had plenty of time. I tried to
say good night to Sally, but the girl told me she was out. I went
down to the Nautico and had a drink, bought two bottles of brandy.
At exactly nine I walked across to the quay.

The *Santa Teresa* was there, ready, her engine chugging softly. She
was about thirty feet long, very broad in the beam, and there was
nothing, absolutely nothing, to stop you going over the side.
Towards the stern the great net was coiled and there were a stack
of fish boxes. Behind them was a small well, where Miguel sat
holding the tiller.

'Welcome aboard, Harry. You sit here with me until we are out
in the gulf, and then you go forward and rest with the others. But
you must obey my orders exactly. It is a condition. You
understand?'

'Of course.'

I looked over my shoulder at the small rowing boat that was

lashed behind us. Only one man in it, and at the stern a tall bracket
with a cluster of five big acetylene lights, still dark. Miguel didn't
have to wait for any query. He looked down at the package I held
in my lap. 'What is that, Harry?'

I opened the package. 'Two bottles of brandy, one for you and
me; the other for the crew, with your permission.'

'You are very kind.' He called softly and one of the crew came
forward. He had a swig at the bottle and thanked me; they came
one after the other then; eleven in all. Only one did not drink; a
slight figure that kept in the shadows of the fish boxes. I thought
it was a boy apprentice who wasn't old enough.

We cast off, towing the boat with the lights behind us. It was
still, soft, and warm as we headed into the blackness. The lights of
Rosas faded to a twinkling cluster. We were alone.

Miguel and I sat side by side, passing the other brandy bottle,
smoking my cigarettes; talking about life. He looked at the sky once,
and then at the water. 'Calm, and not too much moon. They should
rise tonight, my friend, to our lights; slowly, in great shoals from
the bottom of the gulf. And once they are in the light they cannot
escape . . . they are mesmerized, as you would say. You will see a
wonderful sight, something you will never forget. Make the most of
it.'

It was about midnight when we anchored. The sea had seemed
calm when we were under way, but the *Santa Teresa* rolled like a
bitch when stationary. Everyone just lay down on the deck and
went to sleep. 'They have made a bed for you on the port side,'
said Miguel softly. 'I will be here to call you when something
happens.'

I went forward, tripping over bodies that lay all over the deck.
All except one that I passed in the shadows of those fish boxes. The
apprentice, the boy who wouldn't drink. He didn't smell of garlic
and brandy, like the others. We didn't speak, but as I passed there
was a faint smell of perfume. I knew why Sally had been out when
I tried to wish her good night. I also knew what I was up against.

My bed, when I found it, was a couple of boxes, with a coil of
rope for a pillow; it was right on the port side, and apart from the
discomfort of the recorder at my hip, the carbon dioxide in my
armpit, it was impossible to sleep from the rolling, particularly as
there was nothing to stop me from going into the drink at any time.
I tried closing my eyes for a bit, and then sat up and smoked. The
lights in the small boat were on.

'Harry . . .' It was Miguel calling softly. 'Come back to the stern and I think you will see something you will never forget.'

I stumbled up past the fish boxes, and then I saw one of the most beautiful things I have ever seen.

The five lamps in the boat threw out a huge pool of light across the sea. It turned it into a pale shade of aquamarine. 'They are coming,' said Miguel. 'Watch them come.'

The sea was unruffled. The man in the boat with the lights was watching intently. Suddenly he said something in Catalan: a pearly drop jumped into the air, like a raindrop in reverse. 'They're here,' said Miguel.

Another drop of silver, another, all jumping at the light and falling back in the sea. Soon the pool of light was creamed with them, millions of them; like the wake of a ship. 'They can't escape,' said Miguel. Then he turned to me, making no attempt to conceal the ugly determination on his face.

The cards were down. I didn't say anything while I watched one end of the net being thrown to the man in the boat; his slow circle towards the bows, keeping that boiling cauldron in his lights; then the tightening of the other end to the power winch—a quick pull, and millions of sardines came tumbling on board. I didn't watch the sudden activity; the sorting and the boxing of them. I just sat quite still in the stern, waiting for the inevitable.

It came after the crew had gone back to sleep and we were on our way home, with the false dawn just breaking the sky. I was still sitting in the stern when the slim figure of the apprentice, who I now knew was Sally, emerged from nowhere and crouched beside Miguel. I looked at my watch and said, 'I'd no idea it was so late.' He looked at Sally and apparently decided to use the direct approach, for he said bluntly, 'You are twenty miles off Rosas. I hope you can swim that far.'

'No. I wouldn't try.'

'A pity, señor. For in a moment you will have the opportunity. And it is no use you shouting for help to the crew. For one thing, they would not hear you above the noise of the engine, for they are very tired and fast asleep. Secondly, even if they did wake up they have a great respect for their captain.'

'I've got the idea.'

'Good. Then we will have a little talk. It is always interesting to have the truth at the last moment. Now, why did you come here and pry into my affairs?'

'I came to visit an old friend, your wife.'

'And to dig in our property.' Sally spoke for the first time. 'It's no use fooling, Harry. We know you found something. Why do you think Miguel followed you this morning?'

'But he let me mail the package,' I said.

'Oh, Harry, you always were slow to catch on to things. What was it that Colin used to call you? Slow-boots?' Sally laughed. This is Spain, Harry, not London. There's nothing sacred about the mail here. After you left, Miguel just wandered into the post office, said you wanted the parcel back, and the man handed it over. Colin's tapes . . . Well, if he recorded anything against us no one will ever hear it. They're in the stove. Burned.'

As she said this some of the chilling fear that had swept over me eased. The tapes were destroyed. And by the very people to whom they could have been most useful. The thought was oddly comforting, helping me mind refocus on the purpose behind my trip. I looked at my watch and pushed the button for the recorder. 'It seems my visit has been a total loss,' I said softly. 'I'm no better off than before I came. I was pretty sure that you had killed Colin.' Miguel took a quick step forward. 'Wait. I know what must come, but as you said, it is always interesting to have the truth at the end. At least tell me this. Why did you try to involve me? After the book came out Lois provided the perfect scapegoat. What did you need me for?'

Sally smiled. 'You still don't see.'

'No, and I'm surprised you were able to fool Colin. How did you get him to write the mystery? It couldn't have been a coincidence.'

She hesitated and looked at Miguel. He nodded, and there was a moment's pause. Then she said, 'Oh, Harry, you idiot! Don't you understand? Colin knew the truth all along. It was his idea!'

'What?'

Again she turned to Miguel, and though his face remained impassive she seemed to read some sign of acquiescence there, for after a long look out to sea she began to explain.

'It all started long ago. In Ireland. You remember how Colin felt about Clonco. It had been his dream ever since he was a little boy—a gardener's son living off lies and imagination. I think he'd always planned to come back and take over. Then he married Lois and he thought he'd won it all: the position, the background, the respect. But it didn't work out that way. In a short time the villagers saw through him. They didn't like him any the less for it, but they knew he was one of them. It made him furious because they treated Lois, lost money and all, like a queen. I don't know if they ever were a happy couple, but by the time Colin hired me she despised him. And he hated her. Hated her pride, her breeding; hated most of all the fact that nothing he did could break her. It was an ugly situation, but static.

'Then you came along and things began to happen. For weeks after you left she mooned about the house in a daze. Only a blind man could have failed to see she was in love, and Colin wasn't blind. He began to hate you, too. You'd cracked a shell he could never pierce. You weren't quite Lois's class, but you were, well . . . a gentleman. It gnawed at him, Harry. I can't explain, but in some ways he wasn't normal. Instead of letting her go and marrying me he insisted on taking her with us to Spain. Every few months he would taunt her about you, and as his illness progressed the scenes became more and more violent. Then the last year they stopped. By this time I had met Miguel, but was keeping it a secret until he had enough money to take me away. I didn't want Colin attacking me.

'Well, things were quiet for a while. It was obvious Colin was getting worse. Then one morning he called me into his room and said he had found a way to get his revenge. If I would help him he would make me his chief heir. While I was still digesting the announcement he started to explain his plan. In brief it was this. He was dying. He had privately visited a doctor in Madrid and learned he had only about ten months left. During the last few weeks the pain would be agonizing and he did not intend to face it. At the beginning of the eighth month he was going to poison himself. But the twist was he was going to arrange to have you and Lois hanged for his murder.'

'Then he deliberately wrote the book to throw suspicion on Lois.'

'Yes,' said Sally. 'I rather think he liked the idea of having you act as the agent. Of course, if you hadn't given it to the publisher he had left a carbon with me which I would have sent on, but he had great faith in your sense of duty. Particularly to the dead.'

Somewhere in the back of my mind I heard a clear schoolboy treble mocking all those rules that England tries so hard to indoctrinate in her young: the clear-cut codes that in most situations save the trouble of individual decision. 'But he couldn't have guessed Lois would sue,' I said.

'No, that was where I came in,' said Sally. 'After the book came out I was to go to London, quietly draw attention to the resemblance between the main characters and Lois and Colin, and finally press for an exhumation. A post-mortem would immediately reveal poison, and once the fact of murder was established the rest would be easy. A couple of words in the right ear would direct the police to a Madrid chemist where a large purchase of dicoumarol had been made by a redheaded woman who foolishly signed the register, "Lois Headly." '

'The woman being you, I gather, suitably disguised.'

She nodded.

'But what about the forged letters?'

'Oh, Colin wrote those. He remembered you once said you still had your old typewriter. He'd seen it when he stayed with you and simply bought one like it. I don't think he realized how easily a particular machine could be identified, and of course, your repairing your machine eliminated the problem. As for the signatures, you know how those were done.'

'So Colin's frantic request that I come to Spain was just to put me at the scene of the crime shortly before the murder.'

This time she didn't answer. I looked at my watch. Time was running out. I had enough taped to clear Lois, but I still felt there was something missing.

'Once Colin was dead,' I said slowly, 'what made you carry through with his plan? Why didn't you just take your money and clear out?'

Miguel suddenly moved forward and took Sally's arm. All through her story he had lounged quietly against the tiller, only his eyes—black hooded slits—showing his tension. Now he spoke. 'Enough. Let it end here.'

'What difference does it make?' Sally's voice was clear and cold. 'Even if there were no more to tell we couldn't let him go.' She turned towards me. 'It's amazing how little you knew Colin after all those years. He would never have left me a thing without making sure I carried out his plans. He kept hinting that he had something on me, too. By the time he had finished the manuscript I was terrified of him. He kept saying that he would keep me faithful to him. Said he was going to add a codicil to his will to provide that I receive no money for five years and at that time only if I had remained single. Then someone, I think Lolita, told him about Miguel. This was just before your visit. He became furious. Swore he would work out his scheme without me. Leave his money to some charity.'

'So you killed him before he could make the change,' I interrupted.

'He was going to die soon, anyway. We just hastened his death by a few weeks.'

'It all must have been quite easy, what with Colin's foolproof scheme to throw suspicion away from you. Still, you might have left me out of the picture.

I knew this was the showdown and tried to think of a way to get out my gun without alerting them. I was looking at Sally, and never saw Miguel drop the tiller and bend down. One minute I was standing on the deck, the next there was a swift pull at my ankles and I felt myself lifting and then plunging down.

Once in the water I swam quietly until the *Santa Teresa* was out of sight. Then I squeezed the bottle under my arm and felt the life jacket expand around me. The bay was cold, but I was safe. When morning came I was still cheerfully bobbing about, with only a headache to remind me of my experiences. Shortly after dawn one of the day boats, an ordinary trawler, spotted me and pulled me on board. I had ten thousand very wet pesetas in my pocket, and it was not difficult to persuade the skipper with these that it would be better to forego a day's fishing and take me straight to Barcelona. There a taxi to the British Consulate, and a somewhat late breakfast with the consul. He didn't need much briefing as he had had to make the original depositions.

'My God, you took a hell of a risk!' he said, sipping his coffee.

'I don't think so. If you know you are going to be "done" and are prepared for it, it's far more comfortable than something in the dark.'

He looked at me, and then at the little recorder, lying beside us on the table. 'I don't think we dare touch that. It needs an expert. I'll send it to London in the diplomatic bag. You've dried out a bit, but if you don't mind my saying so, you still look like a tramp. We're about the same size, so I'll lend you a suit. I want to get you out of here as fast as I can. You're dangerous. I'll take you to the airport myself, and I have a little influence with BEA . . .

I was back in London within four hours.

CHAPTER 12

There is very little else to tell. The recorder played back perfectly when it had been dried out by an expert; everything was there, even the noise of my splash as I went into the sea. Miguel won't be using the *Santa Teresa* for some time—about ten years. They got him through Interpol, and he now languishes in a Spanish jail, which I understand is not too pleasant. Sally just disappeared. I suppose it was easier for her as she had kept her Irish passport. She will surface again sometime . . . the Sallys of this life always do.

And Lois. The case against her was dropped. They let her out at eight in the morning, and I was waiting with a taxi. She came out slowly, walking, and then she saw me, and she started to run . . . ran straight into my arms, clinging to me.

'Oh, Harry! Oh, Harry!'

'Don't say anything, darling. I've got a cab waiting. Let's just get away.'

When we were inside I closed the division between us and the driver. 'I should have brought some flowers,' I said, 'but I thought it would look a little silly.'

'Don't worry.' She was holding my hand very hard.

'I've got something else in my pocket, though. A special licence. Would you like to use it?'

She stared ahead for a long time. 'Of course, darling. But I'll have to get some clothes first.'

The house in Rosas was empty for some time, and then the lawyers decided we could pay a nominal rent for it and take it over. So we go each summer, and sit in the patio, on the old millstone by the gnarled tree. We watch the cats—they are getting a bit plump now—run up and down the trunk. We talk to the villagers; they never mention anything. They are too polite. They know that Lois and I are deeply in love—perhaps more than the usual, for we have both been through great suffering.

No one worries us there, but in London sometimes when we leave a party or go out of a pub someone says just a bit too soon, 'That's the couple that did a murder and got away with it.'

And that's why I have written all this down. Truthfully. Just as it happened.

The Shadow of Time

Contents

CHAPTER 1

I never saw the man I had been fighting until I faced him across
the well of the court at the Old Bailey. As I walked up the steps
to the witness-box, everything round me was blurred and unreal,
like the bad print of a photograph . . . except one thing in sharp
contrast . . . Jacques in the dock opposite, flanked by his two
warders.

The first time face to face . . . but he was no stranger to me, he
had been described too often: as I stumbled through the words of
the oath, our eyes caught and held for a moment and I thought of
what Joan had said to me once, 'It's as if suddenly shutters fall
down . . . and for a moment behind them you see all that's evil in
the world.'

Through all the long time of my evidence, through all the questions, he did not look at me again; even when I turned to stand
down he was examining his finger-nails, and that was the first and
last of Jacques, with his neat blue suit, a red bow tie, the sallow
face, the pencilled moustache and the sleek black hair, those hooded
eyes. The last time, I am sure, for the judge sent him down for ten
years; yet for a month he had been closer to me than any other
man. He had been the constant, ever-menacing shadow just behind
my shoulder, I had heard him, I had smelt him—that never-to-be-
forgotten scent of his hair oil as I grappled with him in the dark,
towards the end I even knew the way he thought: but now I had
seen him for the first time.

It is a strange story. It started when Joan put the business card
on my desk and said, 'He's in a terrible state.' I read,

John Stebbings,
Ladies' Hairdresser,
The Mint
Rye,   Gentlemen attended
Sussex.   by appointment.

I said, 'I haven't got a clue, darling, but wheel him in.' But even as she went out to the front office, I knew there was a clue . . . in that name. . . . Stebbings. I had heard or read it somewhere before.

He came into the office quietly, almost diffidently, and when I offered him a chair, sat down with an odd, neat little movement as he hitched up the trouser creases of his new suit. He was a small man, with a round, ruddy face and bright blue eyes; the fair hair beautifully trimmed. As I pushed the cigarette-box towards him and held out my lighter, I watched those hands, and the pale tapering fingers were never still. I thought the last thing in the world he looked like was a barber; wondered incongruously if they cut their own hair. But, all the time, that name . . . Stebbings . . . at the back of my mind it was ringing a faint, distant bell.

He waited until the door had closed behind Joan's back, then cleared his throat and said, 'Mr Pemberton, he's got a week-end cottage near Rye. He was in for a trim on Saturday. He told me about you . . .'

'Mr Pemberton—? You mean the insurance assessor?'

He nodded.

I had done a job for Mr Pemberton a month before: a lady had been claiming £700 off one of his companies for a diamond brooch she said she had lost in the Tube between Bond Street and Marble Arch; I found it in an empty coffee tin in the larder of her flat in Sussex Gardens. I would always remember the look on her face when it was uncovered; now it was nice to think that Mr Pemberton had remembered too.

'What can I do for you, Mr Stebbings?' Stebbings . . . there was something there. I wished I could place it.

He didn't answer for a moment; then he said, 'I take it . . . that any business . . . between us . . . is confidential?'

'Blackmail,' I thought. While I had been waiting I had been watching the strain he was trying so hard to hide. I said, 'If there is anything criminal, I couldn't handle it. I'm afraid my duty would be to inform the authorities.'

'No,' he said. 'I meant my wife . . . or that young lady outside.'

I laughed. 'The "young lady" is my wife. She takes her wedding ring off in office hours because she thinks it is better for the business; if there's nothing that I've told you I can't handle, and unless you give your permission, it stays in my head.'

Somehow, I felt glad that whatever he had done was only stupid, not nasty.

'That's all right.' He was staring at the carpet in front of the desk, turning his hat round and round by the brim; then, suddenly; he looked straight at me and the agony and despair in those eyes were like a blow in the face. 'I want you to find my daughter,' he said.

I had written "Stebbings" on my desk pad, and the pencil was poised, ready to go on. I said: 'Christian names, and full description, please. Also when, and exactly how, did she leave home?' I looked up, and across the desk those eyes were staring at me again; I couldn't meet them and had to turn away. I said hurriedly, 'It probably isn't as serious as you think. If it was just a family row, she's probably too proud to come back and admit she was wrong—but she'll be safe. If it's a dash to Gretna Green with the boy friend, they've got to get by the three-week Scottish residential qualification, so there should be plenty of time to step in and stop it.' It was just to reassure, to give him time to hope . . . anything to take that look from his face.

His voice came, very softly, 'It's not like that, Mr Kent. Margaret is only three . . . fair and chubby . . . rather difficult to describe beyond that.' I had to look up then, and his face had started to crumple, and for one awful moment I thought he was going to cry.

Of course, I had it then. I put my pencil down gently. I couldn't help him.

'I remember now, Mr Stebbings . . . I should have before. That tragic case of a little girl vanishing from a village near Rye. I'm trying to think of the name of it.'

'Long Row,' he said. 'We live there—the shop's only a lock-up.'

I tried to be gentle. 'But—the police—they were on the case for weeks. They had their dogs out, they used helicopters over the marsh, they got the Army in to beat an area of about fifty square miles. I read all about it in the papers . . . then, again, only the other day, that they had—'

'—Given up hope.' His voice was flat. 'Yes, they have. And so has my wife. But I haven't.'

'Look—I can't delude you. After those enormous resources have failed, what hope has a single individual got of doing a thing?'

'Because there's something I know that they don't—' There was a pause and then he said suddenly, 'Margaret is still alive.'

My head came up with a jerk. 'Alive—? But how—?'

He looked very carefully round the office. 'You swear you will not tell a living soul without my leave?'

'Of course.'

He felt in his breast pocket and pulled out a bunch of envelopes, which he put on my desk. 'I get one a week,' he said, 'ever since it happened. They don't come like that, but tucked inside a trade circular. Just a photo each time ... nothing else, except what's written on the back. But I kept the wrappers with each one in case the postmark might help. My wife doesn't know. It was lucky I met the postman on my way to work the first time ... and since then I've always been on the look-out.'

I opened one of the envelopes. There was a small snapshot, with a circular wrapper pinned to it, addressed to 'Mr J. Stebbings, Tinmans Cottage, Long Row, Nr. Rye, Sussex'. The postmark was Appledore, Kent. I was pretty certain that the type was that of an old standard Underwood, but that could be easily checked.

'Appledore. That's quite close to you, isn't it?'

'About five miles.'

I folded back the wrapper and had a look at the photo: just the small picture of a plump little girl.

She was standing in sharp sunlight in some kind of a courtyard, and she was sucking her thumb. The print was very clear—you could count the squares of the paving stones all round her feet—and to one side of the picture the bough of some sort of a tree shaded across the foreground. The white wall that was behind her back was part-covered with some kind of creeper, and there was a flower bed below that; the child's shadow was long, so that it must have been taken in the early morning or late afternoon. There was nothing more except a single sentence typed on the back by the same machine.

First a date—this one was August 19th—and then just: 'Yes, she's still alive and well. You know what you have to do to keep her that way.'

I put that down and picked up the next. The same little girl, in the same place, but you could tell by her frock and the way she was holding her hands that it was a different picture. This time the message on the back was dated August 26th, and the message read, 'It's Margaret's bedtime—the time that her Daddy used to play to her. Never again. But any bedtime is better than there being none at all.' I went on through the lot of them. Only three things were constant: the position of the child; the theme of each message—'She's alive, and she'll stay that way, if—' only the if was never mentioned; and the look of lost bewilderment on that little face. All

the fear and horror there is in a child-kidnapping surged up inside
me.

'You must go to the police,' I said.

'I can't.'

I had to look at him again. 'You *must* Mr Stebbings. I know quite
a bit about blackmail, I'm sorry to say, and there are only two
factors that count. One is the amount that can be squeezed out of
you; the other, the hold they have over you. As regards the first, it
will just go on getting more and more until there is nothing left,
and you'll be just that worse off in the end; with the second, there
must be some other hold they have over you—I mean, you can't
take this threat . . . of killing . . . that seriously.'

'But I do, Mr Kent. They wouldn't think twice about it.' I think
it was his flat tone of acceptance rather than the actual words that
made me frightened.

A heavy silence fell between us. Then he said, 'It isn't money
they want. It's something they say I must do.'

'What is it?'

No answer to that; only, '—There is something else they
know—something I did. Criminal, I suppose you would call it, but
not really serious—'

'Then go to the police, man. They are very understanding and
lenient in these cases. They hate blackmail worse than any other
thing. Make a clean breast of it, whatever it was, and they'll forget
it. Then they are on your side, with all their power, to find—'

'I would have done that right away, Mr Kent—whatever the
consequence to me—if that was the only thing. But I dare not,
because the moment they found out Margaret would—' His voice
faltered and once again I had to plumb the depths of misery in
those haunted eyes. The worst thing was that I *believed* him; I knew
it was no idle threat; that there would only have to be one single
false step on his part and it would happen.

'Who are they?' I said quickly.

'I don't know.'

Perhaps he did—perhaps he didn't: it didn't matter, for I realised
that there could be no one for him to trust. The whole thing was
quite hopeless. We sat in silence in the dusty autumn sunshine that
managed to filter through my City window while I put the photos
back in their envelopes and then pushed the bundle towards him
across the desk. I had to end it. 'I'm sorry, Mr Stebbings. I think
I understand why you can't tell me any more, but you must

appreciate, from your side, that with the little I know, I can't help
you. but—' I looked at the bunch of envelopes in his hand—'if she
were my child, I would still risk *anything* and tell the police. I'll ring
them up now if—'

He stood up. 'I've told you I daren't.' There was a pathetic kind
of dignity in the way he tried to straighten his shoulders as he
moved towards the door. Then he turned to face me for the last
time. 'I'm sorry to have wasted your morning,' he said; then, almost
to himself, 'We haven't a great deal of money, but I've had a good
offer for the business. I'd have taken it . . . if you had thought . . .'

That finished me; all I could do was to mutter at my blotter, 'I'll
think it over, but I won't promise anything. Can you come
back—say at three this afternoon—and will you leave those photos
with me till then?'

At once he was wary. 'Who are you going to show them to?'

'Only my wife.'

He thought for a moment. 'All right—but no one else. I'll be
back then. And—' But he checked himself suddenly and gave me
a little bob and then the door closed softly behind him.

First I looked at the engagement book and saw there was no
important entry until I had to give evidence in the High Court in
a fortnight's time; then I looked out of the window and thought
how nice Rye would be after hot, smelly London; then that Joan
looked a bit peeked and could do with a bit of a holiday; last, that
I was soft. Then I went through to the outer office, where Joan was
pounding her typewriter, which looked impressive to any intending
client if they did not know, as I did, that it was part-time work on
chapter five of her novel, the one that was to end all novels. When
she had disengaged herself from a tricky sentence, I pushed her
into my room and sat her down and told her all about it.

When she saw the photos, I knew that we were right in it. It was
not that she said anything, only the way that line of her jaw—that
lovely line—hardened when she saw the pictures of the baby. 'Of
course we must do it,' she said.

'But, darling. The man won't tell me a thing to go on. He won't
go near the police. How can I—?'

'You must,' was all she said.

I got her to go out and ask the café to send up two lunches on
a tray; while she was gone, I spread the six snapshots out in a row
on my desk; I was counting, 'eight left and two back' as I turned
from one to the other. Joan said, 'What the hell—?' and it was

awfully difficult to try and explain just what I was trying to do. 'I'm trying to construct a sundial the wrong way round,' I said.

She looked at me as if I was crazy, and I tried to explain the glimmering of an idea that was at the back of my mind, but I don't think she understood much; we had our lunch in silence and all the time I kept on glancing up at those six photos propped in a row across my desk. When the tray was cleared away, I got out some paper and a pencil and tried to explain again by drawing it for her.

'It all depends on two things, Joan. The time these photos were taken, and the child's height. I'm sure Stebbings can give us the second, and I hope he may have a clue as to the first.'

'How?'

'By a remark on the back of one—someone's been a little bit too clever. But let's leave that for a minute and go back to the beginning. Just take a look at them—is there anything rather odd that you can see?'

'Only that they are taken in the same place.'

'And on the *same spot*. Almost exactly. Look, you can count the squares of the stones of the pavement: it's always eight and a bit from the left hand side, two and a bit from the back. Anything else?'

'I don't think so.'

'They are all taken in bright sunshine. You can see that each is a different snap—and each is dated, with the postmark on the wrapper they were sent inside roughly corresponding. So the sun was shining on six occasions spread over six weeks. Is that likely in England?'

She looked out of the window. 'It's been a wonderful summer.'

'Not that good.'

'Well, it must have been.'

'I don't think so,' I said. 'I don't think they were taken in England at all. But it will be easy to check that from the sunshine records.'

There was a moment's silence.

'Then, from sunshine to shadow,' I said. 'Look at that child's shadow, darling. You can measure that against the squares of the pavement too. Do you see how as the dates go on, it gets longer, swings to the left? The child is the style of our sundial: but we don't want to tell the time, we think we know it. What is the other factor that is left out?'

'Harry, I haven't the slightest idea.'

'Position, darling. The place our sundial is on the globe of the world. At least, a line of latitude that encircles it.'

She was interested at once. 'Then you get the north and south thing—what do you call it?—longitude, and you have the exact spot.'

I shook my head. 'No, you can't get that from a photo. There must be a combination of sun and moon, or stars, for that. But there must be something else—' I peered at one of them—'but they're too damned small to make out any real detail . . . we must get them enlarged as big as they'll go. But, even then, I really don't know enough to be accurate.'

I hesitated, hoping that she would make the suggestion, but she did not, so I had to say it myself. 'I think we'll have to call in Josh.'

I could feel the hostility welling up inside her; when she spoke her voice was sharp. 'Joshua Ponting—? No, Harry.'

'Why not?' This always irritated me.

'Because you know what he's like, you know what happened the last time. He's hopeless . . . utterly hopeless.'

'And you don't like him—'

She swung round on me. 'I don't like anyone that takes my husband out on what he is pleased to call an hour's investigation, and then neither of you come back at all and I'm called up at midnight by the police to come and bail you out over being drunk and disorderly in some low pub.'

I grinned. 'Yes, that one was a bit much. But we got what we wanted.'

'I got much more than *I* wanted, I assure you. And look at the way he treats women—'

'Just because he's been married twice, and both times it's gone wrong, it doesn't say he's always to blame.'

'Perhaps not—' she made one of those faces. 'But—'

'Look,' I said, 'even if I agreed with all that, which I don't, will you grant me that he is brilliant—erratic, eccentric, if you like, but brilliant. He knows a little about everything and the hell of a lot about some things; what he doesn't know he jolly well always finds out. This is just up his street.'

'No, Harry.'

I started to put the photos back in their envelopes. 'All right. Stebbings will be here in half an hour. I don't want to face him. Will you say that I'm very sorry, but I can't take the case on.'

'But that baby, darling. If it's true—you can't!'

'And I damned well don't know enough to do it on my own.'

There was another long silence. 'O.K., Harry. Have it your own way—but I don't want to have anything to do with him.'

For some reason I felt immensely relieved. 'Then I'll see Stebbings, if you will take these round to Robbie's place in the Strand and ask him to blow them up as far as they'll go. And say I must have them by six tonight.' As she leaned over the desk to take the photos, I caught hold of her free hand. '—And, darling, I do promise you that nothing will happen . . . like that last time.'

She was smiling now. 'I'll believe that when I see it. Actually, you're both as bad as each other. You both behave as if you were twelve years old some of the time.'

When she had gone, I looked up the phone number of Josh's flat in the City, but there was no ringing tone and then a sweet voice came in to tell me that the number was 'temporarily out of service.' So he was cut off again. A bad sign. I could hear Joan saying, 'I told you so,' and wondered how long it had been since I had seen him—it must be months. But before I could do any more worrying on that score there was a ring on the outside bell and Mr Stebbings was on the doorstep.

When I had him sitting down on the other side of the desk, I said, 'Mr Stebbings. I don't think I can do anything for you—but I'm going to try. I'm sure I could do far, far more if only you would trust me and tell me *everything*. Please—won't you change your mind?'

'I daren't,' he said.

'Well, your enemies—you said "they" yourself, you know—can't you give me some line on them, that won't make anything worse?'

'I don't know who they are,' he said.

I pulled the few notes I had made towards me, and then tried another line. 'Tell me, how tall was—is Margaret?'

He winced a little at my quick change of tense, then felt in his breast pocket and produced a diary; he looked puzzled as he flicked over the pages, then looked up at me quickly. 'Why?'

'It may be important.'

'Two foot, five and three-quarter inches, in her socks, against our sitting-room door on August the first,' he said. 'She was growing so fast—we did it every month—but that was the last time . . .'

'Say, two foot six now,' I cut in hastily. 'That's very, very useful. Next, on one of those snaps it says something to the effect that you

used to play *to* Margaret—not the usual *with*. Is there any signific-
ance in the change of that word?'

'Oh yes. I play the guitar ... amateur. And I always used to
sing to her—some nursery rhymes—each night when I got back
from work, just before she went to bed.'

Excitement was growing inside me. 'And that would be at a fairly
regular time, I suppose?'

'Yes. Her mother was most particular she went to bed at six,
sharp. So it was always five-thirty, as soon as I got in.'

'And would that be generally known?'

He thought for a moment. 'Most of the village, I suppose; and a
few friends in Rye. But no one else.'

'Now the last one. I'm afraid that it may be rather painful for
you to have to tell me—but was there any detail about the evening
that Margaret disappeared that you did not tell to the police—or I
can't get from the newspaper reports?'

He shook his head. 'No. I told them all I knew—and that wasn't
much. It was the one night we let her stay up a little later. You
see, the Long Row Prize Band always plays outside the pub, the
Horse and Cart. Being musical myself, I liked to go and listen—and
it made a change for the wife to get out and have a sherry. We
used to sit on the benches outside the saloon bar door, and it wasn't
very nice for Margaret to be there, playing about among all the
empty glasses. There was a garden at the side, though, with a thick
hedge all round so that she couldn't stray on to the road, and only
one gate out to the front, that we could watch all the time. We used
to give her a bag of crisps and let her play there. It seemed so safe.
Then, that evening, when I went to collect her ... she was gone.
And no one saw her go.'

In the silence that followed, I heard the outer door open and
close softly and I knew that Joan had come back. 'That was a
Saturday night?' I said.

'Yes.'

'And there's nothing else you can tell me?'

'No. I wish I could—you or the police. But I've told you I dare
not ... because if they knew I had, they'd do that to Margaret.'

'But you told me you don't know who they are.'

'I don't—but I know what they are like.'

Always the same blank wall. I said, 'Now I'm going to tell you
what I propose to do. I'm coming down to Long Row for a week,
just to scratch around. Is there anywhere to stay?'

'The Horse and Cart. The landlord's a friend of mine. I'll fix it up for you.'

'That's just what I don't want. You must know nothing about me. Even if we meet. If I want to talk to you, I'll do it by phone, so give me your number and that of the inn. Then at the end of the week, if there is anything to report, I'll tell you—but I don't think there is the remotest chance there will be. But if there is, I won't go on unless you are prepared to talk. So think hard about that one.'

He rose to go, nodding, and then his hand strayed back to his breast pocket. 'What about a fee?' he said.

'We'll talk about that when you are willing to tell me something. Until then, just our expenses. I shall take my wife down. We'll say it's a late holiday.'

After I had shown him out, Joan told me that Robbie had promised the enlargements by six, and I had to tell her that I hadn't been able to contact Josh, and the reason. She did not actually say, 'I told you so,' but she looked it. There was nothing much else to be done until I could take the photos to Josh in person, or try and find out what had happened to him, so I spent the rest of the afternoon going round the newspaper offices and reading up the files on the Stebbings case. There was nothing more there than he had told me: a band performing outside a pub, the parents of a little girl listening while they had a drink, the daughter playing in the garden. Then she disappeared: no one saw her go; no one knew anything. There followed a county-wide search, dogs, planes, and troops, that went on for three weeks. After that, the story went to a back page, there were strong police hints of murder, and then it died. When I got back, Joan told me she had been on the phone to the pub and managed to get us a double room, bed and breakfast, for a week, as from the next day.

We parted company in the Strand after we had collected the enlargements. We stood on the kerb for a moment while the home-going stream of pedestrian traffic swirled round us and Joan gave me one of those little-boy-of-twelve looks; then she said, 'Try not to get on one of his pub-crawls, darling. There will be cold supper waiting for you at about ten, after they close.' Then she smiled at me and turned on her heel and I watched her walking off: the tall slim figure and the shining fair hair, the high heels going clip, clip, clip on the pavement. I thought that even if business wasn't too good, and this present case was going to prove a waste of time and

money, at least I had everything else that anyone could want. I felt
rather mean about the coming visit. I took the Underground to
Cannon Street and then walked down Upper Thames Street to the
converted warehouse which was Joshua's last known address. It
looked awfully deserted from the outside, and for a moment I was
afraid that my bird had flown, perhaps driven underground by the
usual horde of creditors, perhaps removed for one of his periodic
rests at the taxpayers' expense in Wormwood Scrubs.

But he was in, with a bailiff for company, and they were playing
two-handed whist by the light of a paraffin lamp. It all seemed very
cosy and friendly.

'What is it this time?' I said as I lowered myself into the only
other chair. I had noticed that the furniture had undergone one of
its periodic shrinkings.

'Cannon Street Wine Stores . . . £8 11s. 9½d., dear boy,' boomed
Josh cheerfully. I sat for a moment looking with affection—it would
be impossible not to do so—at the ugly face with the black horn-
rimmed glasses perched on the end of the nose, the great domed
forehead, the broad shoulders springing from a six-foot frame. Then
I took out my cheque book and asked the bailiff if he would take
one, and he said 'Yes,' but really I think he was sorry and much
more anxious to finish the game. While Josh was seeing him down
the stairs—I could hear the great voice assuring him they would
finish it next time—I had a quick look in the kitchen and larder.
There was not enough to feed a cat in the whole place. I went back
to the living-room and waited for Josh to return.

He called himself a free-lance journalist on his passport, and I
suppose that was as fair a short description as any; he was, in fact,
the last of the Dinosaurs, a thing that had outlived its time and
had not been able to adapt. He would have been terrific in Dr
Johnson's day, drinking and brawling in the taverns, with the talk
and writing with no holds barred, but it did not fit any more. He
had been to prison once for criminal libel, twice for contempt of
court, countless times for debt. He wrote well, but anything that
had his name on it went straight to the legal department of the
journal concerned, to be put through a fine-mesh screen, and most
of it came back. He had immense scholarship, and an encyclopædia
of a memory that held more facts, both useful and useless, than any
other man I have ever met. He was big in every way—his frame,
his voice, his tastes, his circle of friends; gin, women, everything
came in large portions. I have never met a man who was not, at

heart, his friend. Women feared or adored him. Joan was in the
first class, his two former wives still fiercely in the second: they had
taken him in turn, would have died for him, but just couldn't stick
the pace. I always suspected that they had formed a sort of club
afterwards to pay him a kind of alimony to keep him going.

He came back into the room now, rubbing his hands and grinning
from ear to ear. He didn't even thank me, and, as usual, I didn't
mind.

'What a pleasant fellow! Well, Harry, dear boy, how goes the
world?'

'Passable,' I said. 'When did you last eat?'

He looked vague. 'Yesterday . . . but what does food matter,
Harry? The book is nearly finished. And then—' He spread out his
arms as if to embrace all the comforts of the world.

'How much do you owe them in the café downstairs?'

I knew "The Book"—had read the first half of it, as had several
publishers. It set out to prove the corruption, incompetence and
knavery of every member of the present Parliament. The publishers
who had seen it had licked their chops, sighed wistfully, and sent
it back wrapped in asbestos with a directive that it must never
darken their doors again; one had told me that it would almost be
worth the five years he would get if he did it, but he had to think
of his family.

'About four pounds,' said Josh. 'And they've put the shutters
up.'

I got up and went down to the café and paid that one off too,
arranging that I would be responsible for another four pounds
credit. Then I collected a double portion of cold pie and potato
salad, six light ales from the pub on the corner, and went back and
stood over him while he ate the food. When we had had two light
ales each, we got down to business.

'Harry, I'm greatly obliged to you.' Josh leaned back, stretching.

'You need not be. I've paid out seventeen pounds odd—which is
your retainer.'

'Retainer . . . ?'

'Yes. You are working for me.' I cleared a space on the table.
Then I undid the packet of enlargements and spaced them out in
front of him. 'You are mine, body and soul,' I said, 'until you can
tell me exactly where these photos were taken.'

He picked them up one by one; held them close to the yellow
light of the lamp. It was quite dark outside now, and quiet in the

City streets after the rush of the day's traffic had gone. At last he said, 'What's the story?'

'I can't tell you. Even if I could, I don't think it would help much. They have been blown up to this half-plate size from snapshots and the bloke that did them for me said they wouldn't go any bigger on account of the grain of the film. You can assume that the date I have pencilled on the back of each is the date it was taken; also that they were all taken at five-thirty p.m. The child is two foot six tall, and you can see for yourself that she is standing in almost the same place in each. Her shadow—'

'Yes, Harry. Very interesting. I follow your line of argument.' He was picking each up in turn again, peering at them. 'As the dates progress . . . so that shadow is a little longer . . . swings a bit more . . .'

'Could you get a latitude fix, do you think, from them?' I tried to sound as casual as possible.

'The sundial in reverse . . . the sun compass principle, you mean. Yes, I think you might, but it would be difficult, and not very accurate. There's the direction and angle at which the camera was held to consider as a factor . . . also the question of different stan-dard time. But it could be done.' He looked up at me again. 'Of course you know that it will only *be* latitude—a band round the earth. There's nothing here to help us with the cross fix, of longitude.'

'I know that.' It was my turn to pick up the enlargements. 'But there may be other indications. These are alleged to have been posted in Appledore, Kent, at weekly intervals: what would you say were the odds against having six Thursdays running as fine as that in our wonderful weather?'

'Twenty to one. But we can check that from the sunshine records.'

'Quite. And have you ever seen a tree with leaves like that one growing in England?'

He snatched it from me, peering at one from a range of a few inches. 'You're right, Harry. You never have. What is it, then?'

'Among your other parts, you're supposed to be something of a botanist. I'm not. So you tell me when you are certain. And that creeper thing on the other side—you might get something from that.'

'Yes, yes . . .' I had ceased to exist. He pulled a sheet of paper towards him and started making notes in a furious crabbed hand-writing and I sat and watched for a little, sliding the glass under his nose when he murmured absently, 'Open me another beer, dear boy.' He didn't even look up to drink it, and when I said, 'You must go over them inch by inch, botanically, architecturally, and sift any minute thing that will help—' only murmured, without stopping his writing, 'Not much in the way of architecture here, old man. Not a bit of roof or window to help . . . only a blank wall.'

'There's a thing that looks like a drain-pipe in one corner—see what you can do with that.' It was only meant in emphasis, I didn't think he could do a thing with something as small as that.

The only thing that did stop him was when I picked up my hat to go and said, 'I want the answer in three days, Josh.'

'Not enough time, Harry. There's an immense amount of calculation to be done, and the electric light's cut off. This lamp tires my eyes if I go on too long.'

'Then go to bed now—and get up at dawn,' I said. 'But I must have it. I'll pay any reasonable expense—which does not include the squaring of slates in pubs. Post it to me here—' I put the Long Row address down on the table—'by Friday. Don't come down.'

He didn't answer. He was pouring over the enlargements again. I let myself out, feeling rather pleased. The machine had started to tick.

CHAPTER 2

It was at eleven the next morning, when we were sorting out the office, that a phone call came through from him, demanding the price of a return fare to Sussex.

'You keep away from there,' I said. 'I've told you the answer is not in Rye or Appledore, and I don't want you there.'

'No intention of voyaging in that direction, Harry. I want to go to Eastbourne.'

'Not at my expense, you don't.'

'Near Eastbourne, dear boy, there is a place called Hurstmonceaux. Where resides the transplanted Greenwich Observatory.'

I felt a thrill go through me. 'Then you have fixed it—?'

'I think so. But it needs the collaboration of better brains than mine.'

I told him I'd meet him with the money at Victoria Station in half an hour.

You could see him twenty yards off, towering shoulder-high above the rest of the crowd as he came across to where I was waiting under the clock. He was dressed in a green open-necked shirt and the most peculiar pair of corduroy trousers; he looked like a refined tramp, but I had no doubt at all that he would finish the day by taking tea with the Astronomer Royal.

'Here is your ticket,' I said, 'and here is a pound for expenses. And here—' pushing him gently towards platform 14—'is your train.' I was determined to see him on to it.

He looked down at me sadly as we stood by the barrier. 'A pound seems a very little for a long day, Harry. Especially when it has to cover two taxi fares.'

'There's a good bus service. I looked it up.'

He sighed. 'You are a hard master. But I think I'm going to surprise you with this. Can't I have a little longer?'

'No. But you can tell me where you think it is now, if you want to.'

'No, I'd rather be sure first.'

'Well, I'll give you one extra day—until Saturday. But I must have it by the first post then, and you had better register it.'

He smiled for the first time. 'That will be another few shillings, Harry.' I gave him two half-crowns and he turned away. The last I heard was a roar of, 'Find me a CLEAN compartment, lackey,' to an astonished porter, and then he was lost in the crowd pushing along the platform.

Joan and I drove down to Sussex directly after lunch. It was wonderful to leave the barren desert of suburban houses and meet the country on that hot, still autumn afternoon, with the trees turning, the hop-poles bare and the scent of woodsmoke in the air. We went easily, for the Rover was getting an old lady, and it was after five before we dipped down the hill from Playden to see Rye mounting bravely with the tiers of red roofs on its conical hill to the summit of the church. Then a sharp turn left on the road to Appledore, with the old cliff on one side and the flat, hazy blue of the marsh stretching away on the other towards the sea.

I had never been in Long Row before, but it was the pattern I had expected: a long straggle of cottages and houses on each side of the road, a post office and grocer's shop, a small garage, a smaller butcher's shop, and the pub. This was set back from the road with a wide triangle of grass between the door and the post that held the sign; there were benches running along the front wall, and to one side a garden, shaded by apple trees that were now loaded with fruit. The front of the house was in board, black and white, with deep thatch and little dormer windows poking out from under it like curious eyes. It looked very pleasant, so were the landlord and his wife when they came out to greet us, so was the long, low bedroom under the eaves.

While we were unpacking, Joan said, 'What comes first?'

'Appledore, I think. I want to check on the letter angle; try and trace them back from delivery to Stebbings to the actual posting—which I'm convinced does not take place in Appledore, whatever the postmark may say.'

'And how do you think you can do that, darling?'

'Through the postmen. Lubricated postmen sometimes talk.'

She turned from where she was folding up underclothes in the chest of drawers. 'You're so certain of your hunch —and that your wonder-boy is going to prove it, aren't you?'

'If anyone can, he will, Joan.'

She snorted.

I got up off the bed. 'Well, I'm going to try it, anyway. I'm going to find the local postman.'

There was not far to go, for when I got down to the bar and asked the landlord where I could find him as I had made a mistake in our forwarding address, I was told he was at that moment in the public bar; I went round to it and was introduced to Mr Norbury, who was consuming his evening pint. The first bit of luck was that we both were wearing R.A.F. ties, and soon he was having the other half with me, while we explored the various theatres of war that we might have fought in together. It was easy from there to get talking about Flight-Sergeant Stebbings and 419 Squadron; I said we had served together, and that one of the reasons for my coming to this part of the world for a holiday had been to look him up. I had been horrified to hear of his terrible family tragedy.

'Ah—' said Mr Norbury, staring into the depths of his pint. 'He's had a lot on his plate, has John. I reckon it was one of those bloody sex crimes.'

'And it isn't finished even now,' I said softly. 'This is absolutely confidential, of course, and he doesn't want anyone here to know, but he's still getting letters, nasty anonymous letters, every week from someone round here, saying he ought to have taken more care of the child.'

'That's bloody wicked.' He was staring at me curiously. 'But it isn't a letter—I mean I knew there was something wrong by the way he grabs his mail from me on Saturdays, but it isn't a letter he shies away from, it's a circular—and that didn't make sense.'

'He told me they do come tucked inside a circular, and it's always postmarked Appledore, eight-thirty a.m. the day before.'

'Appledore—?'

'Yes. And what I want to find out is exactly where it was posted . . . and when.'

He looked doubtful. 'We're not allowed to talk about the mails. It would be Jack Hargreaves of Appledore that would do the collection, probably. But I don't know if he—'

'Look—We're both John Stebbings' friends. I thought that if I could find out exactly when some bastard was posting these things, I could go along and wait, and talk a little severely to whoever it is, and say what we all think about it. I'm sure I could stop them without getting the police in. John doesn't want that. He's had enough already.'

Mr Norbury looked round the bar, had another swallow, and

then bent close to me. 'If it was me—I'd say "yes". But I don't know about Jack. Have you got a car?'

'Yes.'

'Well, I'm on late shift tomorrow—and I know it's Jack's day off. I'll come over with you to talk to him if you like. But it will be absolutely unofficial, if you get me.'

'Absolutely,' I said, 'and just the same—not a word to John Stebbings. He might think I was taking too much on myself.'

We found Mr Hargreaves digging potatoes in his garden at eleven o'clock the next morning. We retired to the parlour and, with a lot of humming and hawing, Mr Horbury explained the position to his fellow postman.

Hargreaves did not seem unduly perturbed at the request he should divulge secret information. 'Circulars—? Long white ones, Ted? Yes, I remember those well, they come so regular. They're always in that box in Crooked Lane when I clear the eight-thirty morning lot.'

'Where's Crooked Lane?' I said.

'Out on the marsh—very lonely spot. Don't know why they had a box put there. There's never more than six letters in it.'

I leaned forward in my chair. 'Mr Hargreaves—this is very important. When you pick the letters out of the box, where is this circular? At the bottom, in the middle, or on the top?'

He thought for a moment. 'On the top—I'm sure of that. Yes, they're always on the top.'

'Posted last—' I said. 'And when is the previous collection?'

'Six-thirty, the night before.'

'So if I get along there—say at nine, and wait, I'm pretty sure to meet up with whoever it is?'

'How are you going to see them?' he said. 'It will probably be in the middle of the night, very dark—' He stopped for a moment. 'And if there's to be another one, tonight's the night.'

'I had realised that. And don't you worry how I will spot him. I will.'

When we rose to go, I asked my last question. 'Is there any cover for me near this box?'

'Yes, there's a line of old willows on the other side of the road, nearly opposite. And there's still plenty of leaves—no gales as yet.' Then he held out his hand. 'I hope you catch him, Mr Kent, and I hope you kick his bloody teeth in. But I can't know a thing about it—I haven't even discussed the matter.'

'Of course you haven't. But still, I'm very, very grateful.'

As he opened the door to show us out he said, 'And after you've kicked his teeth in, there's a damned great dyke just behind those trees to cool him off.'

I went back to Long Row and dropped Mr Norbury, then collected Joan and went into Rye for lunch. We came back by a roundabout way through Appledore and found Crooked Lane. It well justified its name—a narrow secondary road, high above the flanking dykes, that ran due south from the main road over the flatness of the marsh, at intervals, and for no apparent reason, taking sudden left or right hand turns. At one of these, the post-box, mounted on a wooden post, showed its bright red bravely against the drab blues and greens of tree, bank and field.

There was no one in sight; no house visible except one group of farm buildings that broke the flat horizon a mile farther on. Nothing but grass and reeds and hundreds of silly sheep, going on and on until they faded into the afternoon haze. In contrast, the post-box and the willows near it seemed to thrust themselves up into the sky.

I stopped the car on the corner facing down the blind angle of the road, and told Joan to sound the horn if anyone came along in that direction; then I walked over to the trees to see if they would do.

There were seven in a row, very close, very old, leaning back out over the dyke behind, and I don't suppose the withes that sprouted from their pollard crowns had been cut for years. The grandfather of the bunch was second but nearest to the letter-box—not more than ten yards from it in a straight line. I scrambled up the sloping trunk, which trembled so much that I wondered if it would be safe, but the crown inside the ring of withes was hard and fairly smooth, and I reckoned I could manage to survive up there for twelve hours. There was good leaf cover still, as Mr Hargreaves had said, and I got out my pocket-knife and started cutting through the smaller branches until there was a little window looking down directly on the box. Then I scrambled down and had a look at my handiwork from the outside. It didn't really show even if you were looking for it . . . and, of course, when I hoped to use it, it would be dark.

Joan was sitting in the car staring at me as if I were crazy. I got in beside her and said, 'Darling, this is a time when I fear we may quarrel.'

Joan said, 'If it's anything to do with those ridiculous capers up that tree, I'm sure we will.'

'I'm a bird-watcher—did you know? I sit up trees all night and watch birds. I've got to do it tonight, and there's not room up there for both of us, so I'm afraid I'll have to leave you all on your own at the pub, and I know you'll be cross.'

'What kind of bird is this one?' she said in a nasty voice.

'I don't know, darling. I think it will be a "he"—and certainly, it won't have any feathers.'

'So you won't tell me—?'

'Of course I will. On the way back into Rye now, because I want to buy some flash-bulbs for the camera.' And as she drove me back I tried to tell her exactly what I hoped to do.

There was only one question when I had finished, and it was a pertinent one, 'Harry, even if you do manage to take a photo—he'll see the flash, he'll know you've done it.'

'I've thought a lot about that one, and there's no way out of it, only to hope that it is light when he comes. But if not I think that the flash will be so sudden that though he knows it has happened, he will not have the slightest idea of where it came from; all I will have to do is to sit quiet and tight, and then he won't know where to search. And I think he will be too frightened to do anything except run away.'

After we had got the flash-bulbs and gone back to Long Row, I told the landlord of my hobby and my intentions, and while we waited for an early supper, I changed and got together the things I wanted in a haversack. I was wearing my oldest trousers and a dun-coloured duffle coat: in the haversack I put my Leica with the telephoto lens and flash attachment, a rubber torch that gave a long beam and was a handy weapon, the flash-bulbs, a thermos of black coffee, some string, and the last brain-wave of Joan's, an air cushion that she borrowed from the landlord, whose wife had once suffered from a universal and distressing complaint.

Joan was very quiet over supper, and when we went up to our room afterwards to collect my gear, I saw her looking rather wistfully towards the big bed.

'What's the matter, darling?'

'Oh—nothing. But you know how I hate sleeping alone . . .'

'There's a nice long bolster,' I said. 'Put it down the bed and cuddle.'

We left at about seven-thirty and took the long way round to Crooked Lane so that Joan would have the shorter drive home. There was just the tinge of a copper afterglow left in the western

sky and the mist was starting to rise in patches of cotton-wool from
the marsh, blotting out the sheep, making everything eerie and
unreal. All the way down the lane we did not pass a soul; the
headlights stabbed into the snaking fingers of mist, the air that
rushed in through the open window on my side was dank and chilly.
I began to regret a lot of things, but it was too late to go back now.

We stopped just short of the clump of trees by the post-box and
Joan got out and changed over to the driving seat. I slung the
haversack over my shoulder and went round to her side, seeing the
pale oval of her face in the dim light from the dashboard, the drops
of moisture gleaming in her hair. I said, 'Straight off home to bed,
darling. I shall be back before you are up. And if it's any comfort,
I shall miss you just as much, and be a lot colder doing it.' I leaned
in through the window and kissed her and then stood watching the
red light of the rear lamp dwindling down the road, the clank of
the engine growing fainter and fainter. I felt very alone.

When I had climbed up into the tree and lugged the haversack
after me, it was fairly easy to get comfortable on the air cushion,
wedging my back against two of the thicker withes that spread up
from the crown. I propped the haversack by my side, with the
thermos handy, and lashed the torch to my wrist with a length of
the string so that I could not drop it; then I settled down to a little
practice in manipulating the camera.

I kept the strap of it round my neck, and by dint of a lot of
feeling and one or two quick flashes from the torch, I managed to
build a sort of platform out of twigs and string, so that if I placed
the camera square on it, the lens and flash-bulb were trained
through my little window directly on the pillar-box. I risked one
last try with the torch trained beside the camera. It was spot on.
There was nothing to do now but wait.

Darkness was complete, no sight of the mist now, though I could
feel its wet coils drifting across my face. No sound but the dry rattle
of the leaves against their stems and the rustle of the reeds on the
sides of the dyke below me. That was one thing I was glad I could
not see—I remembered the look of it from our visit of that afternoon
. . . wide, entirely covered with a sheet of green scum . . . looking
like a revolting cold pea soup.

Some curlews started calling nearby and made me jump, then
two cars travelling fast south down the lane, their headlights making
weird patterns of light and shadow in the branches round me.
Another half-hour, while I changed my position three times, had a

sip from the thermos and longed for a cigarette; a man passed on
a bicycle, but did not stop. Ten minutes later the footsteps came
down the road from the direction of Appledore.

There were two people, and I think that from the sound of them
I knew they were not for me. Slow dragging—even before the
whispers and the giggle that came from just beneath my perch,
even in darkness, I knew exactly how they looked—the young man
and his girl, arms round each other's waists, walking back from the
last bus, stopping every few yards for a kiss.

I wished them the best of luck and willed them to hurry on, but
those footsteps had stopped underneath me, and the man said
something low and urgent. 'No, Henry—no, not here'—the girl's
voice was sharp: there was a kind of a scuffle, I heard the grass
move beneath me and the faintest movement was transmitted up
the trunk of the willow. They were down on the bank, either leaning
or lying against the tree. I was suspended above what, in all probability, was shaping for a seduction.

I don't suppose any girl has ever had an outsider so much on
her side. I willed her to hold out; projected thoughts on cold and
damp and nice dry haystacks down towards her, cheered mentally
at the succession of 'No's' that rose in volume, breathed a sigh of
relief when there was a sudden squeak followed by the word
'nettles'. I even forgave them the flare of a match and then the
torture of cigarette smoke drifting up to someone who had not had
one for three hours. 'Calm down, Henry. Please calm down—' I
was saying it to him over and over again—'have your fag and take
her off down the road . . . anywhere away from here . . . anywhere
you won't scare my game . . .' At last there was a further sound of
rustling and clothes being brushed down; then the feet and voices
dwindling away down the lane. I had won.

I risked a cigarette after that; the strain was too much. The next
excitement came when I was getting over an attack of cramp in my
left leg; nothing much, nothing that had any bearing on what I was
trying to do, I thought, as I listened to the plane flying overhead
to the north. It was low—too low for safety; and there was something else . . . something rather odd about the sound of its engine.
There had been a deep uneven beat when it had been coming
towards me, but now, going away, it seemed thinner, steadier.
Probably some trick of sound on the marsh.

Midnight, and the quarter-moon had risen and I could see the
swirls of mist; and, through one gap in the branches above me, a

cluster of stars overhead. The thermos was finished and I was still chilled to the bone; that cramp in my leg was starting again. I rubbed and rubbed at my calf, longing for sleep. At one-fifteen exactly, the footsteps first came to me, coming along the lane from the south.

They were loud, ringing on the gravel, those of a man, I thought: a confident man who knew just what he was doing, but at the same time was alert. They came on steadily, and as I peered through my tunnel, I could see the darker surface of the road now against the grass verge, the faint blur of the pillar-box. Another six paces, and the footsteps stopped with an almost brutal suddenness. I had the camera ready, and as I eased it forward on to my platform, I could see the dim square of shoulders and the round blob of a head standing there, opposite the box. There was a scrape on the gravel and the shape moved towards it. I gave him two seconds and then pressed the button.

If I had hoped to be able to see anything of him in the flash, I was disappointed; after so long in the dark, being so close to the camera, I was completely blinded by the searing flash. Only one thing was of any value: a sound . . . a dull plop of something falling into the letter-box . . . I must have caught whoever it was at the split-second moment when he was pushing something into it . . . the jerk of his reaction to the flash must have made him let go . . . and it had fallen inside.

Silence. Complete darkness had flooded down again—except for the waves of red and green from semi-blindness that wove in front of my eyes. The moon had gone behind a cloud; there was nothing to do except ease the camera down on my chest, and wait rigid, holding my breath, hoping he had been blinded too.

Feet . . . the soft pad of urgent running feet . . . coming over to my tree, now on the grass underneath. A voice, soft, but very clear, with a clipped accent I could not quite place. 'What are you doing up there?'

I suppose I should have tried to bluff it out—said something about bird-watching, anything: but there was something rather unpleasant about that voice. I sat still and held my breath.

Then it came again, that voice: just below, and within feet of me. 'I know you're up there . . . I can see the face of your watch.' I cursed inside myself and tried to turn the dial to hide the luminous face, but my sleeve touched a branch and there was the faintest rustle of the leaves.

'And now I can hear you.' It was almost purring then.

There was a long, dead silence: suddenly, one sharp sound that once, heard, you never forget. I had, once before, in a black alley off River Street, Baghdad, when I was in the S.I.B. during the war . . . the sound of a spring-knife clicking open.

Nothing to do except wait: no way down, except on the slope of the trunk of the tree to where I knew he was waiting; no help from my light, for it would only give me away. I shuffled on to my haunches and tightened my grip on the torch. I had to wait for him to come to me.

The slightest tremor came up the old tree trunk; then a faint scrape on the bark. I stared at the withes just in front of my face. Perhaps the dark bank of cloud did lift from the face of the moon for a second, perhaps it was the final effort of concentration, but there *was* a little pale patch a little below me and to the right. A hand . . . ? Yes, it was, and it was gripping the base of one of the branches before a last heave up.

I slashed at it with the torch . . . and missed. Then something caught that wrist and a body came crashing up towards me through the withes and on the other side there was a ripping sound as the thing I dreaded came slashing down at me through the leaves.

It was all so quick, but I remembered the old trick of grabbing at his hair and rolling over backwards, kicking up with one foot at the same time to catch him in the pit of the stomach and send him flying over my head. But I forgot there was nothing behind me to roll on; forgot to let go of his hair. With a snap and a crackle, I was through the protecting branches, pulling him after me, plummeting down into the scum of the dyke.

I think he was just as surprised, for he let go of my wrist in mid-air and we hit the water side by side with a terrific splash. We went down, and it was deep and cold and thick: tasting horribly of things dead and rotting for a long time. When I surfaced, I rolled away from the sounds of struggle beside me, trying to make for the reeds of the far bank. It was pitch dark again, no bottom that my legs could feel in that filthy, weedy muck; then a hand came out of the blackness and caught my hair, another one, gripping my collar, started to twist me over backwards. I felt the strap of the camera go, and then it was first one, then the other, on top as we clutched and kicked, spitting and panting for breath. But the most vivid thing I remember of those few seconds was the smell that came to me . . . whenever our heads came close . . . even above the stench of scum and weeds. A strong scent of sandalwood from his hair.

I think it was the fury with which he clutched me, the uncertain, jerky movements in the moments we broke apart, that made me realise almost at once that he could not swim well . . . if at all. The courage of this conviction made it easy for one who did, and soon I was on top, with a neck lock on him . . . half drowning him as I held his head under water while I struck out with my legs towards the bank by the willows.

He weakened quickly; so quickly that I was frightened I had overdone it. But now one of my feet had found the muddy bottom, so I let go and kicked him away, paddling towards the far bank to lie in the reeds, trying to listen as I fought for breath.

He was all right, but he had had enough. There was no attempt to find me and I could only crouch there, shivering, and try to follow his progress by the sounds that came out of the dark: the slow sloshy noise as he struggled back towards the trees, the heavy dragging of a body up the bank, the retching and the sickness. Then unsteady footsteps sounded on the road again, dying away in the direction from which he had first come.

I had had enough too: so cold and tired that I could not face that journey back across the dyke to salve the rest of my belongings. I crawled out into the field and then made unsteady progress down the side of the dyke, looking for a bridge there must be at its gate; the mist swirled round me, and more than once I nearly trod on sheep that stared stupidly as they started to their knees before ambling away. It was a hundred yards before I found it, and then, at least, there was the firm road under my squelching shoes. The shivering stopped as I started to walk as fast as I could in the opposite direction to that my friend had taken, the road back to Long Row.

Twice I stopped and looked back and listened. There was nothing. I was safe, then, and the only thing to do was to get back as fast as possible before I caught pneumonia; I was so intent on doing this that I did not notice a thing when I passed the next clump of trees, until the beam of a torch jumped at me from out of the darkness.

A pleasant voice said, 'Good morning, sir,' In the reflection of the glow I could see the tall helmet and caped shoulders of a policeman.

I had stopped dead. The voice went on, 'Had an accident?' and

I looked down at myself: soaking, stained from head to foot in green slime, coat torn, buttons missing. The only thing to do was to keep as near the truth as possible.

'Yes,' I said. 'I fell out of a tree into a dyke, I'm afraid.'

'Fell out of a tree, sir?' There was polite disbelief in the tone. I could see him more clearly now, the bicycle propped up against the hedge behind.

'Yes.' I moved over towards him. 'I was bird-watching. I was up a willow tree back along the road trying to photograph a nest, and I must have slipped—'

'Ah—' That summed up the whole situation. You could see him thinking that with a bird-watcher anything was possible.

'I'm afraid that I've lost a lot of kit in the dyke,' I said. 'A valuable camera—and a torch. But it was too dark to see a thing, so I thought it would be better to come back when it's light.'

'It might be as well, sir.'

'Well—I'd better keep on the move. I don't want to catch a cold. Good morning, Constable.'

But the notebook was out now. 'Where did you say you were staying, Mr—?' I noticed that it did not occur to him that anyone like me could actually live in those parts.

'My name is Kent. I'm staying at the Horse and Cart in Long Row. With my wife.'

I held the torch for him while all this was written down. 'For the Occurrence Book, that's all, sir,' he said. I remarked I supposed it was 'an occurrence' and he supposed it was too; then he saw I was shivering and picked up his bicycle and said he would walk back a bit of the way with me—'to put me right.' So, under escort, I started the second leg of my walk back to Long Row.

We did not talk much during the first quarter mile; there was a distinct feeling of wariness that indicated he thought he was convoying a harmless lunatic. One long silence was broken by the sound of another plane, this time coming from the north, and flying as low as the one I had heard before. It came directly over us—and the policeman did not even bother to raise his head to look at it. I turned to watch the navigation lights streaking away from us against the sky and made some remark about 'You must get a lot of them.' I hardly heard his answer of 'Directly on the night freight course to London,' I was listening to the engine beat. It had changed in exactly the same way as the one before, only the reverse way: this time the sound seemed suddenly to get deeper, more uneven as it went from me.

We went on with our walk. It was easier when he noticed me pulling out a sodden packet of cigarettes, having a look at one of them, and then throwing the lot away. 'I think I've got some on me, sir'—this, fumbling inside his tunic—'no, you're very welcome, but I don't smoke on duty.' I took the fag with gratitude and we walked on, chatting about nothing in particular; I think he had decided that I was reliable enough to go on my way alone, when the car headlight beam came flooding down the long straight stretch of road behind our backs.

It came suddenly, almost before the sound of the engine, but when I did hear that, the note told me that something was travelling fast. If I had been alone, I think I would have been a little wary after all that had happened, but now I was walking side by side with the Law, so nothing mattered. The two blazing eyes seemed to spring forward at us, gleaming on the bright parts of the constable's cycle, sending eerie slanting shadows over the tarmac of the road.

Cartwright—he had told me his name, and he was, in fact, the Long Row policeman—stopped and pulled his machine on to the verge and stood behind it. 'Best let them by,' he said.

The road was open there, falling away from the crown down steep banks to the dykes on each side; there wasn't much room to stand beside him. I crossed over to the other verge.

I think that the one thing that saved me was the behaviour of the driver in those last few seconds: when he saw the two pedestrians he did not attempt to slow down, he accelerated. As the engine note rose to a snarl, I took one step back on the grass, another quickly as the headlights swerved away from the far side of the road to point directly at me. There was a moment's impression of two great yellow eyes, with moths dancing in front of them, the dark blur of an open sports car behind, and it was on me. But as I shrank away, my back foot caught in a tuft of grass; I tripped and went spinning down the bank in a shower of dust and grit thrown out by the tyres that came so close that I felt the wind of their passing. I finished at the edge of the reeds by the dyke with one leg under me and when I got up and tried to climb back to the road, I found I had twisted the ankle.

Cartwright made no attempt to help me; he did not even look

round as I hobbled over to him. He was leaning on his cycle, staring down the road and the notebook was out again.

'That was a lovely bit of driving,' I said. 'I hope you got his number.'

'No need, I know the car. I'll have a word with Mr Jacques in the morning.'

'Mr Jacques?'

It was too dark to see his face, but there was a curious, wary expression in the voice. 'A hairdresser in Rye, sir. Been there a good many years, though he's French by birth. Made a lot of money, they tell me—and now I hear he's retiring and going back to live in France. The trouble is that he has never got out of his continental driving habits—all horn and speed, thinks that will look after everything. And now he's going, he seems to care even less. We're always having to pull him up.' Then he must have realised how I was leaning against his cycle, taking the weight off one foot. 'Are you all right, Mr Kent?'

'I twisted my ankle falling down there. But it's not too bad. I can manage.'

'You lean on the cycle, sir. I'll come with you all the way.'

We made a slow dot-and-carry progress, with the ankle throbbing like hell, and I was irritated more than touched by his frequent suggestions that he should put me on the saddle and push. Once, to change the subject, I said, 'Well, you've got something else to put in your bloody Occurrence Book now. But I think there was a bit of excuse. With all this slime on me, I must have blended beautifully with the grass verge.'

'Maybe, sir. But I shall speak to him very sharply.'

'You won't prosecute?'

'No, sir.' It was obvious he wanted to get off the subject.

'He's a late bird . . . this Mr Jacques,' I said.

'Been to one of his card parties in Folkestone, I expect. He goes once a week, regular.' And that closed the conversation on Mr Jacques.

I was parked at the side door of the Horse and Cart and managed to get up to the bathroom without waking anyone. The water was tepid, but I stripped down and washed from head to foot; the ankle was black and puffy, but I hoped it was over the worst. Leaving my clothes in a filthy green pile on the bathroom floor, I hobbled to the bedroom, and there was Joan fast asleep, breathing softly. I slipped her arms from their tight clasp of the bolster and slid into its place. 'Here's the real thing,' I whispered.

She did not waken, just murmured something drowsily, and I lay like that for a long time, dead tired, feeling the soft warmth of her flooding through me, but I could not sleep. It was not only the throbbing ankle, but a series of uncomfortable thoughts that raced round and round in my mind. I had surprised a man posting a letter, and because of that he had tried to knife me. He had failed . . . but someone had then tried to run me down in a car in full sight of a policeman. The stakes must be high . . . to risk a term of imprisonment for manslaughter. Jacques . . . French . . . a hairdresser. My client was one too. It was rather a coincidence . . . the beginning of an equation. I was still trying to work it out when I fell asleep.

CHAPTER 3

Broad daylight: Joan sitting on the side of the bed with a tray of bacon, eggs and coffee, tickling my nose to wake me.

'I've been to the bathroom,' she said, 'and seen the wreckage. You must have had a lovely night out with the boys.'

'Not very.'

'I suppose you started asking some of your ham-handed questions, and then someone threw you in the village pond?'

'Not quite—' I pulled back the bedclothes and showed her my ankle, that now looked far more horrible than it really was; she stopped being angry and got worried, and I had to tell her all that had happened. When I had finished she was quiet for a long time: so long that I took the opportunity to finish my eggs and bacon. Then she said, 'Harry . . . you promised me, when we were married, that there would be none of that sort of stuff. Just straightforward cases.'

I looked up from my plate. 'That's all I want, but—'

She went over to the window and looked out, and I remember a blackbird was singing his last song in the garden. 'You mean Mr Stebbings—and that little girl . . .' She turned to face me. 'All right. What do you want me to do?'

I put the tray on one side and had another look at the ankle, giving it a gentle prod. 'There's nothing there that lead lotion won't cure in a day. But I'll have to rest it. Will you go into Rye and get some? Then go round the hairdressers?—the classy ones, I mean. Jacques' place particularly.'

'And Stebbings?'

'Yes, Stebbings as well.''

'But what do you want me to look for, Harry?'

'That's the difficulty, darling. I just don't know. But anything odd—out of place—anything that may connect this lot. A sort of common factor.'

'But I can't just go into the shops and poke round and stare. Do you want me to have my hair done?'

'No,' I said quickly. 'What's the name of that revolting stuff you squirt on your hair?'

'Lacquer?'

'That's it. You say the brand you like is difficult enough to get hold of in town sometimes. They won't have it here. Make them turn out the shop, and keep your eyes open while they are doing it.'

'This Jacques. How do you know he does ladies' hair?'

'He must—with a name like that. Now I'm going to make up on sleep. Be good.' Then I caught her left hand and started to ease the wedding ring off her finger. 'You had better revert to that happy state when you were Miss Kennedy. And you are on holiday in Rye.'

She smiled at me. 'I might get picked up—'

'No sleep will be lost on that score,' I said rudely. 'Not any more. Time marches on.' I pulled the bed-clothes over my head.

I suppose I did get a couple of hours before there was a knocking at the door. It was the landlord.

'There's someone to see you, sir. I said you were resting, but it seems to be urgent. It's Inspector Fox, of the Rye police.'

'Send him up.'

It was probably some footling detail that Cartwright had left out of his Occurrence Book; so they had to send an inspector to put it right.

He was just like his name—only in a nice way. Thin, wiry, with a lean face from which jutted a long thin nose that seemed to be sniffing for a scent. The brightest of blue eyes, and a fair skin weathered brick-red by wind and weather; when he had sat down and taken off his cap, the hair was sandy. A nice fox. I liked the look of him.

'I'm sorry to disturb you after last night's ducking, sir. But there were one or two points—'

'Of course, Inspector. And I would like to thank you for the constable's great help in getting me home.'

He inclined his head. 'Only too glad. When the report came through, and I knew you had hurt your ankle, I took the liberty of sending a car to the place and recovering your property. I've got it here—' he patted the bundle wrapped in an oilskin that he had put down by the side of the bed—'so if you wouldn't mind giving me a receipt—'

This was indeed service. 'It's awfully kind of you, Inspector.'

The blue eyes were fixed on me. 'How is the ankle, by the way?'

I turned back the bed-clothes and showed him. 'My wife's gone to get some lead lotion in Rye. I think that will do the trick.'

'Yes. A pity it should have to spoil the rest of your holiday.'

Why was there that distinct emphasis on the word 'holiday', why was he staring at me like that? 'Well, it's my own fault, so I can't complain,' I said shortly.

He had picked up the parcel from the floor and was untying the string. 'What particular bird were you trying to photograph, Mr Kent?'

Damn the man; I had not even bothered to think of one. 'A redshank,' I said, hopefully.

He did not look up from his struggle with the knot. 'A redshank, sir? Of course, I don't know very much about it—but I thought they always kept to the ground, never nested in a tree.'

'That's quite right. What I meant was—I started out to look for redshank, and then I thought I spotted something up there . . . so I went up to have a look . . . and fell in . . .' It sounded so weak and futile that I was glad he was not looking at me.

'Quite. Well, here are your belongings. One haversack and one air cushion: they were dry because they lodged in the branches. Then a thermos, broken, I'm afraid, because it fell on the ground underneath. We managed to drag your torch and camera out of the dyke, and the torch is all right; but your camera—' he clicked his tongue—'it's in the most terrible state, full of mud and water. We tried to clean it, but it's an expert's job, the sooner the better—there's a very good man in Hastings I can recommend.' Those blue eyes were fixed on me again, uncomfortably. 'We had a look at the film, but it was ruined.'

I had taken the articles one by one from him and had put them down on the counterpane; I was still looking at my precious, slime-stained Leica when his voice came again, and it was completely different. '—And your knife, sir.'

I looked up at an outstretched hand, holding a long, open flick-knife by the blade, the handle towards me.

'Don't touch it.' Some instinct kept on saying that over and over again as I stared. Perhaps the thing that saved me was that I had never seen it before; only heard it open and then come slashing down through the leaves of the willow in the dark.

'That's not mine,' I said.

'No? . . . That's odd, sir. It was close to the torch.'

'I've never seen it before, someone else must have dropped it in.'

'But it can't have been there any longer than your stuff, Mr Kent. There's no rust on the blade . . . quite clean.'

'It's not mine.' I tucked my hands under the bed-clothes.

Inspector Fox sighed, put the knife back in the oilskin covering, tied it up and rose from his chair. Then he stood quite still, looking down at me.

'How long would you say you were up that tree, Mr Kent?'

'I don't know—about ten minutes, I suppose.'

'And did you find this nest?'

'Yes. And I took a photo.' Even if the film was ruined, they would know I had taken something.

'And did you take the bird's nest away with you when you fell out of that tree?—because there's nothing there this morning.'

Less and less I liked each question. 'If you will be so good as to tell me what all this is in aid of, Inspector, then—?'

'Certainly.' The notebook came out and he flipped over the pages. 'At 01.35 this morning, you reported to P.C. Cartwright that you had fallen out of a tree into a dyke, giving the position of the occurrence as approximately the tree opposite the post-box in Crooked Lane. He assisted you home and then returned to his beat. At 03.27 he reached the position you had indicated, to find that an attempt had been made to break open the box, and this having failed the contents had been set on fire, presumably with petrol poured through the slot and then ignited with a match.' He paused for a moment and then his voice became very gentle. 'I need not tell you, Mr Kent, that tampering with Her Majesty's Mail . . . in any way . . . is a felony.'

'Aren't you going to caution me?' I said.

'Caution you, sir? This is only a friendly chat.'

'But you've just accused me of a felony.'

'Nothing of the kind. We just wondered . . . if you had seen anything while you were up that tree . . . bird-watching.'

More than anything, I wanted time. I said, 'The second occurrence—that I hope is in the Occurrence Book —do you want to ask me about that?'

'No, sir. That seems quite straightforward. An error of judgment. Perhaps the driving was a little fast, but we'll attend to that.'

It is always nice to be on the attack. 'And who's going to "attend" to my twisted ankle?—I was lucky not to be killed by that lunatic—and you damn well know it. I'm still considering whether I shall prosecute.'

'I wouldn't do that. There's not much evidence.'

'Just myself—and one of your policemen. What could be better?'

'I wouldn't advise it, Mr Kent. I don't think there would be a case to go before the magistrates. It might cost you money.' You could almost see him shying away from it.

'Well, to get back to the first point. As this is an unofficial chat—will you tell me something? Are there any prints on that knife—or the letter-box?'

He just nodded.

'Then, when I can walk, which will probably be tomorrow, I'll come down to the Station and you can take mine. I'll bet you a fiver now that they don't match.'

'Fair enough, sir. We'll expect you at eleven-thirty.' There was no question of my convenience, it was a summons. When he got to the door, he stopped for a moment. 'Mr Harry Kent . . . I seem to have heard that name . . . somewhere before.'

'Could be, Inspector. There's three pages of us in the London telephone directory.'

'Probably some other Kent, sir.' He gave me a nice smile and the door closed softly behind him.

I dozed off again until Joan came back, and the minute she came into the room I knew she had got on to something: there was that relaxed, cat-after-a-saucer-of-cream look about her. I determined not to play.

'Did you get the lotion, darling? It's been aching like hell.'

'Yes.' Absently, she handed over the lint and bottle and a *crêpe* bandage. 'The chemist says you must rest it for at least two days.'

'Not much chance of that. I meant to ask you—was there any post this morning? Anything from Josh, I mean?'

'No, nothing. But you did give him till tomorrow.'

'I know I did. It's just that I hoped—I'll ring him up and give him a jog. Hell—! I can't. That damned phone of his is cut off.'

I could see her smiling in the mirror as she took off her hat and started to fiddle with her hair. 'I had a lovely morning,' she said.

I looked up from the winding of my bandage. 'Such as—?'

'All round the hairdressers. There are four that you'd call good class—but one stands out from the others—it's better than any I've seen outside the West End. And that's Maison Jacques.

'How does it stand out?'

'Well, it's beautifully furnished, the work looks first-class, and they seem to stock anything you could possibly want.'

'But did you *see* anything?'

She was not going to be denied her story. 'I went there last. None of the other three, which included Stebbings, had the lacquer. But at Jacques' place they produced it at once.'

'So you had to come out at once?'

'No, darling. I demanded Mr Jacques. I knew he must be the king-pin stylist, because there was an old cow at the reception desk making a terrific fuss that she could not have him—'

' "Cow"—that's a very unladylike word. But go on.'

'I did see him. And I put on a haughty London act. He's going to give me a wash and set tomorrow morning at eleven. Personally. For twelve and six.'

'So what—?'

'Harry, I only pay seven bob in London. So he must be good, very good. And people who are that good don't usually bother with that small stuff: they just wander round and see the girl is doing all right and put in the final touches.'

'Then why are you being honoured?'

'I don't know. When I first asked him to do it, he wasn't the slightest bit interested. But suddenly, and it must have been because of something I said—I mean there could be no other reason—he changed. It was a subtle thing, darling. I wouldn't have noticed it if I hadn't been looking for it. He was alert and ready for something. He sort of looked me up and down and said, "Modom has lovely hair. It will be a pleasure to set it." And made the appointment.'

'Darling—try and think. What was it you said that made the change?'

She wrinkled her forehead. 'I'm trying to, Harry. Really, I didn't say much at all. I told you I put on a haughty act—and I think I said something about being recommended by a friend in London.'

'Any name?'

'No.'

'Well, you had better try that line again tomorrow,' I said. 'By the way—what's he like?'

'Jacques? Oh, sallow and slight. Good-looking in a way, I suppose. That blue-black hair and a little smear of a moustache. Too much perfume about him for a man, though.'

'There weren't any traces of green scum about his person, I suppose?'

She stared at me. 'Harry—what do you mean?'

I looked back at her just as straight. 'That scent of his. What was it?'

Her forehead creased into a frown of concentration. 'Musky. But I don't think I can place it.'

'I can. Sandalwood.'

If it had not been so serious, the way her jaw dropped might have been funny. 'That's right,' she said slowly. 'But how could you know?'

'Because, at times, when we took a bath together last night in a dyke, our heads were close enough for me to smell it.'

There was a long silence. Then I said, as casually as possible, '—He speaks good English?'

'Perfect—there's only the trace of an accent.'

'Was there anything else?'

She swung round to the dressing-table. 'There's something wrong with that place, Harry. Apart from what you've said about him. I know there is. I could feel it.'

'What sort of thing?'

'Strain . . .' She had picked up her handbag and was clicking the clasp open and shut. 'I told you I had to wait a bit to see Mr Jacques, didn't I—?' she was speaking fast, '—because there was another woman waiting in front of me. She was well dressed—too well dressed for Rye, I thought.'

'What happened?'

'I heard her ask for him—it sounded terribly urgent—you could almost feel the strain coming from her. After a few moments he looked out of a cubicle and beckoned her in. She wasn't there for more than two minutes, and when she came out . . . her face . . . it was different . . .'

'What was the matter with it?'

'It had changed. I've seen it before. I mean I don't know her, but I know that look. And when I saw it before, it was somewhere with you.'

'With me—?'

'Yes. It was night, and you took me to some place, and there was a woman there that was just the same way. You told me why—but I just can't remember.'

'Nor can I, darling. But I expect it will come.'

'I hope so. Because I know it is important. Now tell me, what have you been doing?'

'Nothing much; if that's your lot, I'll—'

'Not quite.' She cheered up at once. 'I went on to the Mermaid and had a cup of coffee. I met such a nice young man.'

'So the old charm is still working?'

'It must be. He's asked me to dine with him in Hastings tomorrow night.'

'Now, Joan—' I jerked up in the bed and hurt my ankle in doing so. 'I didn't tell you to—'

'But you did tell me to go as "Miss Kennedy"—so you can't blame him, darling. And you won't blame me when I tell you that before I said "yes", I had found out who he was. A reporter on a local paper. So he might be very useful.'

I could not compete. 'O.K., Miss Kennedy.'

'I found out one thing already,' she said proudly as she put on some lipstick and then made faces at the mirror. 'Your Mr Jacques—he is retiring. Made a packet—so Joe White, that's my reporter friend, said. The business is up for sale as a going concern.' She turned and looked at me. 'Joe added something about "he had got rich too quick to have made it all out of hairdressing." '

' "Joe" is probably jealous. You be careful. Anything else?'

'No, not there—' she said it very casually. 'But I told you I went to Stebbings first. Mrs S served me: apparently she's come back to the shop . . . since it happened. Did you know she was French?'

A hairdresser client with a French wife . . . another hairdresser working in the same town, who I knew had tried to stab me because I had seen him post a letter now destroyed, was also French. Was it the next step in solving my equation, or a side step in an unimportant jealousy? It was an anti-climax to have to tell of a dull interview with the police, even the accusation of felony.

It was while we were having lunch in our room—a special concession by the landlord, on account of my 'bad leg'—that the talk turned to motor-cars. I think it came up because Joan mentioned that the Rover battery was getting flat again, and she had had quite a job to start it that morning.

Then she said, 'Talking of cars—I forgot to tell you. There was a lot of very smart ones parked near Jacques' place in Lion Street. There was one Rolls—I noticed it particularly, because the registration letters were the same as Aunt Bertha's initials.'

'BMG—? But that's a London number. You're not trying to make out that this Jacques is so good that people make a round trip of a hundred and twenty miles just to get their hair done?'

'Well, I did think it rather odd.'

'Cars change hands quite often,' I said, 'but they don't change their registration number. I'm sure there are quite a lot of people in Rye that can afford to run a Rolls.'

When Joan had taken the lunch tray down to the kitchen, I lay back on the pillows, staring at the ceiling, watching the smoke of my cigarette curl upwards. Quite suddenly I said, 'Darling, I want to pack this case up.'

'Why?' I never like it when Joan says 'Why' like that: it makes me feel uncomfortable.

'Because—oh, well, I don't think we're going to be able to help poor Stebbings very much . . . and I've got a feeling that Josh is going to let us down.'

'Those are not the real reasons, Harry. Why?'

I didn't want to say it, but I had to. 'I think we are on the verge of something that's—well, not too pleasant. Something that you, particularly, should be kept out of.'

She didn't answer for a moment; when her voice came it was hard.

'You believe that child is alive, don't you?'

'Yes, I do.'

'And that you can get her back?'

'If Josh gets any fix on where she is, I'm sure I could.'

'Then you are going to.' There was something utterly final in the way she said that. She got up from the end of the bed. 'I'll take the Rover up to London now, if you like, and see how he is getting on.'

'But you don't want to go near Josh, darling. You loathe the man.'

'I don't loathe him. I just disapprove. And even if I did loathe him—I'd go. Because of that baby.'

I looked out of the window; the shadows were just beginning to take a slant. 'No, Joan. I wouldn't let you. It would mean coming back all the way in the dark. I wouldn't like it a bit with that flat battery.' I had turned my head to watch her now; there was something in the way she was standing, the way she held her head, the look in her eyes, that gave the essence of the fierce protection of motherhood in all the women in the world. I wished, so much, that we had had the freedom, and the money, to start a family of our own.

'So we go on?' I said.

'Yes, Harry. We go on.'

'Right. . . . Now sit down again, and we'll think it out. The first thing is we leave Josh alone until his time limit—that's second post tomorrow. If he doesn't show something by then, we'll both go back to town and see what's happened. In the meantime, there is only one other line to try—make the gent we're working for do a little to help himself. He'll have to talk.'

'Where can you see him on the quiet?' said Joan.

'At his shop. This ankle will be O.K. for a little gentle exercise tomorrow; will you be a pet and ring him up? Make an appointment for me to have my hair cut at nine, before I go to the police. The place should be fairly quiet then.'

When she came back and said she had fixed it, I was in the process of lighting my fifth cigarette running from the stub of the fourth. 'I've just been trying to work out if there is anything else we can do, darling—but there's nothing. Nothing to get any sense out of, anyway. Two hairdressers in a small town, one French, doing fine business, retiring, but with jumpy customers; the other is being blackmailed, and has a French wife. Where the hell is the link?'

'There must be one,' said Joan, 'and you and I are going to find it.'

The only other thing that happened that day was the personal telephone call that came through for me at nine o'clock. As a message came through with it from the operator to know if I would accept the reversed charge from London, I was sure it must be Josh and I made Joan help me downstairs.

He was tense and excited. 'I've got it, Harry.'

'Where—?'

I did not mean to be so abrupt, and the moment that one word was out of my mouth, I knew I had hurt him. 'But, dear boy, don't you want to know the arguments—all the chain of proof that I have built up? It will convince you.'

'I'm sorry, Josh. I know it will. But it's so important I know where.'

There was silence at the other end of the line.

'Well, I'll tell you, then. France.'

Real reproach in his voice now, 'If you knew, Harry, then why bother to make me—' It was the small boy robbed of his surprise.

'I didn't. It was only a guess. But if you've proved it, that is the vital thing. Post the stuff down to me at once.'

He cheered up at once. 'Couldn't I come down with it tomorrow, Harry? There might be one or two points . . .'

'No. There's a very good reason why I don't want you to show your face in this part of the world. You post it.'

His tone became very wistful. 'I saw a wonderful bargain in the Edgware Road yesterday, Harry. A little Austin, going at fifty pounds, only done twenty thousand miles—'

'The late property of a country clergyman, I presume?'

'But how did you know—?' There was no sarcasm, like mine; it was completely naïve. In some things he really did need a nurse.

'They always are, Josh: and when you open up the gear-box, there's half the harvest festival inside—with a pound of stewing steak for good measure—to keep the wear on the gear-wheels quiet. Look, Josh, even if I could afford it, I wouldn't buy you a motor-car. Your record isn't conducive. Just forget it and post that stuff to me first thing—better still, go out now and send it from that all-night office in Charing Cross. Registered.'

'All right, Harry.'

I felt I must try to make some amend. 'Have you got a passport?'

'Yes. Why—?'

'An available one—not cancelled, or in pawn, I mean.'

'No. I've got it here.'

'Then, if you do what I say, I may be able to offer you a free and interesting holiday.' I said 'Good-night' and rang off.

The ankle was painful still, but fit to walk on in the morning. As my appointment with Stebbings was at nine, we had to leave before the post arrived, which was annoying, but we decided there would be no time to come back and collect Josh's report between our various dates. Somehow, I was sure it would come, and so I arranged to meet Joan at the Mermaid just after twelve. She dropped me in the Mint, outside Stebbings' shop, and I hobbled in, hoping there would be peace and quiet and no other customers.

When I had closed the outer door, I found I was in the common reception space; a notice facing me said that Mr Stebbings was a Ladies' Hairdresser, Gentlemen served by appointment only; to the left were three cubicles, their green curtains drawn, and from one the sound of a hair-dryer whirring, a woman's voice, and a pleasant smell that came drifting towards the entrance. So Mrs S was busy, which was a good thing. On the other side was a single small room with the door open and I could see the one barber's chair with Mr

Stebbings waiting beside it. He looked quite different in his white coat. 'I haven't taken anything on in here till eleven,' he said, 'and the Missis has three appointments running—so we should be all right.' After he had tucked the sheet in round my neck, he went over and shut the door very carefully.

There is something omnipotent, almost god-like, in the feeling of sitting in a barber's chair and having one's hair cut by an expert; I knew he was one from the moment he started, for he disdained the usual zoom up the back of my neck with the power clippers, and did it slowly, carefully, with the hand tool, stopping frequently to stand back and look at his work. The feeling grew with the soft snip of the scissors, the gentle stroke of the brush as he removed the hair, the firm movements as he changed the position of my head. I was above everything; I had all the answers so far. But he was going to talk to me first.

He did speak first: the steady rhythm of those snipping scissors broke suddenly as he said—and I knew how much it cost him to say it, 'Any luck, Mr Kent?'

I waited to let him trim round my left ear before I answered.

'A bit—but I'm stuck now.'

'Why—? What do you mean, you're stuck?'

'I can't go on until you help me, Mr Stebbings.'

The scissors clattered round my head and then went back to their job in three deft cuts. 'I've thought hard about it, Mr Kent, sir. But I dare not.'

'That's a pity. Because I'm pretty certain I know where Margaret is.' I waited for him to steady himself before I added, 'So, you see, if you don't talk now—it will be no good.'

'Where is she—?'

'What's the point of telling you—if you won't help me, and I can't go on?'

Silence, an obstinate silence, over the clicking. Well, that was that, he was not going to talk, and I would have to pack the case up and hate myself for ever after for so doing. I did not speak again until he had started to lather my chin for the shave, and then one of those million-to-one chances came that gave me everything.

The door behind us clicked open suddenly and Stebbings stood back from the chair; I could see in the mirror in front of me the old, old, man who came in the doorway, a shabby old man with bright eyes and the most wonderful grog-blossom of a nose. He gave a quick look at Stebbings, and then at me, and walked across the floor with a queer shuffling, yet bouncy, gait. 'Mornin', John. All right?' I knew that the last was directed at me.

Stebbings just nodded and jerked his head towards the shelf below the mirror and above the basin. Then he said, 'Put it down there, will you, Joe?'

The old man shuffled over and put a folded piece of paper on the shelf. Then he smiled pleasantly at the room in general, said, 'Thank you, John. It's going to be hot,' and made a slow, creaking return outside my field of vision. I heard the door click shut behind him.

Mr Stebbings picked up the brush and made a few final dabs at my chin, then he started the slow sure strokes of the best feel you can have on your face—a really sharp French blade. The chair was not tilted back so far that I could not see the shelf below the mirror; the folded paper that had been placed there was stiff in texture and lay half opened; in my trade, one has to learn to read things at all angles. I could not help seeing it was a betting slip.

'Bookie as well?' I said.

'Sometimes, in a small way, Mr Kent. Why not?'

'Why not, indeed? If you phone a bet, it's legal. If you do that, it's not. Quite daft.'

'Quite so, sir. But all the same, you won't tell anyone, will you?'

'Of course not.' I hardly heard his question or my own answer to it; my mind was racing over the chain of facts, the sudden, almost certain, possibilities. It was like coming out of a dark wood to an open, different view, where each object stood in perspective to the rest. Everything was dropping into place; so fast that I could not keep pace with it; so fast that I had to say it out loud.

'I've never thought about it before . . . a hairdresser's, what better place to go to leave or collect something illegal, however harmless? People come and go, mostly anonymous, the casual trade . . . and there's more privacy than in a shop. And if that goes for betting slips . . . why not other, more profitable things . . . smuggling . . .'

As I said the last word, Mr Stebbings' hand jerked back so hard that he cut me.

Except for his apologies, we did not speak during the stanching of the blood with cotton-wool and the application of the styptic pencil. But his hand was still trembling, and when I was out of the chair and wiping my face, he said, 'I don't like that kind of talk, Mr Kent.'

'Why not? If it isn't true?' I gripped him by the shoulders. 'Look,

man. I *know* it's true now—and if I'm going on with this, I'll have
to poke around to find out *why*. And I don't want to. Can't you
see—it's so much better for you to tell me yourself.'

He looked round the little room wildly. 'Yes—but not here. My
wife—I told you . . . she doesn't know anything.'

I picked up my hat and the stick I had borrowed from the
landlord. 'You said you hadn't taken on anything until eleven
o'clock? Well, give me ten minutes' start, and then come up to the
Parish Church. I'll be sitting in the little North Chapel—the one
with that mahogany altar that's supposed to have been salved from
the Armada. There won't be any local people about—only trippers.
We can talk quietly.'

'Where is she, Mr Kent?'

'In France.'

His eyes were fixed on mine and when I said those two words, I
think I expected to see surprise in them. But there was none; only
increasing fear. A fear that made me know I was right.

Rye church is on the point of the cone that is the town: it is old
and quiet and full of dignity. The great pendulum of the clock
swings down into the nave, beating out in the slowest tick I have
ever heard the message that is inscribed underneath the face of the
clock outside. I got into the corner seat of the back row of chairs
by the screen and waited. I hoped so much he would come—but
even now I could not be sure. The slow ' . . . tick . . . tick' of the
clock came from high up behind me; all round was the cool, damp
smell of age, and hymn books, and scrubbing.

He came at last, sidling down the row of seats towards me fast,
not looking round. I did not give him a chance to cool off; the
moment he was beside me, I said, 'What was it you were
smuggling—and what was it that they wanted you to change over
to . . . that you wouldn't?'

'It was watches. I didn't see anything wrong in that. Then—'
He dropped forward in his seat, his head pillowed on his arms on
the back of the chair in front. But I heard the one word I had been
waiting for, hoping for. . . . 'Drugs.'

It all came out in a rush after that: the story he had kept bottled
up inside himself for so long. I half turned in my seat as I listened,
watching the slow swing of the golden pendulum, thinking about
the confessional.

It had started after the war, when he had gone back to France
to find the girl he had never forgotten. She had sheltered him when

his bomber had been shot up over Occupied France, and risked her life getting him safely away down the Escape Line. It had been a sort of Crusade, a dedicated thanks, and he had found her, courted her, married her, and brought her back to England. He had been apprenticed to a hairdresser before the war, and Marguerite, the farmer's daughter, had been clever enough to take a course in Ladies' styling and get a diploma. Then they had thrown in all they had and opened up their own place in Rye. But it hadn't been that easy: for the first two years, it had been a question of making inroads on the balance of their savings all the time. Then, when they had taken a cheap holiday by going back to stay on her father's farm, he had met a relation, a cousin that lived in Nevers, who, when he heard of their troubles, had told Stebbings he could put him on to a good thing—if he could be discreet. It would be better if Marguerite did not know . . . women were apt to talk. It was watches—smuggled into England from the Continent; he would not be required to have any part in the operation, just be a distributing point, taking in the large consignment, splitting it up and passing the results on to the smaller people. Of the money he took from them he could deduct ten per cent commission, and post the balance to an address in London. When he gave it to me, it was so obviously an accommodation one that I hardly bothered to write it down. If there was time I would have a go at it. But it always took a lot of time.

It had looked so easy, he said, and what really was wrong with that kind of smuggling? Everyone did it, sometimes, in a smaller way.

For the first time, I interrupted. 'Let's cut the ethics. Just tell me how they were shipped over and how you got them and how they were delivered.'

'I never knew a thing about how they came over, Mr Kent. That's honest. But anyone who lives in these parts . . . could have a good guess.'

'Plane—?'

'I wouldn't know—it was better not to know. But they were delivered by a traveller—or someone posing as a traveller. Once a week, and it was always called "the special lotion". It looked like a carton of bottles, and there were some inside, but there were about forty top-make Swiss watches as well. All I had to do was to break them down into packets of six and sell them at a fixed price to anyone that came in and asked for the same thing.'

'Were they always the same people?'

He shook his head. 'No. I think one man came twice. But most were always different. My orders were to sell them to anyone who gave the right words.'

'These orders. How did you get them?'

'Always by phone to the shop. And he wouldn't speak to any other person except me.'

'Was the call local, trunk . . . or foreign? Was it always the same voice, and do you know it?'

He thought for a moment, and when he answered, I could feel the wariness that shaded into his voice. 'Local, I think. And always the same voice. But I wouldn't be able to recognise it.'

'You still get them?'

'No,' he said. 'Not after I said "no" . . . and Margaret went.'

I changed my tack. 'These consignments. Did they always come on the same day of the week?'

'I can't remember exactly.' He was pressing his head down on the hands that gripped the back of the chair in front of him. 'But they always arrived towards the end of the week. I do remember that I used to get worried about them being in the safe at the shop over the week-end.'

I let him go on talking: of the first hint, when the watches were going well, that there might be a far more profitable cargo to handle, his growing suspicion of what it might be, and then the downright order to be ready to accept a load of drugs.

He had refused at once; finally, absolutely. At first all the phone calls had said that the other line would stop, and when he had said he didn't care, there had been no more watches for a week or so: but something must have made them desperate to make the arrangement—he was sure of that. No more watches came but the calls started again. First they had threatened to tell the police what he had been doing; when he countered with a simple statement that he would turn Queen's Evidence on that and the second part, it had stopped them. For a week, and then Margaret had gone, and the photos had started coming, and the threats. He knew *them*, he knew that they would be ruthless and carry out what they said. That was why he could not go to the police—or tell me until I had stumbled on too much. I can remember him, crouching there, beating the chair-back in his agony, saying over and over again, 'Mr Kent, what else could I do—what would you have done?'

There was nothing much I could do to help him, very little more to ask. It was a matter of form to ask if another photo had come that week-end, to show surprise when he said that it had not. I did not tell him of my night on the marsh, or the extra complication of my coming interview with the police—it would have been too much. When I asked him for the name and address of the relative in Nevers who had made the first suggestion, he could not remember, but said he would find out. He swore to me that he had never handled an ounce of the second cargo, and I believed him.

There was a clatter of feet on the stone floor behind us, and the subdued murmur of voices; a crowd of trippers were filing into the chapel to invade our privacy. 'We've been here long enough,' I whispered. 'I'll give you ten minutes' start. Don't come near the pub. Contact me by phone if you have to, and I'll do the same.'

As he rose from his chair, he said, 'Then . . . you are going on with it, Mr Kent?'

'I am now. Because you've trusted me. I only wish you had in the first place—'

'Then there must be a fee—' His hand strayed to his breast pocket before he remembered where he was. 'I'll send you a cheque,' he said, 'we haven't got much . . . but all of it is yours.'

'Only expenses—let's leave a fee until Margaret's home. But I may have to spend quite a bit. Can you manage two hundred?'

He nodded, and I gave him the name of my bank and he said he would send it there at once. He had started to move away down the line of chairs when I had a sudden, last idea. 'Look, before you said you wouldn't handle this stuff, had they said anything about *how* it was to be done?'

'Just like the watches. In much smaller lots, of course.'

'And a code word?'

'Yes. The—it was going to be packed in shampoo packets—real ones. They were to ask for Stebbings' Special Rinse.'

I had to let him go at that, and spent the next few minutes wandering round the church, though I'm afraid I didn't take in much of the beauty. Then I sat, watching that great golden pendulum in its majestic sweep across the nave, trying to tie up the few ends left.

How had the stuff come over? Or was it still coming?

The suggestion I had made about planes had been a wild guess, but more and more my mind came back to them . . . and the strange engine beat that one had made when I was on the marsh. Coming or going back to France, there had been that deep, ragged tone, only when it was to the *south* of me. Could it be two planes coming in very close together, by design, so that one, the pirate, would be without navigation lights, and covered by the radar 'blips' given out by the innocent on a lawful occasion? Then landing, discharging cargo, and waiting for the sound of an escort coming back to the south, before taking off under the same noise and radar cover? It might be done . . . I wouldn't know. I had forgotten too much in the last ten years. It would be terribly difficult to land a plane, even a light one, on that marsh in the dark . . . but it *was* done: now I was certain of that. It was the only way that Margaret could have been got out to France; the only way the photos, taken there, as I was now so certain, could have been sent back and posted in Appledore so regularly.

I left the church and walked down the steep slope of Lion Street without thinking, or bothering to look at Maison Jacques. Somehow, I was certain then that I was going to find Margaret.

CHAPTER 4

Attack being the best form of defence, I gave my business card to the sergeant at the police station to take in to the inspector. There were bound to be more questions, and I knew I couldn't get away with the bird-watching story for much longer; a little truth would be better than a lot of lies.

I was shown into a small bare room; the inspector was sitting behind his desk, looking more Fox-like than ever. He was turning my card over and over between his fingers. 'Good morning, Mr Kent. Take a chair.' He looked down at the card for a moment and then back at me. 'I'm glad you've given me this information yourself —for, as a matter of fact, we had just discovered it ourselves —from different sources.'

'I would have told you yesterday, if you had asked me.'

'I'm sure you would—but then there seemed to be a particular emphasis on bird-watching—' There was a twinkle in his eyes, and that long thin nose, slanting at me as he leaned back in his chair, gave a hint of friendliness.

'That's a side-line,' I said.

'And the real object of your visit to Rye—?'

'Look, Inspector. I came here this morning to have my finger-prints taken, as I promised. Not—'

'There's no need for them to be taken, Mr Kent. We are quite satisfied that you had nothing to do with that business of the pillar-box.'

'I would rather you took them, all the same. In my profession—' I stressed the word—'I can't afford to have the slightest hint against my integrity.'

'If you insist—' He pressed a bell on the desk. 'And perhaps we may be able to talk afterwards?'

'Perhaps.'

When it was done and I had cleaned my fingers, he said, 'I take it you are here professionally?'

'Yes.'

'Can you give me the name of your client?'

I shook my head. 'I'm sorry, no.'

'Or the nature of the business—his business—that you are engaged on?'

'Blackmail.' I thought that would shake him, but it didn't in the slightest. He fiddled with a pen on the desk for a moment before he said, 'Blackmail, Mr Kent, is best handled by us.'

'I agree entirely, Inspector. I've lost count of the number of times I've urged my client to come and see you, but he won't. And he's pledged me to secrecy. So—'

He was on the one point in a flash. 'He—so your client is a man?'

'Yes.'

'A local man?'

'He lives in Kent.'

He smiled at me again. 'We're not going to get very far with this conversation, are we, Mr Kent?'

'That's hardly my fault, is it? You must appreciate how I am placed.'

'I do. And there's one last question—that I hope you will be able to answer. How long do you think your . . . investigation will last . . . in this part of the world?'

It was the sixty-four thousand dollar question; that was really his only interest in me. I knew it, not only by the underlining of the word "investigation", but the fact that he had kept the question till last. And then, the whole feeling of the interview. Polite, but anxious: just the way one would try to treat a casual guest who had dropped in the moment before someone terribly more important was coming to dinner.

'I don't think it will take much longer, Inspector.' I picked up my hat and stick. 'Is there anything else?'

'Not at the moment, thank you, Mr Kent.' Those blue eyes were fixed on mine, inscrutably.

I hobbled to the door and then hesitated. 'There are just two things *I* would like to say. If the thing that, well—has caused this blackmail, was really serious, then I would not have thought of acting for my client—'

He nodded, without speaking.

'And then—you know I was up that tree to try to find out who was posting letters . . . that contained the demands. I wanted to photograph him, but I had bad luck all the way. First the flash blinded me, and I never saw him; then he spotted me, and there was a bit of an argument, and we both finished in the dyke and the film was spoiled. But I half-drowned him, and he doesn't *know* that I didn't see him. So perhaps that will be enough to make him lay off. Which is all I want.'

'We must certainly hope so, Mr Kent. And if there is anything we can do to help you, you have only to ask.'

'Only one thing at the moment, Inspector. Don't follow me around.' As I walked down the hill towards the Mermaid, I was thinking that the last remark he had made was probably the most phoney in all his life. He did not hope that Jacques—if he knew it was Jacques—would lay off; all he wanted was for him to go on undisturbed. He would only help me in things that kept things that way. I was splashing on the edge of a pond where he was fishing very, very deep. He was not interested in me or my case. All he wanted was to get me out of Rye as soon as possible.

Joan was waiting for me at the Mermaid. There was quite a crowd in the bar, so I gave her a sign and picked up the drinks I had ordered and took them along to one of the side rooms—Dr Syn's chamber, long and low and dark with its lovely panelling. We sat down at a table and I pushed her gin and French across. 'Well, sweet. Any luck?'

'Harry—he *is* good. Never had it done better. 'Look—' She fluffed out her hair and I watched the light ripple over the fairness of it, a perfect contrast to the dark age of the linen-fold behind her head. She was right: he was good—and so was she.

'It's lovely, darling. But what about the other thing?'

She went very still, staring into the bottom of her glass as she swirled the drink round. Without looking up, she said, 'I think so—but I just don't know what I have found out. I'd better tell you everything—just as it happened. It seemed so normal—perhaps I imagined things.' For the first time she looked up at me. 'Harry. I'm frightened.'

'Don't you worry. Just tell me.'

'Well, I was shown straight to a cubicle. I noticed it was not Mr Jacques' special, with his name on it, but the one next door. I thought they were going to palm me off on a girl, and was going to make a row, but then he came in to me—very charming, very smart, red carnation in buttonhole and all that—and said would I mind if the girl did the wash and he would attend to the rest himself. It was done so nicely I couldn't object; he made it sound as if he were giving up a pleasure he had been looking forward to for a long, long, time.'

'Go on.'

'Just after he came in and started the set, the curtain was opened behind me, and someone whispered to him. I couldn't hear what, but he asked to be excused for a moment, and when he had gone I heard the curtain of the cubicle on my left, his own special one, drawn shut. There was a hair-dryer going full blast on the other side—you know what a noise they make—but it stopped suddenly. Jacques was talking to someone next door to me, and it was just like shouting at someone against the noise of a Tube train and then it dashes out of tunnel into the open—you're still shouting, because you can't alter your tone quick enough—'

'I know just what you mean—and it worked?'

'Perfectly, for a few words, until they realised.'

'They—'

'Jacques was talking to a girl; I say "girl", Harry, because it sounded such a young voice. But—' She had been fiddling with her empty glass, twirling it by the stem, and now it snapped with a brittle sound; then there was a faint tinkle, as the two halves fell down on the table.

I said, 'Not to worry—I'll get you the other half,' and without looking directly at her I swept the bits into my handkerchief and took them away to the bar and got a repeat order. When I came back, she was in control again.

'What were they talking about, darling?'

'I'll tell you in a minute—but I must explain that voice first, Harry. There was not much in what was said—it was the way it was said, desperate, almost in agony. A pleading, with the shreds of an old dignity still cloaked around it.'

'What did she say?'

'Just . . . "I *must* have it. Why won't you take a cheque? you always have . . . " And then Jacques, quite different to the way I had heard him talk, "A cheque from you, Miss Harris? You must remember what happened to the last one—it bounced." Then he said, "Careful!" and then they dropped their voices. The dryer started up again on the other side, and then, of course, I couldn't hear any more.'

'Miss Harris,' I said. 'We must find out about her. What happened then?'

'Nothing much. He came back and finished the set, and he talked all the time—snobbish talk, Harry. So I came from London, did I? Then I might know Lady Luddimore, or the Hon. Marcia Peasmarsh? I didn't? Of course I must have had the introduction from one of his other London friends, then—it was so difficult to remember all their names, though some were still kind enough to come all the way to Rye to see him, who had tried to look after them in town in the old days. It was phoney, Harry. Completely phoney. I knew that everything said was a delicate lead for me to say something—but I didn't know what it was.'

'And that was all?'

'Not quite. When he had finished, and I had paid, and said how much I liked it, he stood looking at me for a moment . . . and there was an odd expression in his eyes; then he said, "You are sure—there is nothing Modom requires—to take away?" '

'And you said—?'

'Nothing. I told you I didn't know what I was supposed to say.'

I suppose I should have spilled the lot then; told her that I knew damn well what Miss Harris had been pleading for, what "Modom" had been supposed to take away; I should have said that, while she had been telling me all this, the last piece of the equation had fallen into place, and now two and two most definitely made four. But . . . was it quite as simple as that?

To gain time, I said, 'I suppose you want to powder your nose, darling. I'll take our glasses back to the bar.' When I got there, I ordered a quick drink and let the talk and noise flow round me while I sipped and stared at the bottles behind the counter as I tried, desperately, to work out the right answer.

Proof in my mind . . . was not proof in the hand. But I could get that, or rather Joan could. In some way she must have stumbled on the first code word, perhaps the way she said she had come from London. Jacques had been fishing for it . . . she had only to go back and ask. But . . . if she came out with the little packet I hoped for, would it help us? Not with the police, for I would be fumbling too soon for them in their game, not in the saving of Margaret, because even if the police would act on it and pull Jacques in, there would be other links in the chain, dangerous, desperate men who would carry out that threat, not from spite, but to protect themselves. I remembered that a child of three can talk.

Danger . . . that was the keynote. I would be sending Joan into possible danger if anything went wrong. But it would be nice to have that packet, stowed away, a permanent threat to the other

side. And I could not get it myself. So it was "Yes"; the last thought,
as I walked back to where she was waiting for me in the entrance
of the hotel, was that if she didn't know, if she wasn't scared, then
she would act more naturally; the last comfort to myself, that this
was England, safe England, in a the middle of a town, in broad
daylight . . . nothing could happen to her.

I said, 'Sorry to keep you waiting, darling. Will you do one more
thing for me?'

'Of course, Harry.'

'How much money have you got?'

She opened her bag and looked through the jumble and said she
had three pounds ten. 'Take another five.' I handed the notes over.
'Now listen carefully. Go back to Jacques. Act a little cagey, and
ask to see him personally. If you get him alone, say that you had
forgotten the other thing you wanted—a packet of his special rinse:
got that? —a packet of *Mr Jacques' special rinse:* and whatever he
asks for it, don't look surprised. Pay, and take it, and get out as
quick as you can.'

She looked a bit puzzled. 'Where will you be?'

'Waiting for you in the car. But I'll move it from where you left
it in Lion Street, to down the hill and just round the corner in the
High—'

'I remembered what you said about the battery, Harry. It's facing
down the hill.'

'Good girl. Now off you go, and I'll see you in a few minutes.' I
remember that as she walked off ahead of me towards Lion Street,
I felt thoroughly mean—and for all I had said to myself, a little
frightened.

The Rover was parked just a little uphill from Maison Jacques,
and I got in and just managed to get a kick out of the starter, for
the battery was just about as flat as yesterday's ullage. I coasted
down the hill to the corner of High Street, turned left, and parked,
keeping the engine ticking over hard.

Four minutes . . . eight. How long would it take someone to walk
a few yards and go into a shop and order something and pay for
it? Not that long. I sat crouched over the steering wheel, gnawing
at my fingers, cursing myself, getting more and more afraid . . . ten
minutes, and there was nothing to do—except walk back up there
and bust everything open. I was half out of the driving door, going
to do so—she came before any Margaret—when I heard her, the

clatter of high heels on the pavement that I knew so well, before ever I saw her.

She came running round the corner towards the car, bag clutched to her chest, face dead white; she almost knocked a woman flat as she wrenched open the door on her side, and then she was slumped beside me, crying out between deep, tearing breaths, 'Take me home, Harry . . . please, get me out of here.'

'It doesn't matter, darling. I know you didn't get it. But it doesn't matter.'

She did not answer. I kept quiet as I threaded my way out through the town traffic towards the peace of the Appledore road. All the time, I was thinking of the risk I had run . . . what a mean bastard I had been to let her go back.

At last I ventured, 'Could you tell me what happened?'

'I know you'll think I'm being terribly silly, Harry—but it was *horrible*.' There was still a tremor in her voice.

'Oh, my darling—I don't know what to say . . . I should never have let you—'

'It doesn't matter.' She was looking straight ahead at the road, and the flanking dykes that were running past us. But I'm sure she did not see any of it.

'I went in . . . and asked for him. I had to wait a minute and then he came out of his cubicle. There was no one near us, so I asked straight away . . . just in the words you told me. He just looked at me and smiled, and then he said, "I'm afraid you are a little late, *Miss Kennedy*. That line has *just* been discontinued." Just that, and it wasn't the words or the way that he said them that frightened me, Harry. It was the look in his eyes . . . just as if a shutter had fallen down in front of them . . . and you saw deep inside for the first time . . . yellow . . . like a jackal's . . . all the evil in the world.'

'Oh God—I'm sorry.'

There was a silence and then she said quietly, 'What was it you hoped he would give me?'

It didn't make things any easier for her my having to admit it was a packet of heroin or cocaine.

I had been so sure we had kept apart; that there had been nothing to connect us. But someone had seen, and now there was more danger for everyone; worst of all, my Joan had been brought into the circle that seemed to be closing round us tighter and tighter.

And all because I had been too eager to prove a point. I felt a complete bloody fool.

To take her mind off what had just happened, I tried to explain all that had happened that morning: of what I took to be the police reaction to our visit. 'Their only interest in us, darling, is to get us out of the way. We're treading on their toes, we've stumbled on their deeper, far bigger game—I'm sure what you saw this morning—and they don't like it.'

'But you've got to go to them now, Harry. With this morning, and if you tell them about Margaret, they'll have to—'

I braked the Rover hard, and swung her on to the grass verge so that I could park. Then I turned to face her.

'Can't you see I *can't!* They wouldn't believe a thing about where she is, even if Josh has proved it, and if they did, what do you think would happen then—?'

'They would arrest Jacques, I suppose.'

'On what grounds? What do you think he's doing at this moment, if he's wise? Shovelling all the remaining packets of his special rinse into a nice hot fire, I should think. And you saw him this morning, off his guard for a moment. Do you think he would be . . . squeamish?'

'What do you mean?'

'The threat to Stebbings was that they would only keep Margaret alive if he did what they wanted, and now you can see why it was so urgent for them, for, with Jacques retiring, they had to have another outlet. *They meant what they said.* How much more would they mean it, if someone talked? Me . . . Stebbings . . . it wouldn't matter. Even if Jacques was inside, there are probably others in France just as ruthless. They would do it without thinking . . . just like that—' I snapped the matchstick with which I had just lit our two cigarettes. 'And don't forget they would have a far better reason than spite. Protection, Joan. Margaret is three. She could talk.'

I drew hard on my fag, and then I said, 'When Stebbings first came to me, I cursed him for not going to the police, for not telling me everything. Now I know why: he couldn't, he was so certain they would do it. And that is why we can't risk going now, for I believe it too.'

There was a long, heavy silence. 'Then what do we do?' she said.

'Get out of it this afternoon. Go back to town. Try the French angle—if Josh hasn't let us down.'

'But what about my date tonight: with that nice reporter?'

I stared at her in amazement. 'Joan—you don't think . . . after this morning . . . I'd risk it . . . let you out of my sight? Anyway, we know the lot. There's nothing more to find out.'

'There might be. And I can't put him off, Harry. I don't know his address.'

'Then stand him up.'

'No,' she had put a hand on my knee, her most persuasive. 'Look, darling . . . there can't be any danger. You have just told me how you feel that Jacques would think—now I'll tell you my idea. Yes, he's probably shovelling those packets into a fire, just as you said: but only as a precaution. He thinks we know, but he can't be quite sure . . . sure enough to risk drawing further attention to himself . . . on his own doorstep. I'm safer here than any other place. Because I'm so close.'

It was sense—even though I still did not like it. 'All right—if you must. Where did you say he was picking you up?'

'He's *meeting* me at the Mermaid at six-thirty. I sort of gave the impression I was staying there.'

'Right. I'll take you in, and then come back here. I'll go back to the Mermaid at about ten and wait till you arrive. Just come inside as if you were staying. The thing I don't want is to have you wandering round Rye on your own in the dark.'

'And how will you pass the time—a nice quiet evening's drinking on your own?'

'As a matter of fact—yes. In our bedroom.'

'But, why the bedroom—don't you want to be seen in the bar?'

I said, 'Tonight is the last public appearance of the Long Row Prize Band outside the pub; you can see everything from our window, and I thought it might be interesting to watch the same scene—as was set on the night that Margaret disappeared.'

'But it will be much darker, Harry.'

'All the same, I'd like to watch.'

She was silent for a moment, then she said, 'What do you want me to ask my boy friend?'

'Anything about Jacques—the dirt, I mean. And anything on the probability of smuggling on the marsh—how it is done, if it is done—all that sort of thing.'

'But I thought you said that part was the police end—didn't interest us?'

'Only in so far as I am certain Margaret was got out that way. And the letters to Stebbings come in by the same channel.'

We did not speak again until I swung the Rover into the pull-in of the Horse and Cart. Then I said, 'Really, it all depends on Josh—and if he's let us down—'

But he had not: there was a registered packet waiting for us, and I ripped it open as we went up the stairs to our bedroom. I turned over the four closely-written pages, cursing Josh for not using his typewriter, forgiving him when I turned back to the opening paragraph and found the reason was it remained in pawn. His black crabbed hand was too vile to read fast—words like "azimuth" and "declination" were the only ones that seemed to jump out of the page at me—and, in any case, I wanted to know *where*, not *how;* the next two pages of graphs and calculations were no help either, only on the last, the smallest, clipped to the back, was my answer. A map of France, with a band that looked by the scale to be about thirty miles wide, shaded across it; where the great upward curve of the River Loire cut this band there was double shading, giving the shape of a segment; in this area there were twelve small black dots. I read the short paragraph of conclusions and then looked up at Joan.

'Darling, he's got it—far closer than I had dared to hope. He's prepared to bet she's hidden in one of the châteaux on the Loire.'

I gave the ankle another chance to rest that afternoon, lying on the bed, watching Joan's preparations for her party, talking of what faced us now. She seemed quite recovered from the shock of the morning and was now occupied with the enormous decision as to which of the two frocks she had brought with her would prove the more glamorous. I was glad, I didn't mind, even, when she roped me in to make the final choice; although it ended in the usual procedure of her switching back to the one I had rejected.

'It all ties up,' I said, 'even to the fact that that cousin of Mrs Stebbings who started everything lives at Nevers. That can't be more than twenty miles from Josh's area. We'll have to contact Stebbing and tell him that we are going back to town and then to France—'

'We are going back to France? Who is we?'

'You and I, darling. If we find the child, I wouldn't begin to know how to handle a baby.'

She cheered up even more at this. 'But even if you find the place, and know she's there, how can you get her back?'

'In the same way that she was taken in the first place. Snatch her.' I hesitated for a moment. 'How we can do it will depend on the circumstances we find, but in any case I know it will be tricky—more than two people could handle. I think we should take someone else.'

'Who—?'

'Well, darling, Josh is in on this already. He's tough and strong, and his French is near perfect . . .' My voice trailed away as I watched the back of her head for reaction as she made up her face at the dressing-table.

She put down the lipstick carefully. 'And he'll drink himself silly at the first café he gets into—probably assault the entire Gendarmerie, and land us all in jail—'

'If I can get a promise out of him—and I've never known him break one—that he won't have anything stronger than wine—'

'Water—' said Joan, busy with the eye-black.

'Then there's no point in asking. He just wouldn't come. He *loves* wine—understands it. And I don't suppose he has had the chance to get to France for a long time—especially during the *vendange*.'

There was a long silence. 'All right, Harry. I'll settle for wine. Not for your sake—certainly not for his sake—but because I think there is a very little in what you say about having a tough customer around.'

'Bless you, I promise I'll get that promise. I wish to God we could leave on Monday—but francs are going to be the trouble. I mean the delay in getting them. The money's there. Stebbings has sent a cheque direct.'

'But Mr—what's his name?—Mostyn, has always been very helpful.'

'He can't work miracles—and I'm so terribly afraid there won't be a lot of time.'

We nattered on until it was time to leave, and then there was another delay while I had to crank the Rover, for the battery was now almost non-existent. I got her started at last, we drove into Rye, and I dropped Joan at the back of the Mermaid. As I kissed her, I said, 'Have a good time, darling. Be good—and careful. I'll be waiting for you.' I wished I was taking her out to dinner.

When I got back to the Horse and Cart, the stage was already being set for the evening's performance. The golden evening was shading into those wonderful blues of autumn twilight; a few from the village were sitting on the benches outside the public bar, pints in hand, waiting. As I parked the car, two small boys came round the corner, sagging under the bulk of a big bass drum, which they deposited in the middle of the grass triangle in front of the house. By the time I had got two large Scotches and gained the window of the bedroom, music stands had appeared like magic, standing in a half-circle. Then, resplendent in their red and blue uniforms, festooned in aiguillettes and gold braid, the Long Row Prize Band marched into view.

They were remarkably good for a village of that size. Fifteen strong, ages ranging from a boy of ten, in school cap and shorts, cheeks bulging as he tried to blow himself right through his cornet, to the tuba—seventy at least, looking so frail that it seemed impossible that he could hold up his instrument, a flowing white moustache drooping down on each side of the mouth-piece. Their leader, you could not call him conductor, for he played his own cornet all the time, taking all the twiddly-bits and high notes—at the same time contriving to beat time with his head, was brilliant. I admired him, but was not really interested. I was watching the old man and the little boy: because, if they always stood in the same position each time they played there, those two were the only ones that could look through into the garden from which Margaret disappeared.

After a stirring "Colonel Bogey", we stole through the classics and then had "Poet and Peasant". I was watching the old man all the time. There was a second tuba, wielded by a much younger man, standing close beside him, and I thought that it was rather a ponderous bottom combination for the size of the band. It was in "Light Cavalry" that I found the reason: it was getting almost too dark to see, but in the rising crescendo of the charge, with the tubas running up and down the scale . . . ompah . . . ompah . . . ompah, I could just make out the old man's face going through a startling colour change—pink . . . then dull red . . . then scarlet. Suddenly his elbow shot out, catching his partner smartly in the ribs; the volume from that quarter doubled, but the total contribution of the tuba section stayed the same. The old man still held his instrument to his face and went through the motions of playing: but there was no noise coming from him. He was getting his breath back. And while he was doing so, he was staring straight across through the garden gate. Perhaps he had been breathless on the night Margaret was taken . . . at the critical moment. It was worth trying to find out. I had one last look at the boy—but he was going to be no use to me: his concentration was such that his cheeks were bulging, like tight red apples, round the mouth-piece of his cornet, and his eyes were tight shut. He was trying to blow himself into unconsciousness; he would never have noticed anything.

I went down to the bar, where the landlord was trying to cope with the chaos of dirty glasses in the comparative peace while the band was playing. It was almost dark outside now; through the open door came strains of "In Cellars Cool and Shady". I went up to the counter. 'Sling me over a cloth and I'll polish them for you.'

'Thank you, Mr Kent. It's hard to keep pace on a night like this. And the Missis is snowed under in the public.'

I went round beside him and started wiping the glasses and putting them back on the shelves. 'I think the band is very good,' I said.

'Not bad—are they? But it's our butcher, he's the conductor, that takes the weight of it all. I don't know what they would do without him.'

'I've been watching upstairs. That old man who plays the tuba. He looks quite a character.'

The landlord laughed. 'Old Ben—? Would you believe he was seventy-eight? Been playing in the band for more than fifty years.'

'And looks as if he has used up all his breath doing it.'

He looked up from the sink, grinning. 'So you spotted the way he takes a spell off? Well, the bellows aren't too good now, poor dear soul. But don't you mention it to him—it's a sort of unwritten law that no one notices. He thinks that nobody knows—that he'd be thrown out of the band if they did; of course they wouldn't—they'd keep him there as a sort of mascot, even if he couldn't play a note. But he's touchy, is Ben. So the best thing they could do was to ignore it and put in a second tuba player—his grandson—so that when Ben gets short, young Harry comes in and keeps the flag flying.'

'I'd like to meet Ben.'

'You can. Tomorrow morning. Always comes down before dinner for a game of poker dice on a Sunday.'

I thought it might be worth staying on that long—just in case. 'I'll challenge him, then. I've been told I'm good.'

'And he'll beat you,' said the landlord.

"In Cellars Cool and Shady" was just getting to the last climax; the glasses were finished and it was so dark now that it must be the end of the programme. It might be the last chance I would have.

'By the way,' I said, 'I didn't know until someone told me in Rye today that this was the place . . . that terrible case of the little girl being kidnapped.'

He looked away from me. 'We don't like talking about that very much.'

'I'm sure you don't. But there's one thing I never understood, reading the newspaper accounts, I mean. How was it no one saw her taken? She was in the garden, and I was looking tonight. To get her out of there, whoever did it must have come out of the garden gate, right in front of the pub, the band, and everyone who was listening, including her parents.'

He pulled the plug out of the sink and stared hard at the draining water. 'I don't think it happened like that at all, Mr Kent. It was another way. There's a gap in the hedge side of the road, my dog started it and I went on using it when I want to go that way down the street. I never worried about kids playing there, because there was a deep ditch and I didn't think they could get over it and out on to the road. But someone else must have known about it—she was there, playing alone during one of the intervals, because her father took her a bag of crisps; then, after the next piece, she had vanished.'

'You mean either she *did* manage to cross the ditch and was picked up on the road, or someone who knew of the hole in the hedge—'

'Yes.' The finality of the word ended the discussion. Outside in the darkness, the lights of the Horse and Cart now glowed bravely, and the solo trombone was descending ' . . . drinking . . . drinking . . . D . . . R . . . I . . . N . . . K . . . I . . . N—' I held my breath and prayed for him as he wavered, then hit and held the bottom note in triumph. 'Well, that's that,' said the landlord, 'except for "The Queen". I'd best get ready for the rush.'

I moved round to the proper side of the counter. 'There's one thing I meant to ask you—nothing to do with what we've been talking about—but a man called Jacques I used to know, he's a hairdresser in Rye—does he ever come in here?'

He gave me a curious look. 'He used to—but not any more now.'

We stood silent through "The Queen" and then I had one last drink to strengthen me for the starting of the Rover to go and fetch Joan.

The battery was as flat as I had suspected, and she took a dealing of swinging to get going, so I was late for the ten o'clock dead-line.

Determined not to have to go through that performance again, I drove right up to the Mermaid and parked the car facing down the steep cobbled hill of Mermaid Street so that we could coast down and start her in gear when we left. Then I went into the bar and looked round all the lounges, but there was no sign of Joan. A drink lasted me until the bar closed, and then I asked the manager if I could wait a little in one of the lounges. I went back to Doctor Syn's room and it was quiet, empty, and I sat staring at the panelling, wondering what on earth had happened to her, cursing myself for letting her go. Once I heard a car door slam and went out to see if it was her, but there was nothing but the Rover in the shadow of the wall opposite, the lights burning with a dull glow, a deserted street, and the footsteps of some late wanderer, light and hurried, ringing back to me from the cobbles farther down the hill.

Ten to eleven . . . I was back in Doctor Syn's room biting my nails, thinking of worse and worse possibilities. That reporter . . . ? How did Joan know he was a reporter . . . ? How did either of us know it was not a plant . . . that they had known about us far earlier than we had thought . . . that they were going to do with Joan what they had with Margaret? No, it couldn't be . . . not in England . . . safe England. But it didn't bear thinking about, there was nothing I could do except wait; to keep my mind on other things, I pulled out Josh's report and started to go through it carefully.

It was a remarkable document. He had divided it into three sections: astronomical, botanical and architectural, and each went on to build up a case with exactness that I had not dared to hope was possible. In the first part, he had only two facts to go on: one of length, Margaret's height, one of time, the assumption the photos were taken at five-thirty—four-thirty sun time. The first was used to resolve, by trigonometry, the true, square dimensions of the flagstone of the courtyard which showed in the photo at a slant, and then from these measurements the true length, always an increasing length, of each of Margaret's shadows, and then the difference of the *angle* of the drift; with these figures he had made two graphs, which merely needed "fitting" to the curves he had got from Davis' Altazimuth Tables (Part A)—whatever they might be—and one had the required latitude. It ran on parallel forty-seven degrees forty-five minutes, he maintained, but to allow for any errors caused in the camera angle, etc., he would settle for a fifteen-minute margin each side of this, giving a band some thirty miles wide that cut

across the centre of France, the extreme south of Germany and the
north of Austria. To the west lay the Atlantic—no courtyards there;
to the east the way was barred by a change in Standard Time. He
had even considered the same latitude, or rather, the adjusted
latitude because of the earth's tilt, in the southern hemisphere and
I liked the way he was able to dismiss that one out of hand, as only
in one place on the face of the earth did that parallel touch land
—the southernmost tip of South America.

Section two was not so helpful. The branch that came into the
side of the picture was of a vine, not a tree: a common way of
training them for shade and ornamental purposes in wine-growing
districts, which would include both France and south Germany.
The creeper on the other wall was *Bignonia Venusta*, with its clusters
of long orange trumpet-shaped flowers, very common in that part
of France, so common that no one would think of disclosing
anything by allowing it to appear in the picture, but it grew rarer
as one went north, and was not often seen flowering in England.
No proof of anything here . . . only confirmation.

The key was in the last section: in a prosaic thing, my drainpipe.
I had hardly looked at it when I was studying the photos, but there
it was, on the angle of the wall of the courtyard, square in section,
rather battered, ending in a gargoyle spout over a drain; the picture had enlarged well enough to show the faint impression of a
crest or monogram on the plate of the bracket that held it to the
wall.

The line of reasoning was this. If the pipe was square-sectioned
and battered at the edges, it could not be made of cast iron, but
must be lead: if lead, it was most unlikely to be in existence in
either Germany or Austria after the requisitioning of the war—or
for that matter, in Occupied France. But as the band of latitude
cut just north of the line of demarcation between the two zones, it
could only still exist there if it were a building of beauty and
historic importance . . . perhaps ear-marked by Hitler or one of his
henchmen as a Victory residence. A château? And faintly marked
on the plate of the bracket were two entwined capital C's', back to
back.

. . . the crest of Catherine de Medici, who, Josh remarked dryly,
had spent most of her time turning rival Diane de Poitiers out of

Henri II's residences of the Loire . . . the châteaux. In a courtyard of a château on the Loire—he had marked all twelve in the area—you would find what you wanted.

My head jerked up from the page as the door of Doctor Syn's room opened and Joan came in. I don't think I have ever been so ashamed of myself as I was then in having forgotten her—or so glad to see anyone in my life before. She came over lightly, and her face was flushed and her eyes shining; somehow it made my heart turn over to see her back in the years . . . coming from a party where she had been fussed over . . . not tended to be taken for granted. I had meant to be cross with her, but I just couldn't; Josh's papers scattered all over the floor as I jumped up and held her tight.

'What's the matter, Harry? Why all the affection?' She held me back at arm's length. 'Darling . . . you've been drinking.'

'Only two—but I was worried. You being late. I'm so glad to see you. Did you have a nice time?'

'Lovely dinner—he was such a nice boy.' She had gone over to a mirror and was patting her hair. 'He tried to kiss me on the way back.'

I looked up from the salvage of Josh's report from the floor. 'Darling, I can't even be cross about that. But did you have luck—get anything out of him?'

'Not much. He—'

'Well, tell me in the car. I'm tired. Let's go home.'

We went out and thanked the manager and walked across the cobbles to the Rover. The lights were barely functioning at all by now, and as I held the door open for Joan, I said, 'Lucky I parked her this way. I can start her in gear going down the hill.' It was lucky . . . far luckier than that. Someone must have been watching over us that night.

I switched on and put her in gear and coasted down the hill, bumping over the cobbles to get up speed before I let in the clutch. She fired at last, but as soon as we had turned the sharp corner to the right and were running back along Cinque Ports Street I knew there was something more than a flat battery wrong, she was only firing on three cylinders. Joan started to say, 'He did not seem to know anything about Jacques—' but I cut her short. 'Just a minute, poppet. I've got to concentrate on this old bitch—she's running like a cow tonight.'

We limped on to the quiet of the Appledore road, and then I

knew I would have to do something about it. I pulled up, left the engine running, and groped for the torch in the dash pocket.

'There's a plug oiled up—or loose lead. I'm going to try and fix it.'

The night was still and dark and warm. Very beautiful. I opened the bonnet and I remember looking back through the windscreen at Joan, her face lit by the faint light from the dashboard, and thinking how pretty she looked. I smiled at her, and she smiled back. Then I bent down to check the plugs.

We had had the car for five years, and I like machinery, and I had always tried to keep her shipshape. I knew the layout of the engine pretty well blindfold, and it did not take me a moment to find out what was wrong: one plug lead was loose, just resting against the plug, sometimes making contact, sometimes not. I put it on and was groping in the tool box for a spare terminal when the beam of the torch flashed down for a moment and lighted on something thin and gleaming that was no part of my car.

It was a wire. A bright new copper wire that stretched from down by the starter motor to vanish in the shadow at the front of the dashboard. I flicked the torch down and held it steady, staring at the connection it made with the starter motor, the normal heavy cable disconnected and hanging down loose. Who the hell had been mucking about with my starter . . . and why? That wire would never have taken the load, even assuming there had been enough juice in the battery. I ran the beam of the torch up, following the wire. It was fastened to the front of the dash with those crocodile clips and then it bent down and went out of sight. I leaned over until I could follow it on under the tool box.

It ended in something taped in place on the back of the instrument panel: a white bundle that looked like a packed of candles. But they weren't candles, they looked too greasy and there were no wicks running down the middle of them. There was only one other thing that looked like that, and I knew what it was. Sticks of gelignite.

CHAPTER 5

I stayed crouching like that for perhaps twenty seconds. I felt sick: physically sick. Then I straightened, closed the bonnet very gently and walked round to Joan's side of the car. As I turned the handle to open her door, I could feel my hands sticky with sweat.

I just didn't say anything but pulled her out. 'What's the matter, Harry? Darling!—what on earth is the matter? You're shaking.'

I tried to keep my voice steady. 'Have you got the spare set of keys in your bag?'

She pointed to the dash. 'But you've got a set there.'

'I know,' I said, 'and they're going to stay there. Give me the other set. Quick.'

She stood on the grass verge of the road, fumbling in her bag while I held the torch; all the time she kept on looking up at me. 'Harry—how many drinks did you have in the Mermaid? You're as white as a sheet.'

'I wish I had a bloody great double now. Give me those keys, please.'

She gave a shrug of her shoulders and handed them over; watched as I left the engine running and locked all the doors, without speaking. Only when I took her by the arm and started to march her off down the road, did she try and break away. 'Harry! Stop it. You're drunk. You've left the engine running.'

Ten yards . . . twenty . . . we should be safe now. 'I know I have, darling—' it was almost to myself—'it will keep the lights burning bright enough for anyone passing to see and not run into her. She won't stall now I've fixed the plug.'

I turned and held her close; away down the road the tail light of the Rover glowed bright and steady; overhead the soft night with its million stars; no sound but the whispering of the grass round our feet and the faint purr of the exhaust.

'Darling—someone's watching over us tonight . . . I only parked the car facing downhill in Rye because I knew the battery was flat, and I didn't want to crank her. Perhaps I might have tried the

starter once . . . and if I had pressed that button, we wouldn't be
here now. Someone—I suppose while I was waiting for
you—someone who isn't awfully well disposed towards us, disconnected the starter circuit and fitted one of his own. It went through
a charge of explosive that's under the dashboard . . . would probably
have blown the car to bits . . . at best, we would have had the
jagged wreckage of the clock and the speedometer through us waist-
high. . . . It was just the one chance that I opened the bonnet, and
saw that wire, and knew it didn't belong.'

'Oh, my God . . .'

I held her tight until she had stopped shaking. 'Look, darling.
There's no danger to us now—only other people. I think we passed
a phone box a little way back. I must get on to the police. Would
you—could you—stand here, no nearer, and flag down any traffic
that comes along. That tail light is still pretty dim; they might not
see it.'

'No. I want to come with you.'

'Please, Joan. Don't let's spoil our good luck by not thinking of
other people.'

She was crying softly then. 'All right—I'll stay.'

'Not a step nearer the car than this, then. I won't be long.' I
turned and started running down the road as hard as I could.

The police sergeant on duty was sleepy and pompous and didn't
seem to be very interested in a 999 call; even less so when I
demanded to speak to Inspector Fox personally. 'Not on duty,' he
said, 'at home—you can give me the details.'

'Sergeant—have you got the Occurrence Book beside you?'

'Yes. Why?'

'You write in it that Mr. Kent rang up the inspector on a matter
of life and death . . . got that—?' I could feel the edge of hysteria
creeping into my voice. 'And then you can add that because you
were an obstinate clot and wouldn't give him the inspector's home
number, you lost any chance of promotion. I promise you it will be
right.'

There was a short silence. 'Rye 3155,' he said.

I fumbled for three pennies and dialled the number, praying he
was not out. He answered quickly and let me blurt out what had
happened, only putting in one or two shrewd questions that I knew
were tests as to whether I was drunk. 'I'll be right down,' he said
at last. 'Just stay where you are and don't let anyone near that car.'

'Well, for God's sake be quick—there will probably be a police

car down to check on my 999 call—and they may get ham-handed.
And bring an explosive expert with you to defuse.'

'We haven't got one.'

'Then a break-down wagon to tow her away. She's too dangerous
to drive. The bloke at the wheel might stall her—and forget.'

He was quick, so quick to stop anything that I had only been
sitting with Joan by the side of the road for a few minutes before
the first police car screeched up to us, and the crew knew all about
it. We made Joan get into the back of it, well out of range, and
then I and the driver went a little nearer, waiting for the inspector
to come. He was there within five minutes, with a crash wagon
close behind him.

We walked over to the Rover and he played his torch on the
bonnet as I lifted it. The copper wire looked very bright and innocent in the glare: the inspector bent down and followed it up under
the tool box. Then he straightened and said, very softly, 'You're
right.'

' I hoped I was.'

'Well, don't let's argue the niceties of that one now, sir. Just
unlock the door—and we'll switch her off.'

I looked at him and then round the dim shadows that pressed in
on the torch-light. 'I'll unlock the door. But give me a chance to
get clear before *you* switch off.'

'What do you mean?'

'I had something to do with these little pleasantries during the
war. We're assuming only the starter circuit is involved. There
might be a second string—on the starter switch, the push and pull
idea. Switch on, and it cocks it—switch off, and—'

He was rubbing his chin. 'Then what do you do?'

'There are six strong men here. Leave that engine running and
turn her round by hand. Then tow her in with the engine still
going—and keep it going until you get an expert on the job.'

'You'll steer the car, Mr. Kent?'

'Not on your bloody life I won't. With my wife watching? No.
I'm going to be the citizen who has done the right thing; now I can
watch someone paid to do it finish the job.'

'Well—I suppose that's fair,' he said. 'They are contacting a man
in Hastings who knows about this sort of stuff, but I don't suppose
he'll be here for an hour or more.'

'She will run all night like that. There's plenty of petrol.'

I helped them manhandle her round in the road and then went

to the police car, sitting in the safety of the back with Joan as we watched them hitch up to the crash wagon, then following it at a safe distance to the yard of the police station.

The inspector went inside for a moment; when he came out he said, 'This expert—Mr. Jessop—they haven't found him yet. They say he's gone to the pictures—funny time to be at them.' He rubbed his chin for a moment and looked towards the Rover, parked safe and square, the engine purring gently. 'It may be a bit of time—you'd best let me run you up to my place, and have a drink, or some tea. You both look about cooked.'

We didn't say 'No', and it was nice to be driven in a different, safe car out of Rye and up the hill on the Udimore Road to the inspector's trim detached residence. Mrs. Fox must have been alerted, for she was down on the job, plump, friendly, in her blue dressing-gown, patting cushions and saying 'Sit here, dear: that will be comfortable.' We had tea, laced with Scotch, and it made me feel a lot better. Then Mrs. Fox took her cue, 'Well, I must get my beauty sleep—' shook hands and plodded up the stairs.

Joan was on the sofa; her eyes were closed for a moment, and I saw the dark shadows round them and knew how tired she must be.

'Do you mind, Inspector?' She kicked off her shoes and curled her feet up. '—But I'm so tired.'

'You carry on, Mrs. Kent. We're only waiting for the O.K. from the station.'

Soon she was asleep. The inspector did not speak and I was waiting for him, waiting for what I knew must come; the lights were soft, but all of them were focused on me; I could just see the dim outline of the white shirt and sandy hair in the shadows; from the sofa Joan's breathing came soft and regular.

'You know who did this, Mr. Kent?' It was the expected question, but the suddenness of it made me jump.

'What—? Well, I'm not sure. But—'

'Then, as you *do* know, you must also know why.'

I laughed. 'Someone can't like me.'

There was a silence; then he said, 'You're working for John Stebbings, aren't you?'

'I could be.'

'Looking for his daughter, Margaret?'

'Perhaps.'

He sighed. 'If you care to come down to the station tomorrow,

I'll show you a file on the case—that thick—' he made a gesture with his hands—'and you can read the lot: right to the last page where it just says "case closed". It's no good, Mr. Kent. She is dead—violated and fouled and buried in some dyke.'

'I don't think so.'

'Then where is she—?'

'A long, long way from here. And I'm going to find her.'

'Away from here—' There was a quite different, puzzled tone in his voice. A coal dropped suddenly in the grate; from outside, the long low whine of a lorry going up the hill towards Hastings. 'The tea's cold, Mr. Kent. But would you like to have another drink?'

'I think I would.' I looked towards the telephone on the side table. 'They're taking the hell of a long time, aren't they?'

'I told them to ring the moment they were through.'

He got up and mixed the drinks, then came and sat closer to me, more in the light. He sat staring down into the depths of his whisky and soda as he swirled it in the glass; without looking up, he said, 'Mr. Kent, if there was a patch of jungle, and you knew there was a savage wild animal loose in it, and you wanted to catch that animal—what would you do?'

'Put a ring of men round the place—and then drive him into a corner, I suppose.'

'And what would be your reaction—if there was one place that had not been guarded, and then, just as you were going to make your drive, some outsider—quite by accident, of course—blunders through the open gap and scares your game?'

Parables are best answered in the same strain. 'I think I would be bloody irritated at the spoiling of my party—perhaps a little worried over the safety of the intruder . . .' I hoped that I was saying all the things he wanted me to say: the nearest we would ever get to admitting we both knew most things about each other's business but, for different reasons, could never explain them.

'Quite—' He got up and came over and threw a sheet of white paper in my lap. 'And what would you do with that, Mr. Kent?'

It was typed, without address, without signature. It said, 'Call off your bloodhound and keep his mouth shut—or in just one week from today you will get a parcel that will prove we meant what we said about Margaret.'

As I read it, his voice went on, 'After I saw you this morning, I decided we had better take a much more detailed interest in Mr.

Stebbings' mail. At the sorting office, I mean. This arrived there this afternoon, and he hasn't seen it yet. What would you do?'

'Burn it!' I was surprised my voice sounded so fierce; was afraid for a moment I had wakened Joan. But the soft breathing still went on without a break from the sofa in the shadow. 'Let him alone, Inspector,' I said, more quietly, 'he can't help you—and he's had enough.'

'But he can help you—?'

'No. Not any more. What I want—isn't here.'

'Where is it?'

'In France.'

For the first time, I saw a shading of doubt come into those clear blue eyes. 'That can't be—I know she's dead. You will be wasting your time, sir.'

'Perhaps—but I don't think so. But I've answered all the questions so far. Will you tell me one thing—straight? This little trap of yours, when does it shut?'

He hesitated for a moment. 'If—the game hasn't been scared right away—just exactly a week from today.'

A week . . . I looked down at the piece of paper in my hand. 'It seems to tie up with this very well,' I said bitterly. 'Look, Inspector, your game won't be scared away—it may go to ground, but it will still be where you want it. Isn't there a chance of postponing—'

'No, sir.'

'Not even to rescue a little girl?'

'I don't believe she is alive; nor would my superiors. This thing is big, Mr. Kent. Far above my head in its direction. I'm sorry, but there isn't a chance.'

A week . . . now both sides were against me in this desperate race. There was no time . . . we had to get to the Loire . . . and we had to get francs to get there. Tomorrow—no, today, I thought as I looked at my watch—is Sunday . . . wasted. So one day was wasted already.

I knuckled my hands into my aching eyes. 'You wouldn't happen to know how to get hold of £200 in francs in a hurry?'

'I might. I have . . . friends that could. What's the name of your bank?'

I told him, then looked at that paper again. 'May I burn it?' I said.

'No.' He came over and took it from me. 'But I promise you he won't see it—until after—'

The telephone shrilled suddenly, waking Joan. While I found her shoes and helped her up from the sofa, I listened to the monosyllabic 'yes' and 'no' conversation that seemed to go on for a long time. When the inspector had replaced the receiver he said, 'It's fixed now. There was no second string. Mr. Jessop says that anyone with the slightest knowledge of a car's electric circuits could fit that lot in a few minutes.'

It was a silent drive back to the police station. I broke through the barrier of our thoughts once, diffidently. 'Do you collect car registration numbers, Inspector?'

'Sometimes.'

'There are—or were—a few goods round Lion Street most days. London ones, I think.'

'They were. I've checked them.'

'Planes flying across the marsh—' I said, and stopped suddenly.

'We know all about that, Mr. Kent.'

So there was nothing I could tell him. Nothing I could do to stop the machine working on according to its set plan. Just a week . . .

In the station yard the Rover was waiting for us, ticking over gently: it seemed impossible that she had been a lethal weapon only two hours before. The inspector said, 'Don't go for a moment—' and went into the station. When he came out he had a slip of paper in his hand. 'I'm not going to tell you again that you're wasting your time, but if you get into any—difficulty—over there, contact this Paris number. It's the Sûreté. They know all about it.' So they were working on both sides of the Channel. It was as big as that.

We shook hands and thanked him and got into the car. He was standing on the steps in front of the open door of the station with the light flooding out from behind him, head cocked a little to one side, long nose pointing, a faint smile on his face. I put my side window down. 'You'll keep an eye on Stebbings—after this?'

'Of course. And I should get yourself a bodyguard too. After the sample you've had tonight.'

'I'm going to. There's just one thing that might help. Could you get a message—indirectly—to Mr. Jacques' hairdressing saloon? Just to say that Miss Kennedy won't be able to keep the appointment she made for Tuesday. That's she's been called back to London hurriedly, and she won't be down in Rye again for a long time. It might work.'

He nodded; then raised his hand in a half wave, half salute, that implied more clearly than anything that I was a bloody fool about to waste time and money, but that he was glad to see me go and wished me luck. Then I let in the clutch and we turned out of the yard to start a long silent drive back to Long Row.

I phoned Stebbings the first thing in the morning and told him of our change of plan. He seemed apathetic, hopeless, only cheered up slightly when the thought registered that we were going away. 'When shall I be hearing from you, Mr. Kent?'

'Ten days—at the latest.' If I fail, I thought, you'll know the other way, by then. 'And I am so nearly sure the first news will be a sight of Margaret coming through your front door.' It was futile, almost hopeless, but what else could I say?

'Oh, Mr. Kent—I'm praying so. I can't sleep, I can't—'

'Now try not to worry. Don't take any notice if you get another picture. There's one thing you must do for me if you can, though—' I explained, and made him promise he would, asked one more question, and rang off. It was right that he was not going to see that last letter—the one the inspector had shown me the night before; if he did, I know he would crack completely. But all this lying and propping up of hope made me feel a complete louse.

The journey back to London was very silent. As I drove, there was only half of me that was concentrating on the road ahead; the other, the more important, was turning over and over all the factors—of time, and means, and whether Josh was right. But time was the most important; I kept on glancing down at the clock on the dashboard, grudging even those few minutes that were being wasted out of our precious store.

Joan said suddenly, 'Don't worry, darling. Perhaps the police will hold off.'

'They won't. And it's not only that. The other side won't wait. They'll act as they said . . . in just a week.' And then I remembered she had been asleep when the inspector had shown it to me, and had to tell.

'No! Harry. No! We can't risk—even think of—wasting time if that might happen—' Out of the corner of my eye I could see her hands, knotting her handkerchief, twisting it over and over into a tight ball. 'You must dash straight to France, give everything to the French police—and let them find her.'

'I know all that. But look, sweet—what would happen if I did—and if there was a thousand to one chance that they might believe me? They would check this side, and get a firm "No": more delay. Then even if they decided to go on with it, their search, though far more efficient, would be a hundred times more obvious. Who ever is holding the child would know. And then—?'

'Yes. I do see that.'

'A small group, working independently, unobtrusively, has the one great advantage of surprise. They might succeed. . . . We've *got* to succeed—' In my desperate emphasis, I banged one hand so hard on the steering-wheel that I sounded the horn, and an innocent citizen, proceeding on his way to Sevenoaks in perfect safety, turned from his cycle to glare at me. 'And we must take Josh with us to make it possible . . .'I added, softly.

'All right. As long as you make him promise what I asked.'

Silence again: until the hill that runs down to Bromley. 'I got two things out of Stebbings this morning, Joan. The answer to a question—and a promise.'

'What were they?'

'I asked him—when he used to play his guitar to Margaret—if there was any special tune that she loved.'

'And was there?'

'Yes. "*Sur le pont d'Avignon*".' I started to hum it.

'Don't,' she said.

Another five miles, and then I said, 'The other thing—and he promised he'd do it if he could—was I asked him if there might be any special toy at home, something that she was especially fond of, and she would remember. Apparently there's an old teddy bear she used to take to bed. He's putting it on the first coach up from Rye in the morning for us to collect at Victoria. It might be very, very useful.'

The flat was cold and miserable when we got back to it. After we had unpacked, I told Joan that she had better start getting a new lot of stuff together again, because I was determined to get away the next day, francs or no. There was an awful pressing urgency about it now, a kind of desperation; I remember wandering round the flat, picking up things and putting them down again, stopping to watch the clock on the mantelshelf, listening to the soft tick, thinking there were a few more seconds of my time draining away.

Joan came to my rescue. 'You'll only work yourself into a state if you go on like that, darling. There's nothing you can do tonight—' she hesitated for a moment—'except make plans. Why don't you go round and get Josh, and bring him back here. I can cook us some eggs. Then we can all talk.'

I stared at her. He had not been in the flat since that disastrous evening of the police station, over two years ago. 'But are you sure you don't mind?'

'I've got to start to get used to him again,' she said grimly.

When I had found him, in the local, and sober, I made him go back to his flat and pack some of his more respectable clothes, for I reckoned that if Joan would bear him for a meal, there was a chance she would let him stay the night; and I did not want him out of my sight until we left.

The omens were favourable, for when we went into the sitting-room she had a bottle of whisky out on the table; Josh nearly spoilt it by trying to greet her as if she were his dearest friend whom he had last seen a couple of days before; I think he was going to kiss her hand, but I managed to tread on his foot just in time. When we had got sorted out into chairs, we sat and talked for a little while, but the atmosphere was not exactly easy. Then Joan got up and gave me a look that shifted to the whisky bottle. 'I'm going to finish sorting out my things—then make us a ham omelette. You had better talk over *everything*, Harry.'

I gave Josh a reasonable double and poured one for myself; then I sat down and told him the whole story right from the beginning. He listened carefully, asking an occasional question, once producing a point that had not occurred to me.

'I think, Harry, if I was holding that child—and I knew someone was after her—I'd move her to another place, just to be on the safe side.'

I shook my head. 'No. Because I wouldn't dream I had given anything away in those photographs; and if I had a *really* safe hiding-place—as I must think I have—I wouldn't risk the publicity of making a change.'

'You're so certain I'm right, aren't you, dear boy?'

'Absolutely certain.'

He sighed. 'Well, I hope so very much—for all our sakes—that you are right.'

We got out the big Michelin map of France and spread it on the carpet, trying to work out the best way of getting to the area and how to cover it as quickly as possible. Only the châteaux were to be considered—I was obsessed with this idea now—and they could, I thought, be covered in four days; but it did not leave us much time . . . especially as I thought we would be followed, and someone would have to lay a false trail.

We were so absorbed, we did not notice the way time was going; looked up with a start when Joan came in carrying a tray with the things to lay the table. She put it down and went over and poured herself a drink, eyeing the level of the bottle carefully. 'Well, Harry. Have you told him?'

'Yes. He doesn't think there is anything more we could have done, and—'

'I didn't mean that. I mean the other thing . . . that you promised.'

'Well. . . . No, darling. You see, there was so much else . . . I just haven't had time to get round to it . . .'My voice trailed off into a miserable silence.

She stood very straight, holding her glass, looking down at us. 'Josh—do you remember the last time you had a meal in this flat?'

He looked puzzled. 'No, my dear—I can't say that I can. But I always remember your wonderful cooking—'

'You can cut out the bouquets. It was only bacon and eggs. At two-thirty in the morning. After I had fished both of you out of the police station.'

The words dropped out one by one, almost viciously, but he just leaned back on his haunches on the rug by the map and a great grin cracked right across his ugly face, wider and wider, followed by rolls of great pealing laughter. Then he was wiping his eyes, stuttering, 'Oh, yes! That was a night, Harry . . . do you remember . . . how that little man . . . went through that plate-glass window?'

For a moment I thought Joan was going to throw her drink at him; instead, she put it down and picked up his own empty glass from the side table, jerking in a measure of scotch with a splash of soda on top. She held it out.

'Look. When Harry wanted you to come on this trip, I said "No"—a very definite "No"—because of things like that plate-glass window. But he persuaded me—and I agreed—because of, well, the other things involved. On one condition, though. That he got a promise out of you, in front of me. He doesn't seem to have enough guts to ask it—so I'll have to do it myself.' The glass was right under his nose now. 'If you come, this is the last you have. No drinking.'

He took the drink, looking at it carefully. 'Not even an aperitif—?'

'No.'

Now he was looking up at her sideways: a naughty, overgrown schoolboy.

'No wine?'

I could see her lips twitching as she tried hard not to smile, and knew the battle was won and she would go through with it.

'In very small quantities—but no plate-glass windows.'

'Moderation in all things,' he murmured; then he looked straight at Joan. 'My dear, I surrender . . . I promise.'

Afterwards, in all that happened, I always remembered the way that drink went down in one swallow; the quiet benediction of,' . . . the last of the many . . .'

Things were easier after that, and I enjoyed my omelette; Josh seemed to sense the role he had to play, for he kept Joan in giggles throughout the meal with a wicked and witty exposition on a certain daily columnist of a national newspaper.

Over coffee we went over our plans. Having agreed that surprise was our strongest card, we had to ensure we kept it. And to keep it, we had to make certain there was as little chance as possible of being followed from this side to France . . . even to wasting a day of our precious time in laying a false trail. It was easy to convince them that I, the best known, must be the one to do it, but it took a long time to convince Joan that, as I would not let her travel alone, she would have to go with Josh.

At last she said 'Yes,' with that 'no plate-glass windows' look on her face, and then it was the details of their departure—the morning boat train—and our meeting place, the west door of Chartres Cathedral, at ten o'clock on Tuesday morning. That gave us three and a half days at the outside, so little to find and search twelve châteaux; but there was nothing else to do about it. And all this hinged on one thing.

I yawned and looked at the clock and said, 'I think an early bed, chaps—it will be a long day tomorrow.' Then I said, 'Of course, you both realise—if the francs aren't ready for us—if the bank won't play—all this has been a waste of time.'

But the bank did play: because they had been told to. I was waiting on the steps at opening time, and was ushered straight in to the manager. He tried to hide his surprise and curiosity at what he tersely described as 'the communication' he had had on the telephone at his flat over the bank the previous afternoon, Sunday, his day of rest; tried to enlarge on the trouble he had taken over a very early visit to head office to collect the currency. But there it was. I could have what I wanted.

I drew three hundred pounds—all in cash, then took a taxi to

Victoria to see if Stebbings had remembered his promise as faithfully
as the inspector. There was a parcel waiting for me at the coach
station, and on my way back to the flat, looking out of the back
window from time to time, searching the cars behind to see if there
was any sign of following, I wondered if Josh had been as lucky as
I in the job I had asked him to do while they waited for me: a
quick visit to that accommodation address where Stebbings had
sent the watch money. There was not time to follow it up—but it
would be nice to fit in the last piece of the puzzle.

They were both ready, packed, and waiting for the time to leave
for the boat train. As I split up the money, giving them seventy-
five pounds each, I looked enquiringly at Josh.

He shook his head. 'No go, Harry. Just one of those little news-
agent-tobacconists in the Brixton Road. And a most unsocial type
. . . very suspicious . . . almost got nasty. So I beat it.'

'Quite right. It was only just to tie up another end.'

I walked over to the window and peered both ways down the
street. Nothing. Just the usual flow of traffic, the usual stream of
pedestrians. 'Now, let's get this clear for the last time. You two go
separately by train to Paris. If Joan thinks she is clear then, you
join up, have a meal, and take the night coach to Chartres. Meet
me outside the west door of the Cathedral at ten.'

'What about you, Harry? What are you going to do?' It was
Joan.

'Leave before you do—to draw anything off that may be watching
here. Then, I'm not quite sure. I've got an idea, but it's not certain
yet. I'd better not say. But I'll be there on time.'

I picked up the parcel that I had collected from Victoria and
started to unwrap it. Inside was a yellow teddy bear; bald in
patches, battered, with one eye missing, and a green skirt round its
middle. 'Our talisman,' I said. I passed it over to Joan. 'Keep it
handy always, darling. You never know when you may want to use
it.' Then I took hold of both her hands. 'So long, my sweet; see
you tomorrow. Take care of yourself.'

I looked across at Josh. 'And you take care of her—and don't
forget your promise.'

'I won't, Harry.'

I kissed Joan hard and let myself out of the flat, feeling very
lonely.

I took a slower, cheaper way to my next port of call, for I had
plenty of time. At the bus stop at the end of the road I had to wait

five minutes, but there seemed to be no one about who took the slightest interest in me; I was the only person to board the bus at that stop—at least, I was until another man ran and jumped on just as it was gathering speed. He sat down two seats behind me on the top deck, and I didn't really take much notice of him . . . until he got off at the same stop as I did in Piccadilly. And I was watching him closely when we sat down side by side to wait our turn in the same travel agency.

He was small and pasty-faced. He had on a grey snap-brim hat and one of those military raincoats, also grey; as I sat and waited I thought back to earlier in the morning when I had been at the coach station. There had been a man in a grey raincoat waiting in the booking hall. But there were tens of thousands of grey coats in London that morning: it could all be a coincidence . . . up to now. But not any further.

I had gone in first, so my turn came first. When I was at the counter, I spoke loud enough to make certain he could hear when I booked a seat on the afternoon plane to Le Touquet. Then I walked out quickly and turned right down Piccadilly towards. the Circus; once or twice I glanced back over my shoulder, but the crowds were too thick to spot him . . . if he was there.

I went down into the Underground and over to one of the line of telephone booths; when I was inside a box, I dialled the number of the travel agency I had just left, but asked for a different department, and in particular to speak to Mr. John Tracey.

'Foreign Hire Department. Tracey speaking.' He was an old friend of mine; he knew my line of business, and we had had a car from him before.

'John?—this is Harry Kent. I want a Renault for a week. At Boulogne. At six this evening.'

'Come off it, Harry. You know they want at least a week's notice.'

'Not at this fag-end of the season, they won't. They'll be falling over themselves to do it. And I'll pay the lot the other side.'

'It will cost you a telephone call,' he said.

'O.K.—will you just hang on a minute?' I screwed round to peer through the glass of the box. Pasty-faced was standing not five yards away, on the other side of the hall against the ticket machines; he was watching lazily the ever circling stream of tarts. But not quite all the time, for as I stared, just for a moment his eyes flicked up and held mine. Harry Kent, not love, was his interest.

'Look, John—' I was speaking into the phone again—'this is

worth a thousand francs to someone the other end. I want that car parked in a very special place. You know Boulogne Ville Station—yes, Ville, not the Maritime. There's a station yard, and beyond that, the railway tracks from the Maritime cut across the entrance. I want the car parked in the street just beyond that—facing along the Paris road, without anyone waiting by it, and warm, so that she will start quickly. Got it? Well, ring me back at the flat in an hour—and let me know the colour of the car, and its registration number.'

I went out back into Piccadilly and went into a bar and had a drink; pasty-face didn't actually follow me in, but he was propped against the entrance waiting for me to come out. I took a taxi back to the flat—just for the hell of it, to cost his employers a bit more money.

The flat seemed empty and cold and bare. It didn't make things any better for me to find the note that was propped up against the clock. 'Take care of yourself too. J.' I sat down and waited for Tracey to phone.

He was ten minutes late; but I didn't mind, because he had fixed it. 'I had the hell of a time convincing them you weren't round the bend,' he said, 'but the car will be there. All they are interested in now is when do you pay?'

'I may have to be a bit dodgy for an hour. But I'll come back to the garage and settle up then.'

'I told them that, roughly. What is it this time: divorce?'

'Could be—that car: the colour and the registration?'

'A Renault—that bright blue, 64—EC—62.'

'Bless you, John. I'll buy you a fine dinner when I get back.'

'What about the telephone call? It was fifteen bob.'

'I'll pay that when we have the dinner.'

I rang off, and there was still time to make myself a cup of coffee and a sandwich; as I was eating them I walked over to the front window of the sitting-room that faced out on to the main street; a little farther up there was a pub of sorts on the opposite side, and outside that pub a lamp-post. At the moment it was being propped up by a gent in a grey raincoat. He was eating something out of a paper bag, and for a second I felt enough compassion to lower a notice from the window to say, 'Won't be out for half an hour. Go get yourself a cup of coffee.' But it really was not my affair if his bosses could not give him a relief while he had a proper meal.

I got to the airport early, not bothering to see if I was followed, and was first on board. It was amusing waiting for him to come, as I knew he would come. As with the bus, he left it to the last minute, and nearly missed the plane. I think that I would have been disappointed if he had missed it, though it would have made things far easier for me; but I had decided just exactly where I was going to lose him, and it would not be so much fun if I lost that opportunity through a mistake on his part.

He made it by three minutes, though, and scrambled into the seat just opposite mine on the other side of the gangway; I looked across and smiled at him openly, but he wouldn't play except for one flicker of a grimace. Then he buried himself in a newspaper.

The flight was smooth and quick and uneventful. No one spoke to me and I just sat and looked out down on the glinting Channel below, thinking of all the snags we would have to overcome; but somehow it did not worry me half so much now we had started. The minutes of our time were still draining away; but now we were doing something.

When we had landed and checked through the Customs, I hung about in the entrance hall, waiting to see what pasty-face would do. He did nothing, except wander in and out of the door, peering about, looking lost. I went over to the reception desk and fixed up what I wanted, then walked over to put him out of his misery.

'Excuse me, sir. Are you waiting for someone?'

He jerked round. 'What? Well—er, no. Not exactly.'

'I was wondering if you are in the same fix as I am. I mean, how far coincidence can stretch—seeing that we've met twice today already.'

'What do you mean?' It was aggressive.

'Only that I have to get to Boulogne. And there doesn't seem to be a good train connection. I'm going to hire a taxi. If you are going that way, I'll be glad to share it with you.'

He brightened at once. 'It's very kind of you—'

'Three thousand francs each is what it will cost,' I said firmly. 'Not so bad, really.'

He hesitated, fingering his wallet inside his breast pocket. "Come on, Charlie," I thought. "You've got to do it—unless they haven't given you enough money. Otherwise I'll ditch you here—and go in any direction. You haven't any help, because all the other passengers have gone. You can't say 'No' and then follow in another car—that would make anyone suspicious. You *must* come."

Apparently, he thought the same, and with great reluctance

handed over three 1,000 franc notes. All the way in the car I talked to him, telling him of my proposed visit to Paris. And he was going to Paris too?—well, it was the strangest thing. Did he mind if we travelled together? Not in the least, especially if his French wasn't too good. And I always liked to have a travelling companion. Was he going on pleasure, as I was? Oh, business: and what was his line, if I might ask? The import of handbags—how interesting. I didn't know the first thing about handbags, so I could not trip him up there. Really I didn't very much want to.

The driver dropped us at Boulogne Ville Station at half-past five and I went in and looked up the trains, returning to where my shadow was doing his best to shadow and told him there was a fast train at six-forty. Then I said that, if he would excuse me, I must phone an old friend in Boulogne. He waited where he could watch the phone box while I rang the garage.

Yes, Monsieur Kent's car was already there, as arranged by Monsieur Tracey. It was hot and full of petrol. Yes, they understood that I would not be along to pay for an hour, but the amount—it sounded like the National Debt—would all be set out on the bill and the cashier would wait for me. It was perfectly understood, also, that this was a matter of great discretion.

I came out of the phone box, looking very pleased. 'I just caught my friend. He's got to go out tonight, but he's coming down here for a moment first. You'll like him.'

Pasty-faced said he was sure he would.

Boulogne Ville is one of those stations—like Babylon Halt and Ur Junction—that do not look as good as they sound. There is the feeling of being passed by—in one case by two thousand years, in the second by the virile growth of the new station on the quay; nothing stopped there for a definite purpose—it simply passed, and looked over its shoulder and said, 'Well, we missed that one.' The square forecourt was deserted; no taxis waited. They simply put people down who had mysterious business connected with that point, and drifted off, to better fields.

I waited now, in the empty yard, looking at my watch, sensing pasty-face a few feet behind me; I turned and said, 'I can't think what's happened to him—' and moved a few feet nearer to the gap in the fence where the rail from the quay cut across the opening to the Ville station. I waited . . . and soon I heard the sound I had hoped for: the soft 'chug . . . chug' of the night train coming up from the quay.

I waited, bag in hand, looking puzzled. I looked round to where pasty-face, also holding his grip, was standing behind me.

'I can't understand why he hasn't come,' I said.

The engine of the train had appeared from our left side now, moving slowly, bell ringing, to cut off the traffic; a gendarme was on the far side, baton swinging in those wonderful rhythmic gestures that would stop anything. The engine appeared: one of those wonderful French engines that have apart from their reasonable working entity, everything from a baby gasometer to a large incinerator welded to their body, and all working to some use, by the amount of steam exuded.

It came close, this hundred-ton mastodon . . . and I still tried to look puzzled. In front of me, at a few yards, the red front of the engine frame, the buffers that stuck out like outraged eyes, were closing the gap between me and the fence. I looked round at pasty-face for the last time. 'He can't be coming,' I said. Then I ran in front of the engine.

I almost left it too late: the far buffer hit me on the shoulder and I spun round as I tried a futile gesture of pushing five hundred tons on the move away from me. But I was clear, falling on the road as the engine went by, the driver leaning from his cab to scream abuse at me. I was on the other side of something no one could cross—dare not cross—until the length of the train was past. I got up and dusted my knees, and apologized to the gendarme—who took not the slightest notice; then I ran back a few yards to the Renault, that was waiting as I had been promised, threw my bag in the back and was clear of that part of Boulogne before even half the train had passed.

I stooged around for a bit; then dodged back to the garage and paid their monumental bill; there was no hurry now—because I knew that by the time pasty-face could get across the tracks I would have vanished.

I drove due south, through Abbeville and Amiens, then turned east on the road to Reims; I was wasting petrol and time, but I had to make absolutely sure I was not being followed. I spent the night in a little pub near Laon, then spent the whole of the next day in a wide zig-zag sweep round Paris to finish twenty miles east of Chartres. The weather was wonderful—one of those still golden days of early autumn—and the roads empty now of the summer tourist traffic; at no time was there anything to indicate that I was being watched, or followed. Often I wondered about pasty-face, and how he had explained it to them.

So to the dead-line the next morning: the thrill of cresting the last rise and looking down to see the twin spires of Chartres Cathedral dominating the whole of the great rolling plain to the south; the drive up through the twisting, narrow streets of the town to the car park outside the west door; the cool dim interior, with that wonderful glass glowing like jewels on every side.

And they were there waiting for me: standing close together, looking up at one of the rose windows. I wanted so much to take Joan in my arms and kiss her—but there I couldn't. I squeezed her hand and whispered, 'All right?' and she smiled at me and returned the pressure and said, 'Yes, darling—and you?'

Josh didn't speak, but the minute I was near him I knew there was something different. He was aloof, calm, seemed bigger in stature in every way. I wondered about it still more when we had collected their bags and were packed in the car, heading southwards over the rolling sweep of the Beauce, the great central plain of France. The road went on and on, dead straight, disappearing to infinity with the line of trees on either side, and I kept the Renault at a steady sixty, hardly talking. But there was plenty of small talk going on between Joan at my side and Josh in the back, an easy intimacy that I found almost unbelievable. I, who had worried so that they would not get on, was now uneasy that they were getting on a damn sight too well; I was ashamed at the sudden stab of jealousy that came while they discussed an incident that had happened at dinner on their night in Paris.

'I suppose you were too busy laughing at Josh's wit to bother to see if anyone was following you?'

There was surprise in Joan's voice. 'Of course we did, darling. But we didn't see the slightest sign, ever. Did we Josh?'

'No, dear boy. Not a thing.'

Silence for another ten kilometres; then Joan started laughing softly, and I could see in the driving mirror that Josh was pasting a label on the glass of the window on his side.

'What the hell are you doing?'

'Just reminding myself, Harry.'

Joan said, 'He is a fool, darling. He had it on a little card and he propped it up in front of him every time we had a meal. It says, "PAS DE PERNOD. LE VIN DU PAYS SEULEMENT".'

I blew up.

'For God's sake, man—we're not on a holiday. This is a vital job of work.'

He didn't answer until he had smoothed the last edge of his piece of paper on to the glass. 'I know that, Harry. But don't let us go around looking as if we were already at a funeral.'

No one spoke for some time. Suddenly, ahead of us, the ground dropped away and, as if a boundary line had been drawn, the vineyards started: the long, low lines of the vines heavy with grapes almost ready for picking. More trees now, lush farms, and then the broad silver band of the Loire, etched with its darker islands, lay in front of us.

I was feeling miserable—and ashamed of myself. I kept looking up in the mirror to see the reflection of Josh's face, chin on hand, as he stared out at the passing country. There was something there on it, a shadow, that I had never seen before. And I could not know then that it was the reflection thrown forward in time of a man going to his destiny.

CHAPTER 6

The memory of the next three days centres almost entirely on feet. My feet—hot, aching, tired; rebelling against sharp gravel of innumerable paths; paths that wound up steep slopes to châteaux on the tops of hills, paths that led through mile-long avenues of trees to stables and outbuildings, paths that crossed and surrounded acres of formal gardens. There were châteaux on bridges, châteaux hanging on cliff edges, châteaux in the middle of deep woods. I grew sick of the repeated look of them, the white stone and the blue tiled roofs, the rounded turrets always looking like pepper-pots, the never-changing smell of the interiors; musty, stale, long dead. All the tapestries looked the same ... as did Diane de Poitier's numerous beds.

We worked our strip of territory from west to east; that Tuesday night, we managed to cover Luynes and Villandry; on Wednesday, Vouvray, Amboise and Chenonceaux; Thursday, Chaumont, Cheverny, and Chambord. And always, through the boredom during the tramping of the miles to see and search every stable and courtyard, there was no sign of the place we all had stamped in our minds ... no sign of a little girl; always, over everything, the slow ticking of clocks that drained each second from our precious store of time. I used to wake up in the night and listen, sweating, to their passing. It was like the build-up to a war-time operation all over again: D-3 ... D-2 ... D-1. Only it was far worse than then. It was the creeping towards the carrying out of a threat, not the start of action; the slow progress to the point where you ceased to be of use, instead of starting to be.

It was hot—too hot. That did not help when we were under such a strain; we never spoke to each other of the speed with which the time was running out—*we knew*. All that happened was that the barrier of strain that had built up on the first day at Chartres seemed to intensify.

I could see Joan looking at me sometimes, puzzled and hurt. I knew I was the worst, I knew it was mostly my fault; but there was nothing I could do about it. Over everything, between us all, time, that only certain, inexorable factor was seeping away. One by one the châteaux were behind us . . . and still no Margaret. It came to a head on our night in Chaumont, when after dinner Josh said he wanted to go for a walk, and something snapped inside me and I accused him of going out to get a couple of brandies on the side. It was without foundation, petty, mean: there was no excuse . . . except the excuse of a volcano blowing its top off. Josh was hurt—terribly angry with me, for the first time I could ever remember; but Joan's reaction was the most startling.

I will never forget the crash with which her chair tilted over backwards from the table where we were sitting in a café; how she stood there looking at us in turn, while two bright spots of anger burnt on each cheek. 'I've had enough!—of both of you. Just two silly, squabbling kids, frittering away any chance you might have. And all the time there's a—' She stopped in time, remembering we were not alone. Then she picked up her handbag, 'Well, I'm not staying to see it. I'm going back to the hotel now—and I'm going back to London tomorrow.'

It ended in a council in our bedroom, apologies from me, a few tears from Joan, and a general resolve to carry on to the bitter end. And that would not be long now. Even as we talked, I was not really listening to what they said, only the tick of Joan's travelling clock at the bedside, beating out the last hours before the last day.

'Well, that's all paid, weighed and satisfied, Harry boy,' said Josh at last as he got up and stretched. 'So it's best forgotten. Where do we go tomorrow?'

I picked up the map, glad to change the subject. 'Beaugency, first—then cut back to Chouvray. They're so far apart, I don't see we can manage more than those two.'

'And the same plan—if there's luck?'

If there's luck . . . we had started so grandly, but it seemed so hopeless now. 'I think it's the only one,' I said. 'If we see her . . . snatch her quick, and make for the north side of the Loire, into another *département* of France. As I said before, they are so terribly rigid in their administration, it will make things much more difficult for this side if we're chased, or caught . . . give us a little time.'

Friday. D minus one. It was the afternoon that we came to Chouvray. It was one of the smaller, less visited châteaux, jutting out over the south bank of the river on a spur of a conical hill. The village seemed crushed between this and the silver band of the

Loire—a single straggling row of shops and houses, the church, and
the one auberge.

We managed to get rooms there at a vast price: far more than
they were worth, for the place did not seem to live up to its grand
title of L'Auberge de Chouvray et de l'Univers. It was small, dingy,
and crowded, but seemed clean. Madame received us and showed
us the only rooms available. She did not appear to like the English
and hinted that it was a great privilege to be allowed to occupy
'the suite'—a doubtful term for a single room leading into a double,
off which was a private bath. We argued for a bit, but that was her
price, and it was very hot, and there was nowhere else to go. We
surrendered and trooped back to the hall, where madame settled
herself back behind her desk. It was the only time I ever saw her
out of it. Large and fat, sporting a fine moustache, she was always
there, adding up endless sums . . . and watching. Those beady eyes
darting everywhere . . . at everyone who went out or came in. She
was always in the same place; I think she slept there.

We waited, wondering if we were supposed to take up our own
bags; there was the impression of a small insignificant man hovering
in the background towards the kitchen. 'Monsieur,' I guessed, and
I was right: afterwards we were to learn that, in that fine tradition
of French family economy, he doubled the duties of keeper of the
small bar and first chef.

Madame struck a small bell on her desk. 'The girl—she will
attend you.' She grunted. Then she went back to her figures. We
went out into the bright, hot sunshine and stood by the car waiting
the arrival of 'the girl'.

She came softly over the gravel that lay round the metal tables
that were shaded by the plane trees in front of the house. She was
dark, very slim, and tiny: dark, not only in that close-cropped curly
hair, and the clothes that she wore, but in the eyes . . . those
enormous, deep brown eyes, fringed with long black lashes. She
stood for a moment quietly beside us, etched in that harsh light,
looking up at us—she scarcely topped Joan's shoulder—and then
she said, 'I am Françoise, Messieurs, Madame. I will take the bags
to your rooms.'

They lay on the pavement beside the car, where Josh had just
lifted them from the boot: there were only three grips, not large, or
heavy. But Josh shook his head as he straightened and stared down
at her. 'No, child. I will take them. They are too much for you.'

She tilted back her chin and held his eyes with hers; gravely, unsmiling. 'I am no child, Monsieur. I am nineteen. And I am used to carrying the luggage. It is part of my duties.'

'And what else do you do, Mademoiselle?'

She looked surprised. 'Why—I clean the rooms, and serve the *petit déjeuner*, and wait at table and—'

'But I will still carry these bags.' He gave her one of his slow, gentle smiles that made the ugly face look almost beautiful; his eyes did not leave her face. It was still and hot out there in the sunshine . . . and very quiet. But suddenly it was as if something sparkled between those two; it was so vivid, so almost visible, that I took half a step backwards . . . as if I had been slapped in the face. I know that Joan must have seen it too, for she moved close beside me and her hand touched mine.

No one spoke; it seemed as if that moment would hang between the four of us for all time. The girl's face was still slanting up towards Josh; the oval of it seemed at once sharpened, and pale beneath her tan. I looked quickly at him, and there was that same look that I had seen on his face in the car as we dropped down towards the Loire. Still no one spoke; and then a passing car blared its horn and shattered the fragile thing. Josh picked up the bags and Françoise led the way back into the auberge.

Even when we had reached our rooms, something of that feeling was still there. I could not settle down to anything; I wandered about the bedroom, picking things up and putting them down aimlessly, then wandering off into the bathroom. When I came back, Joan was sitting on the bed, her hands folded loose in her lap; I sat down beside her and took both of them in mine. 'Have you seen it?' I said.

'Seen what—?' It was almost as if she had to drag herself back from her daydream to reality. 'What are you laughing about, Harry? It's the first time I've seen you laugh for three days.'

'I've seen the first thing that's cheered me up. The bath. Did you look at it?'

'No. I thought you meant something else. What about the bath?'

'The shape of it. Like a boat. And just about as deep as it is long. I shouldn't think your head would show over the top if you sat down in it.'

'I'll look sometime—' She got up and went to the dressing-table and started to powder her nose. There was a soft tap at the communicating door, and then Josh came in.

'I've been talking to Françoise—' There was the same quietness, the same withdrawn look about him as there was with Joan.

'What about?'

'Oh, herself—she is an orphan, a niece of Madame. And I should say she must do about half the work in the place. Then I asked her what there was to do here—I take it we're going to have a look at this château at the time we usually pick?'

I looked at Joan. 'What do you think, darling?'

'We might as well—we can't do more than one today. And it will be cooler. I don't feel like plodding round in this heat.'

Anyway, it was the best time. We had found out by bitter experience that at the end of the day, when the guides were tired, they hurried through their piece inside the château—so that one did not have to listen so long—and once the last party was bundled outside the front door, took not the slightest interest as to how long they wandered about the grounds, which made our searching of the stables and outbuildings far easier.

'They close at seven. Let's go up at half-past six, then.'

Josh was staring out of the window. 'What do we do till then? I don't want to sit around here for two or three hours. Françoise said—I asked her if there was anything else to do—that the wine caves are very interesting . . . miles and miles of them. I—'

Joan said, 'I don't think drinking in the middle of the afternoon is a very good idea,' and for the first time Josh turned on her. 'Dammit, girl, I don't want to drink. I want to *do* something. Not sit here listening to that clock of yours . . . just waiting.'

In the heavy silence, I could hear it ticking softly . . . another few seconds drained from our small store of time.

'All right,' said Joan. 'If that's all you want to do. At least it will be cool in there.'

The caves were a little way along the road from the auberge, cut into the limestone cliffs of the hill that was commanded by the Château de Chouvray. The first cave the great cave, was in fact no more than a hollow scooped out of the cliff face, open on one side to the light. Here were the long trestle tables where those shown round could consume their free sample of the vintage, and then buy as much more as they could carry—mainly internally, it seemed, from the noise coming from the French coach party then in occupation. The din was terrific: shouting, laughter and snatches of song, all echoing back, booming, from the low stone roof overhead. We stared at them, at the great vats that lined the walls, and then a man in a white coat came over and said that if we wished to make the tour, a party was starting that moment. As we entered the first of the narrower tunnels, the noise at the entrance died away gradually, first to a rumble, then a faint mutter. We did not talk at all, except in whispers. There was that pressed down feeling of being underground, the complete, velvet blackness in the intervals of the switching of lights to the next gallery, the chill, never-changing temperature. I understood then why they were shouting so loudly outside. It was a relief from this.

The guide was used to it; but even his voice was soft. Each time he switched on a new set of lights, the view was just the same: the grey round of the roof of the gallery above us, the white sand on the floor, scored by the two dark lines of the rails used by the trolleys that moved the wine. Always, by the side walls there were racks, with the bottoms of millions of bottles winking at us from the glare of the naked light bulbs: the still wine stored flat on its side, the *mousseux* at an angle, cork downwards. Once or twice, among the racks of the last, there would be another light glowing, and there would be a man or a girl giving each bottle a quick half twist to get the sediment down to the cork. They did not stop or look up; bottle after bottle was lifted gently, given a quick turn of the wrist and then lowered back in the rack. When we had passed, and the lights were switched off, they remained like glow-worms, the faint radiance of their own lanterns dwindling, then vanishing abruptly as we turned the corner to the next gallery.

The soft voice of the guide went on: statistics of the numbers of kilometres that would be walked to go all round, the total millions of bottles stored, the process of the fermentation. We, of the party, talked in whispers as we moved from point to point, there was no other sound but the pad of our feet on the sand; once, from far away in the darkness, came the rumble of one of the trolleys moving, sounding like a distant Tube train.

The guide made all his stock jokes; he left all the lights off for a moment, to let us feel the cloak of cold darkness that wrapped round each person like a physical thing; he assured us he always counted the party at each turn, for if anyone strayed—and did not know the special signs they had at the intersection of each gallery—they would never get out again to the sun. Last, and I don't know why I remembered it so clearly, he took us to the side of one of the galleries to show us how far we were under the ground.

A ventilating shaft ran up there; far, far above you could just see a circle of sky, the pale light straining down through a grating. It showed as a silver streak on the smooth wet stones that lined the shaft; touched on the thin steel ladder that ran from top to bottom.

The guide said, 'We are now right under the grounds of the château, Messieurs, Mesdames. And at a depth of twenty metres.'

I had my hand on one of the bottom rungs of the ladder. 'What's this for?'

He shrugged his shoulders. 'It has been there for a long time, Monsieur. I think it was so that they could clear away any obstruction—a branch of a tree, or a bird's nest, for example. But now we have the grating on the top, it is much easier.'

We finished the tour and came out almost thankfully into the warmth and light and laughter of the outside cave. Joan relented, and we sat down at one of the tables and had our half bottle of dry *mousseux* on the house. Then we thanked our guide and walked down the dusty road towards the auberge.

There was still an hour until the time we had agreed to be best to go up to the château, so I said I would have a bath. The fantastic shape of it still cheered me, and I was surprised to find it was so comfortable; I am fairly tall, but the depth of the sides made it quite easy to sit almost upright but still have one's head resting on the back, well below the rim. In spite against madame—as I did it, I could imagine her sitting down in the hall, stuffed in that cash desk like a bloated spider, forever, watching and scrabbling with those figures—I ran the hot water right up to my neck. It was most comforting.

When I went back to the bedroom, drying myself Joan was sitting at the dressing table, doing her nails. The door to Josh's room was open, and I could see he was not there.

'Where's Josh?'

'Gone out. Said he would be back by six-thirty.' She sounded very abrupt. She picked up the brush again and started painting her left thumb; there was silence while I found a clean shirt and started to slide into it.

'Harry. You've got to watch him.'

I turned, in that ridiculous position when the head is just coming through the collar and the arms are outstretched trying to work up the sleeves. 'What do you mean?'

'You know what I mean.'

I struggled through the last inch and smoothed back the cuffs.

'Look—we don't want any more trouble. Particularly now. I put

my foot in badly enough at Chaumont. If you're going to accuse
him of slipping out for a couple of quick brandies on the sly, then—'

'You know I'm not talking about that. It's the girl.'

Of course I knew what she meant—but it was another complication, and one I didn't want to have to face. I said, 'Damn it—he
didn't make any promises about that. What do you expect me to
do—? Keep him handcuffed? He's a grown man. He can look after
himself.'

'I'm not worried about him—' she spoke slowly, as she finished
off the last two fingers. 'That girl, Françoise—she's only a child,
really. And you saw . . . didn't you?'

'Yes, I saw.' I sighed as I bent down from the edge of the bed
to put on my shoes. Here was another worry.

Josh came back at twenty-five past six and did not say a word
as to where he had been, and neither of us asked him. We walked
out in silence through the gate of the auberge, and then turned
across the street to the angle of the high wall of the château towards
the wrought iron gates and the lodge; we mingled with the crowd
of French trippers that had just been dropped from a coach, queued
with them to take our tickets from the wrinkled old lady who sat
at an open window in the lodge, and then started the plod up the
steep winding path that led to the château on the summit of the
hill. The shadows were lengthening among the groves of cedar trees
on the lawns, the air was still and heavy: there was a tension in
everything, an almost unbearable tension like that which comes
before a thunderstorm. We walked side by side behind the French
party, with no sound but the crunch of our feet on the gravel, then
the hollow ring as we crossed the drawbridge over the moat and so
through the arch that led to the centre courtyard. I think that I
knew then that something was going to happen.

The guide was waiting for us.

He was a little man, almost a dwarf; he could have been one of
the seven dwarfs—if Walt Disney had tried to make them really
unpleasant. It was not just his appearance—the thick lips, the little
darting eyes, the shining bald dome of his head—that made me
dislike him on sight: it was something in the way he looked at this
new flock that had to be shown round—the stony, contemptuous
stare of a housewife weighing up a lot of doubtful cod on her
fishmonger's slab—that put my back up at once. He stood leaning
against the main entrance door; the big master key, the universal
badge of office, dangling on a chain from one wrist; he looked smart

in his grey uniform, but entirely repellent. I wondered how soon we would be rid of him and getting on with the most important thing, the search of the outer courtyards and the stables.

Having weighed us up, he turned and unlocked the door; then, cupping his hands, he gave two claps that sounded like pistol shots—just as if he was scaring a flock of geese—and jerked his head towards the open door to indicate the tour had started.

I knew that it must be about his tenth round of the day; I knew he must be tired, and that his feet would be aching far more than mine; but he need not have gabbled his way through his piece in the way he did. In all the châteaux we had been to so far, I had known there would not be much hope of spotting anything while we were in the actual rooms, so I had tried to listen to what the guide had to say—as much to pass the time as to acquire culture; I can understand most things in French if it is spoken reasonably, and so can Joan: Josh is far away above our class . . . but this was quite hopeless.

The words seemed to rip out of him in an unending torrent, without pause, without expression; then, with the door behind us locked with great ostentation—presumably to make it clear that no one could get back and steal anything—there would be the two echoing claps and we were all pushed forward to the next room. I gave up trying to follow him halfway through the first lecture, and watched in the second room, with selfish satisfaction, Joan's lips framing the fragment of a sentence four behind the one he was then rushing through, the angry frown that shadowed Josh's face: it was at the moment when he was making preparation to enter the third—just as his hands were opening to make those infuriating claps—that Josh got in first . . . with two much louder ones.

The guide's hands stopped their movement with a jerk; there was a sudden, stunned silence and I saw the concerted swing of the twenty heads of the rest of the party, all turning towards Josh, staring in shocked disbelief. He was standing easily, looking down at the little guide; his face was smiling, but not his eyes. Then he bowed politely and said, 'Monsieur. We are English. It is asked that you speak a little slower.'

The guide did not answer him. He just stared back and there was a glint in those dark eyes. Then he turned his back and tapped on the nearest piece of furniture. 'Here, Mesdames, Messieurs, is the wedding chest of Catherine de Medici—' It was about twice as fast as before.

There was a sudden movement from Josh and I leaned over towards him, treading hard on his right toe; we could not afford to have trouble—even at this stage—before we had explored the grounds. As we were unlocked, and relocked before we went into the next room, I had time to stifle his 'I'll do that little—' with, 'Ride it, Josh—it doesn't matter, think about the outside.'

The explanation was coming so fast now that I doubt if even the French of the party understood half of it; far, far above our understanding, anyway. I got hold of Joan's arm and pulled her away from the current centre of attraction—a great, dingy bed, roped off so that the tourist could not touch the place where the only Catherine had laid her down to sleep. I could not understand, and I did not like the smell of damp, decay, and moth-balls. We walked together to the south side of the room, where the windows were open and looked out on the grounds and the gardens. They were much nicer.

There was a wonderful view from there—we were high now, on the second floor and in front of us was a vista of lawn and yew hedge and then the wide rides that gave perspective—or allowed someone to know that her lover was coming. I looked out over it all, glad that the gabble of the guide had sunk to a soothing undertone that had not to be thought on. But not for very long; suddenly Joan's fingers bit into the tender side of my arm.

She was not looking out over the gardens as I had been, but down, over the sill of the window, directly below us; her face had gone rather pale, and there was that hard line on the angle of her jaw. I gave a little grunt of pain and tried to pull my arm away, but she held it, not speaking, twisting it to force me to look downwards.

There was a courtyard directly below, a small one that was hedged in against the wall of the château on three sides by single-storey buildings; it was not so clean and cared for as any of the parts we had seen, and smoke was coming out of one of the chimneys. Probably the concierge or the guide had it as his living quarters. But whoever lived there had a family: in one corner there was a child, playing with a stick and an old tin can. It didn't matter that her hair was short and dark . . . and Margaret's was long and fair; it didn't even occur to me that there was no reason in the world why the people that lived there should not have a daughter of three. In that one moment, I was completely certain.

I managed to free my arm and turned Joan away from the window, guiding her back to the fringe of the crowd, beyond which the guide still gabbled. He was so short that we could not see him, so I hoped that the reverse had worked just as well. I had time to whisper, 'Not a word—even to Josh—until we're clear of here,' and then the monologue stopped and we were clapped into the next room.

I don't know how I managed to contain myself for the last three rooms. I simply dared not look at Joan. When we got to the final exit, and the guide was leaning against the door-post, one hand outstretched, the other scratching his trouser leg with the key, I gave him a far bigger tip than he expected—or deserved. There was a quick twisted smile, a hissed, *''ci, 'sieur,'* and then we were out in the sunlight, walking on one of the smooth lawns of the formal gardens.

'Keep bearing to the right,' I said. 'It's right round on the other side of the château.' Then I looked at Josh. 'We've found her.'

There was a hint of doubt in Joan's voice now, as it came from my other side. 'We've seen a little girl playing in one of the court-yards down below when we were looking out of a window, Josh. But I don't know—her hair was all wrong: dark and short—'

I said, 'They might cut it off—and I should think it might be an elementary precaution to dye what was left. I'm certain.'

'Well, Harry—' It was Josh in his gentlest tone.

'There is one way to find out. See the child at close quarters, show her that toy you have, and if there is the right reaction—why, then we will all be certain.'

'What—now?'

'I think not, dear boy. I think it would be better to spy out the land first, and then consider our plans very carefully. Somehow, I do not think this will be an easy operation.'

We walked on in silence, edging to the right, away from the main group of the party that was making its way straight to the stables. We dodged and twisted through the flower-beds and yew hedges, trying to turn the corner of the château to get to the far side: but always we came up against a long high wall, blank save for two doors, and both of those were locked. I looked at the sun, disappearing now below the bank of trees to the west, then back to Joan and Josh. 'He's quite right—we've got to think hard about this one. Let's make a show of going to see the stables, and then get back to the auberge. I know we'll all be able to cope with this better when we have had a drink.'

Half an hour later we were all sitting in a row on our big bed.

Josh had been down to the bar and got a half of cognac and a
syphon; the bottle was halfway down now, and I was still trying to
talk down all the arguments that were coming against me.

'But I don't see how anyone would dare hide a child in such a
public place.' It was Joan.

'Look, darling. I know you are thinking in terms of a cave on the
top of a mountain—or something like that. They *ask* to be
discovered. But can't you see that here—with lots of different people
coming through every day—who act as a screen—it makes it ideal?
Nobody actually lives there, you see, because they are all State-
owned. Except the concierge, and if you gave a child into his care,
what better place could you hope to find her?'

'Oh, Harry—I just don't know.'

I knuckled my hand into my forehead, trying so hard to think.

'Look, both of you. Just for a moment assume I'm right; and if
I'm not, I'll take the responsibility. We have seen we can't get back
after we come out of the place. Can anyone remember what it was
like before?'

'A bloody great moat—with a drawbridge across it.' said Josh.

'Did anyone see what happened if you went right-handed round
the place?'

Both of them said 'No,' and I knew that if I had been asked, I
would have to say the same.

'Then after we were inside—does either of you remember the
geography? It was in the fourth room—I'm certain of that—where
that window was.'

There was a silence, and then Joan started to say, 'There was a
staircase between the third and fourth—on the right as we went
through. But it was roped off—' And then the scuffle started outside
our door.

It began with voices: first Françoise, one short sentence, angry,
almost disbelieving; then her uncle answered, hissing and soft.
There was the sound of a blow and the tap of heels running away
over the polished boards of the passage. We were sitting on the
wrong side of the bed to the door, and it was a few seconds before
we could get round to it and wrench it open. I peered round Josh's
shoulder. The passage was empty but for Monsieur busily polishing
a window at the far end. Eight o'clock at night seemed to be a
funny time to clean windows. Josh left the door ajar and went back
to the bed. 'You were saying, my dear—?' His voice was steady,
but when he refilled his glass from his bottle of Montrichard—he

had not touched the brandy—I saw that his hand was shaking. And I have never seen a man look so angry.

There was nothing we could do about it—nothing to show what was already known, or what had been overheard. We decided that it was too risky to go on talking about it in the auberge, and that we would go out for a walk after dinner and try and make up some sort of a plan.

Things were not improved during the meal. When Françoise came to our table to wait on us, it was fairly obvious she had been crying and had the makings of a black eye. It was horribly embarrassing—I could not look at her, but kept my eyes fixed on my plate as she did the serving. Only once did she speak, and that was after the entrée; her head was close to Josh as she brushed the crumbs from the table, and she said softly, 'Is it permitted to speak to Monsieur—privately—at some time this evening?'

And Josh, just as if he had been waiting for it, without a pause, answered, 'Always, after my coffee, I walk by the river.'

When she had gone for the dessert, Joan raised her eyebrows and opened her mouth to say something, but I kicked her under the table. 'We can work everything out first thing in the morning,' I said. She had not seen what I had: that look—the same as it had been that morning—had flashed between them in that instant that their heads had been so close together.

There were black looks from madame in the cash desk as we went out through the hall; Josh vanished and we did not see him again before we went to bed. I took Joan for a walk along the road that passed the château, and tried to argue it out with her.

'But he must be twenty years older than her, Harry. And there have been the times before—and they have all ended in disaster—'

'So what—? You are always the same, you women. You take it for granted that hundred per cent is the man's fault—how can anyone know what really happened?'

'All the same—she's a child, Harry. She's never met anything like him before. And I don't want to be responsible.'

'You're not. I'm not.' I took her arm and pointed up to where the château hung over us on the edge of the cliff, so cold and beautiful in the whites and blues that were reflected from the flood-lighting; it seemed to float there, away from the earth, like a fairy castle. 'That's all we are responsible for, darling. Who we think is inside . . . and how we are going to get her out.'

We walked on in silence. I had meant what I said, but I didn't want her to worry. At last I said, 'But you must have noticed one thing . . . he's got so gentle.'

He did not come in until after eleven: after we had got into bed and put the light out. We saw the light go on in his room, and then there was a soft tap at the communicating door. Joan switched on the bedside light and said, 'Come in.'

He came softly and sat on the edge of the bed; one look at his face was enough to tell me that the best thing in all the world had happened to him. When he spoke, even his voice was different: the way I had described it to Joan on our walk . . . gentle.

He said, 'There's trouble. She wanted to warn us. We're under suspicion, but she doesn't know why. That accounted for the little incident before dinner—she caught her uncle listening at the key-hole and he hit her, but she doesn't think he had been there long. Now she has been forbidden to talk to us, and at their supper there was some discussion on the advisability of asking us to leave in the morning.' He paused for a moment. 'But that's not the worst . . .'he said slowly. 'After dinner, her uncle sent a telegram by phone . . . she couldn't hear who it was addressed to, but the text was something about, "the English have arrived". It was a foreign telegram, she said, and she heard the town it was sent to, because her uncle had to shout it three times at the man in the post office . . . Rye.'

'Does she know anything about the château?' It was Joan who broke the silence. Joan, propped up on the pillows, looking at him with a strange softening of her expression. So she had seen it to.

'I asked about that. There's a niece of the concierge staying with him there, on a long visit from Nevers. And . . . her uncle and the concierge are cousins . . . but I'm certain she doesn't know a thing of what's going on.' He stopped, grinned at us, and added, quite naturally, 'I'm going to take her back to England with us.'

I waited for an explosion from Joan, but none came. Josh got up off the bed and said, 'Well, good-night, good people. Sleep long and well . . . before the assault of the Citadel tomorrow. And in that assault, I hope I have the privilege of committing mayhem on that little basket downstairs.' The door closed softly behind him.

We had just put the light out, when it opened again and he poked his head round. 'By the way,' he said, 'I've asked her to marry me.'

For a long time after he had gone, we lay silent in the dark. Joan was so close, warm, and safe; suddenly she said, 'I do hope it works out for them.'

I was on the edge of sleep . . . that wonderful state of all knowing, not caring. 'For them—for all of us . . .' I said, drowsily, ' . . . but most of all for Margaret. Because tomorrow is her last day.'

CHAPTER 7

There were black looks in the morning, but no mention was made of our having to move. We went out after our breakfast and walked down the river bank, trying to work out a final plan.

'Do you think he'll come?' I said it, but to the others there was no question of who was meant. Jacques, a shadow, was already walking beside us through the lush green grass and bog herbs that fringed the shore.

'Yes.' It was Joan, and I watched her as she said it, and her eyes flicked back over her shoulder, as if she thought he was already there.

'No.' Josh was cheerful. 'Look, Harry boy, work it out like this. He *can't*. If the police are so interested, they would not let him—they want him. There would be some delay, a polite apology about the slightest irregularity in his passport, and when that was sorted out, something else would be uncovered. They are a bloody crafty lot—' he gave us one of those delightful grins, '—I know, because I had to try it once, and it just didn't work. No. He won't have got that wire before this morning, and he won't be able to just motor to Lydd, and take the next plane. He'll have to do a bit of dodging . . . waste time. Which means he can't be here today.'

I believed him; somehow, I always believed Josh. 'So . . .'

'Assume—if he's coming, he can't possibly be here before late tonight. Even with a chartered plane. So you have all day to choose to make your move. Make it at the time, late afternoon, which we have all decided is best. Don't be panicked: he won't come—before we're away. If we are right. So let's concentrate on the snatch at the best time.'

'Cutting out time—just how are we going to do it?'

Joan's cold water; but a good thing. So easy to say, 'Go in and find out if it is the child you want, and take her'—but how?

The only thing that was agreed unanimously was that we could not go back again and make another reconnaissance; the third, the real time, would then be bound to make anyone suspicious. The hour to do it agreed, we had to rely on hazy memories of geography from the night before.

'I know that there was a staircase just before that large room—the one that had the big bed in it. And it was on our right as we passed, the outside wall of the château—' It was about the fourth time Joan had said it.

'Why should it lead down into that courtyard—? It might just go down to the ground floor of the main block—'

'Because, darling, if you remember, we had just come *up* by another one from the ground floor when we went into the second room.' She was being very patient with me.

'Henri II might have had a staircase for each room—'

'I think not, Harry boy, I think not—' Josh picked up a stone from the sandy shore that crunched beneath our feet and threw it hard and far across the smooth fast-moving Loire. 'But as we don't know—and can't find out—we must take it that Joan is right.'

'So we troop round until we get there, and dodge down, hoping that we can get out, and the guide won't see?'

'It won't be as easy as that. Don't you remember how that horrible little man waits at the door and locks it when we are all inside? No—there will have to be some form of distraction for him—' He was silent for a moment and then that great grin split his face. 'Yes, a diversion—and it will give me the greatest pleasure to make it.'

'What will you do?'

The grin got even wider. 'Just leave that to me, dear boy. But you and Joan must be the last two into that room, and when I start something, turn back and make a dash for it. I promise I will keep everyone inside the place very busy.'

'And if we can't get out—or it turns out not to be Margaret?'

He shrugged. 'The only harm will be that we have failed.'

'And if it is Margaret—?'

'Get her out as fast as you can; down through the gardens, down through the thickets that slope to the road, and into the car—we'll leave it at a spot you can mark from the top. Then drive like hell.'

'What about you?—and what about our stuff at the auberge? If we pack up and leave, someone might get suspicious.'

He was rubbing his hands together gently. 'I will fight the rear-guard, dear boy. I think I can be trusted to look after myself; also your luggage, so leave everything just as if you were going out for a stroll. I shall feel far happier if you don't stop until you are in

Paris—' Then he turned and looked at me. 'I assume, of course, that you will take Françoise.'

I didn't know what to say, so I looked at Joan. She was quiet for a long time, looking north out across the broad, shining river to the far bank, the side that I think we all felt was the safe side . . . the last barrier we would have to face if we were right . . . and had some luck. She stood very still, the breeze ruffling her hair forward over her face, shadowing it. Then she said, very softly, 'All right, Josh.'

'Thank you.' He looked at his watch. 'Then there is nothing more we can do until six-thirty tonight—except make ourselves scarce. Do you want the car, Harry?'

I said, 'No.'

'Then I will borrow it, if I may. I'm going fishing. I'll meet you in our room at six, and the car will be full of petrol and parked on the road by the wall of the château—there's a bit where the wall's broken down, and it will be easier for you to get over. I'll tell Françoise to wait there.' Somehow, he seemed to have taken over, to be giving me the orders now; but he was so calm and so sure of himself that I didn't mind.

'Which way will the car be facing—I mean, which way do you think we should go to get across the river?'

He said, 'I've thought about that one—' He was looking out over the silver stream, slashed with broad sandbanks and little tree-covered islands, to where the cliff of the far bank sloped up to the rolling plain of the Beauce. 'East would be quickest, but the first bridge across that way is still one of those temporary ones they put in after the original was bombed in the war. It's single-line traffic, controlled by lights—and the bloke on this end might be a pal of theirs. He could hold you up as long as he liked. West, there's a new bridge, very wide. Go for that—and cut back on the far side.' He had moved close to me now, gripping both my arms. 'And, Harry, there is one understanding in all this . . . *whatever* happens . . . you do not wait for me.'

'But—'

'As long as you look after Françoise, Harry—I can take care of myself.' He nodded vaguely at both of us, said, ''Bye for now. See you at six,' and then wandered off along the shore; faintly the tune of a song came back to us from over his shoulder; I knew the melody, and guessed the version of the words he would be singing; then he was lost to us in a copse of poplars.

'Do you think he will be all right?' said Joan.

'If you mean—will he turn up tonight, and have everything organised as he said, and arrive sober—the answer is yes. There are far more important things in his life than bottles at the moment. If you mean, will he be able to cope with the consequences if we find Margaret, and get her away—I think so, I hope so; but it will need the hell of a lot of coping.'

I don't know if he did go fishing that day, or if not, what else he did and if Françoise was included in the plan; I have never asked him, and we were not able to see if she was present at the auberge at lunch-time, for we decided that we could not stand the strain of waiting there, and bought a bottle of wine, a yard of bread and some cheese and went down to the river, sunbathing and swimming on a sheltered beach of white sand on the lee of one of the islands. It should have been the perfect day; but it was not. The sun was very hot, the air still, and already full, in a mysterious way, of the smells of coming autumn. We waded and swam in the tepid water, or lay on the warm sand and ate our meal, knowing there was no one to see, no one to care, if we had any clothes on or not. Joan said that it would be a good thing if we tried to get some sleep—because of all the driving that might have to be done that night—and I did my best, but I could not. The sun, the sand under my shoulder-blades, the gentle, never-ending rustle of the leaves of the poplars that managed to struggle for existence on the island—most of all, Joan's soft breathing, so intimate, so close—all this should have made the perfect lullaby. But each time I closed my eyes, there in my mind was the picture of the slow swing of the pendulum of the clock in Rye church tower . . . beating off the seconds of the last days of our chance to search; and I would shift and turn on my elbow, looking up over the screen of trees that hid us from the mainland: up to the great bluff of the cliff with the château hanging there, round white towers dazzling in the sun, pointed roofs gleaming blue-grey. Margaret was there . . . perhaps. If she were, then we were justified in waiting like this, having made a decision; though our walk up the hill that evening would only be the beginning of a plan over which I had no control, and of which I could not see the end. But if she were not there . . . if it was a ghastly mistake . . . then we would have failed. And always, when I thought about that failure, I knew I would remember how I had frittered away the time that might have made all the difference.

Once, the tugging of my thoughts became so strong that I had to put them into words. I turned over towards Joan and pulled her head into the crook of my arm; then I kissed her hard—and it was not so much the kiss of a lover, though, God knows, I loved her too much as she lay there, so pale, and straight, and slim, and entirely adorable; it was the kiss of someone who has to draw strength from a source that is—in the long run—stronger.

I said, 'Darling—don't you think we had better go back to the auberge—and get the car—and go and look at another of these bloody châteaux . . . just in case?'

Her eyes opened slowly, lazily . . . those flecks of brown were still there in the blue, and I remembered, in a wave of bitter-sweet tenderness, the change of terms that had come in the way I had described that—when we were engaged, it had been . . . hell, I couldn't even remember now.

She said, 'Josh has got the car, darling,' sleepily; then realising what I meant, sat up with a jerk. 'But, Harry. You were so certain we were right—'

'I was . . . because I thought that you were. But now I'm not so sure . . .' I turned over on my back again and stared up at the château. 'And if we're both wrong, Joan, we're just wasting all this time . . . when we might be trying something else. Remember, tomorrow is the day they said they would—'

There was a sudden rustle in the undergrowth behind us, and then an ancient Frenchman, a fisherman by the look of his escort, a very small boy who carried rods and tins and tackle, stepped out on to the beach beside us. He looked for a moment, grinned a very toothless grin, and said something in French, Joan, going scarlet, trying to clutch a towel round the more vulnerable portions of her anatomy, answered, 'I don't know,' and then waved one hand vaguely downstream. The old man nodded, smiled again, and then started plodding off in the direction she had indicated: the small boy followed in his footsteps, looking like a little dinghy being towed by a large boat. Slowly the crunch of their footsteps died on the sand and then they disappeared from sight round the edge of a the trees.

While Joan stared at me, I started laughing . . . a strange feeling, for it was the second time for about three days. 'I don't see what was so damned funny in that,' she said. 'He might have coughed, or something. I was practically naked.'

'Oh, darling—it wasn't that. It was what he said. What did you think it was?'

'He asked me if the fish were biting.'

'He didn't—he wasn't talking to you—he asked *me* if *my* little fish was biting!'

'Well! Really—' But she started to giggle and I knew it had done us both a power of good. Then she went silent and turned over on her elbows, staring at the beautiful white castle that hung on the edge of the cliff. 'I know she's there, Harry. I'm absolutely sure of it—I don't know why. And it's too late to do anything else now. So don't torture yourself by thinking that there is, you'll only work both of us into a state of nerves by tonight . . . the very time we will want all our wits about us. Try to forget it for the moment, darling. Let's have a happy day . . . as happy as we can.'

We got back to the auberge at about five and had a bath in our peculiar bath and changed; while we were waiting for Josh, we took the most essential things that we could carry on us from our luggage, Joan putting hers, and the battered teddy bear, in her big handbag, I stowing a clean collar, passports, the rest of our money, and a skeleton shaving tackle in various pockets of my suit. We left, deliberately, the rest of our belongings strewn about the room, in case someone other than Françoise came in to turn down the beds, and then I put some money—the sum we reckoned we owed for our stay—in an envelope with a message that we had been called away in a hurry and would come back to collect our luggage later. It was the most we could do, and we did not want to get on the wrong side of anyone without good reason. Then we sat on the bed, side by side, waiting for Josh. Once more those little tingling fingers of fear, and doubt, and anticipation were fluttering in the pit of my stomach.

The auberge was very quiet; we had seen no one when we came in, even the cash desk had been empty of madame. The sun was slanting now, slanting through the shutters to draw a crazy pattern on the polished floor. Ten to six . . . five to . . . where the hell was Josh? I chain-smoked cigarette after cigarette and the ash-tray piled high with stubs. At exactly one minute to the hour he walked in at the door.

He came in quietly, easily, just as if he had been out for a few minutes to post a letter; he said, 'I don't think I'm late—but if I am, I apologise. Are you two all set to go?'

We said we were.

'Then I'll just have a quick wash and I'll be with you.' He went into the bathroom and there was the sound of swilling water; in a few moments he came back, looking clean and well and remarkably cheerful. 'Well,' he said, 'I had just better go and park a few essentials about my person, though—' he stopped for a moment, and that grin split his face like a sudden shaft of sunlight—'God knows, the thing I need most is a glib tongue.'

I said, 'What are you going to do?'

'I've planned a "diversion", Harry, that I wish you could see, but you won't because you will be doing other things; but I promise to give you a detailed description afterwards.'

'I just can't wait.'

He loooked at me and then he looked at Joan; he leaned forward and caught her under the arms, lifted her on to her feet without the slightest effort. 'Are you scared, Joan?' he said softly.

'Yes.' She didn't resist, she didn't look angry; she just looked straight at him and said, 'Yes.'

'And you—Harry?' The pale blue eyes had turned from her and were looking straight at me.

'For God's sake—you know I am. So what—?'

There was another gentle smile. 'For your comfort, both of you, I think I am too . . . for the first time in my life.'

He turned to Joan again; for that moment, I was just not there. 'Françoise will be waiting by the car—I've told her exactly what to do. She knows she's coming with us. With nothing—so please look after her. I won't be there to do it.'

'I will, Josh.'

'Then everything will be all right,' he said quite calmly. 'Now let's go.'

As we walked along the few yards of dusty road that separated the auberge from the entrance to the château, I felt those butterflies fluttering in my stomach again. Josh said, 'By the way—in order to make a pretence that we will be there for dinner—I bearded madame in her desk on my way in. I told her that we will *not*, repeat not, be prepared to eat those filthy little sprats they call "fry of the Loire" again.' He was silent for a moment and then he added, 'Monsieur was with her—I wish I could include that little basket in my demonstration.'

We went through the gates, and just before we did so I could see the blue Renault parked farther down on the road against the wall; I judged that if we came out of the château facing the river, and then turned half right as we came down through the thickets, we would just about hit it. We bought our tickets, and the old lady at the lodge did not seem to remember us, then walked slowly, three abreast, up the steep winding path that led through the grounds. Two French coaches had just disgorged their loads, and as we plodded up amongst them, I was alternately glad that we were to have so much cover, and fascinated by the back view of the three girls who were walking in front of us: the three pairs of long bare legs marching in unison, topped by shorts so short they hardly existed at all—how could anything as tight as that be comfortable? I tried to keep my mind fixed on the funny side of six plump buttocks rocking in rhythm . . . on anything but what lay ahead of us.

Now we were on the drawbridge that crossed the moat, our feet drumming hollow on the wooden slats; ahead the outside wall of the château rose like a sheer white cliff. Suddenly one of Josh's great hands gripped mine and I knew, instinctively, that he was doing the same to Joan on the other side. 'Courage, my friends . . . and the best of luck.' I could only just hear the soft words. 'Leave everything to Uncle Josh . . . and don't forget your promise. Now, let us not speak again.' We passed through the great thickness of the outer wall into the centre courtyard.

Ther were not as many in the party as I had hoped. Some that had crawled up the hill with us must have decided to make do with a stroll in the gardens. I gave a quick look round the fifteen or so that were standing in a half-circle, waiting for the guide, and decided that they were all French, with the exception of a pleasant-looking lady with a row of descending daughters; with their tight yellow plaits, plump cheeks, and those china-blue eyes, they must be Dutch. When their mother spoke to one, I knew I was right . . . but it didn't really matter. My eyes had shifted from them to the guide.

He was leaning against the lintel of the first door, legs crossed and tapping on the wood with his big key, looking the bunch over with precisely the same expression as the night before; then he saw Josh, or me, or Joan—I don't know which—and suddenly, though the look of his face did not alter in the slightest, there was a spark gleaming far back in those little eyes. It was not fear—or hate—but a kind of awareness. The key did not stop its tapping, he did not change his position, but I knew that he . . . knew.

He clapped his hands and made his preliminary speil; then, just as he jerked his head towards the open door to indicate that the sheep might enter, Josh stepped forward, bowed, and made his speech.

It was short—and to the point. He said that yesterday we had come to this particular château because we had heard of its interest and beauty. But—through our own fault, in not knowing the language too well—we had missed a great deal of Monsieur le Guide's most enlightening lecture. So we had returned to try again. He did not ask that there should be a translation into English, but for our sake, and that of the other foreigners in the party—here he bowed charmingly in the direction of the Dutch lady—would Monsieur le Guide speak very, very slowly. He was sure that the French people present, who had the privilege of owning this unique monument, would bear this in patience so that we might have the chance to learn all about it. All this in perfect French and with a smile on his face.

There was a rustle in the crowd, a murmur of understanding and agreement; the three girls in their short shorts stared at him curiously, and the Dutch lady nodded her head with an emphatic '*Ja, Ja*'. The guide remained quite still for a moment; so long that I thought he could not have understood. Then I saw the muscles of his throat and cheeks contracting just as if he was going to spit. For a moment I thought he would—straight into Josh's face—but it was controlled into a swallow, and the hissing, slurred '*M'sieur*' that jerked from the side of his mouth was the most he could manage. Josh, still smiling, towering above the little grey form as he stood there so easily, bowed again. There was another pause, then the hands clapped twice, and we were ushered into the first room.

I don't remember much of the details of that—or the next two, only that the guide was tearing through his piece at about twice the speed of the day before, with sudden pauses while he glared at the Dutch lady as she struggled manfully, and quietly, to translate the gist to her daughters; but it was not really meant, it was only an act—all the time, I knew, he was watching Josh . . . like a cat with a big dog when both are waiting for a meal.

Two rooms on the ground floor . . . clean, but dead and musty, the furniture, the chairs and marriage chest that had once, so long ago, been intimate, loved things, lying there without feeling to wait the daily talks, the daily stares, and then go back to better memories.

In the third room, after we had gone up the smooth spiral ramp that served as a staircase, Joan's fingers locked in mine and she breathed, 'It's just beyond the far door—on the right—leading off a sort of lobby.' I looked over to Josh across the heads of the crowd, and he nodded very slightly. The voice of the guide tore on through the description of the room; there was the usual silence at the end, then the two claps, and the crowd was moving away in front of us through the door to the lobby.

I was still holding Joan's hand as we hung back, determined to be last, uncertain of what Josh planned to do. He did not seem to be in any hurry, for he waited to pass through just in front of us, pressing tight against the jam of people waiting for the guide to lock the door behind before he opened the one in front. As we squeezed past, the little eye flicked over us for a moment, the smell of stale garlic fanned over us; then the key grated in the lock behind and the guide was worming his way through the press to open the door in front.

I tried to keep my eyes straight ahead . . . not look to the right, to see if Joan's memory had been that good . . . but I had to. It was there, not a staircase, but the same sort of smooth sloping ramp that we had just come up: you could see about a quarter of a turn before the side wall shut off the rest. The pressure was easing in front now, as the party filed into the next room, but Josh's broad back blocked the view to our front until he was almost at the doorway.

The guide was there waiting to lock us in; leaning against the lintel, tapping with his key, looking slightly more malevolent than usual. Josh stepped by into the room, then turned quickly and picked the guide up by the shoulders of his jacket, holding him a foot off the ground while he shook him gently. 'Three times,' he said in a loud and terrible voice, '—I have asked you to speak *slowly*...and you take not the slightest notice. Now I will take no further interest in your filthy lecture.'

I suppose we two, the last left to pass through that door, should have moved to our right at once, but in the seconds that followed we stood there rooted to the floor, staring in fascination at the scene that followed.

The little man was chattering like a monkey, a film of bubbles blew from his mouth as he hung helpless, his feet beating a tattoo against Josh's knees; Josh was smiling, but there was no laughter in it, still smiling as he turned from us to walk three strides into the room, holding the guide in the same position before he dropped him like a sack of potatoes on the floor. Behind this, a vista of the party, staring appalled, open-mouthed, and behind them the great canopied bed that was the centre piece of the room. Without breaking step, Josh walked on and stepped over the rope that fenced off the bed: there was a creak from it as he laid his sixteen stone down full length on the brocaded coverlet; then he spread his handkerchief over his eyes.

The guide was on his knees now, trying to get up; he looked at us, outside the door, free . . . and then back to Josh, lying on the bed. You could see in that split second the struggle between his job and his personal interest; the job won, and he screamed, a short, sharp scream of a horse in pain, then he was running towards the bed.

I wanted to stay . . . but there could be no more time; I jerked at Joan's hand. 'Come on,' and then we were running down to our right, fast down the smooth stone of the ramp in the turret. The last sound that came to us was the Dutch lady cheering above the general noise.

We ran hand in hand down the slope; one turn to the next floor, another, silent now, sealed off from the rest of the world, alone in our quest. Then a door on the outside . . . a very solid door that was shut. 'This is the right level,' I panted, 'but it's locked.'

'No—those bolts. Get on to the top one, Harry. I'll try the bottom one.'

They were very rusty and stiff; as I reached up and struggled with mine, even as I ripped a finger on a sharp edge, I was thinking. 'It's a waste of time . . . it will be locked as well . . .' But when we had got them free, the door creaked as we hung on it, and then we were out in a courtyard.

Empty . . . still hot, with the shadows trailing purple from the overhanging points of the roof and the fronds of a vine that hung from one wall; empty—but there was a creeper on the other side, still with some clusters of orange trumpets flowering, and in the angle between them a square, battered drain-pipe running down the wall and ending in a gargoyle spout over a drain. No time to look at the wall-bracket and see if the monogram was there . . . I knew we were home.

We stood there for a moment, panting, while the sour, sick feeling of failure flooded up inside me. We were right, but she was not there; how futile it had been to suppose they would not move her; or that she would be waiting all ready for us to just walk in and take her away. She might be inside any of the five doors that opened into the courtyard . . . the two on each side of us, or the one slightly larger, that lay straight ahead. She might be eating, asleep, watched . . . or not there at all.

No one came out to challenge us; the courtyard was silent but for the faint sounds of battle that floated down from the open windows, two storeys above us. They died for a moment, then there was a splintering crash, and they redoubled in volume: Josh must be doing well, but whatever it was, it could not go on for ever.

I turned to Joan wearily. 'We can't go back, darling—and we can't kick up worse hell than's going on up there. You take the left side, I'll take the right. Just walk in each door and grab her if she's there. If there's any opposition, shout and I'll come.'

'No . . .'She was looking straight ahead at the one single door, the bigger one. 'Try there first. I've got a feeling there is something beyond it . . . another yard. I just saw it when I was looking out of the window.'

No time for argument; we ran across and lifted the latch and pushed and it swung open. There was another courtyard beyond, a smaller one that had been stables; all round the square were the double doors of the horseboxes, and in one corner, staring at us with round solemn eyes, one finger in her mouth, was a little girl with short black hair.

'You try . . . darling.' As I said it I moved back a pace to guard the door we had just opened. I could hardly bear to look as Joan walked forward.

'Margaret . . . would you like to go home, darling?'

The child did not move; only the finger came out of her mouth and she wiped it up and down on the front of her grubby blue frock. Joan took another step forward, and tried again, in French. 'We've come to take you home, Margaret.'

No sign, just that solemn stare. Joan was fumbling with the catch of her big bag now . . . and then her voice, soft and clear as it floated in the hot stillness. '*Sur le pont . . . d'Avignon . . .* ' on, right through the song.

There was puzzlement in those big round eyes now, a kind of doubt; suddenly they switched from Joan's to her hands, hands that were holding out in front of her bag a battered yellow bear, with one eye, and a green skirt. Then in a flash expression came and she was running: running to Joan to hug her round the skirt with one hand, while the other clutched a precious, half-forgotten thing. Always I will remember the sight of those two kneeling in the

sunlight together—and Joan's head turned to look at me, with a
bright smear of tears on her cheek as she ruffled the dark hair. 'It's
cut short, Harry, and badly. It's been dyed too . . . but you can
still see the blonde roots.'

I had taken one step towards them to look for myself when the
tight, clipped voice just behind me said, 'What is it you desire,
Monsieur?'

It was a solid, middle-aged woman who was standing in the door
just behind me, hands on hips. She had one of those tough
unyielding peasant faces which would spell difficulty even if the
eyes had not been so watchful.

I looked to her side, at the back of the door we had opened; there
was a lock on our side, a big old-fashioned lock, and the key was
still in it. I said, 'We make friends with the child, Mademoiselle,
with your permission. We have come down from the château . . .
because we did not like the fight that is going on up there.'

'Fight—?'

'Yes. Listen.' Faint strains were coming through the door, and
for the first time she seemed to hear them. 'What is happening?'
she said. She swung her head round and peered back; then she
stared at me again. You could see the doubt appearing in her eyes.

'A mad Englishman—he is having a fight with the concierge.
And we did not want to have any part in it. If you wish to go and
see if you can help, we will watch the child.'

'It is kind of you, Monsieur—' She took another step backwards,
beyond the swing of the door, just where I wanted her. Then she
looked back past me to where Joan was still kneeling, talking to the
child, and then her eyes narrowed. 'And Monsieur brings his own
toys with him—just on the chance he may meet a child?' The tone
of voice was quite different.

I had never manhandled a woman before in my life: but it had
to be done now. I put my hand flat on her chest and gave the
double push: the first small one that rocks anyone off balance,
followed at once by a second, harder one that tipped her back as I
hooked a leg behind to trip her. She sprawled sideways, inside the
swing of the door, giving out a long, high screech; then I had
slammed and locked it and was by Joan's side. There was another
door on the far side of the stables—I don't think for a moment I
worried as to whether it would be open, and we could get out; it
was too heavy, and the latch too high for Margaret to open it
herself. I swung it open and there was nothing but a drive and

broad lawns beyond, with the ornamental gardens showing away to the right. We turned and ran towards them. As we headed for the cover of the shrubs, a gardener straightened his back from the bed he was tending, dropped his hoe, stared for a moment and then shouted after us. But it didn't matter, because we were running free, side by side, jumping over trim box hedges and skirting borders with Margaret clutched over my shoulder laughing at this new game while she held her beloved teddy bear tight against her cheek.

We slowed up when we got to the shelter of the trees, and I eased Margaret on to the crook of my arm. It was difficult going now, a cross between a slide and scramble down the steep banks of fallen leaves and the outcrops of rock that sloped down towards the road and the river. The child was silent now, looking from one to the other of us as I grunted and strained, while Joan turned from in front to give me a steadying hand. The little mouth was beginning to quiver . . . but it did not matter, with only a hundred yards to go to the wall, perhaps another fifty running along inside it to the gap where Josh had left the car. Then she could cry . . . because we would be inside, and my foot would be hard down. Across the Loire, and then over the northern plain in another, safer, *département:* perhaps even as far as the sanctuary of the Sûreté in Paris. With Françoise, of course . . . I could only hope she would be waiting.

She was. I saw her at a few yards' range through the branches, crouching beside a bush on our side of the wall. Closer, and I saw she was pale and terribly frightened. Something had gone wrong.

'The car, Monsieur. They have taken it away. I waited here, as I was told, and then, a minute ago, my uncle and the other one came running down the road from the auberge and got in and drove it away.'

I stared at her stupidly. 'The other one?'

'Yes, the one that arrived from England this afternoon, the friend of my uncle's . . . Monsieur Jacques.'

CHAPTER 8

I could not speak for a moment; I dared not look at Joan, sitting there beside the wall, holding Margaret close. The chill of the realisation of what this meant was almost too much to bear. At last I managed, 'Where have they taken it to?'

'I do not know, Monsieur. I only heard them say one thing. Jacques said to my uncle, "I'll drop you at the gate —go up and start from there. I'll deal with this, phone Henri at the bridge, and go back and wait at the auberge." ' She stood, looking from one to the other of us, twisting her hands. She made no comment that we had acquired a family . . . Josh must have told her. But there was no time to worry about that; we had to get away . . . and our means of escape had gone . . . one of the routes cut. It was Joan who brought home the final thing. She said softly, 'If he's here—and slipped the police, they'll begin to act *now*.'

I shook myself, trying to clear my head for some quick, desperate thinking. 'We'll have to thumb a lift. Until we can get to some place where we can hire a car.'

'Stand out there, in the village street, almost in sight of the auberge—? Too risky, Harry. We'd be bound to be spotted.'

'I didn't mean here. We'll have to cut back inside this wall the other way—right on to the other side of the caves. There's always a crowd to hide us there. It's the only chance.'

'How far, Harry?'

'About half a mile. And pretty rough going. Do you think you can make it?'

'I'll have to—' She stopped and looked at Françoise. 'What happens about that little one . . . we promised . . .'

'I know, but it wouldn't be fair . . . we might get caught.'

We had been talking in English, and Françoise had been standing patiently; those big dark eyes turning uncertainly from Joan's face to mine. Now I went over and held her gently by the shoulders, trying by touch, as well as voice and expression, to urge her into a course of action I knew she would resist.

'Listen, Françoise. This is what you must do. Go back to the auberge and wait. You know nothing of this. You have not seen us—or the child.'

She twisted uneasily. 'But, Monsieur Josh—he promised. He said we all went together. Where is he now?'

'He is still up at the château, Françoise.'

'Then I shall go to him there.'

'No. That would be dangerous for you. Now that the car has gone, Madame and I must find another way . . . and we *know*—other people—understand our plans. It is better you have nothing to do with them. And I am sure that Monsieur Josh . . . when he cannot find out what has happened . . . will go to the auberge. Then, if you wait, you will be all right.'

'He promised, Monsieur.' She made a sudden gesture of brushing the back of her hand across her eyes; it was frightened, hopeless and somehow utterly dependent, so that I wanted to say, 'All right—you can come with us,' but I knew I dared not.

'I know that he promised, Françoise. And I know he will keep it.'

'Then I will go, Monsieur.' She slipped from my hands and turned, running along in the shelter of the wall without turning once to look back. Soon the light flicker of her frock vanished among the darker browns and greens of the undergrowth and Joan and I turned in the opposite direction to try and find a way past the caves and a lift from a car on the road.

It was all right to start with; I took the child again, and she was heavier now, sagging against my arm, all former lightness gone because it wasn't a new game to her any more, and she did not know where she was going, and was a little cold and tired, and hungry.

Then we came to the first snag—something I had not even thought of: the wall on our right went up almost straight in the air like a buttress, while across our path was a smooth, sheer cliff of limestone about fifty feet high. In one or two places a bush had managed to find a crevice and cling there precariously, but there were not enough of them: the thing was unclimbable. I should have remembered the great bluff of rock that jutted out to hang over the entrance of the great wine cave. This was the side of it.

I looked away to our left, where the ground sloped up away out of sight among the thickets; somewhere up there it must meet the

level of the cliff top . . . somewhere. And to find that would be the
only way to get to the top.

'We'll have to go up that way, darling. Then over the top of the
big cave, and down the other side.'

It sounded so simple: but it proved almost impossible. Not only
was the ground very steep, but it was slippery with dead leaves and
treacherous in rocks and fallen branches. The undergrowth was
thicker: bramble and other creepers twined from bush to bush,
stubborn and cruel in their resistance as I tried to force our way
through. Margaret was a dead weight now, dragging on my arm
and shoulder, crying in a continuous, silent, shuddering that was
the worst part of all. I was so tired . . . so tired. Twice I went down
on my knees, tripped by a hidden root; I was frightened that I
would drop the child, ashamed that I had to ask Joan to go first
and try and clear a path.

She tried so hard, but she was not as strong as me; I remember
once the desperate, beaten look on her face as she turned to try and
give me a hand up . . . a bramble had just whipped back across
her face, and carmine beads of blood were pricked in a line down
her cheek. It seemed as if it would never end; that for each foot we
struggled up, we were slipping back two. But at last the bushes
started to thin, the ground to level. We had made the top.

There was a little clearing, and we sank down on a patch of
grass, Joan taking Margaret from me, rocking her against her
shoulder, holding her close, trying to soothe her with soft words
that came in spasms through her own panting breath.

We did not speak to each other for what seemed a long time.
There had been so much noise in our struggle up that slope that I
had not thought about any outside sounds; now, as the drumming
in my head died, and the breath stopped rattling in my throat,
something of the outer world came to me for the first time . . . softly,
very softly at first; increasing as it came a little nearer and I strained
harder to hear it. A sound that I had heard often before: a sound
that thrilled me always when I was standing at the edge of a covert
with a gun ready, waiting for the pheasants to rocket upwards. The
tramping of feet on undergrowth, the sound of men's voices calling
to each other, the tap of sticks on tree trunks. A line of men were
beating the wood; only this time I was not the gun, but the game.

They were away above us, coming down the hill. I judged about
three hundred yards away, and there was at least ten of them: all
the gardeners and sweepers and friends of the concierge that he had

been able to muster, I thought bitterly, while we had been wasting time. I gripped Joan's arm—and I could see by her eyes that she had heard it too. 'Wait—' I whispered, 'see which way they are heading.'

There was silence then between us, save for Margaret's muffled sobbing. I strained my ears to try and find—not the nearness of the approach, but its direction. Soon it was only too obvious that what I feared most was happening. They were not moving in a straight line, but a crescent. And the curving tip that was on their left, the one in front of us, was moving across our only path very fast. There was little time or space left.

'Come on, darling. Try and make a dash for it—'

She didn't answer me; just picked up the child, and then we were runnning through the trees side by side. But only a hundred yards before another halt and listen made it obvious that I had misjudged the whole thing: the main line of the beaters was not now on our flank but our front; they had turned and were coming towards us from the way of escape.

I swung round in the full circle, searching for another line; through the trees, to the side of us, there was another little clearing and in the middle of it what looked the coping of a small well jutting out from the grass. I think that before I moved over to it and saw the grating that covered the top, I knew what it was, where it led, and that our only chance was to follow that path.

I heaved at the grating and it came away quite easily; just below the lip, a steel ladder went straight down out of sight. The noise of those beaters was louder, and Joan was standing beside me, staring down into that small black circle of darkness. I think she knew before I said anything.

'It's one of the ventilating shafts of the wine caves, Joan. We must climb down—and wait till they've passed.' The noise in the undergrowth was very close now.

She didn't argue. But I knew how frightened she was by the way she gave one last look down before she went. Only, as she swung one leg over the edge, she said, 'Must I go first?' and I had to say that she must because I wanted a clear space to carry Margaret. 'I can do it by wedging my back against the opposite wall, I think, while I shift the grip of my free hand farther down the ladder. But you must keep your hands clear of my feet, darling. For God's sake, get going.' In an agony of impatience I watched her slip down, rung after rung, until she had disappeared.

Margaret suddenly, miraculously, had fallen asleep. It made things much easier for me, but I don't think I could have managed if the shaft had been of any larger diameter; as it was, I could just brace my back against the opposite wall, as I pushed out from the lower rungs with my feet, while I clutched the soft, limp little body across my chest before making a grab at a lower rung with the other hand. Getting the grating back into position from below was the worst thing, but I managed that somehow and then it was down . . . like some grub edging its way back into its hole . . . feet feeling gingerly, terrified of treading on Joan's hands. The light faded; with the darkness came the damp chill of the caves.

I had gone down about twenty feet, I suppose, when I stopped and called down to Joan. 'Don't go any farther, darling. We'll give them a few minutes and then go up again. Lean out from the ladder and rest your back against the wall.'

No answer.

'Joan! Are you all right?' I was shouting, and the echoes of it boomed up and down the shaft; if there had been anyone standing near the top, they must have heard. But I just did not care any more.

Joan's voice came up to me this time: very faintly. 'Sorry . . . Yes, I'm all right . . . I was just trying it out . . . But not too long, darling . . . I'm so cold . . . and tired.'

'Just a few minutes. Please hang on for a few minutes.' I leaned back, staring up at the pale disc of light above me, trying to ease the strain of Margaret from one arm to the other; she woke for a moment, whimpered and then wormed her head a little closer into my shoulder under my coat; the seconds dragged by while the ache in my arms and legs nagged deeper and deeper. If I did not move soon, I knew I would not be able to move at all.

'I'm going up now, Joan. Give me a good start, in case I slip. I think I'll be able to push the grating up with my head.' It would have been interesting to have found out whether this last was true, but I never had a chance to prove it: coming down the shaft, gravity had been helping me to wedge my back against the other wall, but trying to fight up against it, the reverse worked and I found that I could not move at all.

Four times I heaved and strained, trying to reach up and grasp a higher rung, but it was no good, 'I can't make it, Joan,' I panted, 'we'll have to go on down.'

'Oh no.' Her voice was very faint.

'We've *got* to—I shall drop this child in a minute. You can't be more than ten feet from the bottom.'

'All right.' It was a relief to hear the scrape of her feet on the rungs as she started moving down; at last her voice came back again, 'I'm on the ground,' and then I slithered down the last few feet to stand beside her in the silence and the chill and the black velvet darkness of the caves.

Margaret had wakened and was crying again, so Joan took her and tried to comfort her, while I leaned back against the smooth rock wall of the tunnel and tried to get back my breath and my strength. I found my lighter and flicked it: nothing more, or less, than I expected to see. A long grey tunnel, with a yellow sanded floor, and the two dark lines of the trolley rails running down the middle to each side the flat-stacked racks of still wine, the bottoms of the bottles winking at us like a thousand evil eyes in the flicker of the thin flame of the lighter.

'Now to get out of here.' I hope it sounded as cheerful and businesslike as I meant it to.

'We can't.' There was a tremor in her voice and she was shivering. There must be no panic . . . no panic. 'It's easy,' I said, 'that ladder was facing us when we came to the top of the shaft, and we were facing west then. So . . . if we face it now, and then turn right down this passage—' I flashed my lighter again and made the actions, 'you will be facing south . . . and you've got to keep south to get to the entrance of the great cave. But we must remember the turns we have to make to left or right when we come to a cross-gallery.'

It sounded easy: it probably would have been if Joan had not muddled me in insisting that I tried to turn on the lights at the corner of the gallery. She was frightened and tired, and she was coping with Margaret, so I groped my way to find them. It made things much easier when I had, but the concentration of finding how the double switch worked by feel must have made me forget a turn; three later, when I had turned out the light of the gallery we were in and switched on the next one to the left, Joan said, 'No. It's the other way—' and we stood there arguing, trying to check back on past movements until we both realised we had not the slighest idea of the direction we now faced.

The rows of lights in the roof gleamed down on the ranks of bottles; there was no sound but our whispering—somehow one could not raise one's voice in that place—and once, far away, the dull rumble of a trolley . . . too far to have a chance of gauging its direction. We were hopelessly lost.

There was nothing to do but sit down with our backs against one of the racks and wait and try and think of what to do; there was not even the consolation of the tilted bottles of *mouseux* behind us, which someone might have to come and turn, and so lead us out. It was all still wine, lying flat, and it might not be wanted for months. The dank chill of the place was seeping right through me now . . . but it was not only that which started my shivering. We must have been sitting there, without speaking, for quite five minutes before the first whisper of the ghost voices came to us.

It came as a soft whispering to start with: an eerie, disembodied, soft hissing that seemed to creep round the corner from a darkened section of the tunnel; it flowed over us, cleared to a single voice talking all the time with a background of subdued whispering and the shuffle of many feet; a large party was being shown round the caves.

I pulled Joan to her feet. 'We've got to bluff this out. We went round with an earlier party . . . we got separated and lost. We've been wandering about trying to find our way out for hours.' I started shouting as we stumbled down towards the reflected glow of the lights that had gone on in a parallel gallery.

We met on a corner. The guide stopped dead in his tracks, with the party crowding round him, peering curiously. There was a moment's complete silence.

'Thank God we found you, Monsieur. It has been terrible . . . we have been walking and calling for hours.' It was not difficult to make either my voice or manner seem desperate.

'But how did you get separated?' The guide sounded horrified. 'It is most dangerous.' There seemed no doubt as to the truth of our story: there could be no other way of getting into the place. I started to say that it had been entirely our own fault when Margaret began to cry again, more piteously than before, and explanations were forgotten; the party surrounded us, patting, murmuring sympathy; a large lady took Margaret from Joan and clasped her to an ample bosom; I saw another woman put her arm round Joan and offer her a shawl; I found I was being held by a little man with straw hat and pince-nez, who murmured about the fortitude of the brave English. Sympathy flowed around us in a warm, comforting cloak: more than sympathy, I detected by the fine aroma of

Chouvray—the party must have done a considerable amount of preliminary tasting before they started their tour of the caves.

It was the leader of the party who summed it all up; he was red-faced, and fat, and looked like a butcher; he stared at the guide and said, 'I think it is our duty to conduct these unfortunates directly to the entrance; I have seen enough of this tour.' There was more than compassion in it, he wanted to get back to the other half of the bottle.

We were swept along with them on a wave of understanding and goodwill; even the guide, when we got to the entrance and the light blinded us, pocketed my tip with an anxious, 'Do you wish me to make enquiries, Monsieur?' breathed a sigh of relief when I said we did not want to cause further trouble—it had been our fault.

They would not let us go, the party: they took us over to one of the long trestle tables and sat us down to take wine with them. Even Margaret, returned now from the fat lady, was given a mug of wine and water, no one at the table seeing the slightest thing wrong in a three-year-old taking this; we told again the tale of our adventure of being lost in the caves, and in the interval when the fat man called for more bottles, I managed to get a few words in to Joan in whispered English. 'Our only hope is to stick to them,' I said. 'I think I heard someone say they have come by private coach from Blois. If we can get on that—'

'It's this child I'm worried about, Harry. She's had about all she can stand.' She was rocking her to and fro against her shoulder.

'Give her some more wine, then—she may go to sleep.'

'She might be sick. Look, darling, I've had about all I can take, too.'

More spouting of goodwill and shouts and laughter from the French party round us; then I managed to get in, 'They'll be going soon. Why don't you take her to the toilet and get yourselves both cleaned up. You'll feel a lot better.'

'I will—' She got up from the table clutching child and handbag. She looked at me doubtfully. 'Look, Harry. I've got some of my sleeping tablets with me. It would be so much easier—do you think it would do her harm if I gave her half of one?'

'No, too much. Try a quarter.'

When she came back, cleaned and freshened from the wash, I was thankful to see Margaret limp and asleep in her arms.

The fat man, the leader of the party, drained his glass regretfully, and announced they must be going; but, of course, if we had missed

our bus through the mishap, they would be delighted to take us to
Blois. I shouldered Margaret and we walked out of the shadow of
the great cave into the last of the evening sunshine. The bus was
just down the road, the fat man had told me; it shook me for a
moment when I saw it parked right outside the auberge, but the
entrance door, being on the right side, was hidden from any prying
eyes . . . and in the middle of this crowd that exuded such a cloud
of *bonhomie*, Chouvray, and garlic, we must be safe indeed. As we
walked along, heads down, I wondered what had happened to Josh
. . . had he been able to make so lucky a getaway? I started to think
about our own troubles again when the bus conductor would not
let us in.

He was an earnest young man and he stood by the steps counting
his flock home; when we came to the door, he said, 'But Monsieur
did not come in my party.' Someone behind us shouted an explanation over my shoulder, but he shook his head and threw an arm
across the entrance. It was not permitted. It was a private coach
with all seats filled. He was not allowed to carry standing passengers. He regretted, but those were the regulations.

I tried a thousand-franc note; he was tempted, I could see that,
but he still regretted. As I stood to one side and argued, slowly and
inexorably our friendly screen melted as the rest of the party edged
by and climbed in. The final irony was the conductor's information
that it was only fifteen minutes to wait for the regular bus service
. . . and we could be certain of shade and refreshment in the excellent auberge opposite. Then the door slammed and the bus pulled
away. We were left in the empty, dusty road, within ten yards of
the place where we had started. And now it was not only fat,
moustached, madame and her rat of a husband—even the concierge
at the château—we had to deal with. Jacques was there . . . inside,
waiting for us. I looked up at the front of the auberge, the shutters
still closed against the heat, giving the impression of half-shut eyes.
Perhaps he was watching, even now.

The terrace in front, with the long shadows slanting across the
tables from the sheltering plane trees, was empty. But no help to
go there, no help to stay where we were, inviting to be seen. Seen
by those hooded eyes that might be looking down at this moment
from the slats of a shutter. 'Just keep walking, darling'—I had taken
her arm and turned her down the village street in the direction of
Blois—'Hope for the best, we're bound to pick up a car.'

'I can't, Harry. I just can't. I'm so tired.' She was sobbing.

'You must—!'

We had moved forward a couple of steps then, so that the hissed '*Monsieur*—!' came from behind me. I jerked my head round, and there in the shadow of the trees of the terrace was the darker stain of a black dress, the pale oval of a face . . . Françoise.

She moved forward a fraction, jerking an arm in the direction of the alley that ran down the side of the auberge towards the river. 'Back door . . . come softly . . . I will let you in.'

I turned, almost pulling Joan after me as she hung back, whispering, 'No . . . no . . . he's in there.'

'We are on our own now, there's no help from the police, because he's slipped them. We want to be close—because it's safest.'

Françoise was waiting outside the opened door in the yard that looked on to the garden and the trees by the river. She was pale and serious, but no longer frightened. 'Shssh . . . take off your shoes . . . and I will take you up the back way. *He* is in his room, and has not come out since I came back—' Then her face lightened—'and Josh, he is back; we did not know what to do, so he told me to watch. My aunt had gone to the château . . . there is great trouble there.'

We crept along the passage, past the closed kitchen door, with the crashing of pots and pans sounding above the under-chef's nasal singing; then softly along the upstairs corridor to our room, watching the row of shut doors as we tiptoed by, wondering which one held *him;* at last, the safety of our own room, the comfort of Josh sitting at the table by the window, so solid and dependable as he munched the rolls and ham Françoise must have smuggled up to him.

'Hello—' He swung round in his chair to grin at us. 'I saw you in the road. You must be starving. Pull up a chair and have some tea.' We might have been coming back from an afternoon stroll.

Joan shifted Margaret in her arms and went without speaking through the door that connected with our room; she came back empty-handed, sitting down in the chair that Josh had left while he went to turn the key in the outside door.

'Thank God, we only gave her a quarter tablet, Harry. She's in a deep, deep sleep as it is. I've tucked her up in our bed—and locked the door.'

'What happened—?' There was a creak of the bed springs as Josh lowered his great bulk down beside me.

Between us, we told him; and the telling of it made our afternoon sound even more fantastic than it had really been. He did not interrupt us once, but at the end the way he said 'Nice work' made all that cold and tiredness and fear seem worthwhile.

'And you—?' I said. 'We were worried.'

The bed under me started shaking; great waves of silent laughter were rippling down from him into it. 'Oh, you dear people—if only you could have stayed! Apart from the fact that it helped you, I would not have missed that for anything in the world. It was just marvellous.' He stopped for a moment to blow his nose and wipe his eyes. 'I could not see exactly when you left us . . . I was busy. When was it?'

'When you decided to go to sleep,' I said.

'I was on the bed? Well, the guide came and grabbed one ankle, and started swearing at me while he heaved . . . but I'm afraid I was too heavy for him to budge . . . and I couldn't answer him because I had got the giggles. The others, the party, just didn't know what to do . . . they stood and stared. Then that little basket must have pulled just a little too hard—' he nearly choked again—'and one leg of the bed collapsed.'

'We heard that.'

'Well, then things were different. You see, I became at once not the mad Englishman, but the barbarian defiler of French national treasures. All the French were on his side in a moment.'

I said, 'There were about fifteen of them. They must have made short work of you.'

'No, dear boy. That's where you are wrong. That was the funniest part of all . . . do you remember that Dutch lady . . . and her three strapping daughters?'

'Yes.'

'Well, they had had a bad time from that guide, and they became my allies. They got on one side and tried to pull to keep me on the bed, while as many of the French as could get near were trying to pull me off from the other. Then another leg broke . . . I nearly wetted myself laughing.'

'But they got you off in the end.'

'Of course they did. And I was frog-marched down to the main hall, and the concierge was screaming his head off for the police, and the French were screaming at him and me, and the Dutch were screaming for me at all of them. Then, quite suddenly, it all stopped. There was a terrific shindy outside and a woman dashed in and got the guide by the arm and started whispering to him. We were all hustled out into the courtyard and the door slammed on us. I waited for someone to come and arrest me, but nothing happened. So I escorted the Dutch contingent down to the gate through a barrage of abuse. Then I came back here, heard about the car from Françoise, and what you were trying to do. But I thought I had better hang on for a bit, just in case. Thank God I did—'

There was a sudden soft drumming of finger-tips on the outside of the bedroom door; then Françoise's voice calling softly, urgently.

'Josh. . . . It is my uncle and aunt. They hurry across from the gate of the château to the auberge. Have great care.'

We heard the sound of her feet moving quickly away down the passage. The whole room went very still—as still as the quiet of the rest of the auberge outside the doors of our rooms. We were back from things done and past to the unknown future.

'What now—?' said Joan softly.

Josh got up from the bed and walked over to the window, staring down on the garden and the shining strip of the Loire, tinged golden now in the setting sun. 'Dark in an hour,' he said softly. 'At the moment, possession is nine points in our favour—of these rooms, I mean, not of the child. We can hang on in here—and they can't get in to see if what they suspect is right—for a limited period only. Rooms must be cleaned, beds made, and if we go down to meals in shifts, it will tell them all they want to know. But if we can hang on till dark . . .' He peered out of the window. 'It's only fifteen feet drop against a blank wall to the ground, Harry. Do you think that you and Joan could get down that on the sheets?'

'Easily.'

'Then if I made another diversion . . . and I assure you I would enjoy it even more than the last one . . . there are boats all along the river bank—I saw them this morning. Get down there, take one and cross the Loire. It would give you a fine start, for I'm certain they would search the roads each way on this bank first.'

'And you, Josh' Joan said it very quietly.

He gave her that long wide smile of his and rubbed his hands together softly. 'I shall be fine . . . If—' his eyes never left her face—'if you keep your promise about Françoise . . .'

'We promised. You know we will.'

'Good. Then—' He stopped abruptly and held up a hand. Slow, purposeful footsteps were echoing on the boards of the passage outside, coming towards us. 'The first assault, I think,' he whispered. 'Get back to your room—make sure the door's locked. I'll handle this.'

I had tested the key in our lock before the three sharp knocks came, not on our door as I would have expected, but on Josh's. 'Who is it—?' His voice was dreamy as he answered, and, to my amazement, seemed to be coming from somewhere near the floor. I tiptoed back to the communicating door, and he was sitting on the floor, cross-legged, by the bed. He winked at me. 'Who is it?' he repeated.

The voice from the other side of the panelling was that of Monsieur le Patron: not servile as I had always heard it before, but peremptory, menacing almost.

'It is I, Monsieur. I have come to attend to the beds.'

'The beds? They are made . . . and in order.'

'I wish to turn them down, Monsieur. With your permission—' I saw the door jamb move a fraction and the handle turn slowly.

'There is no permission,' said Josh. 'I am doing my exercise of yogi and cannot be disturbed. Monsieur and Madame Kent attend to their toilet. We will turn down the beds ourselves.'

'As you wish.' There was a short pause, and then he said, with venom increasing at every word. 'I have also to inform you that—owing to unfortunate circumstances—the dinner tonight will be late. It will not be before eight-thirty.'

'That will be in order—so long as you do not serve us with filthy fried sprats that we have had to endure for three nights running—' Josh was enjoying himself hugely.

Dead silence at this; then the patron came back with his parting shot, the words rising in fury so that you could almost see them being spat against the door. 'And finally, Monsieur, I must ask you to vacate these rooms by midnight. I have a party coming from Paris by car who need them.'

'Oh no, my friend. My yogi trains my eyes to excellent sight, and even as I sit here on the floor I can read the notice nailed beside the door that you so thoughtfully provide for the information of your guests. It states that notice must be given before noon, or a full day is charged. That works both ways. You give us notice now, if you wish. But we pay . . . and stay . . . till noon to-morrow.'

'———' It was a very rude word, almost stifled by the anger in the voice that uttered it.

'Eat it,' replied Josh with relish. There was nothing more but the

sound of the feet moving away along the passage back towards the
service stairs.

Josh was on his feet in an instant, moving without a sound on
his stockinged feet as he pulled me through the door into our room.
Joan was sitting on the side of the bed in her housecoat, gently
easing the grubby blue cotton frock from Margaret's shoulders;
when she had laid her back on the pillow, we all stood in silence
for a moment as we looked at the tousled black hair, the flushed
cheeks and the dark stains below the eyes.

'How is she—?' said Josh. There was a curious gentle look on
his face that I had never seen before.

'All right, I think.' Joan smoothed the hair back softly. 'Her
breathing is still shallow, but it's regular I'm sure we haven't done
any harm.'

'Good. Did you hear that little sally, dear girl?'

'Some of it, Josh.'

'That one will be back, I think, with reinforcements. We must
decide quickly. If dinner is at eight-thirty, the best time is just
before, when they are all busy. Monsieur will be in the bar, so I
will go there at eight-fifteen and have a little argument. When you
hear it . . . and I promise you that you will . . . slide down your
sheets and beat it for the river. I'll keep up the interest as long as
I can.'

'What about Françoise?' I said.

'I'll see her somewhere, somehow, when I go down. Tell her to
drop everything and join you there. Then it must be "Row for the
shore, my hearties", with all the speed you can.'

'And we meet—?'

He smiled again. 'Where we started. At Chartres Cathedral. At
six. If I do not make it, I should be easy to trace, for I shall certainly
be in jail. But in any case you must get in touch with the police,
Harry, as soon as you feel safe out of reach. Don't forget that today
is the last day of grace.'

'I haven't.'

He looked at his watch. 'Seven-ten. Just an hour to wait. What
are we going to do?'

'I'm going to have a bath,' said Joan, 'I still feel filthy from that
horrible cave.'

'A good idea. I shall sort out the few belongings I shall try to
take with me, and advise you to do the same. If we manage to make
our getaway, we shall have to travel very light.'

The bath water was running and Joan fiddling about with her hair while she waited for it to fill, I had sorted out our valuables and had stowed them in the pockets of my suit, was just licking up the envelope with the money for our bill that I was going to leave on the dressing-table, when the knocking came on the door again: this time on our door, this time slow, heavy . . . somehow official.

'What is it?'

There was no anger in the patron's voice this time. Each word came out with the relish of a final triumph. 'Monsieur Kent, I have with me the gendarme of this village. He wishes to interview your party on a serious matter.'

'I'm changing. He'll have to wait.'

'He cannot wait. He wishes to enter and search the rooms . . . immediately . . . for evidence of a serious crime.'

Anything . . . anything, to gain time. I said, 'You'll have to come to the other door, then. The key has jammed in this lock. I can't turn it. I looked back to where Joan was standing between bathroom and bedroom, frozen, staring. I just jerked my head at her, and perhaps there is something in the affinity of ten years of a lot of love and understanding . . . and a few misunderstandings. She just nodded her head—and I knew that she understood. I walked into Josh's bedroom and closed the door after me. He had heard; he was standing quite still in the middle of the floor, waiting for me. 'Police,' I said. 'He wouldn't dare say it if it wasn't true. And *he* may be with them—so we've had it.' It seemed such an anticlimax, such a bloody shame, to be trapped in the bedroom of a second-class auberge after all we had gone through.

'Never say die, Harry boy. Never say die. We'll fight this to the last ditch.' Once again hope ebbed back by the look on that solid, honest face. 'With your permission, as I am bigger, I will open the door . . . in case someone is lying.'

I think that even to the last moment as he twisted the key and edged the door ajar, I hoped that he might be right. But the first thing I saw over his shoulder was the dark, gold-braided, pill-box peaked cap of a gendarme.

We were polite, but argumentative; we ignored the patron, who stood just inside the door, pulling at his lip and smirking. We demanded to know the meaning of this outrage, and what this 'serious crime' that had been mentioned consisted of. Then Josh cut in. 'If it is anything to do with the unfortunate affair at the

château this evening, Monsieur, I am willing to make a full explanation . . . and if it is judged to have been my fault, full reparation.'

The gendarme was young and nervous and not quite sure of his
ground; he scratched his left ear at this piece of information and
looked puzzled. No, there had been no complaint of anything at the
château that had been reported: but a charge had been laid against
Monsieur and Madame Kent, that they had kidnapped a child, the
niece of Monsieur le Concierge, from the grounds. He realised
it was fantastic: but the charge had been laid, and he had to
investigate.

'Then look for her—' Bluff was the only thing left.

He started poking into cupboards and under the bed rather half-
heartedly; Josh kept up a running commentary on the general dirt
of the place for the benefit of Monsieur le Patron, almost crowing
with delight when a dead mouse was raked out from under the
corner cupboard. 'A rated auberge in the guide to France,' he
snorted, '—and dead vermin on the floor. God in heaven!' Little
daggers of hate were darting from the proprietor's eyes: the
gendarme was getting more and more embarrassed. But the scope
was dying, dying to the moment when the gendarme had to turn
to me and say, 'And your room, Monsieur?'

'Of course.' I put my hand on the latch with only the faint hope
of a prayer that she might have thought of something. The room
was empty: the bed smooth, with no sign of Margaret or her; the
bathroom door was closed and beyond it the sound of running
water. I stood watching while the gendarme made a quicker, more
perfunctory search. He turned and looked at the proprietor. 'I think
you have made a mistake, my friend.'

The patron sneered: a mean, drooping sneer. 'The woman is not
here—' I think that one word finished me, but I had to hang on,
and pray. 'The woman,' he repeated, 'is not here—it is said she is
in the bath . . . with the child. Let us see.'

I leaned back against that door, helpless. What was there to do?
I said, 'Can you hear me, darling. There's a policeman here, who
is looking for a stolen child. He wants to come in and look for it.
Do you mind?'

The answer came back to all of us: firm and clear. 'The door
isn't locked. If he must do this . . . he must.'

I stood to one side and let the gendarme march past me.

CHAPTER 9

I will never forget that . . . or be so proud.

As the bathroom door swung open I could see past the
gendarme's shoulder: the bare white bathroom, that quaint, deep,
old-fashioned bath . . . and Joan standing upright in it, naked, with
her hair piled high on the top of her head . . . so slim and pale . . .
so very beautiful.

She stood quite still, her hands clasped loosely in front of her,
and there was a curious look of contempt on her face as she stared
at the gendarme. Then she said, 'Well?' I wedged myself in the
doorway and threw my arm across the lintel so that the patron
could not come in; quickly, my eyes darted round the rest of the
room . . . Joan, the bath, a chair that had her house-coat and a
towel piled on it . . . nothing else . . . no sign of Margaret.

The gendarme stood frozen; I could see a slow red flush spreading
up the back of his neck below his cap, almost feel the struggle
between admiration and embarrassment that was going on inside
him. He bowed, then he saluted, then started backing into me. 'A
thousand pardons, Madame . . .' he was stammering. I let him by
and reached over and closed the door quickly. If he had had the
time or the inclination to look closer, he might have seen three
things that I had in those last few seconds: that Joan's body was
quite dry—she had not yet sat down in the bath; that she was
leaning forward, pressing against the rim of it that came halfway
up her thighs . . . as if she was holding something there we could
not see; that the top of a vest, a very small vest, far too small for
her, was showing from under one edge of the housecoat.

The gendarme swung round and faced the proprietor; his face
was still very red, but now it was in anger. 'Imbecile—! You shame
me, and insult your guests. There is nothing there . . . but beauty.'

He seized the little man by the shoulder, pushing him out in front
of him, through our bedroom and into Josh's. Still holding him, he
bowed again and made an abject apology. While I was stumbling
through an assurance that all was forgiven, that he had only been

doing his duty, I saw Josh's eyes, fixed on mine over the top of his head. They flicked down to his watch, and, somehow, I knew exactly what he was trying to say to me: 'Keep him here. At all costs, keep him here. He is our only hope of safety. For if he goes, there will be a third assault . . . and Jacques will be in that one . . . so keep him here until I can get below and start something else.'

The gendarme was still gripping Monsieur le Patron. 'Is there anything else, Monsieur?'

'Yes,' I said, 'while you are here—you might be kind enough to interpret your laws of contract to us—and this—' I did not want to call him 'gentleman', could not think of anything else that was not really rude, so left it alone.

'If I can, Monsieur.'

I pointed at the printed notice by the door. 'It states there that notice must be given to vacate rooms by noon, or a full day's *pension* must be paid. We were given notice to quit only a few moments before you arrived, by midnight. But we have had half our day, and propose to pay for all of it. Are we not entitled, therefore, to stay until noon tomorrow?'

He stared at the print, from a distance of about six inches, mouthing each word silently; then he straightened. 'But of course, Monsieur. That is your right.' He glared at the patron. 'And if there is the slightest trouble, please send one of your party to the Gendarmerie at once, and I will attend to the matter.'

'Thank you.' I couldn't help a quick glance at my watch. Seven-forty-five. Another half hour to go—and it was not even dark yet. We could not risk leaving . . . and we could not hold out.

'Is that all, Monsieur?' The gendarme was fidgeting, but he had not let go of the patron's arm.

'No.' Josh spoke quietly. 'There is a matter I wish to report to you . . . to make a statement on . . . in private.' He looked at the landlord. 'Since this gentleman has a hobby of listening at keyholes, I would be grateful if you would escort him to his quarters, and then return. I shall not keep you long.'

'Out—!' said the gendarme, and as he pushed the patron through the outer door in front of him, Josh fired his parting shot. 'Inform him, if you will, that we expect our dinner on time—even after this exhibition. And no fried sprats.'

We stood for a moment listening to the harangue that faded towards the service stairs: 'Attend to your proper duties, fool,

instead of wasting my time . . . kidnapped children, indeed . . .'
Then I said, 'For God's sake—shut the door.'

Josh moved over to it and opened it a little wider. He was
laughing. 'No, Harry, the wider the better. That's the beauty of it.
While he's here, we are safe. And the more people that know it,
the better.'

I stared at him. 'But what are you going to tell him—? Not the
truth, surely, after we've just denied—'

'Oh no, Harry. He's going to get the longest lecture . . . twenty
minutes, if I can string it out . . . on psychology and behaviourism
as applied to the breaking of beds.'

Steps outside, and then the gendarme came back. 'Now,
Monsieur.'

'I wish,' said Josh, 'to make a statement on the unfortunate
incident of this afternoon. The breaking of the bed.'

'But I told you, Monsieur, it has not been reported—officially.
Until then, I suggest—'

'No.' Josh made a magnificent gesture. 'I did it, and I am
ashamed. After all the hospitality and kindness shown in this
country to me, it is my duty to tell all, to explain why, and to offer
reparation . . .' He waved a hand towards the bed. 'Sit down,
Monsieur. Your pencil and notebook? Good. We begin.'

'Statement of Joshua Ponting, Esq., of Llanwrtyd—'

The gendarme's pencil stopped moving over the page very
suddenly, and a baffled face looked up at the speaker. 'Pardon,
Monsieur?'

'Llanwrtyd—in Wales.' He was a quarter Welsh, I knew; he
managed that Ll "click" beautifully.

The gendarme shook his head. 'I regret—'

'L . . . L . . . A . . . N . . . W . . . R . . . T . . . Y . . . D,' said Josh
carefully. Then he looked at me. 'Don't you think it would be better,
Harry, if you went and sat with Joan. After all, she's had a great
shock.'

'I think I will—' Even in the deadly situation we were in, I don't
think I could have stayed there and kept a straight face. As I slid
through the communicating door and closed it quickly, Josh was
plodding on. 'At the age of seven, I lived with my grandmother,
who had a fine four-poster bed . . .'

The contrast between this room and the other made me feel
ashamed: Joan was sitting on the bed, in her housecoat, with a

litter of towels round her; the limp pale body of Margaret was half under the coverlet as she struggled to get her back into her clothes.

'How is she?' I whispered. I sat down beside her and tried to give a hand.

'All right, Harry. She's breathing just the same. But, oh God, I was scared, darling. I just managed to get her in the bath in time . . . and hold her head up with my knees. I was terrified she might slip and drown.'

I kissed her hard once and then told her what was happening next door. 'By the way he's started, he can keep it up till midnight—if the gendarme doesn't die of writer's cramp. We're quite, quite safe—until he goes—if we can keep that child quiet.' I listened to the slow, shallow breath. 'And I don't think we will have to worry about that. It's after—when Josh and the gendarme have gone their separate ways . . . even for that five minutes . . . that it will be dangerous.'

Twice I slipped back through the door to see how they were getting on. The first time, Josh was trying to spell "libido" to a pale, slightly sweating officer of the police; the second, and I could feel the strain, even in him: he was getting hoarse, running down. ' . . . And I will make full reparation of the damage . . . apologise to whoever requires it . . .' The gendarme had given up: the note-book was lying on his lap, his hands idle. Over the top of his head, Josh winked at me, then let his eyes move down to his watch. Eight-ten . . . he had lasted out.

'That is all, my friend. Perhaps you will let me know your decision. I thank you for being so patient. If you will go to the bar, I will join you in a few moments when I have washed. It will be an honour to drink an aperitif.'

Never has a man looked so glad to be quit of a room as that gendarme. He jumped to his feet, bowed, said, 'I will await you with pleasure, Monsieur,' and then scuttled out. As the door closed behind him, Josh leaned over and snapped the bolt. 'The danger time, Harry. Don't open it again, whatever you do.'

I said, 'That was a masterpiece.'

'Didn't think I could last out . . . never talked such drivel in my life.' He was striding about the room, stuffing things into his pockets. 'All set now. Just say "So long" to Joan, and then I'm off.'

He walked through to the other room, and there was Joan, sitting on the side of the bed, stroking Margaret's hair. There was no change in the look of that little pinched face which poked out from under the eiderdown; no change in the soft, shallow breathing.

'I'm off now, Joan. See you at Chartres, tomorrow.' He hesitated for a moment, and then he said, 'In the past —I've had some uncharitable thoughts about you, my dear. I take them all, unsaid, back after what you did tonight.' Then that unforgettable grin. ' . . . And after the flattery, a request. I made you a promise in London . . . and I've kept it. Will you release me? For just an hour?'

I couldn't say anything; only hoped that she would understand; say 'Yes'.

'Of course, Josh.' Five seconds must have slipped by before she said it; but she did say it, and that was one of the biggest reliefs of my life.

He gave us both that wonderful grin of his. 'Thank you, my dear. I shall always remember. Now I shall go and have three large brandies as an aperitif to something I am going to enjoy. You should hear easily, Harry: the bar window is only just round to the side below these rooms. When the fur really starts to fly, down you go on your sheets . . . and don't stop. I'll tell my Françoise to meet you in the garden and show you where the boats are. Lock the door after me—' He gave us a mock salute. 'Now the first wave of the assault goes in. See you in Chartres.' The door closed softly behind him.

Four minutes . . . five minutes of silence, while I stripped a bed and knotted three sheets together and made a running noose at one end. Joan was wrapping Margaret in one of the blankets. 'I'm going to get you on the sill,' I said, 'with one foot in the loop. Then I'll lower you until you can hold the sheet with one hand. Do you think you can manage to hold the baby with the other while I ease you down the rest of the way?'

'I'll try, darling.'

I walked over to the window and looked out into the soft black-ness; with all that had happened I had not noticed night coming on so fast. I lashed the free end of the sheet to a heavy chest that was standing there, and then turned back to the bed. Joan was standing staring down at the pitiful, inert bundle that lay there; she was very pale and kept brushing her long fair hair back from her forehead with quick, jerking movements. I went over and took her hands. 'Frightened?' I said.

'Oh, Harry, horribly—worse than ever before.'

'If it's any consolation, I'm not exactly hilarious. But it won't be long, darling. I promise you.' I was holding her very tight when the noise started.

First it was just Josh's voice from below and to the side of us, that deep rumbling voice that would carry most places, particularly if he wanted it to; there were pauses, but I could hear nothing then, only assume that someone was answering him. Gradually it increased until one was at the level of a bellow, and the other, though still wordless, was recognisable as the high, spitting tones of the proprietor. I picked up Margaret and moved towards the window again, holding Joan's hand with my free one. 'Any moment now, darling . . .'

I was expecting the cue, but the immensity of it shattered me when it came. It was not the volume of sound, it was the length of time that it endured. Not the single crack of a glass broken, or a blow struck, but a long-drawn-out splintering crash that echoed like thunder. It went on and on, just as if Josh was walking down a long shelf, sweeping bottles and glasses to the floor in an endless stream.

'Here we go, darling.' I put the baby down on the chest very gently and then started to hoist Joan over the sill, finding the loop for her foot; as I paid off the sheet, the noise seemed to be increasing from down below. There was a banging of furniture now, screams clearly heard, 'Help! . . . save me! Assassin!' There was the sound of running feet on the ground floor, madame's voice shouting. I steadied the sheet as Joan's head came level with the window-ledge, twisted, and managed to grab the little bundle in the blanket, passed it from arm to free arm. 'Down you go, Joan.' I let her down as slowly as I dared.

The first knot slipped over the edge, the second sheet was half gone before her voice came up to me, 'I'm down.' The din from below was rising to an incredible crescendo; there must be at least four bodies engaged in mortal combat down there. But it wasn't the time to wonder how Josh was doing. I gave one last look to see if the sheet was fast on the chest, scrambled out of the window and slid down.

It was dark and warm in the garden; the frogs were croaking and the cicadas making their unending chirrup as we ran side by side out of the yard and down the narrow path that led down the garden between the rows of vegetables towards the trees by the river. The noise of battle was fading behind us. Then a dark shadow broke away from a row of beans and took Joan's free hand without a word and started running with us. It was Françoise.

She did not speak until we were in the shadow of the trees, the white sand of the shore gleaming and crunching beneath our feet, the edge of the water lapping softly only a few yards away; then she tugged at Joan's arm, 'To the left, Madame. To that next dark clump of trees. That is where Henri keeps his boat for the fishing.' We turned and moved on at a fast walk, with Françoise leading, holding the baby she had taken from Joan. It was very dark under that thick clump of alder bushes and poplar: dark enough to make me stumble and grope for a long time trying to feel for that damned boat, but I couldn't find it. At last I risked using my lighter. I could have saved myself a lot of time in the first place. It wasn't there.

It had been: the faint flicker of the lighter showed that I was standing almost on top of the knife-mark of the keel on the sand where it had slid down to the water, the heavier indents to one side of the feet that had pushed it. It did not matter whether someone had known and taken it away, or if Henri had decided on a night's fishing. There was no crossing of the Loire that way.

I snapped the light out and turned helplessly to Françoise, 'Are there any other boats . . . further down?'

She was nearly in tears. 'Yes, Monsieur. But not for another two kilometres. The bank is marshy . . . and there are no trees.'

Bad going and no cover. It seemed hopeless. 'And the other way?'

'Not until we have gone well past the auberge. And it is too late for that now. They are searching the garden . . . look—' She pulled me a little to one side so that we could see back the way we had come. The lights of the auberge were ablaze and, in front of them, fainter jerking lights that moved close to the ground: four of them, torches. They were searching the grounds. The way past would be cut off now.

She was standing very close to me, and at that moment the quarter moon broke fitfully through the clouds. I will always remember that pale oval face tilted up to mine, the dark eyes searching, the short black hair ruffled by the night breeze. 'When Josh asked me to take you over, I swore on my love that I would. There is another way—' She turned and pointed out over the Loire, a broad strip of grey now, smudged with the darker blots of the islands. 'Walk.'

At first I thought I had misunderstood her, and that she meant to try to swim. It was crazy. 'But, little one, it is half a kilometre wide. It runs so fast. Alone I would not try that swim.'

'No, Monsieur. We can walk all the way. It is very shallow at the end of the summer, and warm. I know. I bathe every day. I can take you—' She swung round to Joan, who, I felt rather than saw, had come close to us. 'It is safe, Madame. I promise the water will not reach higher than your chest.'

There was a long silence. 'I'll try,' said Joan, 'but what about Margaret?'

'I'll take her, I'm tallest,' I said.

The moon came out again for a second and we saw that Françoise was pulling her frock over her head. 'Quick, then—' her voice was muffled. 'There is no time to lose. Perhaps soon they will search the bank this way.'

I went and peered round the edge of the bushes, back towards the auberge: the lights were fainter, they seemed to be moving in a line away from us upstream; I could no longer hear the voices. For the moment we were safe. Behind me, I heard Joan saying doubtfully, 'But, Françoise—do we have to?' and the girl's voice answering, matter-of-fact, impersonal, 'It is warm, Madame, and what use would wet clothes be to us on the other side? You will not be shamed before your husband, nor I before my lover's friends.'

We had started to strip and make our clothes into bundles, when we first heard the feet that thudded along the bank behind the trees; they slowed to a walk and stopped. There was a moment's silence and then a rustling of the branches of the thicket. We crouched back in the shadow, frozen, waiting for what was coming. Silence again; a twig cracked and I could hear panting breath. Then a voice said, 'Is there anyone about, sister Ann?'—a deep, well-known voice, breathless but full of laughter. Françoise sobbed, 'Josh,' and ran towards the sound; for the third time the moon cleared suddenly and I saw her like a slim, pale column, pressed hard against the dark bulk of him as he stepped from the bushes to greet us.

He heard the position and took our decision without comment; told me in jerks of what had happened while I helped him strip and tied his clothes and mine in one bundle. 'Had a wonderful time . . . wonderful. Threw that little bastard . . . right through his shelf of bloody bottles . . . tried to heave madame after him . . . but she was too damned heavy. The worst bit of luck was that nice gendarme. I thought he wouldn't wait for that drink, but he did, and I had to deal with him first. Clipped him one that knocked him cold . . . sorry about that . . . and it will make more trouble. Then I tried to lead them on a false trail—out of the front and back to the château gardens, then dodging back. But they spotted it, and now they've seen your sheet hanging down, so I'm afraid there's trouble for all of us.'

'It doesn't matter. We're together.'

The moon had vanished again, and it was so dark that our bodies were only pale, formless blurs as we stood together on the brink. We moved in the darkness, without touching, feeling the nearness of each other as we groped for our bundles; Josh muttered, 'If you can cope with my clothes and yours, lad, I'll manage the baby.' I heard him stumble, curse, and then say, 'Got her—nearly trod on the blanket.'

Down near the water, Françoise's voice called urgently, 'The lights . . . they are coming this way.' No time to argue now, no time to delay; we formed a line ahead, Françoise first, Josh next, with Margaret bundled in her shawl on his shoulder, then Joan, and I last. Each carried their clothes on their head and steadied them with one hand as they held the shoulder of the one in front with the other. There was no thought of embarrassment only urgency, as we moved forward into the warm shallows of the water.

I shall never forget that wade. We moved very slowly until we were knee-deep, to avoid any splashing; then the current caught us as we moved into the flow of the stream, and the smooth, tepid, Loire was racing past, dragging our feet sideways over the gravel bottom. Thigh-deep . . . waist-deep . . . and then the moon came out again; the water was like a sheet of glass as it slid by without a ripple until it touched our bodies. Then a thousand little fingers pulled and plucked at my waist and legs, urging each step sideways, making our line a ragged diagonal to our proper course. I could see the faint gleam of the three in front now, white columns in echelon, one hand resting on the shoulder of the one that led: clearest the outline of Joan's white shoulders in front of me, the swirl and suck of the water at the hollow of her back. Behind us, suddenly, alien to our world of silent struggle against that unrelenting sheet of water, a voice shouted; I gripped at the smooth, well-known shoulder in front of me and turned to look back; there was a circle of those torches down on the beach that we had left. They had seen us.

I shouted forward up the line and heard it passed on; the tempo of our struggle increased, and then the moon was covered once more by cloud. We pressed on, sullen now, not caring, not thinking much, until the feel of the face of that black water was level with Joan's shoulders. Then a whisper came back down the line to me, 'Shallower now . . . island ahead . . . mind for splashing.'

The water receded, the current stopped tugging; soon we were treading gently in the shallows and on to the beach of an island in the middle of the river.

The torches were still grouped on the far bank, little dots of light at this distance, but now they were not moving. There was no more shouting. As I stared back at them, I said to Josh, 'That's his lot. He won't follow our way.'

'Why not—?' It was natural he did not ask who *he* was.

'He doesn't like getting his feet wet. Do you remember that time in the dyke? They'll get a boat.'

We moved up across the white sand to crouch in the shelter of the close-standing, thirty-foot poplars that struggled for existence on the central ridge; above us their leaves whispered, never still, and the light that filtered through them in the fitful gleams of the moon changed all the time, grey to silver, throwing a faint dappled pattern on our bodies.

Josh said softly, 'Take Margaret for a moment, will you, Joan? I want to find something.' I heard him grunting as he fumbled with his bundle of clothes. 'What's happening on the other bank, Harry?'

As I went to the edge of the trees to look back, I heard Joan say, 'She's fine, Josh. As warm as toast—and not a drop of water on her.' I called back, 'I think I'm right. They're moving fast upstream . . . to find a boat.'

'Or the car, to make for this side by the bridge.' In the dim light, I saw him straighten, holding a bottle. 'I had to slip it in my pocket—I couldn't resist it. Cordon Bleu. Let's have one on the house.'

The bottle passed from hand to hand, each in turn tilting it back and taking a gulp; each in turn half seen by the others in pale flickering light under those rustling leaves. The strangest drink of my life . . .

The bundle was repacked and we walked quickly through the trees and out on the beach the far side. Françoise whispered, and though there was no need to whisper, I knew why she did—'It is much shorter, and shallower this side, Josh.' We went into the water in the same order as before, and the greatest depth was no higher than Joan's waist . . . quicker, with firmer strides as there

was no drag from the current. The quarter moon was riding clear
and high now, but it did not matter about the light any more: we
were nearer and nearer to the far bank, the dark line of trees and
the road to safety that I knew lay behind them.

Firm white sand under our feet now, then the shelter of the trees,
trying to dry ourselves off before we scrambled into our clothes; for
the first time since we had left our bedroom, I looked at my watch.
For a moment I thought it must have been under the water and
stopped, but when I held it to my ear it was still ticking. Nine-
fifteen . . . only an hour since we climbed down that sheet . . . it
seemed an eternity.

Josh was standing a little apart from us now; quite clear in that
half light, I could see him hold up the brandy bottle to see the level
remaining, and then look across at Joan. 'I think my hour is just
about up,' he said, 'and thank you for the indulgence.' One quick
movement and he had tilted it back in his mouth, holding it there
as he swallowed. Without looking at us he walked down the beach
and threw, a long, swinging, underarm movement, so that the bottle
jerked out of his hand in a low arc; for a moment the light gleamed
on it as it twisted over and over; there was a dull "plop" as it hit
the water, then silence. He came back to us wiping the back of one
hand across his mouth as if he wanted to brush something away.
'Well, that's that. We had better go and find ourselves some
transport.'

There was a path up the low cliff behind the trees and an easy
climb over the stone wall that flanked the main road that followed
the curve of the river from Tours to Nevers. It was early, but there
was little traffic and we took it in turns to hold the baby as we
walked in the shadows of the wide grass verge, moving in closer to
the hedge to avoid the lights of the few cars that passed us. No
doubt now that Margaret was all right, that we had not overdone
that sleeping tablet; as I held her she moved restlessly inside the
blanket, whimpered, and then quietened to sleep again with a little
snuffling sigh. Yes, Margaret was all right, she was coming round.
But could we say yet if she was safe?

We had turned west along the road towards Blois, and away
from the direction those torches had taken on the far side of the
Loire. I tried to remember how far down that way the next bridge
was if they hadn't been able to find a boat. Four kilometres? . . .
not very far if they had our car to cross over and sweep back in

our direction . . . and if there was a boat lying nearer, they might only be a few minutes behind us.

I turned to Josh, walking close beside me. 'I'm going to thumb the next thing that passes.'

'Your show, Harry—but I wouldn't. Too many of us. They won't stop and they might report it.'

'What the hell do we do, then?'

'Go on a little . . . something will turn up.'

"Like hell it will," I thought, "we'll still be walking along this bloody road at dawn tomorrow—if that lot on the other side haven't caught up with us—and the girls must be terribly tired, because I know I am. I'll give it another half mile and then I'll flag a lorry down."

But it wasn't necessary, for within the distance I had set as a target, transport was waiting for us at the side of the road. I did not see it at first, I was too busy glancing back over my shoulder, straining to catch the first gleam of headlights coming from behind us, but suddenly Josh said, 'Look,' and there on our side of the road the stone wall curved back and the grass verge gave place to a gravelled pull-in: there was a little bistro at the back of this, no more than a wooden shack, now dark and silent and shuttered. But by the side of it was the grey shape of a closed commercial van.

We circled the place once, warily, like animals approaching a baited trap. There was no one inside the place, no one on the car park, no one near the van; we crouched in the shadow between it and the wall while a lorry roared by, going fast; then I tried the driver's door and it was open.

I flashed my lighter carefully and peered into the cab. 'No ignition key—but we can fix that . . .'

'Dare we—?' It was Josh, just behind my shoulder.

I turned. 'Look—in one day you have wrecked a part of an ancient monument of France, assaulted the proprietor of a hotel and destroyed most of his liquid stock, and knocked a gendarme cold. Why not let me try and get level—by stealing a car?' I looked over to Joan. 'Give me a hairpin, darling.'

Bending it, twisting to get into the lock, was a matter of seconds; the completed circuit showed the tank to be half full. 'Let's go,' I said.

We scrambled in, but there was not enough room for all on the single bench seat in the cab, so Josh slid open the door that led to the body and groped his way into the darkness of the back. I heard his feet scraping on the metal floor, then a curse as he stumbled, followed by an echoing, clanging crash that rolled round the confined space like thunder. 'God—!' His voice came back muffled, '—it's full of bloody saucepans in here.'

'It is the *quincaillerie, chéri*—' Françoise's voice a came softly from where she was tucked in close beside me. 'The travelling iron-monger's shop that goes to all the small villages. And, Monsieur—'

'Yes, Françoise?'

'You may not have noticed—in this darkness—but the outside is painted in bright colour. It is most distinctive. If anyone knows we have it, we will be so easy to follow.'

'Too late now, Françoise.' My hand was on the starter button. I turned towards the back for a moment, and shouted, 'I don't care if it's a hearse. It's taking us to Chartres . . . now.' The motor ground and the engine coughed twice and came to life. No sign of vehicle light on the road in either direction . . . I pulled the wheel over hard and turned away from the side of the bistro . . . west . . . on the road to Blois.

She was an old Renault, with a clanky engine, and the lights not too good; the best I could get out of her was a steady eighty kilometres an hour. The main road was practically deserted at this time, and we only passed about six trucks before we reached the outskirts of the town; nothing passed us, nothing seemed to be following. Packed tight in the front, we hardly spoke; once or twice I let my eyes drift from the road for a moment towards Joan on the far side, Joan nursing Margaret on her knee . . . a half-wakened Margaret now, twisting her head to stare at the dashboard light with dulled eyes, before turning against Joan's breast to drowse again. As the van bumped and swayed, a clang and rattle came from the back, interspersed by a running commentary from Josh, as he felt—or fell over—piles of iron buckets, sheaves of feather dusters and strings of scrubbing-brushes, as he tried to find himself a seat. But I was thinking, mainly, of what Françoise had said; if we were so obvious, speed was the only thing.

'Can you find the switch on the dashboard for my light?' Josh called.

'Not until after Blois,' I said. 'Unless you think we should drive straight to the Gendarmerie here . . . and pack it in.'

'No. Still too close. Get into another *département* of France. It will make things all the more difficult for them —if we are stopped.'

'Then you'll have to clang in the dark for a bit.'

A sharp right turn now and, following Françoise's directions, we lurched and rattled up the hill through the narrow, twisting streets of Blois. Little puffs of sound came to us above our own noise from the radios blaring in the late cafés as we flashed by; there was the flicker of shafts of light that streamed from their doors across the pavements; once, for an instant, the white blur of a group of faces, turned from a table on the pavement to stare at our noisy passing.

At a crossroad, a torch beam stabbed at us from out of the darkness; there was a shout, a moment's impression of the cap and cape of a gendarme, a white baton flashing. I swerved, put my foot down hard on the throttle, and we were by.

'What was that, Harry?' It was Josh from the back.

'Copper. Speeding, or wrong way down a one-way street, I should think. Unless they've . . .'

'Quite. Keep going, boy.'

We rattled on, past the last of the houses, into the darkness of the long straight road that led over the rolling uplands towards Chartres.

Eighty kilometres. That was all I could get out of that old crate, but it seemed fast enough; the road stretched away in the beam of the lights, a straight, black, unwinding ribbon; the poplar trees that lined the verges seemed to split apart in front of us and flicker by like a tall continuous fence on either side until they were tossed away into the noise and the darkness behind. We had found the interior light, and Josh had managed to make himself comfortable before we turned it out again; the saucepans rattled and banged against the sides of the van; Margaret woke and cried a little and then went to sleep again. We didn't talk; there was nothing to talk about . . . nothing except the dwindling mileage to Chartres.

One village . . . a second . . . scarcely any check on our speed as we twisted through the narrower streets past the silent shuttered houses, watching for the flash of another torch, perhaps a road block . . . but there was nothing. The needle of the petrol gauge was flickering on the quarter mark . . . it could be no more than thirty kilometres now . . . she was running rough, but steadily: we were going to make it. Then, as we crested a long straight rise, I saw in the driving mirror, for the first time, the reflection of head-lights behind.

They were a long way back; I just saw them as they came over the top of a hill some ten kilometres behind us, and then they were lost again as we rushed down into the next valley. But they were the first lights I had seen, for nothing had passed us or come the other way since we had left Blois, so I watched for them; watched anxiously each time we topped a rise, and sure enough, not more than five kilometres later, they were there again, two blinding eyes now that winked at me in the mirror, with the distance between us halved.

I put one arm behind Françoise and banged on the sliding door that Josh had closed; in a moment it slid open and his head was bending over close to mine. There was still a faint aroma of Cordon Bleu hanging round it.

'Car coming up fast,' I shouted above the din. 'It's made up five kilometres on us in the last ten minutes.'

'Then put your foot right down, Harry.'

'It is. Right on the floor. She won't give anything more.'

'Right. Keep on going. I'm going to close the door. Then put my light on. Maybe I can fix something.' He returned to the clanging of his pots and pans. I concentrated on the road, trying to get the last ounce out of the old Renault.

A few minutes only—but it seemed an age—and then he was hammering behind me again, and I switched out the light. They must be very close behind now, but there had been two slight bends in the road, so I had not had a chance to see them. Josh's head was close to mine again.

'An excellent *quincaillier* this—' he roared. 'Sells every damned thing a man could want. How close are they now?'

'Don't know. Lost them on that last bend.'

'I'm going to open the back door of the van, Harry. And I shall want the light on again. So shut your side.'

For a moment I thought he was going to try something absolutely crazy; there was a sudden movement beside me that almost jerked the wheel from my hands as Françoise turned, trying to hold him. 'No, no, Josh. Please . . .' It sounded piteous.

'Don't be a fool, Josh,' I said.

'It's all right, Harry boy. I promise to wedge myself firmly amongst the ironmongery. I only want to do a bit of pouring.'

'Pouring—?'

'Yes. There's a couple of large cans of DERV in the back here. The finest thing on a road for skidding I know.' The door slid shut with a bang.

No time to argue, no inclination to argue on the possibilities of an innocent traveller who might be over-taking us. Somehow, I knew that it was not. Just time to explain to a terrified Françoise just what he was going to do, before we were plunging down into a long straight hill of a valley. As we reached the bottom, those following headlights came over the crest behind us.

I could see them all the time now in the mirror; they streaked down the hill after us with a kind of vindictive hate. As we laboured up the other side it seemed as if it would only be a moment before they surged past, to challenge, and then block the way. But it never happened.

They swerved suddenly, those lights . . . right . . . left . . . and then hard right again: to stop suddenly, with one gone, the other tilted up in the air at a crazy angle . . . and even that dwindled, grew faint . . . and vanished as we breasted the far crest. Then only darkness behind us . . . Josh's voice, as he shot his head through the partition, saying, 'That fixed 'em, chaps,' the anti-climax of the rest of the drive towards the slim, twin spires of Chartres, shadowed against the dawn.

CHAPTER 10

The end of the story, really—except for the ends.

We drove straight to the Gendarmerie: roused an astonished sergeant, who became equally horrified when we told him of all the things we had done. It took a long time before he could be persuaded to call that number in Paris that Inspector Fox had given me.

It had a dreamlike quality—that time of waiting. I remember sitting in the charge-room, hugging a mug of strong black coffee that had been given to us out of compassion, and thinking ... 'We're here—but it just doesn't mean anything. We're safe, and someone else has taken over—but there isn't any of the relief I had hoped for.'

Gradually, the importance of our story sank in, and we were interviewed by a series of increasingly impressive officials, dragged sleepy and yawning from their beds. Joan and Françoise and the baby had disappeared in company with a stiff, grey-haired woman whom I took to be the matron; Josh and I sat on, nodding in our chairs, while we tried to explain and evidence of our 'crimes' was taken down with expressions of growing concern. We heard orders being given for a patrol to go out and clear the road of Josh's oil and bring in the car if it had been abandoned; telephone calls went to and fro from Chartres to Paris, Chartres to London, and at last, mercifully, we were allowed to creep off to bed. It did not matter that it was obviously a cell, that the bed was a hard plank, that the blankets were rough and smelt horribly of disinfectant. It was warm, somewhere to lie down, somewhere to relax and drift off into those dark, welling clouds of sleep. The last thing I remember was an inspector standing beside the bunk, smiling as he reached down to grip my hand. 'All is well, Monsieur. There are congratulations for you from London, and we and they together now go into action against these malefactors. Sleep well, *mon brave;* you have earned it.' I was out for nine hours solid.

In the late afternoon, it only remained for the small ends to be tied up—the chief being small matters of assault, damage and theft.

THE SHADOW OF TIME

But they had a charming way out of that. Josh and I, rested clean and fed, were taken to the private room of an examining magistrate. There we were instructed to plead guilty to the lot, and were admonished by someone who smiled all the time he did it: a suspended sentence of three months for each of us, and then we were told we could leave the country whenever we wished.

The most difficult thing was getting permission for Françoise. They said they would want her as a witness, and it was only after we all had signed a most solemn declaration that she would be returned when necessary that they let her go. But Josh wanted more than that: it was at his request that we were driven to Paris, instead of being flown straight home, and there in the Consulate, with Joan and me as witnesses, they were married by a slightly bewildered official, who must have been briefed, but still thought the whole thing was crazy. Margaret was in attendance, a calm and happier Margaret who sucked her thumb and watched the ceremony with round and serious eyes. I could see the Consul's eyes darting from one to the other of us . . . wondering who in fact the baby did belong to. The next morning we all flew home.

We all came out on top, in the end, I think. When the English trial was over, the judge had me out in front and said some pretty nice things; the publicity hasn't done the business any harm, in fact I have all I can handle. As I have said, Jacques and his crew went down for ten years, but the French side of it is still going on.

Margaret is blonde and long-haired again. When we go to Rye we always go and see her. She is a happy little schoolgirl now, and though we have never tried to discuss those days, I am quite certain she has forgotten all about it.

Josh . . . he did best of all. Amid all the arrests and accusations, the counter-charges and the ratting, the delays of trial, that seemed to involve every one of Françoise's relations, only one fact was constant and obvious: the Auberge Chouvray et de l'Univers would have to stay shut as there was no one to run it. Uncle and aunt waiting trial without bail struggled over this for a long time, but at last their peasant greed overcame a natural aversion, and it was decided that Françoise must take over. This was agreed legally in the form of a lease, and she and Josh moved in.

It has been an enormous success; he has found his feet—in running the kitchen, and becoming a first-class chef: his *Sole Bonne Femme* is worth travelling a few hundred miles to sample. He is considered quite mad by the village, but is immensely popular, and

I'm sure will be running for Mayor in a few years' time. He drinks
big still, but only wine, for he has never broken that promise he
made to Joan so long ago.

We go back when we can, and it is a time-honoured custom that
I should sit with him on a corner of the terrace and crack a bottle
of Chouvray before he goes into the kitchen. I remember so well
the last time it happened, when I thought of trying to tell all this.
He was sitting there, huge, red-faced, sweating gently in his duck
coat and trousers, chef's hat thrown carelessly on the table beside
us, shouting greetings and friendly abuse at everyone who passed
along the road outside, from the smallest child to the oldest labourer
plodding home on his bicycle; I caught his eye and we both looked
up beyond the sheltering plane trees to the front of the hotel. First,
to the new sign, painted in bold letters AUBERGE DE CHOU-
VRAY ET DU COSMOS—his last challenge; then the other thing
he has added . . . a sundial on the wall. The shadow of the style
was long then, slanting out over the letters he has had put round
it, the words no one in the village quite understands, and put down
to that mad Englishman who is now French. They say:

> 'We are no other than a moving row
> Of magic shadow-shapes that come and go.'

We raised our glasses to that series of shadow-shapes that had made
everything possible.

THE VICTOR CANNING
OMNIBUS

THE PYTHON PROJECT is Victor Canning's most exciting thriller. The trail leads through Paris, Florence and Rome, to the sandy shores of North Africa.

A DELIVERY OF FURIES – Keith Marchant is a tough, free-wheeling ex-R.A.F. pilot who makes a precarious living transporting shady cargoes around the world. His plan is a bold one; he will hijack a cargo of six Hawker Sea Fury fighters on the high seas and deliver them to the sun-drenched Caribbean port of Acaibo, headquarters of Angelo Libertad, the fanatical Guevara-type leader of an island revolution.

'**THE MELTING MAN** is well up to Mr. Canning's high standard of exuberant ingenuity, with the usual seafaring finale.' *Daily Telegraph*

ANDREW GARVE OMNIBUS

MURDER IN MOSCOW – Verney had been sent to Moscow to report on changes in the Russian scene. When the leader of a British peace delegation is murdered, Verney discovers only too quickly the sort of changes that have occurred; the authorities produce a pseudo-criminal – and Verney soon sees why the truth doesn't make a scrap of difference.

THE ASHES OF LODA – This is the story, told at a gripping pace, of how a man struggled single-handed and in alien surroundings to uncover events, intrigues and passions long buried in the 'ashes of Loda' – and of what he found.

THE CUCKOO LINE AFFAIR – When a highly respected citizen is accused by a pretty girl of assaulting her in a train, and two unimpeachable witnesses say they saw him do it, his position is serious. The incident was only the beginning of troubles for Edward Latimer, sixtyish, lovable and slightly quaint, on a journey to the Essex village of Steepleford by the ancient single-track railway known locally as the Cuckoo Line.